IZMIR

ALSO BY E. HOWARD HUNT

UNDERCOVER: MEMOIRS OF AN AMERICAN SECRET AGENT

THE BERLIN ENDING

THE HARGRAVE DECEPTION

THE KREMLIN CONSPIRACY

THE GAZA INTERCEPT

THE DUBLIN AFFAIR

MURDER IN STATE

THE SANKOV CONFESSION

EVIL TIME

BODY COUNT

CHINESE RED

THE PARIS EDGE

Jack Novak books:

COZUMEL

GUADALAJARA

MAZATLÁN

IXTAPA

ISLAMORADA

IZMIR

E. HOWARD HUNT

DONALD I. FINE BOOKS

New York

DONALD I. FINE BOOKS
Published by the Penguin Group
Penguin Books USA Inc., 375 Hudson Street,
New York, New York 10014, U.S.A.
Penguin Books Ltd. 27 Wrights Lane,
London W8 5TZ, England
Penguin Books Australia Ltd. Ringwood,
Victoria, Australia
Penguin Books Canada Ltd. 10 Alcorn Avenue,
Toronto, Ontario, Canada M4V 3B2
Penguin Books (N.Z.) Ltd. 182–190 Wairau Road,
Auckland 10, New Zealand

Penguin Books Ltd. Registered Offices:
Harmondsworth, Middlesex, England

Published in 1996 by Donald I. Fine Books,
an imprint of Penguin Books USA Inc.

1   3   5   7   9   10   8   6   4   2

Library of Congress Cataloging-in-Publication Data

Hunt, E. Howard (Everette Howard), 1918–
Izmir / E. Howard Hunt.
p.   cm.
ISBN 1-55611-474-5
1. Novak, Jack (Fictitious character)—Fiction.   2. Private
investigators—United States—Fiction.   3. Americans—Travel—
Turkey—Izmir—Fiction.   I. Title.
PS3515.U5425I96   1996
813'.54—dc20   95-46864
                                                CIP
This book is printed on acid-free paper.

∞

Printed in the United States of America

BOOK
ONE

ONE

DON'T TRY to marry in Switzerland. The stuffy Swiss have no compassion for lovesick foreign couples and view matrimony as a business merger requiring certificates, statements of intent, character witnesses, registration fees, and on and on. All that for a mere civil ceremony. Religious nuptials were equally complicated, with banns posted for public viewing, ministerial interviews and church reservations. Neither Melody nor I had a fixed religious affiliation. She was vaguely Catholic, having been born in Brazil, and her mother, Delores, had been married and divorced often enough to personify indifference to the holy bonds, coupled with vampirical lust for a mate's financial blood. So, Delores was no role model for either of us, and in truth Melody and I had a fairly casual attitude toward matrimony. On and off we'd been together for more than four years, and after our most recent reconciliation we decided it was time to stop testing and settle down.

We'd come to Bern for two reasons. Switzerland was a great place to honeymoon, and I had serious business at the Guatemalan embassy. In my possession was a wax-sealed, red-ribboned document issued by the Guatemalan Consulate General in Miami entitling me to one percent of more than one hundred and fifty million dollars looted by dictator Oscar Chavez. After his death I'd located the stolen funds in sequestered bank accounts, and the time had come to claim my reward. According to the Guat National Bank representative in Miami all I had to do was present my document at the Bern embassy and become an instant millionaire. I'd postponed it while I spent a week battling cantonal bureaucrats who seemed resolved to deny us a marriage license. Now I was ready to concede defeat, and told Melody so.

"But, Jack," she murmured, disappointment in her voice, "that isn't like you. I've never known you to give up before." She put down her demitasse and eyed me. "Getting prenuptial cold feet, love?"

"No, dammit, but while you snoozed I was up early and down at the Rathaus expecting to finalize things, and—"

"And?"

"And the license clerk said he couldn't accept your US passport as proof of age. He demanded your original birth certificate from São Paulo."

"Oh, God." She flicked dark hair from her forehead and stared at the ceiling.

"Yeah. Well you may invoke the Deity, He's our only hope."

She pushed aside the breakfast table and straightened the pink silk dressing gown across her lovely thighs. "Aside from divine intervention, what do you suggest?"

"A more receptive venue."

She shrugged. "Obviously. But where?"

"You've skipped around Europe more than I have—like with that Signor Manicotti of recent memory—so what's your suggestion?"

"You would bring up Paolo, wouldn't you? Never a day goes by you don't dig me. What about all *your* women, Jack? You're very reticent about that, you double-standard bastard."

"Now, now, precious, let's not grumble and fret. What's your reading on France?"

"Bad as Switzerland." Sighing, she made a face. "Italy . . . Spain . . . Germany . . . administratively they're all the same."

An idea penetrated the interstices of my thoughts. "Where's Delores?"

"Monte Carlo, I suppose. Or off on her friend's yacht."

"Which is named . . . ?"

"*Le Cygne*, or *Cygnet*, one of the two. Why?"

"We could try Monte Carlo," I mused. "I can think of one American who married there."

"Who?"

"Princess Grace."

"Terrific. Will you get serious?"

"I am." Delores's current companion was a multimillionaire Turkish art collector, who undoubtedly had Monegasque friends able to secure us a wedding license. "Okay. It's now ten-fifteen. I have a couple of things to do before noon. Meanwhile, try to locate Mom, wherever she is, and tell her we need help. Let the old pirate arrange our wedding—she'll love that—and say we'll fly down tomorrow."

Melody nodded slowly. "And how am I to reach her?"

"What's the boyfriend's name?"

"Mehmet . . . ah, Kurdlu. And Jack, he's like, really old, so . . . what I mean is he's just a friend, you know? Nothing physical," she ended ambiguously.

"Sure. Listen, those Turks are so tough even the Russians fear them, and they don't grow old gracefully. Know what they eat? Yoghurt and nuts. Olives occasionally, and sheep's eyes for dessert. They outlive wives three or four to one. So if Mom thinks it's all going to be platonic, she's in for a large surprise." I paused. "Locating her is a job for the concierge. Give him Mehmet's name and the yacht's, probable home port Monte Carlo. And when I return . . . we'll get, you know, like really physical. Okay?"

Her lips pursed in a silent kiss.

"In addition," I continued, "there will be a big surprise I've been saving for my bride. Today all will be revealed."

Her face glowed. "You darling man. A big diamond ring?"

"Wait and see." I bent over to kiss her forehead. "Later."

"Hurry back."

I left the suite and took the elevator down to the lobby. It seemed small for a grand old hotel like the Schweizerhof, but held all the elements essential to Swiss hospitality. The concierge, a white-whiskered man in a claw-hammer coat and gates-ajar collar, was at his station attending an elderly traveler, and I hoped Melody would soon focus his attention on locating her mobile mother. With that thought I went down the steps to the noisy street, glanced at the gray, smoked-stained railway station on the far side, and let the commissionaire open a taxi door.

"Embassy of Guatemala," I told the driver, and we sped off through the narrow streets, across the slow-moving Aare River and onto Helvetiaplatz, where several Meso-American embassies were located—including Guatemala's.

The receptionist was a chunky woman in her thirties, with the olive skin and slightly slanted eyes of a *ladina*. She said I would need an appointment to see the ambassador, and in any case he was in Geneva attending a Unesco meeting.

"Okay, I'll settle for the Commercial Counselor."

"That would be Señor Gonzalez. Your name?"

"Novak. Jack Novak."

She wrote it down. "Your business?"

"Financial. Confidential."

She didn't like that but she phoned Gonzalez's office anyway and told me to have a seat; someone would come for me.

While waiting, I removed my official document from a coat pocket and smoothed it over my thigh before looking around the reception area. It gave out into a dimly lighted corridor, whose walls were of darkly varnished wood. Spidery cracks suggested the paneling had been varnished a century ago and ignored ever since. Like many Swiss-German dwellings the overall atmosphere was gloomy, although what the affluent Swiss had to be gloomy about I couldn't imagine.

Anyway, I sat in almost unbroken silence, and thought of the circumstances that had brought me here.

I'd been recuperating off the Florida Keys when I encountered lovely Anita Tessier, the younger of Colonel Chavez's two daughters. We'd gotten along splendidly until she was murdered by husband Claude, who had been Chavez's strongarm during their years of power and plunder. Then came elder sister Rita, who conspired with me to find her father's looted millions; in the end, a tragic, lost, amoral figure I'd left in Spain. Magnanimously, I thought, I'd turned the Chavez swag back to the people of Guatemala in return for a minuscule finder's fee. Claiming it was why I was in the embassy anteroom waiting for Señor Gonzalez to honor the contract and make me a wealthy man just minutes from now.

Of all this, Melody knew nothing. The Swiss Union Bank's check would be explanation enough. Besides, she knew I did off-the-books jobs for Manny Montijo from time to time and was paid with funds confiscated by DEA. At one time Manny had been my partner when I was with DEA. I'd quit to work independently, but Manny had a family to support and stayed on. Now he was close to being head honcho in DEA's Miami office and I admired and respected him beyond other men.

As for why I'd selected Bern for my Guatemalan payoff, the idea was to insulate the transaction from IRS and use untaxed money for a carefree lifestyle with plenty left over to educate the children Melody and I planned to have. Not right away, but after UM Law School, where she'd enrolled.

So these thoughts, images and memories unreeled in my mind as I waited expectantly, until finally I saw a man coming toward me down the corridor. He was tall and thin, his cheeks sunken, and his facial skin pallid. When he opened his mouth to speak I noticed stained teeth in urgent need of prophylaxis. "Mr. Novak? I'm Gonzalez, Teofilo Gonzalez." I rose and we shook hands. His was thin and bony.

"*Mucho gusto*. If you prefer we can speak in Spanish."

He smiled bleakly. "Either way—I was educated at Tulane." He paused. "So—?"

"What I have is better conveyed in your office, *Señor Consejero*."

"Very well." Turning, he led the way back to his office.

The door opened on a scene of disorder. File drawers were mostly empty, their contents transferred to cardboard storage boxes. Loose papers were scattered across the desk, and a terra-cotta ashtray held scraps of burned paper. Gonzalez removed a stack of books from an overstuffed chair and indicated I should use it. Before sitting, I handed him my consular document and said, "Speaks for itself."

He sat behind his desk and read the document with sober care. Then he placed it on the desk and eyed me. "Can you prove your identity?"

I handed him my passport. He compared my photo and face and returned the passport, then tapped the document. "So, you are expecting your compensation."

"Finder's fee. Exactly."

He looked from me to the document, then back at me again. Licked colorless lips before saying, "Apparently you are not current with events in Guatemala."

"So?"

He shrugged. "Three days ago a coup displaced the civilian government with a military junta."

I sat forward. "Meaning?"

"The authorities that issued this document are no longer in power. Therefore, the document has no—ah, validity."

My hands clenched. "You're telling me I've been cheated out of my fee?"

"Perhaps 'cheated' is not the word, Mr. Novak, but essentially you cannot collect your due." He turned in his chair and waved a hand to encompass the office. "I have been discharged. The junta has frozen the embassy's bank accounts so I cannot pay you even were I authorized to do so."

I stared at him. My stomach knotted and went icy cold.

"As you see," Gonzalez continued, "I'm preparing to leave the embassy." His lips began to tremble. "Probably forever. Cast adrift after years of loyal service. In a foreign land, where I have no money, no resources." His voice was bitter.

"That prick Novarro. If I see him again I'll kill him!"

"If he made the mistake of returning home he may already have been killed. In any case you can hardly blame him for what has happened." He picked up my document and passed it across the desk. Taking it, I stared at the typed words, red ribbon and wax seal. "What can I do with it?"

"You might frame it as a souvenir of services rendered to the people of Guatemala. Beyond that . . ." He shrugged again. "The junta was quick to repudiate all national debts, so—" He shook his head sadly. "Perhaps some day the junta will be overthrown and an honest civilian government installed. You could present this to them."

I got up slowly. "It's a miserable cycle," I grated. "Chavez is booted out, and now the people who got rid of him and Tessier have been ousted." I shoved the document back into my pocket. "Wonder how long the junta will last?"

"Until their greed is satisfied." He got up, placed both palms on his desk and leaned forward. "I'm sorry this has turned out badly for you. Had you come in before the coup . . ."

"Should have," I said, "but I procrastinated."

He nodded. "A poetical phrase comes to mind: 'For all sad words of tongue or pen, the saddest are these: It might have been.' "

"Yeah. Right now I'm short on comforting philosophy, but you've got problems of your own. Wish we could have done business. *Cuídate. Adiós.*"

He gave me a repeat of that thin, bleak smile, and watched me leave. Jesus, I thought as I strode down the corridor, what a royal reaming! The receptionist gave me an ironic smile as I neared her, but said nothing. Maybe her job was secure. I left the embassy and walked to the taxi stand. The day was warm and sunny, the sky nearly cloudless. High above, a jet chalked a thin trail against the pale blue. This was reality.

Even more reality awaited me in our hotel suite. The Big Surprise I'd promised Melody had turned out to be a Big Fiasco for me. I got into the taxi and sat back wondering how I could tell Melody without looking like the improvident idiot I was. "Hotel Schweizerhof," I told the driver, sat back and closed my eyes.

She was standing phone in hand when I went in, and motioned me to be silent. Dressed in a light gray sharkskin suit, white blouse, black string tie and low shoes. I assumed she was talking to her mother because her voice was low, and that made me unhappier than I already was. Confessing my million-dollar gaffe would give Delores yet another reason to sneer at me. I wanted to blurt out my failure, get it behind us, but Melody kept on talking.

I slumped dispiritedly on a sofa and noticed our packed suitcases just inside the door; evidently we were Monte Carlo bound. When pressed, Melody could organize better than anyone I'd ever known, and this was an example.

Replacing the receiver, she turned to me. I said, "Honey, I've got bad news for you—terrible news."

She came to me, leaned over and kissed my forehead. "Whatever it is it can't be worse than mine."

"Delores? Your mother's ill?" I glanced at the suitcases.

She shook her head. "Brace yourself, Jack, that was a call from Miami." She took my hand. "Manny's vanished, kidnapped."

I gaped at her, swallowed, and managed, "Who says?"

"His wife, Lucy. Honey, I knew you'd want to go, so I've booked you on a one o'clock Dan-Air flight to London and home."

"Incredible," I said hoarsely. "You're coming?"

Her hands spread. "What could I do that you can't? No, I'll go to Monte Carlo, visit Mom and wait until you come back. By then I'll have everything arranged—we'll probably be married on Mehmet's yacht."

Dazedly I stood up. "Manny—*kidnapped.*"

"Lucy believes he's a hostage. She says the office isn't talking or doing anything, so she called you."

The buzzer sounded and Melody opened the door. Two elderly bellhops came in and picked up our bags. We followed them to the elevator. As we rode down, Melody lightly kissed my cheek and murmured, "What's the bad news for me?"

I shook my head. "Let it wait. We've got grief enough as it is." We got into a waiting taxi with our baggage and set off for Belp Airport six miles away.

TWO

In Miami it was late afternoon when I left the London flight and walked with the arriving crowd along the airport's endless corridors, arriving finally at Customs inspection arena. From above, people could look down through pane glass and watch our progress—or lack of it. I'd always disliked allowing greeters to see what was going on. For example, a drug or money courier could signal he had the stuff, then if he was grabbed, the contact man—or woman—could disappear. For me, the windows were too user-friendly for the wrong users.

Eventually, my two bags were chalked, and after tucking away my stamped passport I went out to a rank of waiting taxis. I bargained with the nearest driver and got a flat rate of twenty-five dollars to Coral Gables. The outside air was so hot and heavily humid that I began perspiring even before I got into the cab. Surprise, no air-conditioning.

"What's with the a/c, *amigo?*"

"You wanna haysee, mister? Five bucks *mas.*"

We were already beyond terminal confines, where I could have yelled for a cop or traffic inspector, so I said, "Have it your way," leaned over and dropped a fiver on the seat. "Granada Boulevard. Now let's have that Arctic air."

As we drove south from the airport the inside temperature dropped a couple of degrees, but the humidity declined appreciably, and for that I was grateful.

But not overly so. At the curb I took my bags from the trunk and handed the driver two ten-dollar bills. His eyes narrowed and he growled, "Twenny-five, mister."

"That was back at the airport, *pendejo*. The haysee wasn't worth five *centavos*, so be satisfied." I stepped back to study his license plate. He got the idea, snarled again and got behind the wheel. Tires left curbside marks as the taxi spun off, and I picked up my bags, feeling I'd scored one for the traveling public. Only London cabbies were honest and civil, I'd found; in Paris and Rome they were nothing less than brigands.

Going up the walk to our jointly-owned house, I looked around at the neighborhood. It was a few weeks after the big hurricane and a lot of visible damage remained. Once-graceful trees had been cut off knee-high, roofs lacked tiles, and some were still stove-in where trees had crashed against them. But our little love nest had weathered the storm with only minor physical damage.

I unlocked the front door and quickly disarmed the alarm system. I'd left the air-conditioning—a/k/a "haysee"—at eighty-two degrees, more to avoid mildewing than cool an empty house, so I reset the thermostat to seventy-four—Melody's preference—and heard the blower whine into action.

After locking the door I turned on lights and went to the bedroom where I opened bags and unpacked them. Light glinted from the ceiling mirror that so often reflected our pre-nup gambols, and I began missing Melody.

Next, I opened my concealed floor safe and got out ten hundred-dollar bills. Handling the cash reminded me of the morning fiasco at the Guatemalan embassy, so I poured a dram of Añejo over ice and sipped it to calm my nerves.

From under the bed I drew out my MAC-10 machine pistol and its companion H&K. 38. After replacing the MAC-10, I stuck the .38 under my belt against my spine and decided it was time to phone Lucinda Montijo and learn firsthand what the hell was going on.

I was reaching for the phone when door chimes sounded. Glass in hand, I went to the door and peered through the viewer. A light-skinned youngish man stood there. He was wearing a blue embroidered guayabera and looked harmless. Unless he had come to turn off light or water because of unpaid bills that littered the floor under the mail drop. "Who's there?" I asked in a loud voice.

"Name's Jameson." He opened a cred folder and showed me his ID photo. DEA. Thomas F. Jameson. "I work for Manny." He paused. "Or did."

With that I opened the door and told him to come in.

"Spotted you in Customs," he told me, and took the nearest chair.

"And it's up to me to figure how the office knew I'd be on that flight—right?"

"Something like that." He shifted uneasily, and I smiled.

"Easy. You've tapped Manny's home phone. You heard Mrs. Montijo call Bern, checked London passenger manifests and watched me arrive." I sat on the sofa and crossed my legs. "Why the personal attention?"

He sat forward. "Manny disappeared a week ago. We're squeezing all our informants to locate him. The office prefers that you not get involved, Mr. Novak." He swallowed and lowered his gaze. "That's the main message. The second is this: there's reason to believe Manny is dirty, so—"

"Impossible," I said loudly. "Never happen. Manny's as clean as you are, and a lot more law-abiding than me, so forget item two."

He shook his head. "Hell, I like Manny, always have, he's a good supervisor, but there's supposedly credible evidence he's been taking bribes."

"How credible?" I sneered. "Some zoned-out druggie wanting to cut a deal with you guys?" I shook my head. "I'll stake my life Manny's clean." I drained my glass, gripped it hard, remembering how he'd saved my life in Guadalajara a couple of years ago. "Does Mrs. Montijo know your theory?"

"Well, let's be clear—it's not *my* theory, sir—the chief supervisor put out word, and the USA listened. But she doesn't know."

I thought it over. "Okay, anyone can come under suspicion. If you know anything about my DEA time you know I quit because Phil Corliss had a hard-on for me. I exposed him for the incompetent he is, but apparently Fumbling Phil's legacy lives on. So I'm not impressed by your chief supervisor's opinion. Sounds like a McCarthyite revival in your office." I rubbed chin bristles and stared at Thomas Jameson. "Mrs. Montijo said Manny was kidnapped, you said disappeared. From that I gather your scenario runs like this: Manny is dirty, he learns he's under suspicion and takes off. But what's to say he wasn't kidnapped?"

Jameson was silent awhile before saying, "For one thing there's been no ransom note, no demands on Mrs. Montijo."

"Which you'd know about because her mail is watched and her phone tapped." I twirled the glass in my hand, wanting to smash it against the wall. "Is it out of the question he was snatched—even killed—by some guy he put away? Any agent who's worked the streets develops enemies; if he doesn't he's not doing his job. Right?"

He nodded.

"But you're not working too hard to locate Manny because—if he's dirty—letting it all hang out would embarrass DEA. Am I right about that?"

"Guess so," he said reluctantly.

"So let's put another spin on it. Which of Manny's known or potential enemies would have the balls or means to eliminate him?"

He swallowed again. "Well, there's General Jorge Padilla—"

"The Venezuelan drug baron?"

He nodded. "Manny ran a sting against him. Padilla's doing forty in Metro CC—South Dade."

"Any parole?"

"After twenty-five years. Fined four million."

I grunted. "And he's got forty tucked away. Now, if I was running the investigation, I'd check all of Manny's cases for the last ten years—including those we worked together, putting away downy birds. Who's still in the joint, who's not? Who's alive and capable of working off a grudge by snatching Manny? That would be a beginning, but if the office isn't interested in finding what happened to Manny—"

"That's not so," he said resentfully. "*I'm* interested, damn interested."

"Then I'll tell you this: I'm not impressed by your chief supervisor's injunction that I stay away from things—what's his name, anyway?"

"Van Shugrue."

"Sounds like a shoe salesman. As a civilian I can look into anything I damn please. Tell that to Mr. Shugrue."

He looked away. "Mentioned obstruction of justice if you get in the way."

I laughed thinly. "In the way of a non-investigation? Anyone sends the Feds for me I'll have their balls for false arrest." By now my blood pressure was at an all-time high. I tried to calm down by asking, "Is Manny's disappearance public knowledge?"

He shook his head.

"Bureau on the case?"

"Not yet. If there's dirty linen, Mr. Shugrue doesn't want to expose it to the Bureau."

"I'm familiar with the tradition." I stood up. "Anything else?"

He rose slowly, took a card from his pocket and gave it to me. Name and phone number. He said, "I've delivered the office message, done my duty. But I'm with you, Mr. Novak. I think Manny was kidnapped, maybe killed. I want to help any way I can."

"Unofficially."

"Unofficially." He put out his hand and I shook it. "You'll see Mrs. Montijo now, won't you?"

"Give her what comfort I can. Stay in touch." I opened the door and watched him go down the walk. A young agent, not yet coarsened and disillusioned as everyone becomes waging an unwinnable war.

After a shave and shower I got into clean clothes and drove my pearl gray Miata out of the garage and over Shula Expressway to Biscayne Boulevard, then north to the old Morningside section where the Montijos lived.

*   *   *

The house was one of the older ones, built between wars; one-story white stucco with terra-cotta barrel-tile roof typical of South Florida buildings. The house was set in from the Bay, with ample frontage and a well-trimmed lawn and shrubbery. How often, I thought, had Manny begged off from lunch or fishing saying he had gardening to do. Of two royal palms before the house, one's fronds had been decollated by the big wind and the other had only a short stump remaining. Neighbors with coconut palms had seen the big nuts hurled like artillery shells through walls and windows when the hurricane passed through.

I parked in the drive and went up to the front door, taking note of protective iron grillwork installed since my last visit. A wise precaution against home invasion. Windows were similarly barred, giving the Montijos a modicum of security.

Before I could press the doorbell the wooden door opened and Lucinda Paparelli Montijo stood before me. "Oh, Jack," she breathed, "I'm so glad you're here." She unlocked the grille and opened it for me, relocking both doors when I was inside. Then she came into my arms, sobbing and apologizing for her emotion. I hugged her, stroked her dark hair and said, "Honey, everything's going to be okay. I've talked with the office and they assured me everything possible is being done."

"Thank God, thank God." She moved back. "At least they talk with you; they wouldn't talk with me. Can you imagine?" She dried her eyes.

I shrugged. "Well, it's an ongoing investigation, full-court press to work on informants, so the office is reluctant to give details to anyone."

"Even me?" She stared at me, round-eyed.

"Even you, Lucy. Now let's sit down while you tell me what happened."

A door opened and elder daughter Rosario came in. She had her mother's average height, dark hair and slightly olive complexion. "Hello, Mr. Novak," she said and took my hand. "It's so good of you to come. All the way from Switzerland, Mother says."

"How could I stay away? Your father's like a brother to me."

The three of us sat in facing chairs, and I asked Rosario if she was studying at community college. She shook her head. "I transferred to Florida International University and like it a lot better—even though it's called Florida Immigrant U."

"Names, names. Who cares?" I turned to Lucy. "Your younger daughter . . . ah—"

"Carmen," she supplied, and I noticed her exchange glances with Rosario. "Carmen is, well, she's got a boyfriend. She dropped out of Hurley High last spring, but I'm hoping she'll go back and graduate."

"Slim chance," Rosario said bitterly. "Tell the truth, Mom. Carmencita left school to move in with that son-of-a bitch Carlos Stefano. Jack, he's a biker. Black leather and greasy hair. I thought Dad was going to kill him."

"Glad he didn't—I guess. Seems unlikely their social circles would intersect—how did they meet?"

"He cleaned our pool—sporadically."

"And supplied Carmen with pot," Rosario added. "Dad fired Carlos, but too late—the damage was done."

Lucy's eyes were moist as she looked at me. "For us it's a tragedy. I called her when Manny was kidnapped and she came around but hasn't been here since. I don't know what to do."

"Well, Manny has to be our focus," I said as gently as I could. "Now tell me what happened a week ago. When did Manny leave the house? Where was he going?"

Without interrupting I heard her out. On a Tuesday morning Manny had driven off, as usual at eight-ten, heading for his downtown office in the Federal building. He hadn't gotten there, and his car, a three-year-old white Mercury Marquis, had been found Thursday in the airport's B garage, undamaged, no keys. Upholstery showed no bloodstains, no fingerprints but those of the family. "That's it?" I asked, and she nodded. "So it was made to look like Manny flew out of Miami even though his name didn't show up on any passenger lists."

"Manny drive the same route every day to the office?"

"As far as I know. Down Biscayne, over Flagler . . ."

"Any chance he had a meeting arranged before going to the office?"

Rosario's eyes narrowed. "Meeting who?"

"Dunno. You tell me."

Lucy said, "If so, he didn't tell me."

"Would he normally?"

"If he was going to meet someone away from Miami, he usually did. You know—Lauderdale, the Keys, so I wouldn't worry."

"Jack," Rosario interjected, "would you like something to drink?"

"I would. Rum on the rocks if you've got it."

As Rosario left the room her mother said, "I haven't withheld anything. We never quarrel. I've always thought our marriage was ideal."

"From Manny I know it is."

Rosario brought back three glasses and gave me one. After sipping dark Jamaican rum, which I don't especially like, I said, "I think it comes down to kidnapping."

"But why?"

I sucked in a deep breath. "Manny's put away a lot of narcotics guys, big traffickers. General Padilla was one, and there were others. If an enemy was going to kill Manny your husband would be dead now, body stuffed in the trunk of some car, even his own. Or tossed into one of the 'Glades drainage canals that have become a sort of graveyard for drug dealers. Most narcotics types refrain from murdering Federal agents—they know the penalty is sure and sometimes swift. But you told Melody you think Manny's being held as a hostage. What made you say that?"

"No reason, I guess," she said wanly. "I was grasping at straws."

"Because," Rosario said, "if Dad's a hostage, he's alive. He can be ransomed or traded—right?"

I nodded. "It's a workable theory. Has the office offered a reward for information?"

"I hope so," Lucy said tightly, "but I don't know. Nothing was said to me."

I knew the office was saying nothing to Lucy because Manny was under suspicion, but I couldn't tell her that. His unexplained absence was problem enough to deal with. "I wonder," I remarked, "if Carmen could tell us anything?"

"Like what?" Rosario asked angrily.

"Oh, if she saw anyone hanging around the area. Strange faces, strange cars. If her father said anything to her before he drove away Tuesday morning."

"My sister isn't here enough to—" she began, and broke off. "Wait a minute. Mom, was Carmen here any time Tuesday?"

"Let me think . . . yes, she came by to pick up laundry. You were in class."

"Not class, Mom, the library."

"Did she talk to Manny?" I asked.

"Probably. Unless she managed to avoid her father . . . As you might guess they haven't gotten along well since she started going with Carlos. Moving in with him was the last straw."

"I want to talk with her."

"Waste of time," Rosario sniffed.

"Maybe not, and ought to be done. If you ask Carmen, will she come here?"

"They don't have a phone," Lucy said, "and they live in a terrible part of town. A project."

"So I'll go there. Just give me an address. And show me a photo of her. Last time I saw her she was in pigtails."

"Pigtails—" Rosario started to say something but broke off at a glance from her mother. I finished the remaining rum in my glass and got up. "Rosario, you might as well hear what I'm going to say to your mother, and it's this: I want you to consider the possibility of leaving this house and going someplace more secure—for the time being. Have a couple of bags packed and otherwise be ready to leave if I phone and tell you to. Will you do that?"

"Yes, Jack," Lucy replied, but Rosario bridled, "Why should we? This house is barred and grilled, there's a burglar alarm—"

"—And you'd miss classes, right? Well, life's more precious than a se- mester grade. And as for home security, bars, grilles and alarms didn't protect your father. What I'm saying is that if one of Manny's enemies decides to include you in his vengeance he knows exactly where you are. Your only protection is to be somewhere else."

"Until—what, Jack?" Rosario asked. "How long?"

"Can't answer now. Not without more information than we have." I watched Lucy open a desk drawer and take out a photo sheet, the kind that comes with class photographs. Several prints had been cut out, and Lucy used scissors to remove one for me. I held it under the nearest table lamp and saw a brown-haired beauty with heavy eyebrows, sensual lips and baby fat still rounding the contours of cheeks and chin. "Taken last spring," Lucy told me, and gave me a wallet-size photo of Manny. "This might help," she said hopefully.

"Might," I agreed. "Meanwhile, keep your shades down and don't linger when you come in from the car. Okay?"

Lucy hugged me then and started to cry. Rosario turned away and dabbed at her cheeks while I comforted her mother. "Call me any time you want to talk," I said. "Especially if anyone calls with a ransom demand. Rosario, if you've got a tape recorder, hook it to the phone receiver with a suction mike."

She looked puzzled. "What's that?"

"Radio Shack will help you." I turned to Lucy. "Considering Manny's line of work, your house is dangerously vulnerable. You're about fifty yards from the Bay, exposed to anyone who plans a cruise-by shooting or wants to come ashore and leave unseen. Cars can turn in from US 1 unchallenged, bringing God-knows-who to your front door. You have no security fence or even a wall to keep strangers away. Not a good situation, ladies, so be very careful. While I'm out looking for Manny I'd rather not be worrying about you."

Lucy started toward the front entrance but I shook my head and left by the rear. For a while I stood there until my eyes adjusted to darkness, and then

I peered around the corner of the house. Two houses away a car was pulled over at roadside, not in a nearby empty drive. The car was a black four-door Corolla, unlighted. Even so I could make out the dim silhouette of a figure slumped behind the wheel.

Who was the driver? Why was he there?

Crouching, I ran to my car, knelt and opened the door enough to press the light-switch button and prevent illumination. With my other hand I opened the glove compartment and took out a Maglite, then quietly shut the door.

Pistol in one hand, flash in the other, I circled around and came up behind the parked car. Crouching again, I edged forward until I could grip the door handle. Then I jerked open the door and shined my light in the driver's face. ''Security,'' I barked. ''Who are you? What's your business here?''

THREE

ONE HAND shot up to shield his eyes as he gasped, "Jesus, don't—" and then I recognized him. "Shit," I snapped. "you," and turned off my light. My earlier visitor, Thomas Jameson of the Miami office.

"Mr. Novak," he said hoarsely, "God, you scared me!"

"What the hell are you doing here?" I pocketed pistol and flashlight.

"Watching the house."

"Protective surveillance—office orders?"

He shook his head. "My idea. See—I wasn't sure you'd be here so I . . . well, with Manny gone I thought . . ." His head drooped guiltily.

"Hey, great idea. Sorry I interfered."

I heard him suck in a deep breath. "Might as well tell you—I've been dating Rosario."

"No kidding? She's, what, nineteen?"

"Twenty," he said defensively, "and Manny said it was okay."

"What did Mrs. Montijo say?"

"Well, she was less enthusiastic—but we only go out Saturday nights I'm off duty, see a movie, or dance over on South Beach." He swallowed. "Maybe I shoulda told you."

"Maybe you should. Listen, I'm glad you're here, saves me calling your office." I walked around the car and got in on the passenger side. "I want to talk to Carmen but she's sort of left the family circle. I've got an address that looks like Little Haiti, but I'm not going to make the mistake of urging her to move back home. What I want, and what you can give me when computers go on-line tomorrow, is a rundown on her boyfriend Carlos—"

"—Stefano," he finished. "Manny got the printout a while back and showed me." He paused. "What you wanta know?"

"Putting it another way, Jamey, why don't you tell me what it told Manny and you?"

He looked away, and I saw that he was eyeballing the front of the Montijo house. The shades were drawn so that the only light leaked from their oblong perimeters. No one could see inside. Good.

Turning back to me, Jameson said, "The guy's Miami-born Cuban. Twenty-eight or twenty-nine. Six months in the Dade County Stockade for pot dealing. Never finished high school. Runs with a biker gang that does smash-and-grab road stuff, robs convenience stores and strips cars for chop shops. He's been arrested for that but no conviction."

"Christ," I said, "let's pray he hasn't got AIDS. No wonder Manny wanted Carmen away from him." I shook my head. "Sounds like the kind of varlet who needs both knees busted."

Through the darkness Jameson smiled. "I suppose it's really none of our business."

"Strictly speaking. But where friends are concerned I tend to take an elastic view of private doings."

"Me, too." He looked over at the house again.

"I pray I'm wrong, but it's possible the bad guys could reach out for the ladies. I gave them a short talk on personal security and hope it sinks in. Frankly, I'd like them out of town for a while. Disney World, say, or some hideout on the Keys." I remembered my stilt shack on Islamorada, swept away by the hurricane. Leaving memories engraved in my brain. Jameson said, "Would they snatch the women? Harm them?" The idea upset him.

"Why not? Snatching a Federal officer was a major risk. With that kind of steel balls they wouldn't hesitate to grab the family." I swallowed. "If they found reason to do it."

"Jesus," he groaned, "what can we do?"

"First priority is recovering Manny. Number two is nailing whoever's responsible. Number three—well you're doing the right thing now. Stick with it." I patted his arm and got out. He leaned sideways to ask, "Where you going?"

"Carmen," I told him. "If she knows something it shouldn't stay unsaid for lack of asking."

He grimaced as though reaching a difficult decision. "Stefano," he said finally. "An occasional informant for Metro cops and the office—so he stays out of jail."

"Well, thanks, good to know, but my business is with little sister. Keep up the good work."

I got into my car and drove across town into a raunchy section widely known as hazardous to non-speakers of Creole. The address Lucy gave me turned out to be a sleazy two-story motel featuring shattered glass, plywood boarding, stapled eviction notices, and a plethora of sprayed graffiti. Though nearby *Le Soleil* market was closed, its signs offered goat meat, white and black chickens, slithery seafood and doves. Artistic depictions identified these viands for illiterate denizens, and I particularly liked the portrait of a bearded ram with large, curled-back horns. *Kabrit.* Not to be missed if you identified with Miami's increasingly multicultural society.

Up a shaky staircase to a second-floor balcony strewn with garbage, diapers, rum bottles (empties), broken toys, beer cans, a shopping-cart minus wheels, glass shards that ground under my soles, and much more junk and litter too varied to mention. The stench was worse than a garbage dump. Lightbulbs had been taken from overhead sockets, making it difficult to read door numbers.

Nearby a dog barked. A bottle crashed and the dog yelped. Or maybe another dog. In one of the project units a baby began crying. Distantly a dog started to howl. Not far off a speeding rescue wagon's bells and horns slaughtered what remained of evening stillness. I rapped on the door to unit 22 and listened. Rapped again. A female voice called, "Who's there?"

"Carmen? Jack Novak. I need to talk with you."

"Go away."

"No, I won't do that. Let me in or I'll break in."

Prolonged silence. "You want to take me home."

"I'm not here for that, just a couple questions."

More thinking-it-over silence. Finally, "You promise?"

"Promise."

Presently the snub-chain rattled, the door opened. Inside light came feebly from an orange lampshade keeping visibility low. But I wasn't scanning the room; I was looking at the younger daughter of Manuel Montijo, who slouched before me. Carmen sniffled and rubbed her nose. "Am I supposed to know you?"

"You did—when you were younger." At first I thought her face was muddy, then I realized there were bruise marks on her cheek and temple. Her lips were puffy from lacerations. Eyes reddened. Hair and hands hadn't been washed in days. She shrugged. "So, what is it?"

"Your dad's disappeared, you know that?"

"Yeah." She didn't meet my eyes.

"Last Tuesday morning you went home for laundry. You saw him then?"

"Yeah." The top of her head didn't reach my chin. With proper nutrition she might grow another few inches. I asked, "You talked with him?"

She sighed boredly. "*He* talked—wanted me to leave Carlos and come home."

In the far corner there was a low studio bed, sheets in tumbled disarray. On it lay a white male naked but for a black bikini brief. He lifted on one elbow and called, "You rappin' about me? Who the hell are you, man?"

"Friend of the family. Stay out of it."

He sat on the edge of the bed, bare feet on bare flooring. His black hair was shoulder-long; unkempt strands shaded his eyes. His face was thin, cheeks sunken. Thirty feet away I could count his ribs. Either he was anorexic or a drug devotee. "Hey, man" he called, "you hasslin' my woman?"

Turning her head, Carmen said, "It's all right, Carlos."

He ignored her. "Get the hell outa here, man. Get lost."

"Presently," I responded. "Carmen, did your father say anything about going anywhere before getting to the office? Seeing anyone?"

"Shut up, kid," Carlos yelled. "Say nothin'."

"Listen to me, you *comemierda*, stop interrupting."

"Or what?" A switchblade clicked open as he got up. He was about six feet, one-forty max. "C'mon over, Carlos," I invited. "Tell me about Carmen's face."

"Took a fall." He kept walking toward us, bare feet silent on the flooring. "Right, kid? You took a fall."

"Yeah," she said unconvincingly. The knifeblade glinted in the light as he raised it. I stepped around Carmen to face him. "Try that and you'll get grief you've never known. Put it away and go back to your kennel."

His free hand swished hair from his eyes. Their pupils told me he was on the downside of a fix. "Last warning," I snapped. "Put the shank away."

Instead, he stabbed at me—not the move of a knife-fighter—so I slapped his wrist aside. Carmen screeched, and I grabbed his wrist as I turned around. With Carlos behind mc I twisted his arm, dropped and levered his body over me. Yelling in pain he released his knife before his back hit the floor hard. I kicked away the knife and, still gripping his arm, set one foot on his throat. Carmen cried out and knelt beside him, kissing his face until I brought her to her feet. Carlos's eyes were glazed. He whimpered. Carmen tried to wrest free but I held on as I spoke to the man on the floor. "Listen to me, you piece of shit, and remember what I say. I'm not wasting you because there's a witness. Carmen is leaving with me, and if you try seeing her, I'll find a time and place to hit you without witnesses. Understand?"

"Yeah," he croaked.

"Carmen, get anything valuable and bring it. You won't be coming back."

"I'm not going with you," she flared. "I'm staying with Carlos."

"You like beatings?" I picked up the knife, folded back its blade and pocketed it. "Stay there—*man*," I told him, "and think about statutory rape and physical assault. With your rap sheet that equals two dimes in the slammer."

Carmen renewed her struggles. "Nothing you want to bring with you?" I began dragging her through the doorway but she braced herself against the jamb. So I reached over and bore into the neck pressure point with my thumb. She would have fallen, but I lifted her over my shoulder and, carrying her limp body, made my way back along the balcony and down the open staircase to where I'd left my car.

Three black youths were circling it. They wore turned-around baseball caps and trash clothing. "You've checked it out," I rasped, "so make tracks."

"Who says so, man?" one of them jeered.

"My friend here." I pulled out my .38 and fired in the air. Twice. Before the echo faded they were gone. No project doors opened, no shades tilted at the reports. Gunshots were part of area living—if you could call it that.

Opening the near door, I dumped Carmen inside and got behind the wheel. Then I strapped her into the seat and locked the door.

The sound of the engine starting brought her back to reality. "Bastard! Where you taking me? I won't go home, won't stay there." She started sniffling. "I need to go back to Carlos, take care of him."

"That's one place you're not going—back there. We're going where he can't beat you, where you can clean up and get the fist-marks healed." I steered West toward I-95. "Did he put you on the street?"

"No."

"But he tried."

Her face turned away. Jesus, what that scumbag had done to her! "Okay, you had sense enough not to work the street, so he beat you up."

More sniffling, then came honest sobs. I gave her my handkerchief. Shoulders shaking, she covered her face with it. Crying was good for her, purging emotions.

Eighteen minutes later I turned into my drive and pulled her from the car. Sullenly she went up the walk ahead of me, and it occurred to me that any neighbors looking out would think I was arranging to fuck a teenage whore. Hell with them.

I unlocked the door, disarmed the alarm, and pushed Carmen into the living room. I reset the alarm system and turned on lights. Carmen looked around. "You live here?"

"I live here." I went to the bar and poured Añejo over ice. She looked at it and licked swollen lips. "Can I have some?"

"Are you hooked?"

She shook her head, turned arms outward for inspection. No tracks. "A medicinal quantity, Carmen."

"Vodka?"

I poured a shot over rocks and handed it to her. She stirred with a dirty finger and sipped. "I was afraid you were going to kill Carlos."

"Not my privilege—your dad's. No, don't sit down, come with me." I led her to the bathroom and turned on the shower. "Use soap. And shampoo. I'll get clothes for you." I closed the door and went to the farthest phone, dialed the Montijo house. Rosario answered.

"Novak here," I told her.

"You've got—news?"

"I've got Carmen." Dragged her out of that pesthole and she's cleaning up. I want you or your mother to bring her clothing."

"I'll come, Jack, better me than Mother."

"Your call," I said, and gave her my address. "She needs medical attention, cuts and bruises, but I'd rather it not be done at an ER. Do you know a doc who'd come and take care of her?"

"Well—why not an emergency room?"

"Because your sister might take it into her head to run off. Right now she's not testing high for stability."

"I understand. Sorry. Uh—shall I tell Mom?"

"If you have to. But I want to talk with her later, explain some things. What about a doctor?" I swallowed a mouthful of cold rum.

"There's—wait, I know someone. Doctor Ing."

"Get him moving." I looked at my wristwatch. "You can make it here in half an hour."

"Yes—and, thanks, Jack."

I swallowed more rum. "If Jamey's still outside, tell him to stay where he is."

I heard a quick intake of breath. "Whatever you say."

The shower was still running. At the kitchen table I shook out the empty .38 casings and replaced them with soft-nose cartridges. Poured myself another drink, thinking that in Europe it was halfway to dawn, Melody sleeping peacefully, and me with a young sinner on my hands. I couldn't understand why Manny hadn't yanked Carmen out of that filthy pad, must have had reasons—or maybe he'd tried. Anyway, she was among the living again, and I hoped Rosario would treat her with compassion if not understanding.

I heard the bathroom door open, got up and went there. Carmen had a towel toqued around her hair, another around her hips. She held out her empty glass. ''More?''

I poured half of her first shot and went back to where she was standing. As she took the glass she dropped the hip towel and said coquettishly, ''What do you think, Jack?''

This naked teenager was something else. ''I see some contusions I couldn't see before. Any rib pain?''

''No.'' She frowned. ''Not what I mean.''

''Oh. Well, I think you'll develop into a fully formed female within a few years. You've got a pretty good start.''

She touched her unbruised breast. ''Too small, huh?''

''About right for your age, and there's growing time. Eat a balanced diet and stay away from men who try to kill you.''

I knew damn well what she was up to and it made me feel sick. Manny's daughter. Christ! ''Okay,'' I said, ''you pass inspection. Get in that bathrobe hanging behind the door.''

She frowned again. ''You gay?''

''I've got a girlfriend, okay? Consider me Uncle Jack, your father's best friend.'' The hickeys around her neck angered me. That son-of-a-bitch Carlos Stefano. ''Hair dryer in the cabinet. Plug in and use.'' Melody wouldn't mind. ''By the way, are you hungry?''

''A little.''

''I'll see what there is.'' I hadn't been back long enough to stock up but there was probably pizza in the freezer. She went back into the bathroom and closed the door. Presently I heard the hair dryer whirring. Good sign.

I microwaved a cheese-sausage pizza, got out plates and utensils, and after a while Carmen joined me at the table. Her face was still a bruised mess, but at least it was clean. And her hair was a couple of shades lighter.

After she'd swallowed a few bites I said, ''Before being interrupted I was asking you what you and your father spoke about last Tuesday morning.''

''I told you.''

''Carmen, this is important. Your father's life is in danger. He's been kidnapped by enemies and I need to know if he was going somewhere before the office.''

She looked down at her plate. ''I think—yes, he said he had to gas his car because he was going—'' She broke off and gazed at me.

''Think. Where?''

''It was . . . the Keys.'' She nodded. ''What's that town just where the Keys begin?''

"Florida City."

"That's it," she said happily. "Florida City."

"Good. Great. Did he say why? A name?"

"No, but he never does." She squinted through puffed eyelids. "I remember your name—you and Dad used to work together. Everything secret." The ridiculous thought made her giggle.

"So we did. Your father's an important man in the Government, Carmen, and I'm trying to get him back."

She thought it over. "Suppose he doesn't want to come back?"

"Like, what?"

"Like he got a lot of drug money and took off. Maybe Brazil, y'know?"

I grunted. "You don't know your father very well. Either he's dead or a prisoner, not a corrupt narc."

"You're right about one thing, I never got to know Dad very well. Either he was away or working nights . . . Mom did everything for us—Rosario and me."

"And you haven't made it easy for them. Ever hear of gratitude?"

She looked away, her response to everything. Denial. The door chimes sounded and I saw fright on her face. "I'm expecting two visitors, not Carlos. So take it easy."

I opened the door on Rosario, took the small suitcase from her while she rushed to Carmen and hugged her. Both sisters began to cry. After a while they began talking at once. By then I was at the bar, refilling my glass. I poured vodka for Rosario and took it to her. She gulped the straight liquor gratefully and looked up at me. "Oh, Jack, I'm so glad you brought Carmen. She looks so—" She sobbed brokenly. Carmen stroked her hair and asked, "Does Mom know I'm here?"

"No—not yet. I thought you and I—" She broke off again. "If I'd known how terrible you look . . ."

"Doctor on the way?" I asked.

"Said so. Answered his beeper."

Carmen said, "Doctor?"

"He'll start your healing," I interjected. "And don't fight him, or I'll spank you harder than you ever were spanked before."

As though on signal the chimes sounded, and in a few moments I admitted a small Oriental with a black medical bag. Through thick lenses he peered at me. "Is Miss Montijo here?"

"Both of them." I pointed at the sofa. "Carmen, go to the bedroom and show Dr. Ing where the bathroom is." His head tilted as he gazed at Carmen's battered face, and he gave a low whistle. "When did that happen?"

"Days," she said in a subdued voice. "Today was the worst." She got up and left the room with Dr. Ing. When they were gone I looked at Rosario. "Good work."

"No, Jack, you did the really good work. Was—was it hard to get her away?"

"Not really. Now we've got some things to consider. How to factor your mother in, and how Carmen is to be managed. Whatever drugs she's been on, heroin isn't one. Speed, probably, the biker's choice, and pot so there's no problem of a long-term addiction cure. She needs routine detox and counseling." I paused. "I'd like the doc to take enough blood for hepatitis check and HIV, plus the usual VDs. The doc will know combination clinics around Miami that handle cases like Carmen, and home isn't the place. Home comes later—that's why I had you bring clothing. I'm going to burn what she was wearing." I shook my head remembering the filth of that pad.

Her hands knotted into fists. "What about Carlos?"

"I gave him some pain to remember, along with a reality speech."

"I want him arrested. For statutory rape, beating her up." Her eyes filled with tears. Irritably she wiped them away.

"I understand that, but there are other considerations. If he's charged he'll get a free Legal Aid lawyer and you folks will suddenly be on trial."

"On *trial*? Jack, you've got to be kidding."

"Unfortunately not. The defense lawyer will try to have your parents charged with child neglect—tolerating her moving out and living with an adult male; not reporting it to the authorities. No, this is one where the Montijo family takes its lumps and tries to get together again. No recriminations, no reprising what's past."

We heard Carmen squeal—the doc was bandaging or drawing blood. Rosario stiffened, then relaxed. I said, "Depending on what the doc recommends, Carmen can stay here for now—I'll be away part of the time—and you're welcome to stay with her."

She swallowed. "Jack, how bad are her injuries?"

"She's been beaten," I replied, "but I think the damage is only skin deep, no broken bones."

She hesitated. "Internal?"

"Let the doc do his work."

The telephone rang and I went to it. Jamey calling?

"Jack?" Lucy's voice. "A man called. He said he was willing to make a deal." Her voice trembled.

"What kind of deal?"

"A trade—he called it a hostage trade. He'll send back my husband in exchange for General Padilla's freedom.'' Her voice lowered to a whisper. ''He said Manny's alive—for now.''

''Thank God, Lucy, we've got a starting point. Now we know why Manny was taken.''

Her voice returned to normalcy. ''The Government will let that general go, won't they? I mean, getting Manny back is more important than keeping Padilla in jail . . .''

A chill came over me. ''Sure, Lucy,'' I managed, ''but these deals take time, so be prepared to wait. Now, call the office and tell the night duty officer.'' Rosario had come over to eavesdrop, but I hung up and told her the news. Almost word for word she repeated her mother's question about the trade, and I repeated what I'd told Lucy. Rosario's face glowed. ''How wonderful!'' she exclaimed. I glanced at her and tried to smile encouragingly.

Because I couldn't tell her that the Feds would never make the trade. They had a very big fish in prison and were going to keep him as an example to others. They wouldn't trade Padilla for anyone less than the President, and Manny Montijo was only a mid-level government employee. He wasn't even a shitass Senator. Manny was expendable.

Padilla? My thoughts answered Lucy's caller:

Montijo alive or Padilla dead.

FOUR

SUN WOKE me.

Streamed in through the unshaded window and I turned my face away. For a few moments I lay groggily wondering what in hell I was doing on the living room sofa, then bits and pieces of yesterday began flowing together like mercury droplets until a picture formed.

My watch showed four PM. Was it possible? No, I'd never changed from Swiss to local time. In Florida it was only ten. I sat up, felt neck pain from sleeping on the too-short sofa, massaged my neck for relief and set both feet on the floor. I didn't remember removing my shoes, so someone must have done it. Rosario? Carmen? Dr. Ing had come and I'd dropped off before he left. Combination of fatigue and jet lag.

I lurched over to the window and pulled down the shade, eliminating painful rays. Then I looked around.

No change from yesterday when I'd come back from Bern. Except for a group of tubes and bottles on the kitchen counter. Beside them was a hand-written message but I couldn't deal with it until after coffee. After half a cup I propped elbows on the counter and read:

Dear Jack:
It's almost four-thirty and I have to get back home. Dr. Ing left prescriptions for Carmen and I had them filled at an all-night pharmacy. She'll sleep late because of the sleeping pill.

Okay. When my sister wakes please give her a tetracycline cap and three more during the day. The cortisone cream is for her lips. There are pain pills and two sleeping pills if needed. The doctor said the more time she spends in bed, the better.

I've got classes until noon, after which I'll come back and relieve you. Mom wants Carmen home but Carmen may not want to come, so that's up in the air

at this point. In the morning Mom has an appointment at the DEA office to talk
about the exchange message, and plans to go to your place afterward. So you
might prepare Carmen for her arrival.

We're terribly grateful that you got my sister out of that dreadful mess, and
want to uncomplicate your life as soon as possible.

                                                      In haste, Rosario.

Beside the note was a prescription form headed Horatio Ing, MD, Family
Practice. On it he had scrawled: *Carmen should drink a lot of fluid while on
antibiotics. I gave her a DPT booster.*

Okay, doc, I thought, and, okay, Rosario. Your male nurse is back on duty.

I drained my cup and made my way to the bedroom. Carmen was sprawled
on the bed, face up. The right side of her face was bandaged and her lips were
smeared with ointment. I listened to her light, regular breathing and went into
the bathroom. After shower and shave I dressed and began looking for
breakfast food. The freezer held a box of croissants and a package of bacon.
I took them out to thaw while I organized the eight-cup percolator, and then
I sat down and reflected on Lucy's anonymous call.

What she didn't know was that her phone was tapped and office monitors
heard and taped the call, so the office knew of the demand even before Lucy
could tell me. Better she not know should other calls come in; then she could
respond naturally.

The exchange demand complicated the office theory that Manny was a
corrupt officer, but it also gave Van Shugrue a rationale for not pressing hard
to find Manny. The other negative concerned office awareness that no such
exchange was ever going to be made. No exchange, no Manny, the scenario
went, sparing DEA the embarrassment of putting a corrupt officer on trial.
Dead, Manny couldn't be tried, and I doubted Shugrue would try to indict
him now.

I could never share these thoughts with Lucy Montijo, for they would rob
her of all hope for Manny's survival. I had to spare her that. And what
graveled me was office failure to dismiss the slander against Manny as
disinformation circulated by his enemies—most likely agents of General
Padilla. Rumors of corruption were a traditional means of destroying an
effective DEA officer. Even if corruption was never proved the man's record
remained stained by the allegation; in practical terms ending his career and
usefulness. From personal experience I knew about that.

The phone rang and I heard Rosario's voice asking, ''Jack, you okay?
Hope I didn't wake you.''

''No, but Carmen's still sleeping.''

"Good. Uh—I had to tell Mom the situation at your place, and although I'm dead tired I'll be coming with her."

"Should I prepare your sister for that?"

"Probably not, Jack. The idea is to take her home peacefully."

"If she's willing. Otherwise she can recuperate here."

"That's very generous of you, but you've already done more than enough."

"Ah—where you calling from?"

"Pay phone. Why?"

"Just curious. Anyway, Carmen told me your dad said he was heading for Florida City last Tuesday morning. Mean anything to you?"

"No—wish it did."

"Well, she may remember more in time."

"See you later."

I poured another cup of coffee and was adding sweetener when another call came in; this from Jamey on his car phone. "How are things?"

"Very quiet. Rosario and her mother will be here at midday to retrieve Carmen."

"Good idea. Would it help if I came, too?"

"Doubt it. Did you grab any sleep?"

"A little and I need more. Uh—I heard about the call to Mrs. Montijo last night. The office didn't know how to react to it."

"I can imagine. Anyway, Carmen told me her dad was heading for Florida City last Tuesday morning, before the office. Mean anything to you? Did he have a case working down there? An informant meeting?"

"I just don't know. Maybe Manny was snatched there and his car driven back to the airport—"

"—to make it look like he'd grabbed a flight. Yeah. This thing was organized, Jamey, including the corruption smear."

I paused before saying, "I'd like to get a hook into one of Padilla's men. There has to be a couple of them doing time at South Dade Correctional. Can you help me? Preferably one who's vulnerable—you know, wants to avoid deportation or cut a deal for less time. Give me names and I'll handle the rest."

"I'll try. Maybe I'll come by later."

I separated bacon strips and began broiling them in the toaster oven. The croissants I'd microwave after Carmen woke up.

The next call was from Melody aboard the old Turk's yacht. After affectionate pleasantries she asked if Manny had been found. "Not yet," I told her, "and it's not something to discuss on open phones. The family's pretty devastated and I'm trying to help as I can."

"I knew you would. Jack, how long will you be there?"

"All I can say is that I'm here for the duration. Meanwhile, you're okay, aren't you? And Mom and Mehmet?"

"We're all just fine—and, darling, he's an old dear. No wonder Mother's so taken with him."

Him and his millions, I thought, but said, "What's the prospect of us marrying in Monte Carlo?"

"Won't need to, which is really why I called. Mehmet will have the captain take the yacht twelve miles offshore, where the captain can marry us. Isn't that great?"

"Terrific. Why didn't we think of that before?"

"Too many other things crowding our minds. Anyway, Mother is delighted. She and Mehmet plan a fabulous wedding reception. Honey, are you okay?"

"Sure, just tired from travel. Is there a radiophone call number I can reach you?"

"Uh-huh, here it is."

I wrote down the call-sign as she spoke each letter and number, and said, "Presh, I'll phone if there's any news."

"Please do. Good or bad, I want to know."

As I hung up I heard the toilet flush, meaning Carmen was awake. Presently she entered the kitchen wearing bathrobe, my pajamas and bandages on her face. Her left eye was less swollen as were her lips. " 'Morning," she greeted me. "Late, isn't it?"

"How are you feeling?"

"Groggy, sort of like drugged." She yawned and looked around. "That bacon I smell?"

"It is. Have a seat and some coffee while I do the rest."

We ate croissants with apple jelly and crisp bacon, consumed more coffee, and I noticed that her hands and fingernails were clean. "Any pain?" I asked.

"Not much."

I'd forgotten her tetracycline, so I gave her a cap and a large glass of water. "Three more today," I told her, and when breakfast was over I gave her the cortisone cream for her lips. After applying it, she asked about Rosario.

"She'll come after classes."

She stirred her coffee. "Anything new about Dad?" It was the first time she'd expressed even minimal concern for Manny, so I told her about the call to her mother and the exchange demand.

"But that's great news, isn't it? Keeping Padilla in prison doesn't help anything. But getting Daddy back is what it's all about."

I nodded. "That's what it's all about."

"And we know my father's alive, don't we? I mean, without him there couldn't be any exchange."

"Logical," I agreed. "Now, do you remember anything Doctor Ing told you?"

"Oh, he took some blood from my arm, said he wanted to test for various things, asked some personal questions . . . Then I must have fallen asleep." She got up and brought over the percolator, filled our cups. "How long am I going to be here?"

"That's for you and Rosario to decide. You're welcome to stay, Carmen, but I won't be here a lot of the time. Until your father returns all of you need protection, and when I'm away . . ." I spread my hands. "My goal is to locate your father, that's why I came back from Switzerland. I'm sure you understand."

"I do. And I'm grateful for everything you've done. But if it's sort of arranged that they'll let Padilla go so Daddy can come back, then you can go back to Switzerland."

"After arrangements are locked in. But as I told your mother our government moves slowly. For one thing there's a policy of never negotiating for hostages. If the head of DEA and the Attorney General agree to the exchange it can't be publicly known."

"Why not?"

"That would encourage terrorists and narcotics organizations to kidnap Americans around the world in order to force concessions of one kind or another. So your father's exchange would be a very special exception to public policy."

"But they'd make that exception for Daddy?"

Oh, the illusions of the young, I thought before saying, "I certainly hope so." And then I asked, "After talking with your father last Tuesday morning did you tell anyone about his plans?"

"You mean, about going to Florida City." She looked down at her empty plate. "Well, Carlos asked what we talked about—so I told him. Wasn't any harm in that, was there?"

"I don't know. What happened then? Did Carlos stay with you, or maybe go out?"

"Go out for what?"

"No phone in his pad. Maybe he went to a pay phone to make a call. That's what he does, isn't it?"

"Sometimes." She shifted uncomfortably and looked away.

"Well, did he?"

"I—I don't remember," she said huskily.

"Sure you do."

Fiercely, she said, "You're trying to make it look like Carlos had something to do with Daddy's disappearance."

"I'm covering all angles. Did Carlos leave you and make a call? Did he?"

Surlily she said, "So what if he made a phone call—doesn't have to be what you're thinking."

"But could be. Answer my question, Carmen, was a call made?"

Almost in a whisper she said, "He went out, I saw him at the pay phone. I don't know who he called."

"But he made a call."

"And now you're going to try to do something to him—more than what you did."

"He's dangerous company, child. Too old for you, too wasted, too evil. I hear he's a biker—where's his bike?"

She thought about it. "Sold it, I guess. Anyway, it was stolen when he got it."

"Or maybe he was the thief."

Wordlessly, she shrugged. I took our plates to the sink, scraped and rinsed them, and set them in the dishwasher. I'd gotten all I could from this refractory child, but Carlos Stefano was still available for questioning.

"What now?" she asked.

"Rosario brought some clothing, so get dressed before she arrives. You'll look better and feel better."

She left then, and I began thinking what I might possibly do in the event Jamey unearthed a Padilla prisoner for me. I wanted information, but I didn't want to become a target for Padilla troops still on the street. Having put in so much time and concentration on little Carmen, I hadn't had a real chance to organize my thoughts into something resembling a plan. In Florida City there was nothing for me but a bowl of beer-steamed shrimp, if I went there, and I was sure the office had gone over Manny's appointment calendar for clues to his movements. I needed a name or a location, or both, and I had neither.

Where were they holding Manny? Some location remote from Miami? A Beach high-rise? Had he been flown to Venezuela for safekeeping? All were possibilities, singly or sequentially, and I wondered if DEA offices in Caracas and Maracaibo had been told to look for Manny.

I answered door chimes and there were Lucy and Rosario, both looking tired and drawn. Tremulously, Lucy asked, "How is she?"

"Better than last night. She's rested and fed but still pretty edgy. You know her better than I do, but I think a gentle hand is essential right now."

Lucy kissed and hugged me. "I'm so grateful, Jack. And Manny will be—when he gets back." She glanced around, and I said, "She's dressing."

Rosario said, "I told Mom what you said about no recriminations so there'll be none of that. We just want her home where we can give her love and care."

"Really all she needs," I remarked, and then Carmen came in.

She was wearing jeans and a dark blue shirt. Her hair was done up with one of Melody's ribbons, and she looked better than I'd seen her since childhood. Except for the bandages, of course. Lucy went to her daughter, gathered Carmen in her arms, and both began to cry. Rosario looked at me with tear-filled eyes. "Jack, it's a miracle, and we have you to thank."

"No thanks necessary." I looked at my watch. "Got things to take care of, so I'll leave now that the situation seems to be resolving itself. If I'm not back before you go, just lock the door, okay?"

"Okay."

I waved goodbye to Carmen and went down to where I'd left the Miata. I'd forgotten to garage it and by great good fortune the tires weren't slashed or the paint keyed. So I drove down to the market and laid in groceries for a couple of weeks. At the next door liquor store I bought Añejo, vodka, scotch and bourbon. That took forty-five minutes, and when I pulled into my drive the Montijo cars were gone. Carmen with them, I hoped.

Her prescription bottles were also gone, I noticed, responsibility for her care having been transferred back home where it belonged.

In the bedroom I changed sheets and pillowcases, cleaned hair and soap film from washbasin and shower, and made myself a morning bracer—Añejo on the rocks. Then I stowed groceries and was contemplating a return visit to Carlos Stefano, when the phone rang. "Mr. Novak?"

"Yes."

"Please hold. Mr. Shugrue will speak with you."

A gruff voice said, "Mr. Novak, Van Shugrue. Supervising Special Agent of the Miami DEA office. I know that you're aware of certain circumstances affecting the Montijo family, and—"

"You mean the proposed body exchange."

"Exactly. In confidence, you should know that the subject is being handled through official channels."

"Oh, God," I groaned.

"What—what's that supposed to mean?"

"What it sounds like—despair. Manny will die in official channels and we both know it."

Huffily, he said, "I don't know any such thing. I know your background and your disdain for proper procedures, but in this case any interventions you might have in mind will be not only superfluous, but bordering on obstruction.''

"Golly. Give me a moment to wade through those polysyllabic words.'' I paused. "In short, you want me to stay away from the case.''

"You got it. Go back to Bern and get married. We'll work on Manny at this end.''

"Why don't I find that encouraging?'' I asked. "We're talking about a man who saved my life in Guadalajara and you're suggesting I turn my back on him.''

"Not suggesting,'' Shugrue said harshly, "telling you how it's going to be.''

"Mr. Shugrue,'' I said, "you're accustomed to issuing orders to your employees, but you forget I'm not one of them. So I'll take your warning—threat, whatever—for what I deem it's worth. Get it?''

There was a substantial silence before he spoke again. "Not a helpful attitude, Novak. If you're smart as some say you'll reconsider.'' Another pause. "You haven't told Mrs. Montijo about her phone?''

"The tap? Goodness no. That would reveal state secrets. Anything else, sir?''

"One thing. I heard about you from Phil Corliss so—''

"Figures. Maybe he told you I rammed a big stick up his ass. Well, I haven't forgotten how it's done. Consider that my message to you. Got it?''

"Fuck you,'' he snarled, and slammed down the phone. I smiled at the obscene response and swallowed icy Añejo to soothe nerves he'd managed to irritate. Shugrue had shown himself to be another man worthy of shoveling shit in Sioux City and I wasn't going to genuflect in fright. Manny's boss? Jesus!

Door chimes again. This was turning into a busy morning. I opened the door and told Thomas Jameson to come in.

He looked around. "I guess Rosario isn't here.''

"Gone home with her mother—and Carmen. What can I do for you?''

"Got a name for you.'' Smiling, he pulled a piece of paper from his pocket. "A *compadre* of Padilla's. Doing five at Metro Correctional.''

South Dade, half an hour's drive away. "Tell me more.''

"He doesn't like prison. Maybe you could help each other.''

FIVE

OVER COFFEE Jamey gave me details. Tito Gallardo was a fellow *Vene-zolano,* and a one-time military aide to the General. He'd done heavy stuff that couldn't be proved, so he'd been slammed with a nickel for possession with intent.

"Wife and children in Caracas," Jamey went on, "and not doing well if her letters are an indication."

"How about his state of mind?"

"Melancholy, dispirited. Afraid of being hit with another drug conviction before he's served his sentence."

"Is another rap in the offing?"

"Afraid not. He's got another year at MCC before his first parole hearing, and because he hasn't cooperated the USA will oppose parole."

"Good. He's in touch with Padilla?"

"Through the prison underground. Also, despite having a family Gallardo has a girlfriend. She visits him weekly, after which she visits Padilla."

"Regular little courier."

"Better than that, a stripper." His eyebrows lifted suggestively. "Worked at a redneck C&W dive that's been a biker hangout. We busted it last year because bikers were dealing snow, crack and redbirds. Place closed down but reopened under ostensibly new management. The girlfriend may still be there. Marlena Gomez."

"What's it called?"

"El Rancherito."

"Located where?"

"Florida City."

"Florida City," I repeated. "According to Carmen that's where Manny was headed the day he disappeared."

He nodded.

"You say Marlena's workplace is a biker hangout. Well, Carlos Stefano's a biker, maybe with the same *pandilla*." I swallowed the last of my coffee. "So I've got three suspects to see. Appreciate the leads."

"My pleasure," he said but his expression was unhappy. "I'm not using my car phone to call you because the office can monitor it."

"Good precaution. *Señor* Shugrue called to let me know that Manny's fate is in good hands—by which he meant official channels. He was pretty nasty warning me to stay away from *l'affaire* Montijo, so I guess I'm supposed to curl my tail and slink off into shadows."

He smiled. "Van can be a real prick when he wants to."

"Which is probably most of the time. He's a disciple of Fumblin' Phil Corliss, which doesn't lend much luster to his profile."

Jamey chuckled. "Far from it. And while I'm here, Mr. Novak, that was just great, getting Carmen away from Carlos."

"Glad you didn't see her. She was pretty battered but Rosario got a doc to come and take care of her."

"Rosario really cares for her sister," he said in respectful tones, "and I like that."

"Because Carmen might some day be your sister-in-law?"

"Sort of." He swallowed. "Maybe. I'm expecting a grade promotion that can support a wife. And after Rosario gets her degree . . ." His voice trailed off, and I smiled inwardly. This guy was a goner, enraptured by an absolutely perfect girl, and I could only wish him luck. Manny ought to be delighted with this prospective son-in-law.

Jamey got up. "Meeting an informant," he said. "Thanks for the coffee."

"Thanks for your time. Tell Rosario I'm getting back on trail."

I went with him to the door, thinking he wasn't the only one facing delayed vows. I had Melody on my mind, but at least I knew where she was. And Delores was a fierce protector of her only child. The old warrior would keep her far from harm.

Holding that thought, I added our glasses, cups and saucers to the dishwasher and started it. Then I locked up and went out to my car.

The project motel looked different in daylight. Worse. Objects I hadn't seen by night showed up starkly: broken buggies, old tires, rusted air-conditioner, bent shopping cart, shattered door-frame and a bunch of varicolored kids playing around an ugly trash pile. They had toy guns—I hoped they were toys—and took turns shooting each other off the top of the heap. They were wearing tattered clothes but they didn't seem undernourished, and they were having fun. They noticed me climbing the staircase and took a couple of shots at me. I pretended to be wounded, and staggered up the rest of the way. They screamed in delight.

I made my way along the littered balcony to unit 22. The door was shut and I considered knocking. But why bother? It wasn't as though Carlos and I hadn't met before; we weren't strangers. So I gripped the knob and turned it. Unlocked. I pushed inward.

The air was still, the stench of pot less than what I'd sniffed last night. The orange lamp still glowed, but from the floor, partly hidden by a guitar case. Above it posters of Nirvana and Metallica curled from the wall. I took another step and roaches scurried out of my way.

Only then did I see him. He was lying on the mattress, still naked but for the black ball-bra, ribs readily countable, hair back from his forehead showing open eyes, and I wondered why he didn't speak. "Carlos," I said and took three steps toward him.

Then I saw flies around his open mouth, big ugly bluebottles that were working on his lips and crawling into his mouth. I swooshed them away and saw the needle in his left arm. The vein it lay against was slack despite the rubber tubing tight around his wrist. Because his heart was no longer pumping blood. I stepped back and flies returned to his face, settled on his eyes. One more OD'd junkie for Metro's daily tally, but I wasn't the one to inform them.

There was something on his right forearm I hadn't seen before, a blue tattoo depicting a tiger or panther in a stalking crouch. The artwork had been done with punctures of a ballpoint pen, probably when Stefano was in jail—typical of the outlaw culture through which he moved in his wasted life.

Retracing my steps, I left the way I'd come, palming my handkerchief to wipe prints from the doorknob unobserved.

The trash pile kids saw me coming down and targeted me again. My heart wasn't in their game, but I zapped back with my laser-ray Death gun, staggered to the car, and waved goodbye as I started the engine.

Driving away, I wondered if I'd just witnessed death by misadventure, or if a purposeful high-test fix had been administered. I hadn't noticed the usual heroin paraphernalia—candle or alcohol lamp or flame-blackened spoon—but the cops would probably find them. At least Carlos was out of Carmen's life, permanently, and the questions I'd had for him would never be answered.

Next stop, Metro Correctional Center and a prisoner named Tito Gallardo. I'd been there a few times interviewing prisoners, but usually I became aware of it en route to the Trail Glades Range where I shot pistol and sporting clays. The buildings were surrounded by ditch and chain fence topped by rolls of razor-wire. That hadn't been enough to prevent a spectacular escape by helicopter a couple of years ago, but prison security was above average, and General Noriega was still there, snug with his TV, telephone and computer. So I had no doubt that Tito Gallardo was still in residence.

To the admin building's reception guard I showed the DEA buzzer I'd neglected to return when I'd resigned, then signed the register and asked for Gallardo. While waiting for him to be brought to the interview room I inquired about recent visitors.

"Only one," the guard told me. "His girlfriend."

"How recently?"

He flipped register pages until he came to it. "Marlena Gomez, right? Last week."

I nodded. "What day?"

"Sunday—when she usually comes."

"Any complaints about Tito? How's his deportment?"

"Okay. I heard he was suicidal when he first got here. They put a watch on him but he must of got over it. You want more you can talk to Records."

"That's good enough."

He looked me over. "If you're carrying, check it here. You know the drill."

"Clean," I said as a metal-shod door opened. An escort guard crooked his finger and I followed him to the first inside door. Through thick foot-square glass I could see the bare table and bolted-down chairs. In one of them sat a man in orange prison uniform, number taped across his chest. He was short, black-haired, and built like a block. His hairy forearms were brawny, and his upper lip sported a thin mustache. He had scimitar sideburns and skin the shade of old copper. The escort said, "How long you gonna be?"

"Not long. I have a proposition for him; he takes it or leaves it. I hear he's doing time the hard way."

"So he is, so he is. Sticks to himself, reads, listens to the radio, and lifts weights." He unlocked the door and I went in. The guard locked it behind me.

I sat down across the table from him. "Don't know you," he said curtly.

"Ah, but I know you, Tito." I flashed my cred and asked, "They treating you right?"

"I got no complaints."

"That's what I like to hear—a cooperative con. How'd you like to cooperate more than you have? Parole hearing's not far off. I could do you some good."

He shrugged again. I said, "I hear they're desperate to have you home, Tito, but something's come up that could add to your present sentence. More years than you can count on all your fingers."

Pain froze his face. He sat forward and swore. "I can't do more, *hombre*."

"And there's Marlena to consider."

"Marlena?" His small pig-eyes squinted at me. "She done nothin'." He rubbed a coppery cheek and looked away.

"We'll get to her. But for now let's talk about the Mafia connection."

"Mafia?" He shifted uneasily. "What Mafia?"

"The Cuntrera brothers. Pasquale, Paolo and Gaspare. *Sicilianos* who prospered with you and General Padilla. They're back in Italy, you know, awaiting trial. You also know they helped Padilla take over the New York heroin franchise, and with the General in jail they got no rabbi." I paused and eyed him. "Naturally the brothers aren't anxious to do more time than they have to, so at least one of them is talking to the Rome Procurator—cutting a deal."

"So—what's that got to do with me?"

"Suppose I tell you you've been named as helping Padilla get five hundred tons of heroin into the New York market?"

"Lies," he said, but his face tightened.

"Maybe. But one or more Cuntrera on the stand in New York is plenty to convict you, Tito. Think about it. Guilty men testifying against another guilty man. Their credibility will stand up in court because they can supply dates, places, drug tonnages and means of shipment. Major stuff, Tito. Now, it's possible I might be able to keep your name off the indictment—you're not the only trafficker being named—but that would depend on you. Specifically, your cooperation." When he was silent I continued. "You don't like it here? Try Marion, Leavenworth or Lewisburg. Those places are for felons doing twenty-five or more, and the only sunshine those cons see comes from the TV. Plus that," I added, "the slammers are cold in winter, and the guards don't much care how cold the cell blocks get." I paused again to let the concept sink in. "Would a wife visit a husband who's doing life, five thousand miles away, in a country where she could be arrested when she steps off the plane? As for Marlena, those locations are far from her feeding range. Even farther if she's stitching mattress covers in Alderson, where the long-term bimbos are sent."

He swallowed, still avoiding my gaze. "She's no bimbo," he said surlily.

"She's more than that. She's a courier for you and Padilla. She takes messages between the two of you, and delivers word to the outside world. That makes her part of the conspiracy, so if she's grabbed—and you might be able to protect her—she'd do fifteen to twenty-five in the Federal slammer. Maybe a few years less if she gets a sympathetic female judge. But whenever she got out she won't be someone you'd want to see: thick waist, bulging biceps and a butch bob. Yeah, she'll come out dyke, no use for *macho* fuckers like you." I grunted. "Taking care of your grommet? This place is HIV heaven."

His fingers had laced together, and now he strained his palms outward so hard his forearm muscles lifted tight and hard. *"Jesu,"* he groaned. *"Jesu María.* What do you want from me?"

I drew in a deep breath. Finally I'd got him in a talking mood, and it hadn't been easy. "On top of all that, Tito, comes the kidnapping of a DEA officer named Manuel Montijo. We know the snatch was ordered by Padilla through you and Marlena Gomez, who passed the word." I thought he'd dispute it, but when he said nothing I went on. "Kidnapping a Federal officer carries a life sentence. Killing or harming him means a one time visit with Ol' Sparky. That's the sort of danger you're facing, Tito. You and Marlena. Padilla? We have to wonder if he's sane. Thinking he can ship out in exchange for a low-level government employee. Personally, I think the General's brain has gone squishy as a month-old mango, but if Padilla pleads insanity it won't help you or Marlena." I reached across, grabbed his chin and twisted until his face fronted mine. "As a general, Padilla got too used to issuing orders and expecting instant obedience, no questions. I'm pretty sure the snatch wasn't your idea, but you helped instigate it, so you're as guilty as he is." My eyes narrowed. "Am I getting through to you? Do you understand what I'm saying?" I released his chin, and his head snapped back from tension. "All right, that's part of it. The significant part comes now: around DEA Montijo hasn't many friends, he's too ruthless, too mean. Frankly, not many of us give a shit if we ever see him again, but that's not the point. The point is, we don't body-trade for hostages, never, under any circumstances; we can't let you scumbags think all you have to do is snatch another body and you'll get what you want. That won't happen. If Montijo turns up dead, all three of you go down—six feet under." I paused to fill my lungs again. "I came with an offer, a reasonable one: you help me, I help you. Who's got Montijo, and where is he being held?" I sat back, drained, and studied his face. To my surprise, tears welled in his eyes, streaked down his brown cheeks. The strongman breaking down? I handed him my handkerchief, and he blotted his eyes, wiped his cheeks. Weakly, he said, "You promise to help me?"

I sat forward. "I promise to help as much as I can. Where's Montijo?"

"And the General won't know I snitched?"

"Won't hear it from me."

"Okay," he sniffled. "Go to Marlena, she knows who did the snatch. Tell her I said it's okay to talk." He blew his nose noisily. So long, handkerchief, I thought, but said, "You don't know?"

"Names change. I don't know her contacts anymore."

"Suppose she doesn't believe talking's okay? You better write a note." From my pocket I took out a small spiral pad I carry around to note license plates of cars that might graze my Miata. I handed him the Mont Blanc pen I'd bought in Bern to fill in those endless Swiss forms. Tito Gallardo looked at me. "What do I write?"

"Oh, put this down: 'Querida Marlena, I want you to tell this man everything you know about Montijo. It's okay.' Sign it 'Your loving Tito,' or however you sign."

Writing wasn't his particular skill, but he did it legibly. I tucked the note away and shook his hand. As we rose, he asked, "You'll help Marlena, too?"

"Why not? It's as easy as what I'm going to do for you. Ah—she's still at El Rancherito, right?"

He nodded. After rapping on the viewing window I looked back at Gallardo. "Need anything? Cigarettes?"

He shrugged. "I got money, but it don't do me much good here."

Which, I mused, is one reason we put you animals away.

The escort unlocked the door and came in to take Tito back to the cell block. I went into the reception area, signed out and left the building.

From there I drove back to US 1 and headed for Florida City in the Keys, astonished by how readily Padilla's plot was unraveling.

I hadn't really lied to Gallardo. I'd agreed to help him as much as I could, though in fact I couldn't help him at all. Or Marlena. But he'd heard what he wanted to hear without asking the penetrating questions a lawyer would have posed. His IQ was about body temperature, I thought, as I drove through a warm sunny afternoon, sniffing salt air from the marshes, enjoying being alive. And watching sleek white herons gravely stalk their prey in roadside canals along the way.

And after a while I came into Florida City and spotted an ornate arrow-sign that pointed the way to the joint where Marlena worked, a couple of blocks off the main drag.

SIX

THE NAME of the place was spelled out in bright reflector buttons, and fluorescent-colored words announced:

GOOD EATS   C&W MUSIC   NUDE DANCING   EVERYDAY LADIES HOUR
5–6 PM   ½ PRICE DRINKS   BBQ   ICY COLD DRAFT   OPEN 11 AM—?

At each end of the sign nude females were painted in bold primary colors, their mammary development astonishing.

So I followed the arrow and pulled into a large almost-empty parking lot, at whose far end stood a low, wide, rustic-style building with a sloped shingle roof and a neon sign that repeated the place name. Above the entrance steps hung a wooden sign lettered: This Is The Place.

Close to the entrance were two parked cars and a gray pickup with high-rise springs and oversize swamp tires. Spotlights were mounted atop the cab, and gunracks were bolted below the rear window.

Next to the pickup stood two Harleys and a Honda, helmets on their seats. I parked on the far side of the entrance, locked my car, and set the alarm before going up the board steps and through twin swinging doors.

Inside, dimness contrasted with the bright glitter of exterior signs. For a few moments I waited while my eyes adjusted to the change, smelling old beer and fry fat, hearing the rhythmic throb of rock music. When I could see more I made out a room-length bar with five customers on bar stools. The hardwood dance floor was bounded by cypress-top tables and captain's chairs. The left side was given over to table-booths above which hung photos of sports scenes and Nashville stars. Five four-bladed ceiling fans turned lazily. The far end held a bandstand, with mikes, and on its platform a nearly nude female was clinging to a pole and gyrating to the music. She wore hip-length red tresses, and her breasts jiggled as she swayed from side to side. None of the customers seemed to be watching her. When she turned, I could see a narrow waist strip that supported a small cloth V above her loins and vanished in the crack of her ass. I wondered if she was Marlena Gomez.

At the near end of the bar I took a stool and waited for the bartender, a young woman with colored tassels on her nipples, short black hair and a suede cowgirl-style skirt that barely covered her crotch. She set elbows on the bar, framed her face with her hands and stopped chewing gum long enough to drawl, "What'll it be, stranger?"

"Draft Miller's, pard. Icy Cold like the sign says."

"Got Bud, Heinekens."

"Bud."

She resumed chewing as she eased off to the service section. I watched her fish a mug from the water-filled sink and set it under a handle tap. When it was topped with foam she leveled it off and slid it along the bar. I stopped the mug with one hand and noted other offerings set out along the bar in two-gallon jars. Red sausages, pickled eggs, dill pickles, and so on. A clip rack held peanuts, beef jerky sticks and nacho chips. Thirst-making snacks.

Using a paper napkin I dried the mug rim and sipped. The beer failed the Icy Cold test but was welcome after the drive down, and I avoided thinking of the sink water the mug had come from. The wall behind the bar sported a large mirror and in front of it were long racks holding liquor bottles. On the mirror's corners small lascivious scenes were painted. As music volume increased I noticed the dancer rubbing her crotch on the pole in apparent ecstasy. Well, I hadn't sought El Rancherito for moral uplift, so I took things as they came.

Behind me the doors opened for three more customers; two young, bearded men, and a woman in black Spandex shorts and matching bra. They joined the other bar customers, exchanging hugs, kisses, high-fives and cries of jubilation.

The bartender busied herself drawing beer for the arrivals, then leaned back and eyed them. When she glanced in my direction I beckoned her over. " 'Nother?" she asked.

"Not yet. Happens I'm looking for Marlena—Marlena Gomez."

"Yeah?" She eyed me suspiciously and her chewing slowed.

"Yeah. A good friend of hers asked me to stop by, and—well, that's private. Is she here?"

"What good friend?"

"Let's say he's in a situation where he can't come himself. Not today, not tomorrow. Not for a long time. Is Marlena here?"

"Could be."

She lingered while I passed over a fiver, and then she walked the length of the bar and opened a door faced with a silver star. The rock music crescendoed and stopped. The dancer sank to the floor, the spotlight went out. Presently I saw her strolling toward the bikers. She took a stool, wiped sweat from face and chest, and looked around for service. After a few moments the bartender appeared, and walked back to me. "She says take a booth, she'll be with you."

The dancer pounded the bar. "Hey, Trudi, I'm a person too."

"Since when?" the bartender called, but went down and took her order. Tequila on the rocks, I saw, and the dancer drained it in two swallows. I carried my mug to a wall booth, sat down, and waited. After a while a woman came out of the starred door, glanced around, and crossed the dance floor toward me. Setting palms on the table, she asked, "Who's our good friend?"

"Tito," I told her, "so take a seat. Drink?"

"Good idea." She went over to the bar, and while her drink was being poured, I surveyed the woman who was going to tell me all I needed to know. She was about five-four, maybe one-thirty. Bare, mango-size breasts; cellulite-dimpled hips and butt, skinny legs, muscular thighs and shoulder-length blonde hair with dark roots. Her belly bulged above the pube-masking V, and when she walked back her spike heels click-clacked on the hardwood floor. She eased onto the opposite seat, swallowed from her glass and set it down. "So Tito sent you—what's on his mind?"

I got out my wallet and separated five hundred-dollar bills, set them under my mug, and brought out Tito's folded note. She looked at the money and the paper in my hand. "For me?"

"Sequentially."

"You mean, one thing after the other." The frown made her face rounder than it was. Lips, eyes and eyebrows were heavily made up, but no rouge disguised the paleness of her cheeks. Another Snow Queen.

"Read the note," I said, and passed it to her. She squinted to read the handwriting and put it down, fear in her eyes. *"Who are you?"*

I took back the note. "Someone Tito wants you to talk to."

"Why?" she husked.

"To save both of you from the chair." I leaned forward and pushed aside my mug.

"The *chair?*" She drew back, and I said, "Exactly that. Now let's not waste time. Where's Montijo?"

She shrank back. "I—I don't know."

"But you know who kidnapped him. Talk, Marlena. I'm giving you and Tito a chance to save your lives so don't hold out on me."

She swallowed, licked her lips. "If I tell you, Padilla will have me killed." Her eyes moved around as though searching for help, and I noticed that the bar customers were no longer talking; they were watching us. I didn't like the attention but I had to press on. "If Montijo's killed you and Tito will roast in the chair. Padilla won't have you killed unless he knows you talked." I shrugged. "Who's to tell him? You? Tito won't because he loves you, so listen to me. All I want is Montijo alive and well. That's it. More than one man snatched him, so more than one man could talk. You were a big part of the conspiracy because you carried messages and passed word to the kidnappers. And you lured Montijo here last Tuesday morning."

She began to whimper. "Tito told you?"

"Your name was on Montijo's desk pad. So, talk."

A large biker got off his stool and walked toward us. Ignoring me, he spoke to Marlena. "Honey, this guy hasslin' you?"

She shook her head. "He's okay, just go away, Donny."

But he persisted. "Then why you cryin', sweet thing?"

"He brought—bad news from—you-know-who."

For the first time he looked down at me. "Yeah? Maybe you better tell me."

"Maybe you better ask the lady."

"Hey, man, you tellin' me what to do?"

"Just a suggestion," I said mildly. I didn't come for a barroom brawl, didn't want one. What I wanted was names from Marlena. She grabbed his hand and said, "It's okay, Donny, really okay. It's just that—oh, maybe I'll tell you later." She took a paper napkin and dried her eyes. The runny mascara gave her features a grotesque appearance. I took another napkin from the stack and dabbed at the wet mascara. Donny looked on uncertainly, finally said, "Okay, hon, but if this citizen don't act right, I'm here, okay?"

"Okay." Her gaze followed him as he went back to the bar, then she looked at me. "Ready to talk?" I asked. "The atmosphere's getting oppressive and I have things to do." Country music came from a hidden speaker— Willie Nelson whining a self-pitying rustic ballad. Gimme Wynonna or Johnny Cash anytime.

Looking down at the table top Marlena drew in a deep breath, spoke in a low voice. "The contact is Hector Munguía."

"Who's he?"

"Works for Colonel Lozano."

"First name?"

"Antonio."

"Where do I find them?"

"All I got is a phone number."

I pushed the note to her along with my Mont Blanc pen. She picked up the pen, hesitated. I took my beer mug off the banknotes and edged them toward her hand. She wrote down a number and after I read it I said, "Where are they keeping Montijo?"

She pulled over the banknotes and put them in one of her shoes. "Told you I don't know."

"Make a guess."

"You got what you came for, leave me alone."

"Not yet. Carlos Stefano phoned you early Tuesday morning. He told you Montijo was heading for Florida City, right?"

"Yeah."

"But that didn't give Lozano and Munguía time enough to get here first. So you had to tell them before the morning. When, Marlena?"

She swallowed again. "I called Mr. Montijo the day before—Monday, I guess—told him to come here."

"Why would he want to come?"

Her eyes were tearing again. "I told him there was a big load of drugs nearby, said if he came alone I'd show him the stash."

I sat back. "Glad you got it out?"

"Yeah—I suppose."

"Now tell me the Carlos connection."

"He was into the Montijo kid's pants."

"That's known. Who pointed him at her? You?"

"Not me, Hector. Carlos got drugs from Hector so he did Hector a favor."

"Some favor," I said bitterly. "Balling a kid, taking her from her family . . ."

Her smile was thin, cynical. "Cruel world, ain't it?"

"And you don't know how cruel it can get." It was time to leave but I had a parting thought. "What was Carlos to you? Boyfriend?"

"You can call it that."

"Let's call it that. But Tito's supposed to be your boyfriend."

"Yeah. But Tito's in the joint, right?" She left the rest of the thought unspoken. I said, "If Tito knew he wouldn't like it. Could have your legs busted."

"Maybe, only who's gonna tell—" She broke off and stared at me. *"You wouldn't do that?"*

I grunted. "If this number turns out bogus I sure as hell would, so keep that in mind, sweet thing."

"No, no, it's okay, I swear it is."

"Then your two-timing's safe with me." I paused. "One last thing, honey, what's that tattoo on Donny's arm—some kind of animal?"

"Blue panther." She gestured at the bar crowd. "They all got it. In the joint where they got nothin' else to do."

"Thanks for the information," I said, "I was wondering about that. Where's yours?"

"Mine?" She grinned lewdly. "Carlos put it where the sun don't shine. Get it?"

"Got it. Invest that money wisely and you'll be set for life."

"Yeah? Ain't enough to wipe ass with. Maybe I'll buy some good shit for Carlos."

"Don't bother," I told her, "he went away."

As I left the table I heard her gasp but didn't look back. I wanted the outside, clean air, sunshine, blue skies. I'd seen all I wanted of El Rancherito's daytime habitués; I wondered if the nighttime crowd would be an improvement.

Back on US 1, I reached for my car phone to call Jamey for an address to match Lozano's phone number, then decided we could be overheard. I didn't think it wise to reach him at the office, and I didn't have his home number, so I tried the next best thing. I drove back to Miami and headed for the Montijo home.

It was a wise decision, because Jamey's car was parked in the drive. Rosario answered my ring and put a finger to her lips. "Mom and Carmen are sleeping."

"Good." Jamey was stretched out on the sofa, coat off, revealing his shoulder holster. "Looks like one tired soldier."

"He is, Jack." She gestured me into the dining room. I sat at the table and Rosario asked if I wanted something to drink. "Anything," I said. "Water, soda, whatever's handy."

She opened the fridge and got out a two-liter bottle of Coke. "This okay?"

"Perfect." I looked back at Jamey, who was beginning to stir. The clinking of ice cubes in my glass roused him. He sat up, looked blearily around and spotted me. "Hey, hello," he said, "been here long?"

"Maybe a minute, don't let me disturb you."

"Didn't mean to fall asleep," he said irritably, "but it happens."

"But never on stakeout," I reminded him, and took the filled glass from Rosario. She sat across from me and laced her fingers. "Any news?"

"Maybe. Everything okay here?"

"Yes—thanks to you."

I drank thirstily before saying, "One thing I can tell you—you'll never see Carlos again."

Rosario regarded me with suspicion. "Jack, did you kill him?"

"Would I tell you? Uh-uh. I went back to ask some questions and he was already dead. Needle in arm."

Rosario clapped a hand to her mouth. "Oh, Jack, how dreadful!"

"Hey, he found an endless dream of peace. And that's not dreadful for the Montijo family."

"Well, no," she agreed as Jamey came over. "You report it, Mr. Novak?"

"Hardly," I replied, "so forget it."

Rosario asked, "Should I tell Carmen?"

"Poor idea. Eventually she'll find out, but we shouldn't be the ones to tell her. Anyway, it's time to steer her back to school and conventional family living. Right, Jamey?"

"Absolutely. Let dead dogs lie."

I finished my Coke and stood up. "I need a private word with you, Agent Jameson," and we went back to the doorway. Rosario took my glass back to the kitchen. Jamey said, "You saw Tito?"

"Spun him a tale, and got to Marlena." I gave him the paper with Tito's note and Lozano's phone number. "What I need now is an address matching the number. Get it from the office reverse phone book and come to my place. I'll tell you what it can lead to."

His face lighted. "Manny?"

"With luck." I looked beyond him at Rosario. "Business concluded. Thanks for the drink. Love to your mother and sister."

"We love you, Jack," she called and I went out to my car.

When I turned onto Granada Boulevard, I saw a car parked in front of my house. Black four-door Ford with trunk-lid antenna and local plates. Federal official. I pulled into my drive and was walking toward the front door, when two men got out of the Ford and approached me. One called, "Mr. Novak, need a word with you."

I halted, turned and saw they were wearing light-colored rack suits and conservative ties. Special Agents Harlan Doak and Walter Rennie. I'd dealt with them on Guatemalan matters, not always comfortably. They stopped a few feet away, and I looked them over. Wayne and Garth of Federal law enforcement.

"What's on your mind?" I asked, and Doak grimaced before saying, "The kidnapping. Can we talk about it?"

SEVEN

"**W**HY NOT?" I asked. "Doubtless you can add to my limited knowledge." I paused. "The Montijo snatch, right?"

Rennie nodded. "Federal officer—so we're involved."

"Thank goodness," I said. "I was afraid recovering Manny was being left to Mr. Shugrue et al. Welcome news, so what can you tell me?"

Harlan Doak wet his lips. "Anything we might have is sensitive-classified. I hoped you might know a few things we've missed."

"Doubt it," I told them, "since Mrs. Montijo is my sole source of information. Anyway, I believe in reciprocity: you reveal what your investigation has picked up, and when I have significant information I'll eagerly share it with you." I smiled. "If and when."

Rennie edged forward. "Past contact indicates you tend not to be forthcoming, Mr. Novak. So, we're here to warn you against withholding any information you have or may acquire."

I nodded thoughtfully. "That sort of echoes Mr. Shugrue's words about obstruction of justice. Wait a minute— you're carrying water for him, right?"

The special agents exchanged glances. Doak said, "We always cooperate with DEA."

I laughed shortly. "Except, maybe, when it doesn't suit you, and I can remember busts that went sour because the Bureau failed to cooperate in timely fashion." I paused again. "Or share pertinent information. So, you're leaning on me not because you think I might have any real information but because Shugrue doesn't want me sniffing around—right?"

"Substantially," Doak conceded, "and he's very serious about that."

"Nothing personal, Mr. Novak," Rennie said unconvincingly, "it's just to keep things orderly."

"Well, hell, I can identify with that, no problem. Who wants amateurs goofing up the scene? Incidentally—and here's something Van might have neglected to share with you fellows—he's crediting a smear by unidentified informants to the effect that Manny's dirty.''

''I take it you don't believe that?'' Doak ventured.

''No way. Never. For God's sake, you know the deal—Padilla's freedom for Manny's, and you've got the General in custody, so that's not only part of the problem, it's part of the solution.''

''How do you mean?'' Rennie asked with genuine interest.

''Figure it out, fellas, I'm not paid to do your thinking for you. Meanwhile, I'm doing what little I can to provide aid and comfort for the family. They're good people, and Manny's a good man. So if you're looking for corruption, look elsewhere.'' I glanced at my watch. ''I know it's hot out here, but if I invited you in you'd poke around and try to build a case against me. Without a search warrant yet.''

Doak's eyes narrowed. ''What kind of case?''

''Oh, I dunno—unregistered peonies—whatever. Is the interview over?''

Doak nodded, and as he turned away I said, ''One last thing, lads, if I'm tailed or my phone tapped I'll have Neal Sonnett get an injunction against harassment—maybe file a suit for monetary damages and injuries to my sensitive psyche. You'd be named defendants, personally liable for the judgment.'' I paused. ''So you understand my position.''

Doak said, ''Doesn't have to be like this, Mr. Novak—the hostility.''

''On my part? C'mon, Harlan, you guys come here with threats and warnings and I'm supposed to lick it up like honey? Get real.''

I watched them go down the walk, and unlocked my front door. When I looked back the black Ford was gone.

After shedding my coat I poured Añejo over ice and sipped with gratification. Then I noticed the red light blinking on my answering machine. Melody again; why hadn't I called?

Damn! I put through a call to the yacht's radio operator, learned Melody, her mother and Mehmet were ashore at the casino. Well, that was to be expected. Monaco was a fun place if you had no spending constraints. Delores, for one, would never see the inside of a Budget Inn.

I drank more rum and thought about my recent visitors. I didn't enjoy contact with the FBI, even though it was no more than an irritant. The pusillanimous Shugrue had set them on me, but that was to be expected from a sycophant of Phil Corliss's.

Self-Seeking Shugrue, I thought, and smiled, though if it was left to him, the search for Manny would likely prove fatally long.

Sun no longer struck my blinds and I felt vague stirrings of hunger. There was plenty of food to satisfy my yet undefined appetite, but I thought I'd wait until after evening TV news before coming to a decision. Beside, I was anticipating a serious talk with young Jameson as soon as he arrived, so dinner could wait.

As I reviewed Marlena's information I thought it unlikely that the two kidnappers were holding Manny at their phone location. They could be among the thugs guarding their hostage, but he was probably kept in some other place. What would be gained, I wondered, if I told Shugrue or the FBI the alleged kidnappers' names? Not many judges would issue warrants based on an unsupported allegation; but even if a go-go judge were found, what value was an arrest? The perps had only to deny involvement, retain counsel and bond free. Meanwhile, Manny's guards might take fright and kill him— which was precisely what I craved to avoid. The Feds wouldn't sweat the two scumbags interrogation procedures forbade that lest a good case be soured. I could understand that, even empathize with frustrated law enforcers. But the delicacies involved in today's criminal justice system deterred the enforcers, not the thugs.

After I was no longer part of DEA my value to Manny—and the country— was precisely because I chose to ignore legalities when I worked for him abroad. I could zap malefactors, burn their properties and confiscate their cash. But I realized that even my most successful efforts did little to reduce the invasion of narcotics from abroad. Putting down a few drug barons could slow things temporarily, but most had families who buried the fallen, and took up where they'd left off. And I assumed that Padilla's organization was still in business even though his Mafia connections were in Italian custody, on trial.

Not long ago I'd admitted to Manny that I thought the drug war was unwinnable; logic likened it to Prohibition and the Vietnam War, for all lacked public support. Were I President, I mused—as often before—I'd declare victory and legalize narcotics.

Chimes rang and I opened the door for Jamey. His face was flushed and his tie unknotted. "Take it easy," I told him, "have a drink and settle down."

"Ice water," he said, and wiped his wet forehead. "Air-conditioning broke down," he explained, "but you know office cars."

"Bad memories, except for an occasional forfeited Porsche or Mercedes. Get on the list for one."

"There's a list?" He sat down heavily.

"Shugrue keeps it so his favorites get the good wheels." I brought a glass of ice water and sat across from him. "Got an address?"

"Yeah—but I almost got caught using the reverse book. My supervisor asked what I wanted from it, so I told him a girl's address—all the single agents do it.'' He drank deeply and fished a piece of paper from his pocket. ''Colonel Lozano has a house on North Bayshore Drive—El Portal section. I drove past it on the way. The back has a fenced swimming pool and a boat dock on Biscayne Bay. There was a gray BMW in the drive.'' He wiped his forehead again. ''I didn't see anybody around.''

''Satellite dish?''

He nodded.

''Should have mentioned it, Jamey. Lozano could be in satellite communication with Caracas. Don't overlook a detail like that.''

''Sorry.'' He looked contrite and I told him why I wasn't going to share our information with Federal law enforcement. My reasoning went against his training, instincts and ethics, but after thinking it over he conceded I was right. ''So, what's to be done?''

I strolled back to the bar, splashed more Añejo into my glass and returned. ''The perps have to tell where Manny is.''

''That's obvious.''

''Take it easy, kid, I'm trying to think things through. Obviously, they have to be bagged. A SWAT team could do it but I ain't got no SWAT team to guard the rear exit while the front door guys slam through and toss in stun grenades.''

Jamey said, ''Jack, I'm on the office SWAT team.''

''And you've a career to consider.'' Suddenly he was calling me Jack. ''No, this has to be done by civilian risk-takers.''

''I had an infantry platoon in Desert Storm.''

I looked at him with new respect. Manny was going to get quite a son-in-law, I thought—after he was free. ''Even so,'' I told him, ''you're not part of bagging the perps, so forget it. And you're not to be around when I squeeze them.''

He shrugged. ''I could do some surveillance.''

''Thanks for the offer.'' Was there anyone in Miami I could get to help? Someone trustworthy and unafraid of a firefight? On Cozumel I could get a dozen volunteers, but this wasn't Cozumel.

Jamey said, ''Rosario said I should tell you Manny's cousin is coming from Spain.''

''Oh? Maybe he can help out—if he's anything like Manny.''

He shook his head. ''It's not a he, it's a she.''

''Rats. What's she coming for, routine visit?''

''Actually, she's coming as a visiting professor at FIU. For the time being she'll be staying with the family.''

"Well, there's safety in numbers," I remarked, and Jamey said, "Her name is Pilar Marisol de la Garcia y Montijo." He stumbled over pronunciations, so I said, "Better sharpen your Spanish if you're marrying into a Hispanic family."

His cheeks colored. "Yeah, I should, but I never seem to have time to listen to the language lab tapes."

"Does La Profesora speak English?"

"Didn't ask, and she's not arriving until tonight. I'm going with Rosario to bring her from the airport. Anyway, to teach at FIU she has to speak *some* English, doesn't she?"

"Guess so, I've never taken classes there." I visualized a gray-haired super-religious old spinster with pince-nez lenses and a sour outlook on life. But maybe she could lend some comfort to a distraught family. God knows, they needed it.

"Okay, kid," I said, "thanks for the location, I'll take things from here on."

He drank the rest of his glass and got up. "But I'm available for odd jobs."

"I'll bear it in mind."

"Like a couple of stun grenades the office wouldn't miss."

"I'll let you know. Meanwhile, you could find out where Padilla's cell is at MCC, the guard situation."

He stared at me. "You're not thinking of busting him out?"

"Anything's possible—but that's a last resort. What I have is fifty thousand dollars for the family of the con who kills him."

His cheeks paled. "You're serious?"

"It's a solution. No Padilla to exchange, no Manny to hold. I'll let the idea ripen. And tell La Profesora I look forward to meeting her."

"Will do."

"Incidentally, we know each other well enough so call me Jack. And if you didn't know it the Montijo family in Spain is large and wealthy. They produce some of the best Spanish wines."

"Rosario never mentioned it."

"Modest people," I said, "so treat the professor with respect. You and Rosario may be vacationing there one day."

"Great idea." He adjusted his tie and left.

There was a sort of innocent, unworldly quality about Jamey that I liked. Maybe I resembled him before I went to Vietnam. I wanted to think so.

Añejo had quelled my appetite and I had other things to do. Checking Lozano's abode topped the list.

*   *   *

The house was set on a five-foot berm at 86th Street on the water side of
Bayshore Drive. Single-story ranch with yellow stucco walls and red-tile
roof. A sort of campanile or watchtower rose from the roof and resembled a
very large chimney. Beyond it a large black satellite dish.

No BMW in the drive, or any other vehicle; no lights inside the house. The
only visible lights illuminated davits on the north side of Lozano's dock, but
I could glimpse lights sparkling across the Bay in high-rise condos and hotels
along Miami Beach.

Now in late evening the area was peaceful, but I remembered nocturnal
disruptions by high-speed Cigarettes outrunning Customs boats along the
Waterway. Thundering engines and gunfire had reduced real estate values,
but now with major drug deliveries moved well north and west of Miami, El
Portal was beginning to revive.

The whole waterside zone had suffered from drug trafficking. Customs and
DEA seized Cocaine Cowboy houses and let them decay from inattention.
Here and there were overgrown lots that once had houses on them. Other
homes showed unrepaired damage from the last hurricane, and some were
shells, burned out when illegal immigrants built cooking-fires on living room
rugs and floors. Where once there had been well-kept lawns and trimmed
shrubbery, tall weeds and kudzu vines stirred in the onshore breeze. Hurricane Andrew couldn't be blamed for all the city's ills.

As I idled past the house I could see a reminder of former times tethered
to the dock: a shorter Cigarette formula racer named *Sabre* that could run as
fast while carrying a smaller load. I turned onto 86th Street heading inland,
and reflected that the black *Sabre* could roar up from Florida City faster than
a car could make it through work-hour traffic last Tuesday morning, when
Manny disappeared. Had that been Manny's route to his place of imprison-
ment? Was Lozano's house an intermediate stop, or was Manny there now?
All things seemed possible.

Driving back to I-95, I reflected that putting a contract on Padilla might be
counter-productive. Once their leader was dead, Padilla's henchmen would
have no reason to keep Manny alive, and alive was how I wanted him. So
once again I'd spoken impulsively without thinking things through. At all
costs, General Padilla had to stay alive and well. But after Manny was free
a hit might serve as a warning to others.

The day's stress plus a continuing sleep deficit had tired me more than I'd
thought. I realized it when I found the Miata straying into the left-hand lane,
with traffic rushing at me. I corrected quickly, sucked in a deep breath and
leaned close to the steering wheel. If I was going to die a violent death I
didn't want it to be on I-95.

I had enough residual energy to garage my car before going into the house, where I downed a shot of Añejo and tottered off to bed. If the phone rang during the night I didn't hear it. But I heard it early in the morning when Rosario's call woke me.

"Jack—are you all right? I thought you might be—"

"Dead? Only to the world." Slowly my mind was getting up to speed. Too slowly. "Is there—?"

"No, no news. But Cousin Pilar arrived last night—Jamey told you?"

"He did."

"And she's very distressed about Father's disappearance."

"Well—understandably."

"And she wants to see you right away—thinks she might be able to help."

God keep me from well-intentioned female kibitzers, I groaned inwardly, but said, "Look, I'm far from organized, and figuring the drive to your place . . . I can't be there for, say, an hour and a half."

"Not necessary, Jack, she'll meet you there."

"Here? Can she locate my house?"

"She knows Miami, let her find her way, okay?"

I sighed. "Well, if that's what she wants."

"She does, and she wants to help as much as she can."

"Okay, Rosario, tell Cousin Pilar to come ahead. I'll be getting myself together."

"Thanks, Jack. She's really distraught. Daddy was like a big brother to her."

I replaced the receiver, perked coffee and carried a cup to the bathroom, where I sipped between shower and shave. Fresh clothing enhanced my morale, so I 'waved an egg, muffin and ham sandwich, dutifully downed orange juice, and was putting things away when door chimes sounded. I dried my hands and opened the door.

"Mr. Novak?"

"Yes. Please come in."

She was about thirty-two, I judged. Blonde hair pulled back from her forehead in a bun. No pince-nez, just clear-blue eyes surmounted by light brown eyebrows. Cheekbones accented her pale skin to advantage, her nose was small and straight, and she was dressed in a beige linen pants-suit that fitted her curves to perfection. She walked slightly ahead of me into the living room and I followed, admiring a figure that was far from the usual notion of a Spanish female. And even farther from the gray-haired, squinty-eyed, blue-stocking schoolmarm I'd ignorantly envisioned.

Tapering fingers clutched a suede handbag, and she turned to face me.

"Mr. Novak, please forgive the early hour, but I felt I had to do something immediately to help bring my cousin back."

"Quite all right, I understand your concern. Please be seated."

"Thank you." She chose an upholstered chair, crossed her legs and smoothed fabric along her upper thigh. "The family feels that if anything is to be done, you're the one to do it. So I have this suggestion. Can you offer ransom for Manuel's return?"

"How much do you have in mind?"

"A million dollars."

EIGHT

"**A** *MIL—?*" I stared at her.

"Or should we offer more?" She looked down at her purse. "Two million? As you may know, my family is wealthy, and I have personal resources as well. So I thought a substantial ransom offer could gain the kidnappers' attention."

La Profesora had spoken, and awaited a response.

Finally, I said, "It might, and the idea deserves consideration. Only tell me why you—?"

"To an extent, family honor is involved—is that difficult to understand?"

"Not at all."

Her features relaxed. "You seemed taken aback."

"By the sum, not the offer. Ah—shall we discuss it over coffee?"

"By all means. Black, please. You see, Mr. Novak, in practical terms, money is replaceable, my cousin is not, so the conclusion is obvious."

"Hadn't thought it through," I admitted, and left to draw cups from the percolator.

When I came back she was sitting forward, opening a gold-washed cigarette case. "Mind if I smoke?"

"Not at all." I set an onyx ashtray on the coffee table and lighted her cigarette. After inhaling, she said, "You Americans with your—shall I say puritanical—efforts to limit life's simple pleasures . . ." She shook her head. "I flew over on Iberia because I enjoy smoking on long flights—passes the time, and relaxes my mind."

"Mine, too—though I find brandy an excellent trip companion."

She nodded. "We produce a rather good but limited amount of brandy— Tres Reales—are you familiar with it?"

"Mainly with the price, but, yes, it's excellent. I've found it in Mexico, where it costs a good deal less."

"I'm glad you enjoy it." She tapped ash from her cigarette and looked around the room. "You're not married."

"How can you tell?"

"This is a very male ambiance, not feminine at all."

"Male, or—*macho?*"

"Male. The pejorative doesn't apply—or does it?"

"Not for me to say." I sipped more coffee, set down the cup. "I haven't shared the totality of my thoughts with Lucy, not wanting to alarm her—perhaps needlessly—but I feel I can be frank with you."

"Yes, I hope you will. Actually, I came here to speak privately, away from the family. So, please be entirely frank, Mr. Novak, and I will preserve the confidence." She sat back in the chair and let smoke drift slowly from her nostrils. There was a sort of unintentional hauteur in her pose, but then she possessed every characteristic of a Spanish aristocrat.

"We go back a few years to a sting operation that Manny conducted in person," I began. "You know the word 'sting'?"

"I saw the movie."

"Good. Manny persuaded the Venezuelan general, Jorge Padilla, to come to Florida. Padilla thought Manny represented a consortium of Miami traffickers, but when the General got here Manny sprang the trap and arrested him."

"Good for my cousin!"

I nodded. "Padilla was sentenced to forty years, not at all to his liking. So, in keeping with the rough-and-tumble tradition of Venezuela's underworld, Padilla had Manny kidnapped, the idea being to release Manny in exchange for Padilla's release."

Again she tapped cigarette ash, recrossed her legs and gazed at me. "Is that likely to happen?"

"No. But I haven't told Lucy. And I might as well tell you that Padilla won't be interested in one million ransom or even two. He's got millions stashed all over the world, and he wants freedom to enjoy them. And he wants revenge."

"I see his point of view. So ransom—"

"Still a worthwhile idea. Because—well, there's a development I haven't told Lucy, but I'll confide in you."

"Please."

"Yesterday I managed to learn the identities of two *Venezolanos* who snatched Manny."

"Wonderful! Can they be arrested and questioned?"

"Possibly."

"Or—bribed?"

"A more practical move. Ah—coffee?"

"Yes, I'm still in jet-lag and want to stay awake and alert. Lucinda brought you back from Switzerland, didn't she?"

"A few days ago, but I'm adjusted to local hours." I took our cups to the kitchen, refilled them and uncapped a bottle of Veterano. Added some to my cup and looked questioningly at my guest, who said, "Not just now."

After we'd sipped I said, "I can see definite risk in trying to bribe the kidnappers—a Colonel Antonio Lozano, and one Hector Munguía—because if they don't agree they may well decide they're in danger and dispose of Manny to eliminate problems."

"You mean, kill my cousin."

"I do." I studied her face and decided there was strength in it as well as intelligence. The Spanish cousin was also a very attractive woman, and I wondered why she had never married. She said, "I understand the risk, Jack—may I call you Jack?"

"Of course."

"And I'm Pilar." She smiled, showing white, perfectly even teeth. "Pilar," I repeated. Was I crazy, or did I sense occult vibes being transmitted, however unconsciously? What I knew was that I had all along sensed a magnetic aura surrounding this unusual woman, but I was ignoring it in order to concentrate on business.

"So, the alternative to ransom and bribery is—what?" Her question cut across my thoughts and it took me a moment to get back on track. "I haven't decided," I admitted.

"But involving the police or FBI, or whatever, isn't it contemplated?"

"The FBI is already involved, Manny being a Federal officer, but if they've made progress I'm not aware of it."

She shrugged. "Lucinda suggested they weren't doing much—yet you know who the kidnappers are."

"She may also have told you Manny's office hasn't done much."

Pilar nodded.

"Unfortunately, there may be a reason for disinterest, or inaction." I cleared my throat. "The head supervisor thinks Manny may be dirty—his word—meaning corrupt."

Her head shook angrily. "No, no, I won't believe it. Do you?"

"Not for a second, Pilar. I believe *narcotraficantes* circulated the smear to discredit Manny, destroy his usefulness after he's freed—assuming he is recovered. It's a pretty standard tactic, discrediting a really good agent who can't be bribed.''

"So, why would the office believe it?''

I grimaced. "Unfortunately, there's a mind-set against Hispanics, and there's very likely envy of Manny's accomplishments. Office politics aren't pretty but they exist. Lucy's not to know about the smear.''

"My lips are sealed.'' She took another cigarette from her case and I lighted it. Settling back, she said, "I don't want to interfere, understand, but I want to help wherever I can. Just tell me.''

"Your money gives me options.''

"It's available whenever needed. Meanwhile, I have confidence in your approach, and shan't ask for details.'' She breathed deeply and exhaled smoke. "Carmen seems to be recovering well,'' she remarked, "and I also want to thank you for bringing back my niece. I won't even ask the question, but if you killed her boyfriend in the process that's quite all right with me.''

"Didn't have to,'' I replied, "he killed himself with his own needle.''

"So much the better.'' She finished her coffee, and said, "I'll have that brandy, now, if I may.'' And while I was filling a snifter for each of us she said, "I met Rosario's young man last night and I'd like your appraisal of him.''

"First-rate, no known or suspected failings. He may be more serious than Rosario is, but I suspect a deep relationship may grow.''

"She's young, but so is Jamey, and that's not all bad—assuming they don't rush into things.''

"Well, I see them both as pretty levelheaded and I see only good things for them should they share their future. Now, because of my curious nature, tell me something of yourself. Your English is perfect, for one thing. Did you learn it in Spain?''

"I had grammar in convent school, but I perfected it—if that's the word— while I studied here at Barry.''

"Up in the Shores?''

She nodded. "Two years. Then I graduated from the University of Salamanca, where I teach.''

"You enjoy it?''

"Most of the time, but Spanish academia is largely a male domain.'' She sighed. "Salamanca is a religious institution, very old, very conservative, but faculty nuns accept me as I wasn't accepted at the University of Madrid. I did my doctoral work there, my dissertation was on the political and economic dynamics in post-Franco Spain.''

"A rather large subject. So, you're a *Doctora.*''

She smiled. "Does that bother you?"

"Hardly. In my line of work I don't encounter many intellectuals."

"I've been wondering, Jack, what kind of work you do. Lucinda was quite vague."

"Odd jobs for Manny. Things that can't be done officially."

"Narcotics?"

I nodded.

"Enjoy it?"

"I get satisfaction from a job well done," I paused. "While you're at FIU what will you teach?"

"The subject of my dissertation. Sort of relevant to Hispanic students."

"North or South campus?"

"Both, but I don't have to begin for a few days. I came early to look for a comfortable place to stay. FIU offered accommodations but they're dormitory-style, and I prize privacy."

And can afford it, I thought.

She put out her cigarette and sipped from the snifter. Both of us had relaxed considerably since her arrival, and I felt at ease with Doctor Pilar Marisol de la Garcia y Montijo, who said, "I'll be looking for an apartment or condo, I don't want the demands of a house."

"How long will you be at FIU?"

"This semester, then back to Spain for Christmas." She laughed pleasantly. "My father didn't want me teaching at a secular institution, but I persuaded him that things were a little different here. Besides, Barry didn't invite me."

The brandy was getting to me. "Forgive me for noting that you're a very unusual woman—all your accomplishments. Why didn't you join the family business?"

"Yes, that would have been the tradition, wouldn't it? What's expected of the daughter of a well-to-do family. But I thought there was more to life than growing grapes, making wine, marketing it."

"And brandy."

"Yes, Tres Reales has an excellent reputation. My brother Pablo manages that branch of the business—his MBA is from Stanford and he's very good at what he does. Three children, a comfortable lifestyle . . ." Her voice trailed off.

"Pardon the personal note, but you're so thoroughly attractive I've been wondering why you're not married."

Her features set soberly. "Ten years ago I was engaged—but my fiancé got himself killed racing at Monte Carlo. I'd never been serious about another man, and his death affected me deeply. I found solace in study and—I guess I never looked back. Being independent, respected as a teacher, is an accomplishment I value.''

"As you should.''

She finished her brandy and stood up. "I'm grateful for this talk, Jack. Helps me deal with Manuel's family, with the situation that's agonizing them. They're very fortunate to have you as a friend—a friend who's doing all you've done for them.''

"Thank you. Do you have to leave?''

"I really need to sleep a few hours, then go apartment-hunting with Rosario. Right now I'm feeling depleted, not at my best.''

"Well, if you have nothing else in mind, how about dinner with me?''

"I'd love to. When and where?''

"There's a good restaurant here in the Gables—Charade. Why don't you come here first, we'll have cocktails and go on. Say, about eight?''

"Eight it is.'' She offered her hand, and I took it before walking her to the door. Opening it, I saw a gunmetal Jaguar in the drive. "Nice wheels,'' I remarked admiringly.

"Leased while I'm in Miami.'' She started out but I held her arm. "Please tell Lucy the next time the kidnappers call—and they'll call—she should demand to hear her husband's voice. Insist on hearing proof he's alive if exchange negotiations are to continue.''

"Excellent idea, Jack, and I'll tell her to be firm.''

With that she continued to her car, unlocked the door and waved goodbye. She backed out and turned down Granada—taking with her most of the psychic electricity I'd felt around us. Cousin Pilar. What an exceptional woman!

I collected our cups and glasses, emptied the ashtray and began thinking of ways to deal with Lozano and Munguía. Thanks to Pilar I had two million dollars to back me up.

A few minutes after eight the door chimes sounded, and Pilar came in. Sleep had washed tenseness from her features and she looked refreshed and lovely. Tonight her hair was styled in a French braid, and in contrast to the morning's beige pants suit, she was wearing a knee-length black lace dress with three-quarter sleeves. A small diamond-set gold watch circled her left wrist, and a gold crucifix depended from a gold-link necklace. The black suede clutch purse had a gold clasp and fittings.

After pleasantries, I suggested an *apéritif;* hesitantly, she wondered if I had *manzanilla*—a dry white sherry favored in Spain—but when I confessed to having none, she opted for a vodka martini with me.

While I was making a small pitcher—Stoly and a few drops of dry vermouth—Pilar said she'd found a furnished apartment in Miami Shores. "I used to walk past the building when I was at Barry, and always admired its old Spanish-Mediterranean architecture. The furnishings are, oh, elderly and darker than I like, but I can move in tomorrow." She sipped, wrinkled her nose, and said, "Excellent, Jack. While I was resting, what did you do?"

"Drove past Lozano's house but saw no activity. No car in the drive, nobody outside. Speedboat still docked. From a pay phone I called the house, got no answer. Lunched with Jamey and asked for a printout on our two suspects. He said the office computer was down but thought he could manage it tomorrow." I shrugged. "No real progress."

"You've accomplished so much in so short a time; there are bound to be delays. You're not—dispirited, I hope."

"Not at all." I noticed a gold crest ring on her left little finger as she lifted her glass.

"Do you know Spain?" she asked.

"Visited Madrid a few times, and spent a week at a hacienda in Asturias."

"Oh? Which family?"

"Castenada."

"Jaime Castenada," she said musingly, "the old *réblan*. You knew him?"

"His wife, Rita. Through her younger sister, who was murdered last spring, down in the Keys."

"Oh. Well, Rita was recently widowed. Jaime's death was in the papers. I suppose she'll inherit whatever properties Jaime still had."

"Probably. You called Jaime a *réblan*—I'm not familiar with the word."

"Means—oh, a spent force." She looked away. "Implies limpness, impotence. Madrid society gossiped cruelly when he married the much younger Rita." I knew why, but wanted to leave the subject. Still, Pilar said, "As you must know, she and her sister were daughters of Oscar Chavez, the one-time dictator of Guatemala."

I nodded.

"Jaime squandered most of the Castenada fortune," Pilar continued, "and tried borrowing money from my father. But Jaime refused to entail his properties as security, so my father declined the loan."

"Wise decision."

"Yes, though the Castenada and Montijo families had a common political bond. Years ago we were Carlists and that was very useful during the Civil War. The Communists thought we were probably Progressives, and the Na-

tionalists assumed we were Conservatives, so neither side harmed our properties.'' She sipped again. ''Now, of course, the Carlist cause is no longer a
political factor.'' She looked at me, and her cheeks colored slightly. ''Forgive
me for boring you with Spanish history—I suppose it's the professor in me.''

''Not boring at all,'' I replied, though her mention of Jaime's widow
brought back an unpleasant memory: Rita *in flagrante* with another man. I
finished my martini and put down the empty glass. ''Ought to leave,'' I said,
''they'll only hold our table so long.''

The restaurant was set in an old Gables mansion that retained much elegance
from a storied past. Petit-point chairs, silver candlesticks, white linen napery,
glistening chandeliers, and a menu of which any Paris restaurant could be
proud. We had duckling and trout with a bottle of white Riscal, and after
coffee we left Charade and said goodnight beside our cars.

I drove slowly back to my place, aware of a subtle, unspoken bond de-
veloping between us, and knowing that I wanted to see as much of Pilar as
possible before leaving Miami.

When I entered the house my phone was ringing. Melody, I thought
guiltily, as I picked up the receiver; instead, I heard Lucy's voice.

''Jack, he called again—the same man—and he threatened Manny with
death.''

She began to sob.

NINE

"LUCY—LISTEN to me. Exactly what did the man say?"

"He—he said he was losing patience. If General Padilla wasn't released within the next few days I could . . . I could forget about seeing Manny again. Oh, Jack, Jack," she wailed, "what are we going to do?"

"We'll get to that. Lucy, are you sure it was the same caller?"

"Yes."

"And he spoke in Spanish?"

"As before." She was breathing in short gasps.

"Did you tape the call?"

"Yes—yes, I did."

"And did you tell him you had to hear Manny's voice for proof he's still alive?" In the background I could hear Rosario trying to calm her down.

"Yes, Jack, I told him that. Insisted on it."

"So—what did he say?"

"Well—it's all on the tape: said I was asking too much but he'd think about it."

"And—?" I pressed.

"He hung up." She was sniffling, but at least the deep sobs had stopped.

"That means," I told her, "he'll call back. And my guess is you'll hear Manny."

"Oh, that would mean so much to me!"

"And to me." I paused while I thought things over.

"Notify the office—they'll send someone for the tape. Maybe FBI techs can learn something from background noise—was there any?"

Rosario broke in. "Plane flying, jet engines."

"That's a start. Rosario, call the office now."

"If you say so—you don't want to hear the tape?"

"Your mother's summarized the conversation, so just get the recording in official hands. The sooner the better."

"Well—okay." She hung up, and I swallowed a quick shot of Añejo. Cold out of the bottle, it tasted like stone. I shivered and drank again. This was the real thing.

Lucy's call had helped me in two ways. Although she didn't know it, her tapped phone was feeding everything into a central listening post, where maybe twenty other wiretaps were monitored. So the Feds heard her incoming call while it was being made. They didn't need her tape, but I'd suggested she turn it over because our conversation was also recorded. Soon, Van Shugrue and Special Agents Doak and Rennie would hear me urging her to contact the office without delay. Proving—should the question arise later—that far from obstructing justice, I was giving it a helpful shove.

I hadn't carried iron to the restaurant, but now I fished my .38 from its cache under the bed, and stuck it in my belt. I left house lights on, set the burglar alarm and drove my Miata from the garage, then locked the garage door and drove up I-95.

Lucy's dialogue with the unknown caller might have gone on long enough that the Bureau could trace the phone location. Probably a pay phone distant from where Manny was being held. Routinely, the Bureau would speed agents to the site, but I was sure they'd find nothing but a deserted phone booth.

While they were wasting time responding by the book I wanted to run a parallel check that might prove more profitable. So I left the Interstate at the 95th Street exit and drove through dark, shuttered Miami Shores to 10th Avenue. Turned south to 86th Street, where I cut headlights. Then I parked on grassy swale and walked toward the Bay until I could glimpse Lozano's house.

Moonlight limned roof and watchtower but I saw no inside illumination. What light there was came from the back swimming pool and the dock's boat davits. There was no car in the drive.

But maybe one would come.

My watch showed midnight. I'd wait until twelve-thirty and—and then what? Have to think about that. I took position partly behind a Royal Palm trunk and watched the house.

Time passed, and I began wishing I had a cigarillo to smoke. Out of deference to Pilar and restaurant management I hadn't taken one to Charade, and had none now. But I wanted one clamped between my teeth, giving off soothing smoke and connecting me to reality.

The .38 was digging into my spine so I dug it out and transferred the pistol to my right-hand pocket, while reminding myself that I wasn't going to kill the perps—tonight. The piece was mainly for protection.

As I watched and waited, I debated letting the Feds know about Lozano and Munguía. If they netted the house to bag them and Manny wasn't there, my old friend was as good as dead. Conversely, the Feds could tap Lozano's phone, bug his car and add an electronic beacon. Then they could follow the BMW from a distance and bring in a surveillance chopper with SWAT team to surround the suspect site. Things I couldn't do. So there were reasons to divulge what I knew. But suppose Manny were killed in a firefight? I'd never forgive myself for sharing potentially crucial knowledge. Or if mobile surveillance was so clumsy as to alert the perps, Manny's hours were numbered. Either way my choice could have unintended consequences.

Clouds slid past the moon and the target house seemed to recede and vanish in the dark background. I was tired of standing and watching. Twelve-thirty. Time to move forward or retreat. I heard a footstep behind me, but before I could turn I felt something hard poke my spine. "Security," a voice hissed. "What's your business here?"

I put up my hands and turned to see Jamey grinning at me.

"Scare you—like you scared me?"

I couldn't get mad at him. Shrugging, I said, "Probably. Now, what in hell are you doing here?"

"You weren't home, and I was pretty sure you weren't doing the South Beach scene, so I figured you might be poking around here."

"I told you to stay out of this, Jamey."

"Right. But the office computer came back on line, and I sneaked the printouts." He nodded toward Lozano's house, tapped his coat pocket. "Munguía's on parole, and Lozano's under deportation order."

I grunted. "It's as hard to get a parole revoked as it is to force deportation. Anyway, Lucy got another call."

"Rosario told me she notified the office to pick up the tape. Frankly, that surprised me."

"Let's not fence, Jamey. The Montijo phone is tapped, so the incoming was monitored—also her call to me. I'm not supposed to know that, so I used it to let Shugrue and others believe I'm cooperating. What worries me is the Feds getting ahead of me, moving prematurely and getting Manny killed."

"Yeah, that worries me, too. But if the perps let Manny talk to his wife we'll know he's alive."

"No small thing." I squinted at the dark house, wondered if Manny were somewhere inside—chained, bound and gagged. This might be the time to find out.

"Don't you want the printouts?"

"Later. If I'm found with them we'd both be in trouble."

"Sure would," he agreed, "so I'll drop them off tomorrow."

"Anything significant?"

"Beyond what I told you?" He shook his head. "They've both had traffic accidents for speeding—Munguía was on a motorcycle clocked at one-fifteen. Spun off the road into a canal or they wouldn't have caught him. Venezuela background missing, except their military ranks: Lozano, colonel; Munguía, captain." He snorted. "Both in narcotics intelligence before coming here. Can you imagine that?"

"Easily. And what a help to Padilla they must have been. Okay, it's after your bedtime, so be off with you."

"How long you staying around?"

"Ten, twenty minutes. I want to see if anyone leaves or arrives."

"And?"

"Place looks empty to me. By now they could be in Caracas, with or without Manny. Where's your car?"

"Behind yours."

We walked back together. I unlocked the car door and activated my car phone, then punched Lozano's number. The phone rang six times before a male voice grunted, *"Sí?"*

"Domino's Pizza? I wanta order two large with—"

"Hey, you gotta wrong numba. *Adiós.*"

"Adiós," I replied, and cut off. Jamey looked at me. "So?"

"So a guy answered the phone. Goodnight, Jamey."

"Sure you don't want me to stick around?"

"I'm sure, and thanks for coming."

He smiled slowly. "That Cousin Pilar—she's something, isn't she?"

"Overwhelming," I agreed, and walked him to his car.

He backed around in a U-turn, lightless until the car turned onto 10th Avenue. I watched his taillights disappear.

I'd been considering a surreptitious entry into Lozano's house, but the male voice killed that idea. Instead, I took my Maglite and walked toward the Bay.

The hurricane had torn man-sized chunks of concrete from the seawall, but the tide was low and I was able to find dry footing until I reached the south side of Lozano's dock. From it steps led up to ground level, where entry was barred by a wire-link gate. The pool's submerged lights were off, probably by timer, so the Bay side of the house was dark. Except for the davit-mounted lights.

Now that my vision was adjusted to darkness I made out a pole-mounted switch so, keeping low, I went to it and clicked off the lights. Beside me the long, low *Sabre* rolled gently against dock fenders. Its cockpit was covered by a fitted black tarpaulin but I wondered if the engine compartment was open.

After looking for trip-wires and pressure pads, I crawled onto the stern and lifted the compartment's flush handle. The hatch was metal-framed and heavy, but I pried it up, and found a notched support to keep it from closing. That done, I lay belly-down and played the Maglite over twin twelve-cylinder engines. From them came the usual smell of oil and gasoline, telling me a dropped match would blow the *Sabre* out of the water. I moved the light aft and saw the copper tubing that delivered gas from tank to carburetors. I reached down for the brass coupler flange and turned it to disconnect the flow line. Gas poured out—too much, so I repositioned the coupler with a half-turn—enough to stop gas loss, though a few hard wave knocks could jar it loose and kill the engines.

What I'd done was promote the possibility of the *Sabre* going dead in offshore water and attracting Coast Guard attention. If the boat carried no contraband—human or otherwise—Coast Guard boarding would only irritate captain and crew. But if Manny were aboard . . . well, anything could happen.

I heard a car coming down 86th, so I lowered the hatch cover and slid back onto the dock. Just before the car braked in Lozano's drive I switched on the davit lights, and retraced my steps along the seawall. Two houses away I climbed onto land and made my way between houses until I reached the street. From there I could glimpse Lozano's garage door closing behind a gray BMW, then it was down and the garage light shut off.

I wondered who the driver was, where he had been and what he'd done while away. Had he called Lucy from a distant telephone? About two hours had passed since the call, so he could have been fifty, sixty miles away. Or passing time in a congenial lounge, of which there was no shortage in South Florida.

As I walked back to my car I recalled Jamey's mentioning Munguía's arrest for speeding on a bike. I'd visited one biker haven and wasn't eager to return. Maybe the driver had visited Marlena for an intimate chat over a few cold ones—or gone there after a warning call from the dancer. For a few moments I sat behind the wheel pondering the prospect of a long drive down to El Rancherito. The idea was unattractive, and supposing I went there, what was to be gained? Another dreary exchange with Marlena. For that it was too late, and I was too tired. I started the engine, and U-turned away from the house before I switched headlights on. And while I drove west to the Interstate I thought about my dinner date with Pilar and the vibes I felt whenever she was near. She was even more attractive than Rita Chavez de Castenada of triste memory, and a lot more intelligent. And I wondered what Pilar felt—if anything—when she was with me.

Then, guiltily, I thought of Melody, so far away. At least she was in her mother's watchful care, not in the hirsute embrace of Signor Fettucini, and that comforted me. I could rationalize my attentions to Pilar as disinterested concern for Manny's foreign cousin. That would hold until Melody came face to face with Pilar, after which my rationale would be ruled invalid. So I hoped the two would never meet. But why was I getting all apprehensive? It wasn't as though La Doctora and I were lovers—hell, we'd barely met— and Pilar could be virgin or lez. I didn't think so, but I had a premonition that fairly soon I might be given a chance to find out.

These thoughts occupied my mind until I pulled into my drive. After I garaged my car I found a business card stuck in my door jamb. Special Agent Doak's official card, and on it was written *Call me.*

My message machine showed a red light, but I ignored it and got into bed. Before sleep came I thought of Lozano's *Sabre,* and wondered how soon he would be taking it to sea.

TEN

MORNING ISN'T the best part of the day for me. I prefer slow waking, restorative coffee, mildly-stimulating shower, more coffee, substantial breakfast and time to contemplate the day's agenda. That's the ideal scenario, but oh, how seldom it occurs.

This morning was no exception. The telephone woke me around ten. And I let the answering machine kick in with an invitation to leave a brief message, though with no promise I'd call back. Whoever called broke the connection, relieving my mind of the conditioned reflex to communicate promptly with the caller.

Okay. I lay on my back eyeing the mirrored ceiling; it showed an unshaven face with eyes as red as Wolfman's. The bristles were natural overnight growth, but the eyes—? I conceded that I'd been imbibing alcohol to excess, quite probably because Melody was not around to monitor my intake. As an Olympic athlete she was an alert nay-sayer when it came to items injurious to my health, pointing out that a vibrant sex life depended on healthful diet and sufficient sleep. So I was glad she couldn't see me now—my mouth tasted like mushroom compost, and that drove me from bed.

I brushed my teeth vigorously, gargled with mint mouthwash, and kicked back a dram of Añejo to steady my hand as I shaved. A steaming shower cleared respiratory passages, after which I draped a towel around my middle and gulped instant coffee, having neglected to load the percolator last night.

Coffee started the mental gears grinding, and I recalled a waiting phone message, plus Special Agent Doak's terse demand. I played back the message, and to my intense pleasure heard the soft voice of Pilar: "Jack, thinking it over, I don't feel I adequately expressed my appreciation for a wonderful evening. It's been a long time since I had such an enjoyable experience, and—'' she faltered ''—it's difficult to put into words, but for a few hours you freed me from academic prison and allowed me to feel, well, feminine.'' Pause. ''I hope we'll see each other soon again.'' *Click, click,* and the message was over.

Well, hell, I thought, no one hopes it more than I, and we'll have to see what can be done about an early reprise. I reset the machine, and found Doak's card on a table where I'd dropped it last night. Before calling him I made another cup of instant and flavored it with tiny drops of Añejo, sat at the dinette table and pulled over the phone. After a couple of intra-office holds and transfers I heard Doak's raspy voice. ''Novak? How about coming in for a chat?''

''Should I bring my attorney?''

''Now why would you want to do that?''

''Maybe it's fear of authority and not knowing what you guys are up to. But since I'm not being charged with a felony today, why don't you drop by? Bring along your partner and we'll have coffee. Bring your own Danish, I'm barely vertical and haven't checked outside weather.''

''Well, I guess we can accommodate you. An hour too soon?''

''Just make it before noon.''

I dressed slowly, theorizing that the FBI reps planned to inform me of the kidnapper's second call. They had it on tape, but didn't want to let me know Lucy's line was tapped, or that they'd also heard her call to me. That way the fiction could be maintained.

Along with that time-waster I suspected that SA Doak was going to admonish me for giving Lucy advice, such as demanding to hear Manny's voice during the next call, whenever it came.

Well, admonish away, I reflected. We were all in the same ball game, though some of us were scoring while others seemed to be still warming the bench.

I added prime Colombian grind to the percolator basket, spring water to the jug, and set it on timer, wondering why I was wasting superb java on a couple of Feds. Maybe to flaunt the rewards of working on my own.

The postman dumped mail through the slot. A letter from the Principality of Monaco on yacht stationery, which I set aside for uninterrupted reading. Four bills, including Coral Gables taxes and water/sewer/trash collection fees. The joys of home ownership. No wonder Pilar opted for a rented pad; one payment and she was finished for the month. Melody didn't know it, but after we were united all financial matters were going to end up in her pretty lap to deal with at her discretion. Our roles would be as follows: I to bring home negotiable green, she to spend it as she chose. But I hadn't yet fully contemplated what it was going to be like living with a first-year law student, though I could anticipate her absence in classes, long hours in the law libe and more hours at our home computer.

Irritably, I mused that there was already an overabundance of lawyers in South Florida. I didn't need one in the family because I had enough stashed away for paying the likes of Neal Sonnett and Roy Black, should need arise. Why couldn't Melody get into a socially useful profession like real estate? There her charm, intelligence, looks and languages should make her a million-dollar broker in no time.

During the night I'd slept hot and my sheets were damp, so I stripped them and set them in the washer, then remade the bed. The motions reminded me of Annapolis mornings when my roommate—still listed MIA in Vietnam—and I hurriedly made our sacks, testing blanket tension by bouncing a dime. Had I gotten through four years of it? All I wanted to bounce on the bed was Melody, as the ceiling mirror could attest.

With the washer churning along I checked the percolator, set out cups and saucers, then door chimes sounded. Fifty-two minutes since calling Doak. The Bureau was nothing if not prompt.

Doak wanted his joe black, with sugar, and Rennie asked for a dollop of milk. We faced each other across the coffee table before the senior agent began.

"Did Mrs. Montijo tell you she received a second call from the assumed kidnappers?"

"She did."

"I assume you suggested she insist on hearing her husband's voice."

"Right."

"Can't really object to that, but we feel it would be better all around if you didn't offer advice. Dealing with kidnappers is a very delicate business, and our people are trained and skillful."

"Glad to hear it," I remarked. "Too many clowns in law enforcement are indelicate and heavy-handed."

"Well, I can't subscribe to that characterization, but my office has assumed full authority for managing the Montijo case."

"DEA out of it?"

"Except for collateral support."

"Good news. I was afraid Van Shugrue was clumping around, muddying waters."

"Not anymore. Besides DEA informants have come up with zip, so—who needs them?"

"Exactly." I sipped from my cup and looked respectful and humble.

"You wouldn't want to talk about your visit with Tito Gallardo?" Doak asked.

"Why not? Tito was so close to General Padilla I thought he might know something about the kidnapping."

"So you asked him."

"I did."

"Using an expired DEA credential to gain access."

"Mainly to save time. Ah—you've questioned Tito?"

"He's been interrogated. The Sheriff's office coordinated with us—Tito being a Federal prisoner—and—"

"Sheriff's office?"

"Investigating a murder. Tito's girlfriend, one Marlena Gomez."

I sat forward. "When?"

"Body was found in her car parked behind a South Dade biker dive, El Rancherito. Yesterday." He glanced at his watch. "About twenty-four hours ago. When Tito was informed he went crazy, blamed a nameless Federal officer he'd given her name to. The visitor register had your name on it." He put down his cup. "Didn't cut her throat, did you?"

"Not into knifing females."

"But you visited her where she works—worked."

"To give her money."

"Why?"

"Tito asked me to. He wanted pay for talking with me."

"How much pay?"

"Five large."

He turned to Rennie. "That explains the four hundred in her purse."

Rennie nodded soberly and I shrugged. "Is it a crime to give money to a stripper?"

"Well, she was something more than that, wasn't she? When you gave her the five hundred, what did she say?"

"Thanks."

"I can imagine," Doak said thinly. "But if she hadn't been murdered we wouldn't have known you visited Gallardo." His hands spread, palms up. "These things come out."

"Implying I was trying to conceal something? I didn't think it prudent to trust Tito with my name. Or Marlena."

"But it was okay to interrogate a prisoner with ties to Padilla, a prisoner who might have significant knowledge of the Montijo kidnapping."

"Seemed like a good idea."

"And now that the stripper's dead?"

"The Sheriff's office will assess blame, not you. No, I don't know who killed her. But I can't have Tito thinking I killed his woman, now that he's learned my name."

"Well, if you're lucky the Sheriff's deputies will make an arrest, solve the case, clear you."

"That lucky, I'd play the state lottery—and win. Okay, all the talk's been about me—let's talk about you. Made any progress in retrieving Manny? Arrests? Suspects?"

"That's privileged information."

"Meaning no progress. Meanwhile, the kidnappers are getting nervous and itchy to free Padilla. If that doesn't happen we all know they'll kill Manny."

The SAs glanced at each other, said nothing. So I asked, "What's your sense of things in Washington? Is the Attorney General going to authorize the exchange?"

"Haven't heard," Doak said curtly.

I sighed. "If the AG stalls a few more days Manny will be dead and the problem disappears. Sort of the Washington way of dealing with a crisis. Right?"

My visitors said nothing.

"So, despite your hostage experts' special training and experiential skills nothing's moving toward getting Manny back."

Doak cleared his throat. "I wouldn't say that."

"Don't have to. Manny's absence speaks for itself."

SA Rennie muttered, "You're really fixated on the guy, must think a lot of him."

"Fact. In Guadalajara—that's Mexico—Manny got me out of a torture cell where cops were beating me to death. Why were the cops beating me? Because I'd sabotaged a drug operation they were paid to protect. Yeah, I think a lot of Manny Montijo and I'll do whatever I can to free him."

Doak's chin lifted pugnaciously. "Meaning you're going to stick your nose into things, cross wires with an authorized investigation—"

"If there was a wire to cross I'd be happier than I am, but you fellows haven't even begun looking. All you've accomplished is eliminate DEA to get sole jurisdiction. The snatchers would be paralyzed with fear if only they knew." I stood up. "I've had it with you guys. No more informal chats, no phone calls, no notes stuck in my door. If I have something to share with the Bureau I'll call you. Until that times comes, stay off my screen. Tail me or tap my phone and I'll get an injunction that'll roast your balls."

Doak and his partner got up. "Sounds like a threat."

"Threat? Prediction of things to come. Meanwhile, I'll assert my right as a private citizen to advise Mrs. Montijo as circumstances suggest.'' I paused. ''By the way, has anyone talked to Padilla's lawyer?''

''Jay Gerschwin?'' Rennie blurted, and got a dirty look from Doak, who said, ''No point, he'd only tell us to get lost.''

''I understand. Everything's hopeless, nothing to be done. Goodday, gentlemen.'' I closed the door behind them and felt tension drain from my body. I opened and closed my hands, quaffed a short slug of Añejo, and remembered Melody's letter.

The yacht was bound for Athens, then Crete, possibly a cruise among the Greek Islands before heading for Izmir. ''Though maybe not in that order, geography not being my best subject at Ransom Everglades. Anyway, Mehmet wants to show Mom and me his beloved Turkey, and I sort of look forward to it—it would make a nice honeymoon trip when you join me. I know you'll phone or cable when Manny's safe again. In the meantime I miss you desperately and love you in boundless ways.''

Yes, I love you, too, I thought, and I wouldn't mind touring Turkey either. But, first things come first, and Manny comes before nuptial pleasures. Putting aside her letter, I got out the phone book, and found only an office listing for Jay Gerschwin, Esq. Following Joel Hornstein's murder, Jay had become the top narcotics lawyer in Miami and prudently concealed the location of his home. It was probably close to the mansions of Stallone, Madonna and Julio Iglesias, access protected by gates and guards. I dialed his office number and asked to speak with Mr. Gerschwin.

''Sorry, sir, Mr. Gerschwin's in court. May I connect you with his secretary?''

''Please do.''

After a short delay a female voice purred, ''This is Mrs. Margolis—may I help you?''

''Yeah. I'm Flaherty, Braman Service Department.'' Braman imported, sold and serviced every make of upscale cars. ''Got a service order for Mr. Gerschwin, car pickup, okay?''

''Go on.''

''Need an address.''

''Oh. Um. Well, is it the Mercedes or the Rolls?''

''Mercedes. If I can get it now it'll be ready today. Where's it at?''

''Hmmm. Well, unless he drove it to the office it's in his condo garage.''

''Swell. Address?''

''Villa Moravia, South Brickell. Penthouse— Ah, what about keys?''

''We got dupes here in case like a customer loses a set or gets robbed, y'know.''

"What a great idea! Only last month my purse was snatched with my car keys and I had dreadful trouble replacing them."

"Buy your next car from Braman, Mrs. Margolis, and I'll be glad to service you, night or day."

"I'll remember that, Mr.—?"

"Flaherty. Dennis M. Flaherty."

"Ah—your service policy intrigues me—Dennis. You said night or day, did you not?" Her voice was low, intimate.

"That's right, ma'am, but we better keep it to nights."

"Oh? And why is that?"

"We both work days." Smiling, I put away the phone book and wondered briefly if I'd ever see the face behind the playful voice. Probably a Gerschwin paramour, but she'd supplied useful information. Gerschwin's place wasn't on Fisher Island, Star Island, Palm Island or one of the other islands referred to as "exclusive haunts" of the rich and famous. Villa Moravia was approachable by land, and I planned to reach it that way. But later. Although the FBI visitation was mostly wasted time, their impotence persuaded me to run a scam on Jay Gerschwin—at his lair. It was now noon, too early to brace the lawyer, so I phoned Lucy Montijo and asked to speak with Cousin Pilar.

"Jack, she's moving into her apartment. Let's see—here's her number." She read it off, I repeated it, and thanked her before asking about Carmen.

"She's much better, Jack. Thank you again for—"

"Please, Lucy, I did less than Manny would have done, no thanks necessary." I paused before saying, "You'll let me know when the next call comes?"

"Of course."

"And notify the office, as before."

"Yes. Jack . . . you do believe we'll get Manny back, don't you?"

"Never doubted it, honey." I hung up, wrote down Pilar's phone number and dialed. When she answered I said, "Thoughtful of you to leave a message, and I enjoyed the evening as much as you did. This is a new day, it's noon, and I thought we might share a crust of bread somewhere."

"Oh, Jack, I'm just moving in, hair's a mess, I'm filthy and not fit to be seen."

"Tell you what—take a quick shower, pull on jeans and a T-shirt, and I'll pick you up in an hour. Okay?"

"Well—you're sure you won't mind how I look?"

"You said you hoped we'd see each other soon, and this is the first opportunity."

"So it is." She paused. "Actually, I'll welcome getting out of here, and I do have to eat . . ."

"Exactly. See you in an hour."

She came out to the car wearing light-pink tailored jeans, matching silk shirt, tails tied around her waist, pink bow in her hair, neutral lipstick and white alpargatas. In short, sensational.

"What a great idea," she said as she got in beside me. "I'm ravenous. Where are we going?"

"Little place that caters to nice people. You should know about it."

She nodded. "But when I'm teaching I'll only have time for cafeteria lunch, I'm afraid. How far is it?"

"Ten minutes." I drove far down 2nd Avenue and pulled into the public parking area. After feeding quarters into the meter I saw a raggedy-looking creature lurching toward us. "Watch your car, mister?" he croaked.

"Yeah. Here's five. Stay awake."

Pilar linked her arm with mine and we walked a few steps to the Charcuterie entrance. The place was crowded with young professionals so we waited for a table. Pilar said, "If there were any news about my cousin I know you'd tell me, so I won't ask. But I know you're doing all you can, and that comforts all of us."

A waiter came to us with a tray bearing glasses of white and red wine. We took white, touched glasses and sipped. Pilar said, "What a nice idea. More restaurants should do it."

"More restaurants should have French owners."

A party left and in a few minutes we were shown to a quiet nook at the far end. Pilar ordered lobster mayonnaise, and I asked for calves liver, medium-rare, hold the onions, and a chilled bottle of whatever we were drinking.

The wine bucket came first, and while the Sancerre was chilling, Pilar said, "Lucinda is very reticent about you, Jack, but she did say you're engaged to a lovely young woman."

"I am. Engaged, not married."

Her eyebrows lifted. "Even so, we probably shouldn't see each other as much as I'd like."

"But looking at it another way, we have the Montijo family in common, making contact inevitable."

She gazed at me. "Inevitable," she echoed, "and that would be fine except that I find you very attractive. What am I to do?"

"My dilemma, too," I admitted, "but it doesn't need resolving over lunch. Let's take things as they come, see what happens."

She smiled then, the waiter came back to open the wine, and when our glasses were full we touched them and Pilar said huskily, "To whatever happens."

"Sin compromiso."

She nodded agreement, our orders arrived, and we ate hungrily.

Afterward, I found my car untouched by vandals, although the watcher was sitting on the paving, back to a wall, sipping from a bottle in a brown paper bag. He waved sleepily, I unlocked the door for Pilar, then we drove back to her apartment building.

I parked in the turnaround and said, "I've got plenty of time, and it occurs to me I could move furniture, be helpful some way."

For what seemed a long time she studied my face.

"Are you sure you want to?"

"I'm sure."

She sighed, got out of the car, and I followed her up the walk.

Her apartment was on the third floor. No elevator, so we took the banistered staircase that gave out onto a carpeted hallway. It was dark and cool, and when she handed me her key I opened the apartment door.

The place was furnished in a style reminiscent of the Thirties when the apartment had been built. Ceiling fans and window air conditioners. A desk held books, papers and a laptop computer. Beyond the living room I could see a small dining area and a fairly modern kitchen

"Only one bedroom," she told me, "and that's where you can help."

Together, we moved the heavy, old-fashioned bed, and I put tables and chairs here and there as directed. From a linen closet she brought sheets and pillowcases and we made the bed. There was light perspiration on her forehead when we finished, so she went into the bathroom to rinse her face. When she returned, her feet were bare, shirttails unknotted. I noticed high color in her cheeks as she came hesitantly toward me. She halted a foot away, close enough that I could kiss her forehead, and then I circled her with my arms and she flowed against me. Our lips met, and I felt electricity entering my body with almost paralyzing force. Her cheek pressed mine, and she whispered, "Should I undress?"

"Let me." I unbuttoned her shirt and peeled it from her shoulders and arms. Then I undid her jeans and they pooled around her feet. I unhooked her bra and kissed her warm breasts. She gasped and shuddered, pulled down her panties, and stood naked before me, arms crossed before her breasts. Stripping took me much less time. I sat on the edge of the bed and kissed her nipples until her pelvis began undulating, and then I drew her down beside me.

For a time our hands and mouths explored each other's bodies with the intense curiosity of first-time lovers. She was soft and warm and passionate, her loins damp with desire. I entered her slowly and carefully, because her tense vagina was almost virginal, and as she began moving against me she whispered, "Don't make me conceive, Jack, please."

"I promise." Then flames enveloped and consumed us, little cries coming from her throat until she climaxed. After I showed her I'd safely spent, she lay back, contentment on her features. "Inevitable," she murmured, and her eyes closed.

Side by side we slept for an hour before making love again, and this time uncertainty and subliminal fears were gone, replaced by deep, mutual fulfillment.

When I woke again it was evening. Her perfect body lay in a child's innocent repose, perfect study for a Goya. I brushed her lips with mine, but she did not wake, so I dressed, covered her with a sheet, and looked back longingly as I went away.

Her conscience was clear. I had work to do on mine.

ELEVEN

RUSH-HOUR traffic was almost over when I turned off South Brickell toward the Bay and took the access road to the Villa Moravia. Built some ten years earlier, the building added height and controversy to the Miami skyline. Its construction was the dream of Jiri Vlasic, a Czech immigrant financier who commissioned a Czech avant-garde artist to paint each level a different pastel hue, making the condominium distinctive among its neighbors, some of which sued to have the building redone in conventional tones. But even before construction ended Vlasic fled to his native Europe, barely ahead of liens, subpoenas and indictments, denouncing bank failures of the Greedy Eighties as responsible for his fall from glory. Over ensuing years the fugitive had been sighted at Costa Smeralda, Naxos, Nice, Monaco, Capri and other watering holes of the very rich, always in the company of young and attractive females. Reports that made his creditors groan and redouble efforts to bring him to the bar of justice. So far Vlasic had eluded them, and seemed likely to continue to do so until graveside.

I looked up at the garish facade and smiled, thinking, a cat can look at a king, or in this case, a king's manor.

Ahead, a gated guardhouse. As I neared, a uniformed guard stepped out and held up one hand. I slowed, braked, and before he spoke, flashed my DEA credential. "Has Mr. Gerschwin arrived? Mr. Jay Gerschwin?" I pocketed the cred as the guard frowned. Unaccustomed to answering direct questions, he scratched the point of his chin. "I can phone," he suggested, and started back for the guardhouse, but I said, "Uh-uh, don't alert him. What I want from you is a simple answer—yes or no. And while you're considering where duty lies I should warn you that lying to a Federal officer is a felony. Obstructing justice is another. Make up your mind."

His frown deepened. Doubtless Mr. Gerschwin slipped him big-time green on holidays and he didn't want to risk losing it. Finally he grimaced, and said, "Okay, he drove in about twenty minutes ago."

"Rolls or Mercedes?"

"Rolls. Silver—"

"I know, I know. Penthouse, right?"

"Yeah," he answered resignedly.

"So far, so good. The reason I warned you officially is that I'm here on a law enforcement matter. If you tip Gerschwin to expect me I'll know—and you're in for a night or two in the slammer. Got it?"

"I'm cooperating, right?"

"Keep it up. Move."

From inside the guardhouse he raised the barrier and I drove through. Parked by the entrance, and saw a uniformed senior citizen hustle down the steps, waving me off. I locked the car door and faced him.

"You can't park here," he blustered, "there's a place around back for visitor parking."

I opened the cred case long enough that he could see it—if his eyesight was better than I thought. "Law enforcement," I snapped, "and I won't be long. Anyone tries to move this baby, big trouble. Understand?"

He nodded hastily. "Who you wanta see, sir?" Respectfully.

"That's my business, Pop. If I need help I'll let you know."

"Okay, okay, do what you gotta do."

"And keep your mouth shut. If the suspect expects me and there's a shootout—well, accessory's a mean rap to beat." I brushed past him, went through the lobby past his desk, and entered an open elevator. I pushed the lighted PH button and the doors closed. The upward rise was like jet acceleration, and when the ride ended I was glad to step off.

I was in a narrow hallway. One door, walnut-paneled, no name, just a peephole lens. I covered it with my hand and rang the doorbell, heard faint ringing in the interior distance. Rang again. Put my ear to the door and heard a sort of rhythmic grinding that halted. Feet pounded toward the entrance. I rang again to unsettle him, and then the door flung inward. "Okay, okay, what the hell do you want? Who are you?"

For the third time in recent minutes I flashed my cred and put it away. I'd seen newspaper photos of Jay Gerschwin and in living TV color as the lawyer walked clients to and from the city's courthouses. But this was a Gerschwin I'd never seen before.

He was short, fat, nearly bald, and he wore a red velvet jogging suit, black

Nikes, and on face and forehead a lot of beaded sweat. Squinting at me, he said, "Didn't get the name."

"Wear your glasses," I told him, "next time. Right now you don't need them because we're going to talk. I do better sitting down, but if you want to hang there like a piece of red shit, that's up to you."

"Hey, fella, I don't get talked to that way. Be civil or I call the U.S. Attorney and you wake up in Fairbanks, Alaska."

"Don't obstruct justice, Mr. Gerschwin. I'm here on a matter of mutual interest. Call it a mission of mercy."

"Mercy?" He laughed shortly. "Okay, fella, you got big, tough balls, you get to come in."

I eased past him into a room that was a decorator's dream. Chinese furnishings, Chinese wall scrolls, Chinese vases and soapstone animals. Except for the sand-colored carpet, the prevailing color was red. "Okay, guy, what is it? Police Benefit tickets? Call the office tomorrow."

"You're wasting time, sir. Instead of temporizing bullshit, your response should be, 'How may I assist your inquiries?' "

"Yeah. Okay, consider I said it. What's the beef?"

"You're the attorney of record for General Jorge Padilla. He still your client?"

"Sure is. He in trouble again?"

"Heavier than you can imagine."

"Son-of-a-bitch! How can you get in trouble in the slammer?"

"Scores of ways." From beyond the big Chinese room came the rhythmic sounds of an exercise machine. "You got a bimbo there, tell her to turn on the shower and cover her ears."

"*Bimbo?*" He nearly shrieked. "My fiancée's working out with me and she's no bimbo. Happens to be a lawyer."

"There's a difference? Tell her, Jay. This has to stay between us."

Irritably, he left the room. Exercising stopped, and presently I heard running water. When Gerschwin came back I said, "Settle down, Jay, and hear me. How do you like the sound of kidnapping a Federal official, extortion and attempted murder? Does it resonate?"

"*Kid*—What the hell you talkin' about? *Padilla?* What's that got to do with him? With me?"

"From his comfy cell your client, Padilla, ordered the kidnapping of a Federal officer, and—"

"Oh, Jesus," the lawyer groaned.

"Mary and Joseph," I finished. "Padilla thinks the government will free him in exchange for the officer, Manuel Montijo by name. Are you listening? Do I have your attention?''

He licked his lips, wiped sweat from his face. ''You got it,'' he said, and slumped into a chair. ''Whatcha want from me?''

''Coming to that. Padilla thinks it's a smart deal, body for body, but though that's the custom in Venezuela it doesn't fly here. Now, for the moment I'm willing to assume this act was done without your advice, consent, or knowledge—''

''It was, it was,'' he yelped. ''If in fact Padilla provably did it.''

''Oh, it's provable. We've got the actual perps under surveillance, can bag them in five minutes, but what we don't want is a nasty shootout with maybe Agent Montijo getting killed in the line of fire. See, Jay, like it or not, Padilla's dirtied your hands. So what I want from you is assistance in clearing things up. Help us now, and no one suggests you gave him criminal advice. Tell me to fuck off and tomorrow morning I'll have Marshals subpoenaing every file in your office, with a moving van to cart the stuff away.''

''Okay, okay.'' His hands waved agitatedly. ''What can I do to cooperate?'' Smart enough to know when to surrender.

''All right, you're being reasonable, I can be reasonable, too. You didn't get where you are being an asshole, so here's what you do.'' I sucked in a deep breath. ''At an early hour tomorrow you go to MCC and see Padilla in that interview room. Tell him the exchange idea is a no-brainer and he must have Montijo released. Tell him if he doesn't, and the officer is harmed or killed, the Government will take reprisal in ways that will be painful at first, fatal at the end.''

His small eyes opened wide. ''You serious?''

''Bet your ass. Think it doesn't happen? You've never been in a joint with lifers. Most are broke from lawyers' fees, their families destitute and their women turning tricks in cars and alleys. For a few thousand paid to their loved ones they'll tear off a warden's head and drink his blood.'' I paused to gaze at the sudden pallor of his cheeks. ''There's an executive fund pays for wet jobs, Mr. Gerschwin. Not in any overt budget, not subject to Congress, and we like it that way. Yesterday the kidnappers called Mrs. Montijo a second time, threatened to waste her husband unless the General was promptly freed. Now we can't have that sort of thing in our society, so the counteroffer you take to your client is this: Montijo alive and free, or Padilla dead in a week. My office has talked with two prisoners who have access to Padilla. The one who kills him, his family gets fifty thousand, the backup gets half. That's already agreed.''

''Holy God, I never knew anything like that existed!''

"If you'd known about it you'd file some sort of bullshit lawsuit or bring in the Criminal Liberties Union to destroy the fund. So, what I'm saying is, do what I've told you to do and no one gets hurt. Not Montijo, not you, not even Padilla—if he follows your sage counsel."

He sat forward, hands over ears, and slowly moved his head.

"If Montijo isn't delivered safe and sound within forty-eight hours after you've advised Padilla, I'll trigger the hitters." I laughed mirthlessly. "Hell, for fifty thou I could recruit a guard to whack him. For forty I'd do it myself."

"Who—who *are* you?" he stammered.

"A friend of the court. I wasn't here, you never saw me. So, Jay, it comes down to this: I was brought in to handle things, when it's all over you'll never see me again. Meanwhile, I expect you to do your part. If you don't I'll know by noon, and your office will see a lot of buzzers and papers and TV cameras, and then nasty rumors about your criminal complicity will begin. And, so you understand motivation—the fight against crime is uneven, the white hats are outnumbered and scumbag shysters like you make it even worse. We have to fight back as best we can before legal niceties strangle us entirely. That's why I'm putting the arm on you, and why you'll lean on Padilla." I stared at him. "Need I say more?"

He shook his head, eyes wild. "You—you're a death-dealer," he blurted.

"You should know the breed, you defend them. All right, Jay, if I see you again it'll be because you broke faith." I pulled out my .38 and touched the muzzle to his nose. "Bang, bang, another drug lawyer slain by a dissatisfied client. Like Hornstein and St. Armand." I stuck the pistol in my belt, got up and went to the door. Opening it, I glanced back. The lawyer hadn't moved.

At his lobby desk the old elevator-watcher didn't move either. His gaze barely cleared the racing form he was studying. I went outside, unlocked my car, and drove past the gatehouse. The guard looked at me, yawned, and turned away.

Driving toward my place, I reviewed the penthouse scene, feeling less sure I'd done the right thing. But having found a pressure point in Padilla's lawyer I had to try retrieving Manny without bloodshed, sooner than anticipated.

The downside of my scenario had Padilla telling the lawyer to get lost. The General wasn't accustomed to taking pacific advice, and I had no way of predicting his reaction. Ordering Manny kidnapped was an extreme act that demonstrated Padilla's pathological fixation on freedom. In his view it was a card worth playing, the only card he held. But perhaps my death threat via Gerschwin would alter his perspective and produce results.

I'd risked little or nothing against the prospect of high gain—Manny's freedom—and the worst outcome of my ploy would be Padilla's refusal, and Manny's continued captivity.

As I turned into my drive, I recalled Padilla's henchmen and their offshore racer. Even were Manny returned undamaged, Lozano and Munguía had to be sanctioned for capturing and holding him. I could do something about that, but not until Manny was safely home.

Inside the door was a scatter of mail and a large envelope. Opening it, I found copies of the NCIC printouts Jamey illicitly obtained. Frontal and profile photos showed a square-faced Lozano wearing pointed sideburns, a man about forty-five or so. Captain Hector Munguía was in his thirties; lean face, thick black hair, flat nose and a pimp mustache. Now I could recognize them on the street. Thanks, Jamey.

The percolator still held warm coffee, so I poured a cup and added a shot of Añejo to enhance flavor. For a while I watched the usual disquieting news on CNN, then my thoughts turned to Pilar.

I was still feeling the afterglow of our amorous encounter, while marveling that it had occurred so soon. I wanted to see her, be with her—hell, I wanted to move in with her, though that would be a little much for Manny's family to condone. We had made no commitments or anything resembling long-range plans. Our understanding was *sin compromiso*—no commitments at all. Better for Pilar, better for me. And I sensed that after I married, Pilar's moral code would keep her distant from me. But that was an eventuality I wasn't ready to deal with.

The phone rang, and I answered on the second ring, hoping it would be Pilar. Instead, Jamey's voice. "You've been out."

"Shopping," I lied, in case my phone was tapped. "Getting my oil changed. I'm sort of at loose ends if you want to stop by for a brew or two."

"Good idea. Hmm. Say forty minutes."

"How's the family?"

"Very tense—waiting for the next call. Hoping they'll hear Manny's voice. They're desperate for assurance he's alive."

"So am I. How's Carmen?"

"Looking a little better every day. More importantly, she's becoming one of the family again and next week she'll go back to school."

"Let's hope she stays. Wanna eat in? Bring Chinese, Cuban, ribs, whatever you like."

"I like them all."

"So do I."

He arrived with large bags from Tony Roma's rib joint and Wong's Chinese take-out, for which I insisted on paying. "Hell, Jack, I gotta eat," he objected, but I told him his money was better spent entertaining Rosario at the Hard Rock Café. I produced plates, cutlery and chilled bottles of Corona, Tecate not being available in Coral Gables.

As we ate I asked if he thought the FBI was making any progress in recovering Manny.

"Don't know." He licked a rib-greased finger. "I'm cut out of the info loop, and so is Shugrue, which makes him madder'n a skunk in a steel trap. But I picked up one collateral byte, Jack. Carlos Stefano having OD'd, his file had to be retired. Whatta ya know—*he* was the informant who claimed Manny was dirty." He grinned. "Saw it myself. I suppose Munguía put him up to it."

"That's a break for Manny." I chopsticked a load of lo mein into my mouth and chewed thoughtfully. "Shugrue must really hate Manny to take the smear of a strung-out hophead against the record of an officer like Manny."

"Well, that's office politics—what can I say?" He tipped a Corona bottle and sipped.

"Shugrue's a piece of shit, and an insecure one at that. Where does he come from?"

"Last post Costa Rica. Tried a sting operation that got the informant killed and Shugrue expelled. Should have been fired, but instead he was sent here, the equivalent of promotion."

"Sounds like old times," I remarked bitterly, "so we gotta get Manny back." I laid down my chopsticks and swallowed more cold Corona. "To that end," I went on, "I've activated a situation that could produce results in a couple of days, but—"

"Like what, Jack?"

"I don't want you knowing details. If you don't know, you're not implicated if things go wrong—and they easily could. Leave it at that."

"Not even a hint?"

I shook my head. "If you're ever questioned, follow the Reagan precedent—you didn't know such things were going on. Okay?"

"Okay—but you've got me plenty curious." For a while he gnawed a barbecued rib, before saying, "And all the time I thought you were occupied with Cousin Pilar." He grinned slyly.

"We've shared a couple of meals, sure. Like you said, a guy's gotta eat. And a little hospitality to a visitor from a far country is never amiss."

"You're right about that."

"And once she starts teaching she won't be around," I remarked for lack of anything else to say. "By the way, last night after you left, a gray BMW went into the target garage. I figured he could have driven an hour distant, called Lucy, and driven back over a two-hour span, but that's speculation.''

"So, what do you think?''

"Either they've got Manny in that house, or some other place. But I'm certain they know where he is. What I'm hoping is Padilla will have a change of heart, let Manny go.''

He looked startled. ''Is that likely?''

"It's possible.''

"Because of something you set in motion, right?''

"Look, anything's better than having Manny in that middle of a firefight. And if the perps sense danger their first reaction could be to kill Manny, who can probably identify them. So those are two situations to avoid.''

He nodded slowly. ''Leaving—what?''

"I may be able to tell you tomorrow. Lo mein?'' I added a pile to his plate.

We'd pretty well finished dinner when the phone rang. I answered, and heard Lucy's voice. ''Jack, I heard from Manny, so I know, thank God, he's alive.''

"Or was,'' I told Jamey after Lucy hung up. ''What she heard was a pre-recorded Manny, saying he was being well treated and hoped his exchange was imminent. Good for Lucy's morale, but useless for our purposes.''

"Yeah, guess so,'' he said dejectedly. ''What now?''

"Grab some sleep, I'll do the same.''

"If you're going back to Lozano's—''

"I'm not. There's a limit to my curiosity about that house.'' I got up and began clearing away dishes. Jamey rose and looked around. I said, ''Take the surplus, lotta good food there.''

"Sure? I'll leave the onion rings.''

"Take it all. Enjoy.''

After Jamey left I phoned Pilar, heard her answering voice, and said, ''*Doctora,* are you settled in?''

"Almost, and I'm glad you called.''

"I was afraid you might be sleeping.''

"No—you left so quietly I didn't wake until an hour ago. It was wonderful—and I don't mean only the sleep.''

"Me, too. You didn't think you'd seen the last of me, did you?''

"Well, it occurred to me that your motto might be fuck and forget, but now I know better.''

"I certainly hope so, *querida.* When can I see you again?''

"I'm not sure. I have to be at the university tomorrow to get organized, find out class schedules, and so on. And there's a departmental buffet in the evening—would you want to come?''

"Uh-uh, sounds deadly.''

"Afraid you're right, but for me obligatory. Still, there's the weekend.''

"Definitely. We might drive down the Keys, see what the hurricane left.''

"I'd like that. You'll call?''

"I'll call. Oh—almost forgot—Lucy got another of those calls, heard Manny's recorded voice.''

"How wonderful!''

"It's a favorable development. Things are—well, moving along.''

"And I'm so relieved.'' She paused. "Jack, do take care of yourself.''

"Always.''

Before turning in I thought again about Lozano's house, and again decided not to return. Jay Gerschwin was to brace General Padilla in the morning, and depending on the outcome, further steps might be unnecessary. I'd rolled the dice, let's see how the spots turned up.

TWELVE

I SLEPT late, drank a lot of coffee with breakfast, tidied the house and dressed for the day. By then it was nearing eleven, and if Gerschwin had seen his client per instructions, Manny's release might be at hand. I combined a visit to the wine shop for *manzanilla* with a stop at the gas station's pay phone. When Mrs. Margolis came on the line I said, "Dennis Flaherty, Braman Service, Mrs. Margolis."

"Oh, yes, Mr. Flaherty, is there a problem?"

"Hope not. I've got a reminder about Mr. Gerschwin's Rolls—routine maintenance—and I wonder if he wants it done today?"

"Umm, well I really can't say. I'll have to check with him when he comes in."

"Is that, ah, likely to be much later, ma'am?"

"He left a message on the office machine, said he'd be delayed with a client, so I can't give you an estimate. It's, oh, almost lunchtime, so I rather doubt he'll come until afterward."

"Then he can't expect the work done today. Okay, you've been helpful and I'll just reschedule. Thanks a lot." I hung up before she could offer to call me at Braman's, and walked toward my car. Before unlocking it, I went back to the pay phone and dialed the number I'd noted on Gerschwin's penthouse phone. After five rings I was ready to hang up, when I heard Gerschwin's hoarse voice. "Cheryl? Have to call you back, I'm busy right now, okay?"

"Okay," I replied. "Busy doing what?"

"Oh, God," he husked. *"You!"*

"Friend of the court, counselor. Collect yourself, Jay. You saw Padilla, what did he say?"

In a strangled voice Gerschwin said, "Told me to get out, threatened to have me killed for suggesting he release Montijo."

I gripped the receiver. "Bad as that? Surely you used all your forensic skills to persuade him?"

"I did, I did, I swear I did. He was threatening me when the guard came in and hauled him away. It was really scary. Now *you* . . . oh, Jesus," he wailed.

"Hey, you followed instructions, you're off the hook with me, so take it easy."

"But Padilla—God, he could have me *killed!*"

"Not if he's killed first."

There was silence while he thought it over. Finally he said, "Too risky, I can't wait for that. I'm getting out of town."

"Where to, Jay?"

He laughed hollowly. "Think I'll tell you, you killer? It'll be far, far away, that much I'll say. Goodbye, you death-dealing son-of-a-bitch." The phone slammed down, and I replaced the receiver with a smile. Gerschwin's fright was all I had to smile about, though, because Padilla's monomania put me back to square one. My dice roll had come up snake eyes.

But as I drove back to my place I reflected that the con had been worthwhile because it told me Padilla was immovable, and I couldn't put off working on his henchmen.

Turning into Granada, I saw a brown four-door at the curb in front of my house. That was okay, except for the whip antenna and the white lettering that read: Sheriff Dade County. Oh, oh, I thought, and decided not to keep driving. Instead I braked the car in my drive and walked back to the parked car. Two brown-uniformed officers were in the front seat, wearing DI hats. The engine was running so their a/c was probably keeping them comfortable despite the midday heat.

The nearest man opened his door and peered up at me. "Mr. Novak?"

"Right. What can I do for you?"

"Got a few questions, sir. Mind if we come in?"

"I do. You stay there and I'll stand here. What's the problem?"

The one with three sleeve-chevrons said, "Concerns a murder. Young woman knifed outside a biker dive, El Rancherito."

"Ummm. Let's see—Marlena . . . Dietrich? No, can't be. Chavez? Doesn't sound right . . ."

"Her name was Gomez, sir, and you were known to visit her a day or so before her death."

"Gomez, right. Lady seemed harmless enough. Who'd want to kill her?"

"That's what we want to find out. Mind telling us the purpose of your visit?"

"Not at all. I already told the FBI but maybe they don't coordinate timely with your office." I shrugged, got out a handkerchief and wiped my face. It was hot in the sun. I wondered if the recent hurricane was worsening our seasonal weather pattern.

"So, you talked to the Feds."

"Special Agents Doak and Rennie. Too bad about Marlena. Now all the rednecks who used to enjoy watching her display her tits and pussy'll have to find a substitute." I paused. "Around Miami that shouldn't be too hard."

"Guess not," the sergeant said sourly, "but for the record, what was the purpose of your visit?"

"A friend of hers asked me to give her some money. I did and we parted friends. No big secret."

"And that friend's name?"

I sighed, wiped my face again. "Tito Gallardo. You know that because you got my name off the prison visitor list."

"Yeah," the no-striper drawled, "that's a known fact. How much'd you give her?"

"Five hundred."

"Well, there was four in her bag, so it wasn't strongarm robbery."

"And I didn't return by night to get it back."

"No one's sayin' you did, sir. Just checkin' facts. But mind sayin' again why you gave her the money?"

"Gallardo asked me to."

The troopers exchanged glances. The sergeant said, "Could be you're a nice fellow to know, free and easy with the green."

"Sometimes. Also for the record I didn't pay her to perform some unspeakably perverted act or even a hand-job. Anything else?"

"Yeah—Gallardo says you killed Marlena."

"Then he's stir-crazy." I shook my head. "What's the rationale? I give his girlfriend five bills, then kill her? Where's the satisfaction?"

"Yeah, it's a little crazy," the sergeant conceded. "Just where were you the night Marlena Gomez was killed?"

"Not knowing what night that was, I can't say. But it seems to me those Blue Panthers ought to be worth looking into. Who knows if one or more of them was insanely jealous. Or Marlena—to put it delicately—declined the back seat advances of some biker stud?"

"*Back seat!*" How'd you know she was killed in the back seat?"

"Relax, it was on the airwaves. And I don't know she was killed there, I heard that's where the body was found. Right?"

The troopers looked at each other. The stripeless one closed his book. "Have to check every angle."

"Sure." I paused. "While Marlena and I were talking a big nasty biker came over, name of Donny. She said I was okay and he went away."

The sergeant sighed. "Guess we better talk to Donny, see if he's got any ideas who'd want to harm her." He looked up at me. "That'd be Donny Simpkins, mean bastard. Rap sheet long's my arm, including manslaughter."

"I believe it." I wiped my face again and stepped back from the car. The nearest trooper touched the brim of his DI hat and they drove away. As I walked up to my house I theorized that Donny or another barfly had reported my chat with Marlena to—to whom? Munguía? Lozano? Then someone had forced her to admit she'd named names, and she'd been killed for it. Despite the heat I felt sudden chill. Marlena hadn't known my name, but the troopers had, because it was on the prison register for the whole world to see. And that world included Munguía, Lozano, and—Gallardo. Unwisely, I'd signed my true name, never thinking it could endanger me. And danger was real, as proved by Marlena's brutal murder. Even behind bars Tito Gallardo could put out a contract on me, Padilla, too.

The mail included a card from Melody at Piraeus, the yacht's port of call. She loved the Aegean almost as much as she loved me and when was I going to join her?

Good question. When was I going to find Manny Montijo?

I sat at the dinette table, quaffed a cold Corona, and made out a shopping list, a short one; Home Depot warehouse could supply most of my needs. So I drove off to buy them.

At five the alarm woke me from an energizing nap. I phoned Pilar, who was dressing for the departmental buffet, and suggested she limit intake to social nibbling then meet me for dinner at La Paloma on Biscayne.

"It won't look well for me to leave early, you know. I'm supposed to meet faculty and they're supposed to meet me," she said dubiously.

"Faculty'll be around a long time, but I'm a short-timer. Eight o'clock?"

"Hmmm. I can probably meet you at nine."

"Nine it is." I gave her the restaurant's location and got dressed for the evening. After that I undid parcels and set out my purchases on the dinette table: bolt cutter, machinist's face mask, powerful slingshot, golf balls, can of white gasoline and a pair of Bic lighters. A reel of primacord and a can of black powder would be useful, I thought, but I didn't know where to get them without signing a dealer register as the law required. So I'd go without them. But not without a Colt .32 ankle gun.

By eight it was dark. Lozano's house was dark, too, except for the davit lights by the dock, and the neighborhood was quiet. I continued around the block and parked at a shopping plaza a few blocks away. From there I used a pay phone to call Lozano's number and when a male voice answered I said, "Ginny there? Tell her Roy—"

"No aquí. Equivocado," the man snapped and slammed down his receiver. At least one of the perps was home; where was the other?

I drove back to Bayshore, cut off headlights and set a shiny golf ball in the slingshot. I opened my window and braked in front of the target house. Then I pulled back the rubber sling and aimed above the grilled front window. The missile hit the wall and bounced off. I aimed lower and saw the ball slam into the pane, shattering it. Instantly the alarm erupted, piercing the night with a cacophony of shrieks and howls and siren sounds that faded behind me as I drove away. It took the IDT response van two minutes and forty-three seconds to reach Lozano's house. The vehicle was large and shiny black, with a light bar atop the cab and the bold IDT logo on the door.

I drove slowly past, saw the grounds bathed in light and two IDT security types at the front door. They seemed to be demanding entry, but Munguía kept shaking his head and brandishing a long assault weapon. Finally the two arrivals gave up and started down the walk. One peeled off and went around the side of the house where he unlocked the system box and turned off the alarm. I assumed he wouldn't reset it before the window glass was replaced along with new metallic sensor tape; meanwhile the house was vulnerable to entry.

As I drove off, neighbors returned to their houses, Lozano's exterior lights went out, and the night was calm once more.

In disabling the alarm system I'd learned that it wasn't linked to any police department, and that the security firm's response time was just under three minutes. I'd learned, too, that the occupants didn't want visitors, not even IDT security men—meaning they had something inside the house to be kept unseen. And that something could be Manny Montijo.

At La Paloma I took a banquette and ordered a bottle of white Rioja to chill while I waited for Pilar.

Twenty minutes later she slid onto the seat beside me, apologizing profusely for being late, but I kissed her cheek and said, "What's important is you're here. How was the social hour?"

"Pretty boring—so I'm grateful you asked me here."

The headwaiter came over, twirled the Rioja in its icy bath and looked at me questioningly. "If it's ready, we're ready," I told him, "and then we'll have a menu."

The wine was cold and dry and light to the tongue. We ordered crab-stuffed shrimp with saffron rice, and while it was being prepared we talked of what our lives had been, and Pilar described her sheltered childhood, the annual ritual of grape harvesting, and the academic prejudice she'd had to overcome after leaving home. She spoke openly and effortlessly, without affectation, telling me that she doubted she could ever chair a department in Spain, and so she would be looking for academic openings while in the States. "So much has changed in Spain since Franco, but the status of women is pretty much what it's always been. And having tasted real freedom when I was at Barry, life in Spain is suffocating by comparison."

"Does your family understand that?"

"Not really." She lifted her glass and sipped. "I've given up trying to make them understand. So, I do what I choose to do . . ."

"They ought to appreciate what you've accomplished, what you are."

"In time, they probably will. Meanwhile, I want to achieve as much as I can for myself. Fulfill my ambitions."

"Like the Army says, 'Be all you can be.' "

She smiled mischievously. "Did the Army say that to you?"

"Guess I wasn't listening. Maybe I'd have turned out better than I have."

"Oh? I think you're terrific just the way you are."

"And you're sensational, *mi amor.*"

Her cheeks colored at the word. Presently she said, "I have to keep reminding myself you're spoken for. Otherwise . . ."

We were nearing deep water so I lifted her hand to my lips. She smiled, murmured inaudibly and looked away. Then for a while we spoke of other things, without any reference to our passionate encounter the day before. After espresso Pilar looked at her watch and said she had an early lecture to give. "It's almost eleven, Jack, and I must get my sleep."

"See you home?"

"Not necessary, it's so near."

But I waited with her while the valets brought our cars, we kissed and said goodnight, and I watched her drive away.

I headed back toward the Lozano house, pausing at a bridged canal long enough to toss away slingshot and spare golf balls, and then I cruised along Bayshore Drive, noting that the house was dark again and the neighborhood tranquil.

The setting was right for my purposes, but I wanted to wait until reasonably sure the occupants were asleep. Manny, too, if he was there.

To kill time I drove across the causeway, admiring Miami's spectacular night skyline. Among tall buildings Villa Moravia was one of the tallest, and I thought of Jay Gerschwin feverishly packing to leave town. I couldn't judge how real his danger was, but in his mind it was authentic, and that was enough for him. His keen little ears had heard the starter's gun and he was off and running. The Bar wouldn't miss him, I reflected, Miami was bulging with lawyers eager to defend narcotics clients, the specialty being the most lucrative around, except for S&L bankruptcies. Still, it was hazardous to the rainmakers, lawyers who promised acquittal and couldn't deliver. In the drug trade a promise is a promise no matter how fanciful.

At a Bay Harbor movie house I caught the last part of a new Spielberg picture, and left with the crowd. Time: one forty-seven. I turned onto 86th street at two-fifteen and parked behind a stand of scrub palmettoes that concealed the car from Lozano's house. Maglite clamped between my teeth, I opened my trunk and checked contents, got ready to move. My principal risk, I thought, was a prowl car spotting me with burglar tools and a can of gas.

When clouds obscured the moon I followed the swale to Bayshore and scanned the outline of the house. No light leaking from inside. I listened for a few moments, and looked carefully around before crossing the street to Lozano's lawn.

Keeping to shadows, I fitted on the machinist's mask and reached the side of the house near the telephone lead. The bolt cutter's jaws severed the wire easily as a licorice stick, and I moved farther along, kneeling where the satellite dish cable led into the house. Even though the coax was as thick as my thumb the cutter parted it with a single snap. Without communication, the house was now isolated. I hadn't cut the electric cable because I needed interior light to search the house. Emptying it was my next project.

Ducking low, I skirted the swimming pool's glow and descended to the dock. Wind had risen and the *Sabre* bumped noisily against dock fenders. I didn't want to damage the racer, but that was up to the wind.

I uncapped the metal gas container and emptied it along the dock's wooden planking, recapped the can and laid it on the dock. Heated by dock flames its confined fumes ought to explode like a mortar round.

Breeze freshened; waves slapped the *Sabre* hull a few yards away. Moonlight glinted along the racer's brightwork, outlining it like a ghost vessel. I knelt on the wood planking and touched lighter flame to the near end of the gasoline stain. With a *whoosh,* blue flame flared down the dock, and I sprinted for shore.

From concealment beside the a/c unit I watched fire catch the sun-dried wood, offshore wind whipping flames away from the snubbed *Sabre*. Okay, their boat was usable—if they could reach it. Anyone leaving the house would have to pass me, or exit along the swimming pool. Either way I could see them.

By now the fire had a good foothold on the dock. Smoke and flames had nearly obscured the racing boat when the gas can exploded. From fifty feet the shock wave hit my eardrums like a bazooka blast and rattled window panes.

Inside lights went on. The rear door slammed open and two men raced out. One wore jockey shorts, the other sweatpants, yelling at each other as they ran to the dock. They hadn't tried telephoning for help, didn't know their line was cut. One jumped into shoulder-high water and disappeared around the prow while the other shielded his face from heat and loosed the bow snub line. Current began swinging the bow from the dock, and he jumped for it, catching a gleaming handrail to pull himself aboard. Catlike, he went aft and dropped into the cockpit just as his partner pulled himself over the stern. He threw off the stern line and the heavy roar of twin engines smothered the crackling of the flames. Freed, the *Sabre* turned from the burning dock and then swung around, heading for deeper water. When their backs were to me I left my hiding place and went through the open doorway, bolting it behind me.

I was in a lighted kitchen. Ankle .32 in hand, I moved into the dining room, whose table was littered with dirty dishes, wine and beer bottles. Next the living room. Liquor bottles and glasses on coffee tables. Nothing moved.

A corridor led off the living room; two open doors showed rumpled beds. *"Manny!"* I shouted, and checked the deep, walk-in closets. Clothing on hangers, dirty clothing on the floors. "Manny!" I kept yelling, and returned to the corridor.

The third door had a hasp and a Stanley lock. Cutters sliced through the lock and I kicked the door inward, found the wall switch and turned on ceiling lights.

On the mattress lay an assortment of automatic and semi-automatic weapons, full magazines and shells spilling from open boxes. M-16s, Uzis, MAC-10s, Ingrams, a Galil and a pair of Kalashnikovs. Enough firepower for an infantry platoon. Under the bed, more ammo boxes. The room was an armory.

"Manny!" I yelled again, and went into the closet.

No clothing, but shoe-shelving held bag after plastic bag of white powder.

Could be flour or sugar, but I didn't think so. Opening one, I tasted a sample: cocaine. Thirty bags, I estimated, thirty keys, sixty-six pounds of white shit. I left the closet stash and took a MAC-10 from the bed. Full magazine and silencer. I jacked a shell into the chamber, replaced my .32 in its ankle holster, and turned off every light in the house. Manny wasn't there, but the occupants, now busy with their boat, knew where he was.

Finally, I entered the garage through the living room door and turned on the overhead light. The BMW was there, fenders dented, right door badly scraped from hard or drunk driving.

Three sides of the garage were given over to a tool bench with a power saw and grindstone, a newly sharpened machete beside it. There were hedge-trimmers and lawn hoses, a gas mower and a red can of gasoline, sprinklers, and a dusty set of louvered doors. With the machete I slashed the car's front tires, then re-entered the house with machete and gasoline. Turned off the garage light and closed the access door.

In the dark kitchen I turned a chair to face the rear door, then unbolted it. By now, fire had consumed most of the dock. Wind-fanned embers resembled a long row of campfires. Farther off, the Bay was dark, no boat lights, no sign of the rescued *Sabre*. I settled into the chair and waited.

They came back sooner than expected.

THIRTEEN

M̲ungUÍA and Lozano came in wet, furious and cursing the son-of-a-whore who set their dock afire. Both were well-muscled and hairy, Lozano the taller by half a head. Munguía switched on the overhead light. Seeing me, they froze. Then Lozano lurched at me until he saw the weapon pointing at him. He froze again. In the suddenly silent room the off-click of the safety was loud as the crack of a .380. Lozano stepped back, looked at his partner, then at me. "Who . . . who are you? What do you want? Money?"

"How much?"

"You count it."

"Later. Hector, bolt the door. Both you *señoritos* lie down. Face down." Lozano got down first, then Munguía. Lozano muttered, "Son of a whore. Son-of-The-Great-Whore." I flat-bladed the machete against the back of his skull and he yelled in pain. "We'll have respect around here," I announced, "or you'll be missing fingers and hands." I stabbed the machete point into the floor, and they stared up at me, hatred in their eyes. "Where's the boat?"

"You want the boat? It's yours."

"*Bueno*. Where is it?"

"Tied to a channel buoy off Eightieth Street."

"Keys?"

"In it—fuckin' engine stopped, won't start."

"Well, you made a smooth getaway. Each of you did the right thing, great cooperation."

Lozano started to rise, but I fired a shot over his head, slug burying in the wall. The sound was a mere *phhhht*, like air escaping from a punctured tire. I aimed the muzzle at his forehead. "Who knifed Marlena Gomez? You, Colonel? Captain? I won't kill you for that, I just want to know." When neither spoke I said, "Talk, dammit," and fired between them. The bullet furrowed the linoleum and glanced into the dishwasher. When they came in their faces had been flushed from exertion and rage. Now their cheeks and foreheads were fish-belly white. Munguía moaned, "A biker did it."

"Blue Panther? Which one?"

"Rusty."

"Why?"

Munguía looked at Lozano before saying, "Talked too much."

"Who said? Donny?"

"Yeah. But he didn't want to do her."

"So Rusty did it for drugs."

"*Sí.*"

"All right, now we talk about why I'm here. Any ideas?"

Neither spoke, so I said, "Anyone ever suggest General Padilla is crazy?"

Colonel Lozano swallowed, stared down at the floor only inches from his eyes. He shivered. I said, "Only a super-*loco* would try to get free by snatching a Federal officer. It's never been done, never gonna happen. If Agent Montijo lives or dies, Padilla stays where he is. If he dies, you two will be burned for felony murder. If you don't know what that is, it's when someone dies in the commission of a crime." The mask muffled my voice, hid my face but for my eyes. My captives were probably trying to remember if they'd seen me before, heard my voice. I said, "Before I leave you're going to tell me where Montijo is being held. Both of you know considerable about torture, but I doubt that you've *been* tortured. Think about it." For a while I said nothing, then I broke the silence saying, "The Arauca *indios* favor having an anaconda bite off a captive's balls. Ever see that? The poor *pendejo* dies on the spot or goes crazy. Now, I haven't got a snake but I've got this machete you sharpened so nicely." I touched a finger to the shiny edge. "Fingers first, then hands, toes, and, finally, cock and balls. I'll practice on one while the other makes up his mind." I sat forward. "Who's been calling Señora Montijo?"

"Him," Lozano spat.

"Figures. Let the Captain do the dirty work. Stretch out your hand, Colonel, palm down." I jerked the machete free. "Show Hector how brave you are." I lifted the machete menacingly. Colonel Lozano hid both hands under his chest. His body began to shake. Munguía looked at his superior with contempt. I said, "I'm waiting. Who'll it be?" I wanted to kill them both, kill them both painfully for the agony they visited on the Montijos, but not until I learned what I'd come for. "You kidnapped Agent Montijo and took him where?"

Lozano elbowed his partner. "Don't talk," he snarled.

"No prompting." I flat-bladed his skull again. His face hit the floor and

Munguía winced. "While the Colonel's in dreamland, you can confide in me, Captain. Where's Montijo?"

When he said nothing, I drew the machete blade across his rump. The fabric parted like wet Kleenex and a line of blood appeared. I dipped the machete tip in it and held it before Munguía's eyes. "Want more?" Blood dripped to the floor. Munguía closed his eyes, gasped, "No more, no more, I'll tell you. The bikers have him." He opened his eyes. "They get *cocaina* for keeping him. He's—safe."

"Where?"

"Everglades—they have a camp there."

"And what's supposed to happen if there's a rescue attempt?"

He didn't reply until I prodded him with the machete. "Kill him."

"Maybe he's to be killed anyway, since he can identify you and Colonel *Cobarde*." The coward.

"I—don't know. The Colonel gives the orders."

"But it's a reasonable assumption, right?"

Munguía sighed. *"Sí, señor."*

So, a call from one of them wouldn't release Manny; the Blue Panthers would follow previous orders and kill him. *Shit!*

Lozano groaned and stirred. I cut long cords from the Venetian blinds and had Munguía tie Lozano's hands behind his back, hobble his ankles. Then, with Munguía lying face down on the floor, I tied his wrists behind his back, prodded him to his feet. "Help the Colonel up," I told him, "we're taking a walk."

Maglite between my teeth, a weapon in each hand, I lighted the way to the garage door, kicking Lozano when he staggered.

Inside the garage I turned on the light and opened the car trunk with keys from the ignition lock. Forced Lozano into the trunk and closed it. I considered letting the engine run in the closed garage, asphyxiating the trunked Colonel, but decided against outright murder. Besides, I had a now-cooperative Munguía, and the way to Manny was opening.

After a few more details.

I turned off the garage light, got Munguía into the living room, and bolted the access door. "Lozano offered money—where is it?"

When he hesitated I jammed the MAC-10 muzzle against his spine. "You'll never get to spend it. Show me."

To Lozano's bedroom. I slit open the mattress and pulled out decks of hundred-dollar bills. Five thousand per deck, thirty-five decks, totaling a hundred and seventy-five thousand dollars. Walking-around money for drug dealers. "That it?"

"All the cash."

I stripped off a soiled pillowcase and put the money in it, knotted the top and put it aside to work on the closet stash.

With Munguía watching I shoved all the plastic keys onto the floor and slashed them open. Drenched the cocaine with lawn-mower gas, and picked up a spare MAC-10 magazine from the bed along with my cash-filled pillowcase. On the way to the back door I checked kitchen drawers and found a box of green plastic trash bags. I fitted one around the pillowcase and knotted the drawstrings, making the container more or less waterproof. Then we went out into air that was fresh and free of cocaine-gasoline stench, and walked down to the narrow beach.

Breeze wafted dock smoke into my nostrils, but there were no flames, just smoldering embers. As we stood there I said, "You use the *Sabre* to reach the biker camp?"

"*Sí, señor.*" He shivered in the sea breeze. Rump bleeding had stopped, the underwear hung loosely from his hips. Hands bound behind him, he looked ridiculous in his near nudity. I said, "We're going there, Hector. Keys in the boat?"

"*Sí*—but the engines don't run."

"They will. Move." I prodded him ahead of me, coral chunks cutting his bare feet as we followed the shoreline south. Along the way I noticed a thick clump of palmetto, and cached the money bag under its low-lying branches and fronds. Five minutes later I could see the *Sabre*'s dark bulk at a channel buoy. "We're going to swim to it," I told him.

"I'll drown," he whimpered.

"You didn't drown coming ashore. Get in the water. Now."

From where we were I could see an occasional car crossing the 79th Street Causeway. Bridge pylons were dimly lighted. On his back, Munguía kicked toward the tethered boat. I stuck the machete in my belt and used the MAC-10 as a paddleboard as I moved toward the boat. The stern dive platform was down, and I climbed onto it. Nearing it, Munguía was coughing and swallowing water. I hoisted him onto the platform and told him to stay there. Then I opened the engine hatch and recoupled the gas feed line to the twin carbs. The engine space was filled with gasoline fumes, so I left the hatch open while I brought Munguía into the cockpit and looped a waterski towline around his bound wrists. For warmth he huddled into a seat corner, and watched me with eyes like wet flint.

I turned on engine compartment blowers and let them run until the dash sensor light showed no combustible fumes remaining. Then I ran the bilge pumps to purge water, gas and oil, hoping no environmentalist was nearby to witness such overt lawbreaking. When the bilges were clear I started the engines, startled by their ear-shattering roar, and cast off from the channel buoy. Running lights on, I clutched forward, running slow past Belle Meade Island, gaining speed off Morningside, where Manny's dependents were sleeping unaware of the night's events.

The tachs showed well-tuned engines whose throttles responded to light touch, reminding me of a chopper's collective control. Beside me Munguía said, "You sabotaged the boat."

"Burned your dock, destroyed your coke and disabled your colonel." I glanced at the fuel gauges; the tanks showed about a hundred gallons each— plenty to get where we were going, but at the big engines' consumption rate probably not enough high-test to make it all the way back. I set course due south and locked in the auto before looking down at Munguía. "You've got no future here, Hector, you or the Colonel. If you survive the night you'd do well to head back to the Big V."

He thought it over. "And the Colonel?"

"His chances are less than yours—figure slim to zero. As for Padilla, I haven't decided: let him live in his cell until he's too old to care, or have him put out of his misery. Anyway, he's not rational, and irrational, once-powerful men are a menace to society."

Ahead, the light-chain marking Venetian Causeway. The *Sabre* rode low enough that raising the bridge wasn't necessary, and I didn't want bridge-tenders recalling our passage. I kicked the controls back to manual and swung around Watson Island, where the Goodyear blimp used to stay in years when Miami had a competitive NFL team.

Government Cut now, turning east-southeast past the long cruise-ship docks and the port of Miami. I slowed to avoid tarpon fishermen, steering well clear to avoid swamping their much smaller boats with my heavy wake. Finally ocean chop, spray breaking over bow and coaming.

Gradually I eased the throttles forward, feeling the stern dig in as the bow lifted and began to plane. Except for Yard craft at the Naval Academy I had never handled as big and powerful a boat, and I respected its potential. There were stern vanes that acted like a plane's trim tabs, but I didn't know the angle/speed equation and so I ignored them.

Clouds obscured the moon again; my running lights gave off a ghostly glow that made Munguía's face resemble a corpse. Ahead in the ocean blackness pinpoint lights located distant buoys, Intracoastal channel markers and fishermen. By now I was accustomed to the throb of the engines and the monotonous burbling of the exhausts, and my mind began to wander.

How would it be, I wondered, to steer this baby into Havana harbor, and go ashore for a cold Hatuey at Sloppy Joe's?

Well, it would be great, the apogee of a long career in risk-taking, but I'd need a pair of deck-mounted Bofors, a rocket launcher and a recoilless 75, none of which I had any prospect of acquiring. Yeah, I could get to Havana, but getting out alive was not a bankable risk.

The cockpit clock showed a few minutes after four, giving me maybe three hours before daylight. We were off a lightless coastline that I knew to be heavy mangrove swamp, and a few minutes later I spotted humpbacked Card Sound Bridge. I slowed to pass under it, noting hurricane damage to the planking, then accelerated through Barnes Sound, Key Largo off to the left. I toed Munguía awake and asked, "How much farther?"

"Blackwater Sound." He licked his lips. "What are you going to do with me?"

"Cooperate and I won't kill you. Where do I put in?"

"There's a hook of land with a small wood pier. A dirt road leads to the camp."

"How far?"

"Not half a mile."

I could see Jewfish Creek Bridge ahead, another wind-damaged humpback I was glad I didn't have to drive over. I guided the *Sabre* under it and followed Intracoastal markers west toward the mainland. "What's the camp layout?" I asked.

"There's a clearing with an old log cabin, a cookshed, some lean-tos for hammocks."

"How many bikers guarding Montijo?"

"Sometimes four, sometimes two."

"Perimeter guards? Fencing? Dogs?"

He shook his head. "They don't expect visitors."

"Women?"

"Not supposed to be any."

"But there could be."

He shrugged. "Those scum have no discipline."

"But if there's a rescue attempt they're to kill Montijo."

"*Sí.*"

"And may already have killed him?"

He shook his head. "That would have to be ordered by General Padilla."

"How?"

"Through Colonel Lozano."

"Or you."

He nodded reluctantly.

"Then you can order Montijo's release."

"Only Lozano." And Lozano was in a car trunk, maybe alive, maybe dead.

I didn't want to risk Munguía trying, so I was going to have to get Manny the hard way. *"Bueno,"* I said, "we're in Blackwater Sound. Stand up and look around, show me where to go."

He got up and peered at the dark shoreline. After maybe a minute he pointed off the port bow. "There."

"Where?"

"Tall palm—no top. Bear left and you'll see the pier."

To reduce noise level I killed one engine and throttled back the other to 400 rpms. The boat was moving slowly enough so that I wasn't worried about damage from a sunken log; besides, the *Sabre* had come this way before.

Aside from the palm landmark I could see nothing ahead. Then clouds cleared the moon and within moments I was able to make out a rustic pier jutting into the water. It was extended forty-odd feet from shore, supported by palm trunk pilings set at intervals, and looked far from sturdy. I cut off running lights and we moved darkly toward the pier. Hoarsely, Munguía said, "What are you going to do?"

"Check out the camp."

"There could be four bikers there," he warned.

"I like the odds."

He looked away. "What if you don't come back?"

"Your biker friends will take care of you." I cut the other engine and we glided silently toward the pier. Presently the port side of the bow angled against the pier, scraped along and came to rest against a piling. The boat shuddered and lay dead in the water.

I looped a snub line around the piling and came back to the cockpit. From the transom toolbox I got out rolls of electrical and duct tape, told Munguía to sit while I taped his ankles together. That done, I taped his mouth for silence while serious work went on. Then I pocketed the ignition keys, and picked up the MAC-10 and its extra magazine, heart pounding from awareness of imminent danger and the prospect of freeing Manny. Before stepping onto the pier I looked down at my prisoner. "If I find you've tried to get away I'll drag you back to Miami at the end of the ski line, so if you value your life you'll stay where you are. Understand?"

He nodded docilely, and I stuck the machete in my belt, wondering about this tough army officer who kidnapped a DEA agent and taunted the agent's agonized wife—he had *cojones* for that. But when it came to standing up to a determined male—myself—what happened to his *machismo?* Apparently it dissolved like coke in a toilet bowl. But if he got free he could be dangerous, I reminded myself. Desperate men are.

The trail led into tall grass and stands of scrub pine; it was just wide enough for a narrow car or boat trailer, and rutted with tire tracks. I figured there ought to be another way out of the old fishing camp, a trail that led eventually to a 'Glades road usable by bikes, but if all went well I wouldn't need it.

At that point my main worry was stepping on an unseen rattler or cottonmouth waiting for a swamp rabbit to hop along. So every now and then I'd shine the Maglite ahead for a couple of seconds to make sure the path was clear of reptiles. If any campers saw it they'd figure a giant firefly was flashing for a mate.

When I'd covered a hundred yards I stopped to slow my breathing and think things through. It seemed unlikely that any of the biker-guards were sleeping in lean-to hammocks, exposed to spiders and mosquitos: more likely they were in the cabin where Manny was supposedly kept. That put a maximum of five people in the cabin, only one of whom I didn't want to kill. I sucked in another deep breath and plodded on, thinking that most fishing camps were built much closer to the water, and wondering why this one was so far away. Presently I discovered why.

The trail ended at a clearing fifty yards in diameter. In the center was a small log cabin with a closed door and two windows. Extending from it was the open cookshed, and nearby, a pair of palm-thatched lean-tos with hammocks but no occupants. On the cabin's side were nailed half a dozen alligator hides, telling me the camp was set inland by 'gator poachers to conceal their activity from Rangers and passing fishermen. For jungle bums the hides were a ready cash crop, even the meat could be sold. But these hides were hung and dried so long ago their edges curled inward. Either the poachers had died or been evicted by the bikers—and probably killed. My problem was to neutralize the guards without harm to Manny, but without stun grenades or gas bombs how could it be done?

The answer came from a yard away. I heard brittle rattling and shined my light in that direction. What I saw was a big diamondback reared up from its coils, swaying back and forth to get a distance fix on me. The tip of its tail vibrated furiously as I pulled off my jacket. This was one pissed-off rattler. I hung my jacket from the end of the machete and trailed it back and forth in front of the rattler's eyes. He reared higher, getting ready to strike, and when he struck he came full-length at the jacket, burying his fangs in the fabric. I dropped the jacket over him and watched the jacket twist and turn and revolve as the snake flailed around. I shined the light to locate his head under the jacket, got behind it and grabbed the snake just behind its head. I lifted it from the ground and held on while the body thrashed and coiled like a powerful cable. The rattler was as determined to get free as I was to immobilize his head, and my arm was tiring from the struggle. So I jogged across the clearing to the cabin door, listened for inside sounds and flashed the Maglite across the interior.

Three leather-jacketed bikers were sleeping on army cots, weapons on the floor. At the far end stood a bunk bed and mattress. On it lay Manuel Montijo, wrists and ankles bound. Absorbing this took only a second, so I pushed the door slowly inward and tossed snake and jacket at the farthest cot. As it flew through the air the rattler shook off the jacket and landed across the biker's thighs. The biker woke and yelled just as the snake sank its fangs in his bicep. I backed away, stood outside the cabin wall and cocked the MAC-10.

FOURTEEN

TWO BIKERS burst out of the cabin, followed by the third fighting to tear away the snake. I shot the first two from ten feet, and drilled the snake-fighter through both thighs. He went down screaming, but alive. On the ground, the snake opened its jaws and crawled away from its victim. I gave its body a three-shot burst before the receiver caught on the empty magazine. I extracted it and slammed home the spare, chambered a slug and looked down at the poisoned man. He wasn't Donny—none of them were—but his red beard suggested he was Rusty who'd knifed Marlena to death. He was screeching and yelling, clutching blood-drenched thighs. Snake venom was racing through his veins and he was beyond any help I could give him—if I'd wanted to. My light showed a knife at his belt, no pistol. As I'd hoped, fear of the snake drove all three outside without their sidearms.

Time to tend to Manny.

I went inside, pulled off my mask, shined the light on my face, and said, "It's okay, pal. Everything's okay. Those creeps are dead and we're going home."

"Oh, Jack," he said hoarsely, "oh, Jack. Jesus. Oh, Jesus, I'm so glad you came!" Tears trickled down his dirty, unshaven face swollen from insect bites. I hugged him and felt tears spilling from my eyes. Then I wiped them away and cut his bonds with my machete. Shakily, he stretched his arms and I saw ugly wrist burns where the ropes had been. From outside came a series of yells and shrieks. Snake poison makes a painful death.

I helped Manny get his legs over the edge of the bunk. "Not sure I can walk," he whispered. "Help me."

"That's what I'm here for." I went over to my fallen jacket and held it up. Under the light I could see yellow venom stains on the fabric. The rest had gone into Red Beard, now thrashing around in agony. "Any liquor here?"

"On the sink." Manny sat staring down at his feet as I went to the filthy sink and brought back a bottle of cheap bourbon that had been worked on. While Manny drank I poured bottle water on the rattler venom, then looked around the cabin. Lewd posters were tacked to the walls, a litter of beer cans and bottles filled one corner. Canned food, paper plates and plastic utensils. "Been eating well?"

"Not exactly." He managed a weak grin, then his face contorted and he began to weep.

"Let it out," I counseled, "and help me figure out how to explain all this."

He swallowed with an effort. "Explain? You shot these bastards and freed me. What's to explain?"

"Too much." I took the bottle from him and swigged until the raw liquor flashed fire through my veins. "Needed that," I coughed, and handed it back. "Any drugs here?"

"Some pot—bag under Rusty's cot."

"White shit?"

"Snorted. Eddie left yesterday to get more."

"Left on what?"

"Bike."

"Feel like a bike ride?"

"To get out I'd ride the Devil's chariot."

"Won't have to—we're going back in style. Stand up, compadre, let's see how steady you are."

Slowly he pushed himself upright, wavered and sat down suddenly. "No strength, Jack. Weaker than a kitten."

"It's natural. You'll get it all back." From outside came hoarse rasping rales. I looked out and saw Rusty's body arched like a bow. His convulsions reminded me that venom-induced contractions could snap a man's spine. As I watched, the body collapsed. Adiós, Rusty, have a long slide to Hell.

I borrowed the bourbon from Manny, drank again and told him to down the rest. Then I sat beside him. "The tale to be told goes like this: I wasn't here—ever. Gunshots woke you. You think only one man did the shooting—outside. You didn't see him so you can't identify him, and you didn't see the killing. You speculate it had to do with a soured drug deal, but have no way of knowing. After the shooting, after everything was quiet, you crawled over to the doorway and saw the bodies. You managed to get the knife from Rusty's belt and cut your ropes. Be vague, okay? That's basically the story. Later, if you feel expansive, you might suggest the camp's original owners—

'gator poachers—came back for revenge. But don't vary from this scenario: some unknown savior killed your captors, and you cut yourself free.''

He shook his head. "Hell, Jack, you did it all, why not take credit?"

"Long story. I need to get back to Melody and get married. If I'm a material witness they'll never let me leave Miami. Besides, a couple of FBI mooks and Van Shugrue have a hard-on for me. If it's within their power to make my life miserable, they'll do it. Not to mention the Sheriff's office." I gazed around. "I guess we're in Monroe County, and those deputies have hard memories of me from when Anita Tessier was killed—remember? I don't want to tangle with those pricks again."

"Ummm. I hate lying, but I owe you that much—and a great deal more."

"Hell, a man who's gone through what you have wouldn't have total recall, so don't sweat details. Now, Lucy's okay, and so are Rosario and Carmen—you'll see them today." I helped him upright, then gathered his severed bonds and carried them outside, dropping them beside Rusty's body. Under the red beard smiled the rictus of death. I pulled his knife from its sheath and told Manny to grasp the handle. "For fingerprints," I explained, "in case they test your story."

"Test—? Why would they?"

I ignored the question, not wanting to tell him he'd been suspected of corruption, and toed Rusty's swollen arm. "Recognize the tattoo?"

"Blue Panther. Small-time."

"But big enough to keep you prisoner, *amigo.* Padilla's people pay them with drugs."

"Padilla," he muttered. "Was the AG going to let him go?"

"You know better than that, *compadre.* Unfortunately, Padilla didn't." I dropped Rusty's knife near the cut ropes. Manny looked at them before gazing steadily at me. "Then who brought you in? I figured it had to be—"

"That's for later, there'll be a lot to talk about, clarify. Put names under faces. Trust me."

Manny's arm across my shoulders, we moved slowly through the clearing. Let absent Eddie explain the killings, I thought, and bent over the snake's body to cut off the rattles. Later I'd give them to Manny as a souvenir of the critical motivating force.

I recognized one of the dead bikers as a Rancherito beer-belly, the other I'd never seen before; he was probably stuck at camp. The trail was hard going for Manny; he'd slip on ruts, stumble and begin to cry. Finally he said, "I'm so ashamed, *amigo,* you've never seen me like this before."

"No one ever will—and what the hell have you got to be ashamed of? You were captured and held hostage, lucky to be alive. And I will shortly show you a major surprise.''

"I'm too confused to guess.''

"Don't try. Meanwhile, your cousin Pilar is in Miami, and did a lot to shore up your family. Beyond that she offered two million dollars ransom to get you free.''

"Jesus! Little Cousin Pilar,'' he said in tones of wonderment.

"Not so little any more, Cousin Manuel. An incredible woman in every way. And—well, you'll see for yourself.''

He eyed me suspiciously but said nothing. We paused for him to rest and gather strength for the final distance. Then we moved on, and finally beyond where the trail met the beach, I could see light gray rimming the horizon. "Almost there,'' I told him, and helped him along until sounds from the boat halted me. I moved Manny to trailside and told him to stay while I investigated. Was Munguía free and trying to get away? I cocked the MAC-10, slipped off the safety, and scanned the pier from behind a tree.

A second boat was tied there, a twenty-foot sport fisher with Bimini top. No one in it. Voices came from the *Sabre,* two men speaking terse Spanish. I heard metallic banging. Hector being helped by a stranger? Didn't seem right. Something wrong. More banging.

Invisible from the pier, I called, "Boat ahoy.''

A head popped up above the *Sabre* coaming, then another, and the banging stopped. Dark as it was I could see neither was Hector Munguía. I hailed again. This time I saw the barrel of an automatic rifle thrust skyward, then lower in my direction. A long burst slapped leaves from shrubbery to my right. Dropping prone, I sighted at the shooter. In Spanish I called, "Lay down your piece, hands up, both of you.''

But these were hardass muthas, resolved to finish whatever they came for, and it wasn't honest toil. The shooter fired again, bullets whining above me, and I let out a loud scream. The shooter stood up, and I had a clear view of his silhouette. Two bullets hit his chest and dropped him out of sight. *"Carajo!''* his partner shouted, and snatched up the weapon to fire at me. The idiot emptied his magazine, and when he slid over the *Sabre* coaming for a spare in his boat I shot him on the pier. He screamed and yelled but didn't rise. I waited until he lay silent, then edged closer. As in 'Nam, I kept the muzzle trained on his body, so when the *pendejo* sat up, pistol in hand, I shot first. The impact slammed him a foot backward and he died against the *Sabre* hull. His pistol hit the pier with a dull sound.

Was there a third robber? I took cover again and waited, heard Manny moving toward me and hissed, "Stay down, don't leave me now.''

"*Cabron,* you have all the fun," he grunted in his first attempt at humor. I fished out my ankle .32 and passed it to him. "Cover me."

"Like old times," he muttered, as I went slowly toward the pier.

"You'd have loved 'Nam," I told him, and kept going.

Cautiously, I stepped onto the pier, rounded the slumped corpse, and peered over the gunwale into the cockpit.

The first shooter's body lay half-off the transom. His guayabera's chest was stained with blood. The M-16 they'd both used lay at his feet. I looked around for Hector Munguía; in the cockpit area he wasn't hard to find. Still bound and taped, as I'd left him, but the robbers had sliced his throat wide open.

I cupped my hands, and called Manny to come aboard. Expecting him to emerge slowly from the foliage, I waited a few moments before yelling, "C'mon, Manny, let's move!"

His response was a strangled, "Need you here, Johnny."

I froze. No one ever called me Johnny, so it had become our code word for trouble. But what kind of trouble? "Okay," I called back, "take it easy, I'm coming."

MAC-10 beside my thigh, I walked down the pier, stepped on land, and called, "Where are you?"

"On the trail, not far." Hoarse voice, harmonics of danger.

"Okay, on my way." I entered the trail, keeping to the side for cover, walking naturally until I saw him.

He was standing, but bent backward, because an arm was around his throat. The man's other arm held a pistol to the side of Manny's head. I couldn't see him clearly, nowhere clearly enough to risk a shot, so I said, "Hey, what's happenin'?"

"Put down your piece, man, hands on head an' no one gets hurt."

I kept walking, stopped ten feet away, "What's this all about? You want the 'gator hides? They're yours. Let him go."

"You listenin'? I said drop the piece or I blow off his fuckin' head."

"Why? Where's the profit?" I shrugged and thumbed off the safety. "Manny, this guy reminds me of Valdez, remember?"

"Valdez—yeah. Okay, I remember. So do what the guy says, Johnny."

I bent over as though to lower my MAC-10, snapped, *"Now!"* and watched Manny go limp. The gunman's arm couldn't support his weight and Manny slipped down and free. Startled, the gunman hesitated, pistol wavering between Manny and me. By the time he decided who to shoot I was belly-down on the ground and squeezing the trigger.

A three-shot burst tore through his upper chest and toppled him backward.

Manny flung himself across the body and scooped up the fallen pistol. He jammed it against the man's head as I got to my feet. I slipped on the safety and went to Manny, helped him off the still body. "Good reaction," I said, and took the pistol from him, replaced it in the gunman's hand. "Would this be the missing Eddie?"

"Yeah—and coked to the ears. Came up behind me while I was watching you—never heard a sound. Sorry, Jack."

"Well, that accounts for all four." Eddie's arm had the Blue Panther tattoo plus a pair of SS blazes that marked him as a White Supremacist nut as well as an outlaw. Staring down at him, Manny said, "Lucky I remembered Valdez."

"Figured you would." We'd been looking for Julio Valdez in a Baltimore alley when he grabbed me from behind. I'd dropped and Manny drilled him through the throat. Yeah, we remembered Valdez. "So," I said, "that sort of evens the score, *compadre*."

"Whatever—I don't want any more of this shit." He walked back and picked up my ankle .32 from where he'd dropped it, brushed off dirt and gave it to me. I put an arm around him and we walked to the pier. Manny shuffled unsteadily to the *Sabre* and clutched the gunwale. He peered at the carnage and shook his head. "Jesus, who were they?"

"Thieves, robbers, pirates, hijackers . . . who knows?" I shined my light on Munguía's face and Manny sucked in his breath.

"Meet Captain Hector Munguía, late of the Venezuelan Army."

"Why—he—he's one who kidnapped me."

"Right. He and Colonel Antonio Lozano did the dirty work— on Padilla's orders."

"Damn! Where's Lozano?"

"Not sure," I replied, "but time will tell. Anyway, Munguía was my big surprise for you—alive."

"You mean—these bandits killed him."

"Carved him a second grin."

He looked around the cockpit. The thieves had been working on the boat's electronics, cutting Loran, radar and radio from their mounts with mallet and chisel. The radio was almost out, its wires dangling near Munguía's dead face.

"Show time," I said, and got out ignition keys. One engine caught, and when it was throbbing rhythmically, I fired the other. Over the combined roar Manny asked, "Whose boat?"

"Lozano's."

"It brought me here," he said, taking a seat across from the dead robber. He covered his face and shivered at the memory.

I killed the engines and touched his shoulder. "We've got a disposal problem, so while I deal with it, you take it easy, okay?"

He looked up at me. "When can I call Lucy?"

"Soon. Now keep clear." I hoisted the robber's body over the coaming and slid it down onto the pier, repeated with Munguía. Then I dragged each body to the robbers' sport fisher and levered them into it. Finally, I got into the boat and arranged the bodies for visual effect, then pulled the tape from Munguía's mouth and cut his bonds, discarding them in the water.

By killing Hector the thieves had resolved my dilemma: alive, Munguía could talk and implicate me, but I hadn't wanted to execute a cowed and defenseless man. So I'd decided Manny should judge him. Now, neither of us had to make a hard decision. I checked the bait well for narcotics, found two yard-long snook they'd caught out of season, but no coke keys or pot. Then I transferred the M-16 and handgun to the robbers' boat, polished off my prints and dropped the weapons on the duckboard. Their outboard engine was a big Evinrude 250. I started it and switched on the boat's running lights to suggest the killings had happened at night.

While the outboard burbled noisily I set the rudder seaward and untied the bowline. Then I clutched forward and climbed onto the pier as the boat moved away. I watched it fade into darkness.

When I got into the *Sabre,* Manny was pulling off his shoes and socks. He looked at his urine-stained trousers with loathing. "I need a bath."

He entered the water from the beach, ducked and scrubbed his face, combed wet hair through his fingers. "God, this feels good," he called, then wrung out his wet clothing, and after a while got back in the *Sabre* cockpit. Naked, he arranged his shirt and trousers to air dry, then lay down on the transom. I gave him my dirty jacket for warmth and said, "We'll make a short run, *'mano,* then I put you ashore. Phone home and they'll come for you."

He pulled the jacket around his neck.

"Your phone's been tapped ever since you vanished, so your office and the Bureau will hear you call Lucy. She doesn't know about the tap and I'm not supposed to, so I mention it to remind you about saying nothing. Give only your location. Your family will be so euphoric they'll ignore details, okay?"

"Whatever you say. You've managed everything so far."

"One other thing: there's been no publicity about your disappearance. What Van and the Bureau know has been kept quiet."

"Good. I don't want a lot of press and TV cameras around the house."

I looked at the gas levels, quarter-full, and figured I could get back to Lozano's place running slow, or on one engine. The sky was lightening and I didn't want to be out in broad daylight. So I slipped the bowline and let current push the *Sabre* around until it was heading toward the sea. "Meanwhile," I advised Manny, "grab some Zs," and punched the starter buttons.

I made the run to Jewfish Creek in under an hour, nosed up to the nearest empty pier, and gave Manny pocket change for the phone. "Now, tell me how you got here."

Like a schoolboy reciting he said, "After shooting stopped at the camp I took the trail to the beach, waited there until a fisherman in a small boat drifted by. He gave me water and brought me here. Gave me coins for the phone."

"What's his name?"

"Wouldn't say—because he was fishing snook for market."

"Describe him."

"About seventy, gray whiskers, leathery face, straw hat. Old scars on his hands. Worn jeans and a torn denim shirt."

"Good, say no more." The description would fit a hundred fishermen on the water, any morning. I gave him an *abrazo,* his eyes grew moist, and he turned away, got onto the pier and walked toward shore. Before he got there I backed off the *Sabre* and headed up the Intracoastal.

I would have liked to deliver him to his loved ones, but that would further complicate my life. A truthful recounting would have hurt Jamey and done no one any good, least of all me. Silence was golden.

As I hauled north into Biscayne Bay, big Bertram charter boats raced past me heading for Government Cut, rods and outriggers ready for sail and marlin when they reached the offshore fishing grounds.

A little before seven I eased under the 79th Street Bridge and began looking for a place to leave the *Sabre.* I chose a narrow strand of sand and coral to ground the bow. Even before abandoning Manny I'd deep-sixed the MAC-10, machete, mask and bolt cutter, so I had only to scan the cockpit and clean off fingerprints before jumping onto dry land.

Sunrise was beginning to cut through morning haze as I retraced last night's footsteps, searching for the palmetto clump where I'd stashed the green trash bag. Found it in under five minutes and slung it over my shoulder like a beach-bum's bindle.

By then, outgoing tide had freed the *Sabre* and was drifting it down the Bay. I paused long enough to scan in the direction of Lozano's pier. A Marine Patrol craft was tied up at one of the pilings, but there wasn't much to see.

Some of the supports had burned to the waterline, and the cross-planking was entirely gone.

I made my way between houses to 10th Avenue and walked unhurriedly to 86th Street. My Miata was there, dew-wet but untouched by human hands. Just a parking ticket under the windshield wiper. Fifteen bucks. With a hundred and seventy-five thousand in my bag I could handle the fine.

I locked the bag in my trunk and drove off, turning past Lozano's house. The front window was still smashed from my golf ball but I was pleased to see no police cars or yellow Crime Scene tapes. Lozano? I'd finished with him. The coke and guns in his house would put him behind bars for the rest of his life—if he was still alive.

Morning traffic was heavy as I drove south to the Gables. By the time I reached my house, early haze had burned off and the sun came down through nearly cloudless sky. I garaged the car and carried the trash bag into the house, picking up the morning paper from the lawn. Before anything else I drank a lot of orange juice but no coffee. More than anything I needed sleep.

My message machine was blinking but I ignored it; later would do as well. I stripped off my filthy clothing and got under a hot shower, brushed my fingernails clean of engine grease and gunpowder specks, and shampooed my hair. Drying myself, I felt human again, and wondered if by now Manny was in the bosom of his family. When she thought of it, Lucy would phone me; Pilar later on, after classes. My job was done, and it was time to leave Miami and return to Europe and Melody.

I silenced the phone ringer, got into bed and stared up at the dark ceiling mirror. In it I thought I could see Melody's moving figure, and turned on my side. Unbidden, visions of Pilar merged with those of my fiancée until they became a single beautiful woman, who seduced me into sleep.

FIFTEEN

$\textbf{W}$AKING WAS as torturous as clawing my way out of a deep well and I kept slipping back despite insistent ringing of door chimes. Finally I managed to sit upright and focus on my surroundings. Back, arms and legs ached. I eased off the bed, wrapped a towel around my hips and plodded to the door. The spy-hole showed the face of Thomas Jameson so I unlocked and opened the door.

Pushing in, he said, "Manny's back! Did you know?"

"Great," I said. "How is he?"

"C'mon, Jack, don't con me. You got him, didn't you?"

"Who says?"

"Me."

I shrugged. "Let's have coffee. How's Manny?"

"Alive, scratched up and worn out but very damn alive."

"Wonderful news." I made my way to the kitchen, Jamey following.

He watched as I measured coffee into the filter and turned on the percolator. Then I sat at the dinette table and looked up at him. "What time is it?"

"About three." He drew back a chair and sat across from me. "Everyone's been trying to call you, Jack. Where were you last night?"

"Drinking."

"Yeah?"

"Yeah. So—Manny's free. Bureau retrieved him?"

"Shit, no."

"So—?"

"He tells an involved tale that—"

"Tell me." I got out the Añejo and poured myself a therapeutic portion, sipped while he repeated the cover story I'd confected for Manny, and felt life beginning to infuse my veins. Jamey repeated it all, down to the fortuitous fisherman, then watched my reaction. I got out two mugs and filled them with steaming coffee. Jamey sipped and said, "Well?"

"Terrific," I resumed my seat. "Lotta dead perps, and Manny in the bosom of his family. What could be better?"

He blinked uncertainly. "You weren't involved?"

"Listen, kid, I had a hard night and I'm in no mood for questions. Bottom line: Manny's home. Right?"

"Right. But I'll always believe you were responsible."

"Think what you want." I added Añejo to my mug and stirred with one finger. "Family happy?"

"Euphoric. They asked me to come and bring you."

"And the office?"

"Well, if Shugrue isn't rapturous the rest of the office is. Naturally, the Bureau wants to talk with Manny, but Dr. Ing says Manny's too exhausted to be coherent."

"Good man, Ing."

He eyed scratches on my arms and face. "You didn't get marked up fighting a bottle, Jack. Maybe Ing should see you."

"I'll think about it."

He smiled. "Couple other things. Lozano's *Sabre* was found off the Beach, vandalized. That took the cops to Lozano's house, and they found him in his car trunk."

"No kidding. Alive?"

"Barely. He expired on the way to Jackson Hospital. No loss, eh?"

"Drug war casualty. Munguía?"

His hands spread. "Hasn't been found." When I failed to react he asked, "Think he will be?"

"No opinion." I sipped again. The warm rum was dissolving muscle pain—a sovereign remedy for physical ills. Jamey said, "The family, especially Manny, is really eager to see you. How about getting on some clothes and coming with me?"

"I'll go later," I countered. "I'm going to get a flight reservation and close up the house. Manny's safe, and I can return to my fiancée and get married."

"Yeah." He paused. "Cousin Pilar wants to see you—can't imagine why—and said she'd come here after classes. Around five."

"Great, I'll be waiting."

He stared at his coffee mug. "Jack, I'm gonna miss the hell out of you. You've become sort of a big brother to me, given me a role model I badly needed."

"Thanks, Jamey. I'll miss you, too, but, hell, I'll be back with my bride, and we'll pick up where we left off. Okay?"

"Sure. Oh, I ought to mention the Bureau is having Padilla transferred to Terminal Island, where the sun don't hardly shine."

I nodded approval. "Tito Gallardo?"

"Lewisburg for the rest of his time."

"Yeah, good idea to separate them out of Miami."

His pager sounded. He checked the calling number and used the kitchen phone, grunted some and hung up. Turning to me, he said, "They found that camp where Manny was held, bodies all over the place like Manny said."

"Solid corroboration," I remarked, stretched and yawned. "Munguía among them?"

"Maybe." He stood up, extended his hand and I shook it. "You're some guy, Jack. Have a happy wedding and honeymoon."

"That's the plan." I showed him out and locked the door. After a long hot shower I got dressed and turned on the bedroom TV. Channel 7 was into early news and I watched until satisfied there was nothing about Manny or the dead scumbags, so I was reaching for the remote when a photo of Jay Gerschwin filled the screen. The voice-over said, "Sources close to the office of noted narcotics defense attorney Jay Gerschwin say that he has suspended practice indefinitely while recuperating from what an associate described as overwork. 'Jay is traveling abroad, taking it easy and considering future options,' the associate said, asking not to be named.

"Gerschwin's longtime companion, Cheryl Ribotsky, admitted his sudden departure surprised her. 'We had some definite plans—social things, y'know—charity balls, like that, so I guess I'll be going alone.' " The screen showed a hard-faced young bimbo with metallic blonde hair and thin lips. She was going to miss Jay, but would he miss her?

"Asked if she anticipated joining Mr. Gerschwin on his foreign travels, Cheryl said, 'Anything is possible, and you can quote me.'

"Meanwhile, the Gerschwin office announced that pending cases will be transferred to Quim, Mentule, Tush and Merkin, a firm that specializes in criminal defense and sexual assault litigation.

"One former Gerschwin employee theorized that the lawyer would be meeting abroad with Villa Moravia developer Jiri Vlasic to sort out the fugitive financier's many legal problems. However, the scenario lacked corroboration, and the office of the United States Attorney for the Southern District declined comment."

One less Miami mouthpiece, I mused, and flicked off the set. With Gerschwin gone, and possibly conspiring with Vlasic in less threatening crimes, I didn't have to worry about Jay spotting and identifying me. So putting the arm on him was having an unexpected benefit.

I gassed the Miata and drove up to Morningside, where the Montijos—and Jamey—were celebrating uninhibitedly with champagne. Manny and I greeted each other as though we hadn't been together for months, and his womenfolk covered my face with teary kisses, including Carmen who appeared uncharacteristically happy. Manny wore bandages on face and wrists but his eyes sparkled, and when no one was looking he gave me a broad wink. "Everything's okay now, Jack, and will be. Can't thank you enough for all you did." His face sobered. "When are you going back to Melody?"

"Probably tomorrow."

"We'll all miss you, believe me."

"Well, I'll miss all of you, and I'm glad Lucy thought to call me."

"How did Melody react?"

"Urged me to come. She and the Dragon Lady are cruising the Aegean with a Turkish billionaire, and I'm to join them."

"Well, you deserve the best, Jack." He paused. "Any time I can do anything for you—"

"Sure, Manny. Now enjoy life again."

"Ah—you'll see my cousin before you leave?"

I nodded.

"You made a big impression on her."

"Mutual." I looked at my watch. "Maybe our paths will cross again."

"She'd like that." Jamey came over and said, "Manny, office call—want to take it?"

"Might as well," he sighed. "They'll probably mark my absence against annual leave."

"The office can wait," I suggested. "You need sleep. Jamey, tell them that."

He smiled. "Yes, sir," and returned to the phone.

"So," I said to Manny, "this is so long for a while."

We shared an *abrazo*. I blew kisses to the ladies and left the house, eyes moist.

As I drove back to the Gables I reflected that the Bureau would take credit for Manny's return, and that was fine with me. I didn't want Doak and Rennie interrogating me, and my strong preference was never to see them again. Kidnap experts? Yeah.

At home I put fresh sheets on the bed, revived the percolator and poured

Añejo over ice. I uncorked the *manzanilla* and found a wineglass for Pilar, poured a welcoming dram.

Spanish-style, she arrived late, pink-faced and flustered. Wordlessly we came together, and while she held me, very softly she began to cry. Puzzled, I asked, "Why the tears, *querida?*"

"Because . . . because—" her face lifted, "I could say tears of joy because Manny's safe, and that's part of it. But—oh, well, I know you're leaving, and I don't want you to go—only it's right that you should." Looking away, she dried eyes and cheeks. "I've loved you, and that's *not* right," she said tightly.

"No guilt," I told her, "no place for it, no reason." I kissed her damp cheek. "I'll never forget you, never."

"And you'll always be in my heart." She drew in a deep breath and looked around. I brought her the filled wineglass and touched it with mine. "Should we toast?"

"Yes, but silently." She sat on the sofa and looked up at me searchingly. "I don't want this to be as difficult for you as it is for me, *mi amor,* so let's change a doleful subject." She hesitated. "The family is overjoyed that Manny's home safe."

"So am I." Sitting beside her, I took one hand. Quietly Pilar said, "You did it."

"Did what?"

"Freed my cousin. Jack, I *know* you did."

I shrugged. "Then you know more than the FBI—they claim they got him back."

"But it was really you. All during the night I tried calling you—never an answer, so—"

"Proving nothing," I said, "because I silenced the phone so I could sleep. So please put that idea out of your mind." I kissed her cheek again, patted her hand. "Jack, stop patronizing me. Admit you freed my cousin," she said irritably.

"Should I lie?"

"Of course not—we've been truthful about everything." She gazed at me. "So far."

When I said nothing Pilar sighed. "I'm sure you have excellent reasons for keeping the truth from Manny's office and the FBI, even his family—but I'm your lover, you shouldn't even be evasive."

"Don't want to be."

"And I speak for the Spanish Montijos, who would be profoundly grateful if they knew."

"I'll remember," I replied, and drank deeply from my glass. "Suppose we lighten up. You've had a demanding day, and—"

"—you a dangerous night." She smiled. "Yes, since this will be our last night together I don't think we should waste time. Do you?"

"Not a second."

She sipped *manzanilla* and rose. "There's perspiration all through my clothing—I think I noticed a washer beyond the kitchen?"

"And dryer." Nothing if not forthright.

Her blouse was off before she crossed the dining room, then her bra. Shoes clattered on the kitchen floor, and presently the washer began its monotonous drone. As Pilar entered the bedroom I saw a flash of white flesh, gulped and swallowed the rest of my drink.

As things turned out, we showered together and made love on the bedroom rug before we were even dry. Her soft moanings and tender embraces made my heart choke in my throat. God, I didn't want to lose this unique, loving woman!

Toward eight I called Charade and asked the *maître d'* to send dinner by taxi: giant prawns for Pilar, rare lambchops for me. Over dinner we talked of everything but Manny's captivity and release. She said she was reasonably well satisfied with her classes and teaching schedule and might extend her stay. "After all, my goal is a permanent faculty job in this country."

"Not necessarily Florida."

"No. So I'm going to begin checking professional journals for possible openings, send out résumés, and see what happens."

I nodded, thinking it would be a lot easier to avoid temptation if Pilar were away from Miami.

She sipped wine and said musingly, "I suppose Manny will be all right now—I mean his office work."

"It's a difficult profession at best and all the adversaries aren't on the street."

"But that General Padilla isn't a threat—is he?"

"No," I replied, though I wasn't sure. There was just no way to keep him from communicating with men willing to carry out his orders. Suffering one setback wasn't going to keep him from trying again. For vengeance he could order a straight hit on Manny or a loved one. Lucy, Rosario, Carmen, even Pilar, were easy targets for a killer with a gun. But I didn't want to worry Pilar. Changing the subject, I said, "I've been thinking that Carmen would benefit from schooling in Spain, under your family's wing, of course. What do you think?"

She nodded. "I like the idea, but would Lucy and Manuel?"

"After what they've gone through with Carmen I should think they'd welcome it. But Carmen would have to go willingly. Could your family manage a streetwise American teenage delinquent?"

"Probably. But I'll sound them out before talking with Lucy."

"With Carmen you might have to do a selling job."

"I know. You raised the subject, I'll see what can be done." She looked away. "How long do you expect to be in Europe?"

"A month or so, maybe less. My fiancée's missing law school classes."

"I'm sure she'd rather miss them than miss her honeymoon."

"I guess. Wine?"

She nodded and I refilled our glasses.

"You'll live here—the two of you?"

"The location's convenient to the university, shops and restaurants, so we'll probably stay."

Her expression was wistful as she said, "Seems we've set our courses, Jack. I could wish otherwise but that's the way it is. After all, your plans were interrupted by Manny's abduction; otherwise you'd be married by now."

"True." Why wasn't the prospect exhilarating? Probably because we'd been together, lived together so long. We'd played house and simulated marriage. All that remained was documentation to make it official, a condition long awaited by Mama Dragon.

"Will you miss me?" murmured Pilar.

"You doubt it?"

She shrugged. "I'd like to hear you say it."

"I'll miss you. Dreadfully. We've enjoyed a rare gift, *mi querida,* and I'll treasure the memory."

Her expression was elfin. "Truly?"

"Truly." I emptied my wineglass, got up and cleared away our dishes. Then I filled liqueur glasses with Tres Reales and joined her on the sofa. As I gave her the glass I noticed that the bathrobe had slipped revealingly from her thighs. She kissed my cheek and asked, "Are you sleepy?"

"Somewhat. You?"

"The same. So I think we should have coffee. If I slept the night away I'd never forgive myself."

"Small chance of that." Our glasses touched, I sipped the rich Montijo brandy, and charged the percolator. Before leaving the kitchen I drew a bottle of Piper from the refrigerator and placed it in an ice bucket to really chill. I set two champagne glasses in the freezer and rejoined my guest. "Coffee underway," I announced, and drank half my brandy. Somehow, in my brief absence, even more of the bathrobe had slid aside, revealing the fullness of

both thighs. The device was one Melody employed as a silent way of communicating her desires. Leaning over, I kissed bared flesh and felt her shiver.

"Nice," she murmured. "Will there be more?"

"In time there will be everything."

She pressed against me, clasped my hand in hers. I kissed her brandy-wet
lips and explored her mouth as she reciprocated. I was relaxing into a dream-
like state when I remembered the coffee. So I left her to pour two cups, and
returned with them. Her head was tilted back on the sofa, eyes partly closed—
catlike. "Don't slip off into slumber," I warned.

"No danger of that. I was thinking what life is going to be like without
you. I'm not looking forward to it, not at all." Her head moved forward and
she gazed at me.

"Now, Pilar, you could meet a perfectly enchanting fellow tomorrow or
next week."

"That's true, but he wouldn't have your courage and generosity, your
ways. Unfortunately for me, you're unique, and others will always be measured by you." She sighed, lifted her coffee cup and drank, then emptied her
liqueur glass. "We have to deal with Fate as best we can, don't we?"

"We do." We kissed again, and after a while I opened the champagne and
took it with our glasses to the bedroom. As I filled our glasses Pilar turned
down the bed and shed the bathrobe. Then she lay down and took the glass
from my hand. We drank together and then I gathered her in my arms.

During the night when we weren't making love we held each other quietly,
and toward dawn—before we finally fell asleep—I tasted salt tears on her
cheeks.

Morning sunlight woke me; I was alone. I called her name but there was
no answer. I got up, aware of a brutal headache from strong drink, and
trudged to the bathroom for Tylenol. There on the mirror was a lipsticked
message: *Te amo.*

It was like her to avoid a prolonged parting, I reflected as I got back into
bed; less stressful and embarrassing that way. And I felt deep gratitude for
everything she'd given me.

By noon I had the house shut down, the Miata's battery disconnected and the
newspaper terminated. The travel agency delivered a first class ticket to
Athens on a British Airways flight leaving at three. Waiting for the taxi, I
thought of calling Manny but then realized his phone might still be tapped.
The cover story had held so far and I didn't want it broken by chance
indiscretion. So I turned the a/c up to eighty-two degrees and unplugged the

televisions. From my safe I took five thousand dollars and fitted the bills into my money belt.

Presently the door chimes sounded and I gave my two bags to the taxi driver. Then I locked the front door and followed him down the walk. Looking back at the house, I felt as though I'd left Bern months ago, so much had happened since then.

Now I was going to join Melody, we would be married as planned, and a new life would begin. No obstacles, no complications. Padilla was locked up on the far side of the continent—but I had to stop thinking of him. From now on my thoughts should be only of Melody. Despite the incredible interlude with Pilar I was eager to see Melody and I promised myself to be a good and faithful husband.

The taxi pulled from the curb and I settled back, wondering where I would find Mehmet Kurdlu's yacht, the *Cygnet,* and how hospitable the old Turk was likely to be.

BOOK TWO

SIXTEEN

TIME-ZONING eastward, I was fed three times before the big Airbus landed at Rome's Michaelangelo Airport. The British cuisine was heavy on calories only a *sumo* wrestler would need: chops and joints served with browned potatoes and lathered with glutinous gravies, and sauces with beguiling Continental names. I washed it all down with select wines and brandies, rationalizing their intake as conducive to sleep. It was, but not a refreshing one. Rather, my between-meals dozing featured cold perspiration, feverish breathing and frightening flashbacks to Manny's rescue. So I was glad when the Rome layover ended and we were on our final leg to Athens. At cruising altitude I put on the blinders again, telling myself that if I was going to swill like a shoat I shouldn't complain over consequences.

The cabin speaker provided advance notice of landing—meaning no more drinks and uncomfortably upright seats. So for the last few minutes I watched our wide sweep over the emerald green Aegean, with its countless islands and their foam-flecked shores. The view was worth the price of the trip, and I recalled seeing it on a previous occasion when I was flying tourist-class to a DEA conference in Ankara. Not an enjoyable place, Ankara; remote, dusty and cheerless, in contrast to the robust vitality of Istanbul and the busy, glittering Golden Horn. Well, that was all in the past. Who remembered the subject of the conference, even the participants? Whatever its purpose, the westward flow of Anatolian poppy juice never diminished.

Flaps and wheels down, the huge aircraft settled into its final approach, and I could see the port of Piraeus below, and then ahead rose the distant Acropolis and its chalk-white Parthenon. This was Greece.

Elliniko Airport then, noisy, crowded and hot. I claimed my bags and followed the Green lane through Customs, having nothing I wanted to declare. At the exchange bank I got about ten thousand drachmas for five hundred dollars and carried my bags to the telephone counter. I told the operator I wanted to call the *Cygnet* somewhere in Greek waters and supplied the yacht's radio call sign. Within five minutes the operator directed me to a phone cabin where I identified myself to the radioman and asked to speak with Miss Melody West. "I'll connect you with her cabin, sir," he replied, and presently I heard my fiancée's voice. "Jack! Where are you?"

"Athens airport—where are you?"

"Oh, honey, I'm so glad you're back. Why didn't you let me know you were coming? Is Manny okay?"

"Just fine, and I have much to tell you. Now, how do I get to where you are?"

"Hold on, dear, I'll ask one of the officers."

Another wait, interrupted by an accented male voice. "Sir? Second Officer Costas. We are now north of Crete and making course toward the Cyclades. We will put into Santorini Island late this afternoon."

"How do I get to—Santorini?"

"There is air service, flight time an hour and a half. The island airport is near Firá." He broke off to consult with Melody, who returned to the phone. "Honey, we'll send a car for you, so just wait at the airport, okay? I'm absolutely thrilled you're coming, and Mom will be too. Mehmet's anxious to meet you, having heard so much about you from us both. So don't hang around Athens, okay? See you soon. I love you."

"I love you," I repeated dutifully, but the words were cut off by carrier hum. I paid the operator, who directed me to the domestic airline's counter. There I learned that the feeder flight would leave in just under two hours and I was taking one of the last available seats. "How many seats in all?" I asked as I handed over a sheaf of drachmas. "Twenty-one, sir," the clerk replied, "and there is no buffet or other amenities."

"Soda?"

She nodded and gave me back three banknotes and some coins. I checked my bags and made my way to the airport bar, ordered scotch and aspirin and swallowed both. With two hours to go I spaced my drinks to avoid total inebriation, but I needed something to fortify me for the rigors of a small plane and a Greek pilot.

We flew south, not above five or six thousand feet, and I fell asleep counting the islands below. An olive-skinned young sailor met me at baggage claim. His cap had a black ribbon with *Cygnet* in gold letters, and his English was limited. "We go now to yacht, sir," he told me and carried my bags to a black Rolls Corniche with a brown fabric top.

As we drove over third-class roads the sailor told me that the island was the cone of an ancient volcano, accounting for its steep rise from the sea. The crater was more than four hundred meters deep, providing safe harbor for the largest ships and boats. *Cygnet* had put in for fresh meats and vegetables. From the road all I could see was barren, rock-strewn landscape that looked hostile to agriculture of any kind.

Darkness had fallen before we climbed over the summit and began zig-zagging down the cliff face to the harbor. The driver pointed out *Cygnet,* the largest by far of all the boats in the basin, and the yacht looked as long as a football field. It was gaily lighted and painted a dazzling white. From above I could see a group gathered on the fantail, but I was too distant to identify anyone. Then the driver turned down another sharp decline and the yacht was lost from view.

Finally, we reached the foot of the cliff and the Rolls moved down the pier to the landing stage. From it a gangway slanted up to the main deck, and I saw Melody hurrying down it. I met her on the stage, hugged and kissed her as she murmured, "Oh, darling, I thought you'd never come."

"Well, I did, and we'll never be apart again."

"Swear it?" she breathed.

"I do." A cargo boom was lifting the Rolls toward the foredeck and what looked like a steel cargo container. Secured inside, the Rolls would ride protected from rain and ocean spray. "Come on, come on, honey, we've been waiting for you." She tugged me toward the gangway and went up ahead of me.

At the top Delores waited. We exchanged dutiful kisses, after which she said, "So you're really here. I'll admit I began wondering if Manny's abduction was going to be an excuse."

"For what?"

"For not marrying my daughter." A basilisk smile. "How *is* Manny? One of my favorite people, you know."

I hadn't known it and couldn't imagine it, but I said, "Manny came through like a star performer."

"So you didn't really have to go?"

I took Melody's arm and began moving away. "I ran errands for the family, made myself useful."

"I'm sure—now come along, Mehmet is eager to welcome you."

So we followed her to the fantail, where our host was seated in a large rattan chair. He wore a white mess jacket, and his thick hair and small goatee were almost as white as the deck chairs' linen coverings. He half-rose to extend his hand, and when we'd clasped he relaxed again. "Welcome indeed, Mr. Novak. I've heard tales of your deeds that seemed truly incredible. But now that I see you''—he shrugged—''I can believe them all.''

''Thank you, sir. I've looked forward to meeting you. You've been most kind to my loved ones.''

''Do call me Mehmet.''

''Jack.''

''Yes. I understand I'm to have the pleasure and honor of giving the bride away—with her mother's consent.''

Melody squeezed my hand. Mehmet beckoned slightly, and a tray of champagne appeared beside us. Four glasses. We each took one, and Mehmet lifted his. ''A toast to happiness, good health and long life.''

''Hear, hear,'' Delores intoned, and we drank. Over the rim of my glass I studied Mehmet's features. Heavy eyebrows over deepset, dark eyes; aquiline nose and swarthy skin, less lined than I'd anticipated in a man of more than seventy. But he could afford the best cosmetic surgeons for a nip here, a tuck there. His hands were old, though, spotted and shrunken, veins standing out like long blue worms. Hands were a dead giveaway.

He said, ''The plan is to sail well out to sea where my captain can perform the marriage ceremony. This is a first for the *Cygnet,* and I'm delighted the wedding will join such a handsome couple.''

Delores sat in a chair next to Mehmet's and took his hand.

Melody asked, ''What's our dinner hour?''

''Whenever you like, child.''

''Well, I'd like to show Jack around, help him get settled in his cabin. Say an hour?''

''An hour it will be.''

We toured the weather deck, peered in at the dining salon whose long table was set with white napery, candles and gleaming sterling. ''Honey, I could get used to this, couldn't you?'' Melody murmured.

''It would mean a major effort, but yes, I probably could.'' I took her in my arms and kissed her deeply. Her body pressed into mine, and I felt the tingling of desire. ''Where's that cabin of mine?''

''Next to mine, precious—I'll show you.''

Her body was tanned the color of the mahogany that paneled my cabin walls. All over, except for a light line that girdled her hips and marked the support cord of her modesty patch. She lay face down beside me, one arm across my back, her breathing shallow and regular. Lest she drift into sleep I spanked a bun lightly and said, "Okay, immediate needs having been met, we need to change for dinner."

Raising on an elbow, she gazed at me. "Thank God you're here, really here. For a while I thought it was just another erotic dream."

"You have them, do you?"

"When you're not around, presh."

I kissed her cheek and swung off the bed. A steward had unpacked my bags and hung my clothing. Melody picked up her strewn apparel and opened the connecting door to her cabin. I shaved, had a quick shower and donned my least wrinkled clothing. Melody came in fluffing out damp hair, and had me button the back of her blouse. "I let you go to Miami—willingly," she said, "and I expect a full account of everything that happened."

"You'll get it."

"I'm really proud of you, love, and thrilled to have a husband who can do what you did for your friend."

"That's what friends are for." We left my cabin, and walked down the carpeted, paneled passageway. Mehmet's stateroom comprised the far end of the passageway, and Melody had told me that it also contained an office filled with computers and other electronic equipment. As we went up the ladder I asked, "What's his line of business?"

"Oh, I'm not sure, but whatever it is he runs it from the yacht."

"Did your mother ever mention it?"

"No—but she wouldn't care how he got his money, just that he has plenty."

"That's Mom," I agreed, and then we entered the air-conditioned dining salon.

Mom and Mehmet were there, and I was introduced to the Captain and the First Officer; all hands were enjoying cocktails. Melody asked for sweet vermouth *au glace* and I requested Añejo on the rocks. Melody said, "They have it because I told them you'd like it. See how thoughtful I am?"

"Just don't let thoughtfulness end after the knot is tied, okay?"

"Beast!" She pinched my wrist. Our drinks arrived and while Melody chatted with the ship's senior officers, I went over to Mehmet and Mom. "This must be one of the finest yachts in the Mediterranean," I remarked.

"Thank you," the owner replied. "Built to my order in Holland. Steel hull eighty meters in length. Interior fitted out at Cyprus." He sipped from his glass. "When next in Izmir I am having some of my art treasures installed."

Like Onassis, I thought. Old Ari had set the standard for all yacht owners. Delores gushed, "And what treasures! Picasso, Mondrian, Dufy, Rouault, Van den Boek." She sighed admiringly. "Mehmet's home is—well, aside from being a palace, it's a veritable art museum."

Mehmet inclined his head modestly. "I like beautiful things," he explained, "and having the means, I indulge myself."

"I can understand that," I responded, as Melody joined us.

Mehmet said, "Jack, I understand you were a naval officer at one time." I nodded.

"Then you will doubtless be interested in *Cygnet*'s computerized navigation. What is the phrase? State of the art. Captain Staloniku will delight in showing you."

"I don't want to represent myself as a qualified ship handler, because I went into flight training after Annapolis."

"And flew in the Vietnam war," Melody added. "Has his own plane in Mexico."

Dinner chimes sounded and we took our places. Mehmet was at the head of the table, Mom on his right. Melody on his left, me next to her, and the officers across from us. We were served by a steward and a stewardess: shrimp cocktail, seafood consommé, portions of a large baked fish, assorted vegetables, salad and sherbet. Then coffee and liqueurs. Hearing the breathy beat of helicopter rotors, I looked questioningly at our host, who said, "My secretary, Giorgio, returning from Crete. Perhaps you and Melody would like to see Santorini from the air before we leave port tomorrow. Unfortunately, the island itself is uninteresting. There is very little water, and so the land is without trees." He paused. "The volcano, of which the island is a remnant, exploded some three thousand years ago. I have heard that the force was far greater than the explosion of Krakatoa. Some scientists relate the volcano's submergence to the disappearance of Atlantis. In any case, what remains is hardly worth notice. But for this sheltered deepwater port, no one would ever come here."

The First Officer said, "There are some hot water springs said to be beneficial to bathers. Mud baths, too."

Melody giggled. "But no mud-wrestlers."

"Hardly," Mehmet said reprovingly. "The Greeks leave that to the Germans."

After dinner, Mehmet took me out on deck and we strolled forward, pausing beside the Bell helicopter's secure stowage. The yacht's Third Officer doubled as its pilot, he said, the chopper being useful when he had urgent reason to fly to inland destinations. Then he moved to the rail and stared seaward. "I want to confide something in you, for I feel you will not betray the confidence."

Thinking he was going to reveal his feelings for Delores, I said, "I can be closemouthed when necessary."

"Good. In addition to modern art I have an interest in Mediterranean antiquities. A few days ago our sonar gear detected an underwater wreck and I sent down a diver with a camera. My thought was along the lines of a sunken Allied or German vessel, but the diver reported the outlines of an ancient galley with amphorae and ballast stones strewn around—photographs confirmed the find.'' He paused. ''Ever since Lord Elgin stole the Parthenon's friezes the Greeks have been very sensitive about their antiquities. I decided to have a few amphorae brought up, leaving the rest on the ocean floor, but deep within the remains of the hull some remarkable statuary was discovered. Knowing the Greek bureaucracy as I do, it would be useless to try to obtain a salvor's permit, so I am in the process of taking what I most want, eventually notifying the Greeks where the galley can be found.''

''Finders keepers.''

''Eh?''

''American expression. He who finds it keeps it.''

He smiled. ''American practicality. Now, the undersea work need not delay your and Melody's wedding unduly but it will postpone the Monaco reception a few days and I apologize for that.''

''No need to. Does Delores know?''

''About the amphorae, not the statuary. Experience has taught me not to rely excessively on the prudence of women.''

''What about your crew?''

''I pay them well. The Greeks would not reward them for the information. One sees to one's own interest, eh?''

I thought it over. ''Always. How deep is the galley?''

''Thirty meters, a hundred feet.''

''No color at that depth,'' I remarked.

''None, though halogen lighting brings out the original colors—what remains of them. I don't want to linger overlong near the wreck lest Greek naval patrols become suspicious—or pirates. Another three days at most. By then you and your fiancée will be married, and we will proceed to Monaco without further delay.''

''We're in your hands, Mehmet, and I'm eager to see what you recover.''

''And you will. So, that is what I wanted to reveal to you, man to man.''

''I appreciate your confidence.''

Mehmet nodded, and I said, ''You mentioned pirates. Do you feel the yacht's security is adequate?''

''I believe so. Several crewmen had military or naval training and there is a supply of weapons that the captain controls. The radar operator keeps us informed of any approaching vessels.'' He shrugged. ''I am more concerned over being boarded by the Greek Navy than by pirates.''

Melody and her mother were approaching and we turned to meet them. Mehmet said, "I was telling Jack something about this area. Notice the absence of shore lights, so unlike other ports of call."

"Just the boats in the harbor," Delores said, as the faint sound of music drifted across the water. Melody took my hand, snuggled against me catlike. "My last night as a maiden, dear."

"And mine as a bachelor." I smiled winningly at my almost-mother-in-law, who shook her head. "I'll confess I never really believed you two would end up at the altar."

"But now you're resigned to it," Melody said wickedly.

"Resigned? My dear, I'm thrilled. Handing you over to Jack will be a monumental relief."

"Oh, Mother," she pouted. I yawned, and said, "Sorry, folks, jet lag has set in. Goodnight all."

"Rise when you choose," Mehmet said. "We'll be underway, and breakfast is buffet-style. Sleep well."

Melody kissed her mother and we left them in favor of our cabins. In mine there was a bottle of Veuve Cliquot in an iced bucket, and two glasses. I filled them and Melody came in wearing a filmy nightgown with a pink bow. Our glasses touched, and she said, "This is the life, dear."

"Enjoy it while we can, it'll never get this good again."

"Don't be a pessimist."

"Me?"

"You. And when are you going to tell me about Manny?"

"Not tonight. You look so gorgeous I'm speechless."

"And exhausted, I know the signs. So let's turn out the lights and snuggle."

We did.

Toward dawn I heard the hum of the yacht's big diesels, felt the motion of the yacht clearing the pier and turning toward the sea. This was my wedding day and I hoped it wouldn't be marred by Greek boarding parties interrupting Mehmet Kurdlu's criminal enterprise. And I reflected that whether by intention or not the old Turk had revealed an interesting aspect of his character: he was avaricious, and accustomed to taking what he wanted despite troublesome legalities. But why should that surprise me? Someone with his immense wealth had to have acquired at least part of it by questionable means.

As sleep returned, I wondered how long it would be before Delores got her hooks into it.

SEVENTEEN

MID-MORNING sun reflected from the calm and glittering Aegean. The yacht was at anchor and a boom had been lowered from the starboard bow. Bubbles off the tip marked where divers were working below. Melody said, "Isn't this exciting? Who knows what they'll bring up."

"Mehmet said terra-cotta jars—amphorae."

"I know what they are, silly. There's plenty of diving gear—why don't you go down for a look?"

"Not before breakfast."

A canopy shaded the fantail where a buffet table waited. Two chefs tended steam trays and an omelet burner. We began with juice and assorted fruits, graduated to solid food. Melody had sautéed squid and sweet rolls, while I consumed a three-egg omelet of cheese, ham and sliced mushrooms, English muffins on the side.

Delores joined us for coffee, saying she hoped we'd slept well, and not quite smirking. She looked as though she'd barely slept at all but I reminded myself that Melody's mother was never her best in the morning.

Not far off the boom several round, white objects were floating. "More Greek jars," Delores announced, with distaste.

"White jars?" I asked, knowing better.

"Of course not, Jack. Those are plastic parachute-type things, the jars are hanging below. What they do is tie the jars or whatever to ropes that are attached to the plastic, then blow air bubbles into the canopy. The jars come to the surface and they're brought aboard. See?"

The boom's cargo net was lifting the sea-parachutes and their attachments from the sea, dripping mud and water. A crewman hosed the amphorae before they were lowered to the foredeck. Delores sipped coffee and sighed. "You've seen one jar—"

"—amphora, Mother."

"—and you've seen them all. Dear, this is supposed to be your wedding day, but Mehmet says the Captain is too occupied bringing all that old junk aboard to perform the ceremony at noon—which is what we planned."

"A few hours or days won't make any difference," Melody said soothingly. "If marine archaeology is Mehmet's hobby let him pursue it."

"I suppose you're right, dear, but now would be ideal, while we're anchored and no waves or rolling around. And we're far beyond the twelve-mile limit. She shaded her eyes. "No land in sight, not even a fishing boat. I mean, how long can the ceremony take? The Captain reads from a book, we all sign the wedding document, and that's it. The officers sign as witnesses." She sighed again, and I noticed that the chopper was gone. Mehmet probably had it out working a search pattern to give early warning of vessels heading in our direction. He hadn't amassed his fortune by ignoring available tools.

Still dripping, six amphorae were lowered down a hatch out of sight, and I wondered if the far more precious statuary was going to be brought up in daylight. The boom swung outward, lowering cargo net and plastic lifters into the sea. This could go on indefinitely, I mused, until Mehmet picked the bottom clean.

After brunch and a third cup of coffee I went forward and down to the weather deck to watch the recovery process. Never having seen the retrieval of objects submerged for a couple of thousand years, I was curious about Mehmet's booty. As the boom swung aboard another load I stayed clear of the hatch while the old jars were hosed down, then watched them being lowered into the cargo compartment. The interior was lighted, and I could see Mehmet standing by the long row of amphorae already aboard. He looked up expectantly, and almost on signal one, then two, of the jars slipped through the mesh and crashed to the deck where they smashed into shards.

Exposing their contents.

Amid dark chunks of what looked like old cement, scores of small objects glittered with a hue that could only be gold.

Mehmet yelled furiously, swore in an unfamiliar language at the boom operator, and caught sight of me. Startled, he stepped back, then shrugged. "Come down, Jack," he called, "and see what the sea has yielded."

By the time I got there a crewman was shoveling the debris into a barrel, Mehmet watching. "An unexpected dividend," he said, as he bent over and picked up a handful of coins. "Aside from the intrinsic value of the gold, their historical value is immense. Here, take some." His hand opened. "One," I said, and picked out a wet coin the size of a nickel. Its roundness was uneven, crudely stamped by the ancient coiner, but the ruler's profile was still distinct, as was the inscribed rim.

"Phoenician coins make the galley Phoenician," he said excitedly. "I'd heard that coins were occasionally sent from mints hidden in amphorae that usually contained oil and wine." He turned over a thick round plug with his foot. "Pitch used to seal the jars. No telling how many contain coins until I open them all—but that is for later, on land."

I could picture him gloating over his treasure, and hoped these coins were the only ones to be found. "May I make a suggestion, Mehmet?"

"By all means."

"Weigh the amphorae, any heavier than one known to contain wine or oil could be opened."

"Exactly. An ingenious idea, and I should have thought of it myself." He smiled appreciatively.

I heard the chopper coming in and saw it beyond the hatch opening. When I went up on deck it was being refueled from a drum by hand pump. How often I'd seen that done in 'Nam.

On the fantail I showed the gold coin to Melody and her mother, who exclaimed over the find. "How many coins are there?"

"Hundreds, maybe thousands in just two jars. Mehmet hasn't said so but I predict he'll bring up every amphora before we leave the site."

Delores's eyes narrowed. "And how long will that take?"

"Without knowing how many remain in the wreck, I'd guess a couple of days." And there was the statuary as well.

During lunch in the salon Mehmet distributed a selection of gold coins to the ladies, offered more to me but I declined, saying one was a splendid souvenir of the expedition. The captain stayed on the bridge overseeing the loading and Delores said irritably, "How long before he can take ten minutes for the ceremony?"

Mehmet smiled apologetically. "There is a rhythm to the work that I prefer not to be broken just now. I'm told that most of the work can be accomplished by nightfall, so let us say definitely that the wedding will take place tomorrow." He touched Melody's hand. "I regret the postponement, my dear, but I want to accomplish all we can while the weather remains favorable and the sea calm."

"And then there is the Greek Navy," I remarked.

He nodded. "Taking a few amphorae would be seen as a minor infraction compared to the coinage we've discovered."

"I understand completely," Melody said diplomatically, "so the skipper can hitch us whenever it's convenient."

"Thank you, my dear, for your understanding."

Delores grumped but our host took no notice of it. Instead Mehmet said, "Separating gold coins is difficult and fairly time-consuming. The process involves acid baths and electrolysis, and can be accomplished at my home."

"And where is that?" I asked.

"In the hills above Izmir. I propose to unload our Phoenician cargo at the port and see it safely to my place before we head to Monaco. From here the distance to Izmir is something over two hundred nautical miles, and we will move into Turkish waters as quickly as practicable."

"Two hundred miles," Delores repeated, and Mehmet nodded. "No more than an overnight cruise, my dear, and if you like we can stay the night there and leave in the morning."

"That might be a nice change," she said, somewhat mollified, "and the young people could see some of your art treasures."

Through salon windows we could see the boom lifting and dipping, lifting again. I wondered how long the divers were supposed to work at that depth before decompressing and surfacing. Dive tables would tell me but I thought half an hour at a hundred feet would be a safe margin before a measured ascent. But there were probably more than two qualified divers among the crew, working in relays. Still, the physical strain would be considerable.

I excused myself and went up to the bridge. Captain Staloniku was supervising the boom operator from the port wing. Just aft of the bridge I could see the radioman through the open passageway. He was scanning the radar screen with undivided attention. The ship's electronic steering controls seemed to consist of a pair of small handles that fed into a computer console. No old-time engine telegraph, everything was digitalized today. On the aft bulkhead a glassed weapons rack was positioned. The wood-framed doors were secured by a hasp and lock, which I felt was minimal security. Break the pane and grab a weapon. Among them were three AR-15s, some old British Enfield rifles and half a dozen Webley and S&W revolvers. I assumed the pieces were loaded because I saw no ammo stowage. At the bottom of the rack lay a Very pistol with two red star shells for emergency signaling.

Noticing me, the Captain came over and said, "You like my armaments?"

"Very impressive," I lied.

"In addition I keep a twelve-bore trap gun in my cabin for guests' amusement. A Greener," he said proudly. "When we are less occupied you might care to shoot a round or two."

I nodded. "Does Mehmet shoot?"

Staloniku shook his head. "He seems to have a fear of firearms, but I feel every able-bodied man should be able to handle weapons—self-defense, of course.''

"Of course."

"Excuse me, I must get back to work. If anything went wrong with the loading I would be responsible." He touched his cap visor and went back to the wing. I'd half-expected him to apologize for delaying our wedding, but he had his orders from the owner, and I understood that.

Another dripping load of amphorae was being lifted from the sea and swung aboard, then lowered into the open hatch. There must be a hundred in the compartment already, I thought, and tried to visualize how they had been stowed in the twenty-four-oared galley.

The Loran navigational gear was more modern than anything I'd seen before. With it the wreck's location could be pinpointed in case Mehmet decided to return later. By then, I mused, little would remain on the seabed beyond wormy wood and bronze nails.

There being nothing else of interest topside, I went down to my cabin, and found Melody in the shower. She wrinkled her nose and called, "Siesta time—or have you forgotten?"

"How could I?" I called back, undressed, and joined her in the shower.

We surfaced for cocktail hour, dined in splendor with all the ship's officers, and watched a taped movie in the salon. I was fond enough of *Lonesome Dove* to sit through three hours of the Western saga, after which I surrendered, said my goodnights to the assemblage and led Melody below.

Again there was an iced bumper of Veuve to provoke cordiality and invoke slumber, and since tomorrow was definitely going to be our wedding day, why not?

I popped the cork, and as I was filling our glasses I heard the cargo boom's engine start up. Melody said, "How odd—working at night." Our glasses touched, and I said, "That's so we can leave tomorrow," but I knew it was to hoist galley statuary under cover of darkness. I sat on the edge of the bed and drew her beside me. "C'mon, let's put aside Mehmet's piratical ways and make like man and wife."

"In a hurry? We've a lifetime ahead of us."

The boom's gears ground noisily as they took the cargo load. Melody frowned. " 'S'pose that's going on all night?''

"Let's hope not." How much statuary could there be? I emptied my glass and lay back. "Douse the light, will you, sweet thing?"

She did, and then stretched out beside me. ''I do love you, Jack, you know that, don't you? I mean, despite everything?''

''I sensed as much,'' I admitted, and closed her lips with mine.

Much later a foreign sound woke me. The boom engine was silent, and the sound wasn't the kind you expect to hear when a ship swings at anchor, so what was it?

Again the sound, and with senses alert I realized it was a cry. Sitting up, I pulled on shorts, tore out my suitcase lining and chambered a shell in my S&W .38. Still on my knees, I clamped one hand over Melody's mouth, and as she struggled awake, I whispered, ''Something's going on. Lock yourself in the bathroom and stay quiet while I have a look around.''

''Jack—please be careful.''

''Probably nothing more than champagne hysteria.'' I moved to the door and was about to open it when through the air vents I heard feet running down the corridor. Toward us.

EIGHTEEN

A**s soon** as the footsteps went past—toward the owner's suite—I cracked the door and looked out. Although the corridor's only illumination came from spaced night lights I could see a man in tight-fitting black that could have been a diving suit—except for a sort of black ski mask covering his head. For a fraction of a second I thought the visitor might be one of the wreck divers reporting bad news to his boss—until I saw the gun in his hand. A silencer extended the barrel. His other hand curled around the suite doorknob and he shoved against the door. When it didn't give he grunted, took three steps back and got ready to crash it. Before he could shove off I covered the twelve-foot distance in a silent rush and kicked the small of his back. Air emptied from his lungs in a stifled gasp, the gun flew out of his hand and he fell face down, head a scant foot from the door. I set my foot on the back of his neck and bore down. The body twitched spasmodically and lay still. To make sure he was out of it I slammed my pistol into the back of his head, then scooped up his 9mm Beretta. With it I knocked quietly on the suite door, and presently heard Mehmet call out in an unfamiliar language. Kneeling, I spoke through the door's air vents. "Mehmet, Jack here, you're in danger, open up."

A muffled exclamation, then the door opened. In purple silk pajamas, Mehmet Kurdlu stared at me, then at the fallen man. I grabbed the man's hands and dragged him into the suite, closed the door. "I think we're under attack," I said, and jerked off the black head covering. "Anyone you know?"

Mehmet stared in horror at the motionless eyes. "No, no, I never—" He gulped and broke off. I handed him my .38 and said, "Protect yourself and Delores. I'm going to find out what this is all about." My future mother-in-law was asleep in the twin bed. "Better not wake her. Get dressed and don't open for anyone but me, okay?"

He nodded and stepped back, turned and made for his clothing. I pulled off the dead man's costume, not rubber but black nylon with stitched-on *tabi* soles, and drew on the pants, then the tight-fitting top. Mehmet was putting on his pants as I drew the headpiece over my skull and face. I figured disguise was my best chance of surviving. They'd shoot a naked Novak on sight, not one of their own. Who were they? How many? What had they come for? Hijacking the yacht? Its treasure? But how did anyone beyond the yacht know what cargo it held? Hissing, "Lock the door," I stepped out into the corridor. Then I squared my shoulders and strode to the companionway.

From the top I could see two black figures pointing guns at Captain Staloniku. His face was twisted with pain, his left hand pressed against his right shoulder, and I could see blood coming through his fingers.

Where the hell were the yacht's able-bodied seamen?

My guess was they were shut in the crew compartment or being held by gunmen. The other three officers? Dead or locked in their cabins. Shit!

I took steps to bridge level and opened the door. One of the gunmen whirled, gun pointing at me, lowered it and spat a question. I shrugged, lifted the Beretta and pointed at the muzzle, nodding. Before he could turn to the Captain I shot him through the chest, and as he fell I dropped the other bandit. The silenced shots wouldn't be heard away from the bridge. As the Captain stared in astonishment at me I pulled up the mask to let him see my face, then drew it down. One of the gunmen was writhing on the deck. I slashed the silencer against his head and said, "I nailed one outside Mehmet's door. How many are there?"

Grimacing, Staloniku said, "Five, I think."

"The other two?"

A burst of noise from the boom engine told me where one was. "Are they hijackers? Pirates?"

"They want money, the gold we brought up today. And they plan to kidnap Mehmet and the woman, hold them for ransom."

"Who told them about the gold?"

"I—I don't know."

"If you can lock yourself in your cabin, take care of your arm, and I'll get back to you." I smashed the gunrack glass with my pistol and handed him a Webley, then pulled out an AR-15. "Magazine's loaded?"

He nodded and I unlatched the other two magazines, stuck them in my waistband beside my silenced Beretta. Then I chambered a round and flicked the firing level to full auto. Fuck these bastards.

Gunman Four was working boom levers, positioning the boom over the open cargo hatch, so he didn't notice me approach from the side. Holding my left forearm to steady the pistol barrel, I sighted on a spot between his shoulders just below his neck. Fired.

The heavy, high-velocity slug slammed him forward against the levers. His arms hung down like black ropes. I climbed up and stopped the boom's swinging, shoved the controls to neutral. Then I pushed the black-clad body to the deck, dropped down beside it and decided Gunman Five was probably down in the cargo compartment getting ready to load the hoist net. When the boom didn't respond he'd come up to find out why. I wanted him on deck, not down below. I stuck the Beretta back in my waistband—no need for silenced shooting now.

I thumbed off the auto-rifle's safety and walked forward past the helicopter to the protection of a broad air scoop that rose from the deck. From it I could hear pounding below—the crew trying to get out. Patience, I thought, and waited. In less than a minute I heard shouting from the cargo compartment. You shoot woodchucks and prairie dogs by whistling until they stand up, and curiosity kills them. I didn't have to whistle for this dog, he was going to come out of his hole, pissed-off at his partner. And curious. I aimed at the hatch corner where the ladder was, and after another round of furious shouting, a black-clad man climbed out. He'd pulled off his headpiece and the lighter outline of his face against darker background made a splendid target. There was a holstered gun hanging from a gun belt and I didn't want a firefight. He saw his partner's body splayed out on the deck, halted and reached for his gun. In that frozen moment I pulled the trigger and cut him down with a three-round burst. The triple impact slammed him backward and he was dead before he hit the deck. If the Captain was right, that took care of all five boarders—but were there more? I stayed behind the air scoop waiting for others to show up, drawn by my shots. Reaching the fantail, I could see an inflatable boat tied up astern, decided to postpone sinking it. Time to review the body count: one in Mehmet's cabin, two on the bridge and two by the cargo hatch. Five. The rubber boat could carry six, but not if they expected to take away heavy loot; five would be plenty. Still, it was possible a sixth gunman lurked unseen. I moved forward, slid down the companionway and entered the cabin corridor. Mehmet's door was open and I could see him lying on the carpeting, face up, Delores beside him. The reason they were on their backs was because Gunman Six had them covered with a silenced pistol. He was barking questions at Mehmet who gave choking answers. I went to my knees in combat crouch and sighted on the gunman's back, just below his neck. But Delores had seen my movement and screamed. The gunman whirled around and fired. The slug whistled over my head, and before he could shoot again I pressed off two rounds. He fell backward, tripped on Mehmet's legs, and his pistol went off. Mehmet yelled in pain, sat upright and grabbed his thigh. Delores screamed again—screaming was her contribution to the night's activities—so I pulled off the face mask and entered the suite. "Boarders neutralized," I told them. "Unless there's more than six."

Delores was rocking back and forth in shock. I slapped her face—something I'd wanted to do for years—and snapped, "Stop it! Make a tourniquet for his leg, do something useful for God's sake."

"A—a—?" She blinked uncomprehendingly at me, so I said, "Tear strips from a pillowcase, wrap it around his thigh above the wound, twist it tight."

She didn't move. "Where—where's Melody?"

"Safe."

I went to my cabin door, rapped hard on it and called her name, then mine. In a few moments the door opened and she stood there, staring at me, then flung her arms around me and began to sob in relief. "Easy," I said, "there's work to do. Help Mom with Mehmet. The Captain's wounded, too." I pulled away her arms and jogged back to the companionway.

On the bridge the surviving gunman was groaning. I watched him trying to crawl to the gun rack, and when he was nearly there I kicked him on his back. Then I knelt and shoved the silencer in his mouth. "Move and you're dead," I snarled, not knowing—or caring—if he understood English. These pirates—for what else could they be?—deserved no mercy. Getting up, I pointed the pistol at his crotch and went down the passageway past the empty radio shack to a door with a brass plate engraved *Captain*. I called his name, and presently the door opened. His face was pale, and he was pressing a thick gauze pad against his shoulder wound. "I've accounted for six," I told him, "and Mehmet's got a bullet in his thigh. Where's your medical kit?"

He pointed at his bunk where a large medical box lay open. I got out a morphine Syrette and injected it in his left arm close to the shoulder. He winced slightly, and said, "I need an antibiotic shot."

"That you do." I found a prepared syringe and stuck the needle in his butt. "When you can manage it, get your officers together. I'll take care of Mehmet and free the crew. Understand?"

He nodded, sat on the edge of his bunk. I hoped the morphine would lessen pain enough for him to be useful, not chill him out. From a fitted liquor rack I got a bottle of Stoly and swallowed three beneficial slugs, took it with me as I left with the medical kit.

In Mehmet's suite Melody had applied a tourniquet to our host's thigh, and was twisting it with a hairbrush. Good field expedient. Delores was sitting on her bed staring vacantly at Mehmet and her daughter. I handed Mom the Stoly and ordered her to drink. Then I got down beside Mehmet and opened the medical kit. As with the Captain, I injected morphine near the entrance wound, followed it with antibiotic in the back of his thigh. As I feared, there was no exit wound and I lacked skill and willingness to plumb for the slug. Big arteries there, I could sever one and kill him. He'd have to get to a hospital. I voiced my thoughts and Mehmet nodded. To Melody I whispered, "Is he bleeding much?"

"Quite a lot, I think—but I've never seen real bleeding before. God, Jack, what a night!"

"If the pilot can fly the chopper I want Mehmet out of here without delay. Your mother had better go with him to manipulate the tourniquet, otherwise he'll bleed to death before he can get help."

Melody said loudly, "Hear that, Mother?"

She nodded. "I'll get some clothes on. Yes, I should go with him"

To Mehmet I said, "As soon as you're airborne we're going to move the yacht away from here. Our position is known and we risk more trouble if we stay."

Thickly, he said, "Go to Izmir," and closed his eyes.

I went back to the bridge where the Captain was talking with his officers. They looked at me and my commando suit in a kind of stupor, and I pointed at the surviving gunman on the deck. "He may not live long, so he better be questioned, now. Who they are, who sent them, what they came for, and—most importantly—who among the crew betrayed us? Keep him alive as long as necessary. Meanwhile, Captain, Mehmet will bleed to death unless he reaches a hospital damn soon." I turned to the Third Officer-pilot. "Get the rotors turning, man, no time to waste."

He nodded. "The nearest hospital is on Crete—Iráklion—an hour's flight away." He left the bridge, and I told the First and Second Officers to get a stretcher and bring the owner topside. When they departed I told the Captain I thought he ought to go with the chopper. When he started to protest, I said, "Mehmet wants the yacht in Izmir, and I assume the First Officer can get us there. I'm speaking for the owner and I order you to leave with him." The Captain grimaced. "I should see Mehmet now."

"You'll have an hour with him before you reach Crete. How are you feeling?"

"Less pain with the morphine."

"Good. I'll give you a couple of Syrettes to take along. Stick yourself if you need it, but check Mehmet's pulse before you give him more morphine."

He nodded, and I asked, "Did you bring up the statuary?"

He shook his head. "The pirates boarded us while we were trying. Mehmet will be very displeased."

"I'm not sorry. I don't like looters."

"The Second Officer freed the crew, none was harmed."

I heard the chopper engine fire up, the breathy flutter of turning rotors, and went down to watch them load Mehmet into the chopper. Before the Captain arrived I opened the medical kit and got out two Syrettes, gave them to him before he got aboard. Delores was last. She had a glazed expression and vodka breath. Melody kissed her goodbye, and said, "We'll see you in Izmir." I kissed Delores's cheek and said, "No need to hurry, be a comfort to Mehmet. Tell him it was a swell cruise—while it lasted."

She nodded and the pilot helped strap her in. She gave us a vague smile and waved. Melody and I stepped back and the chopper lifted off. We watched it vanish in the night sky until its running lights were pinpoints smaller than the smallest star. Melody took my arm, clung to me, and I saw her looking at the two dead gunmen. "How many were there?" she said huskily.

"Six. And I hope that's all there were. C'mon, I'll show you how they got here."

From the fantail we looked down at the bobbing boat. "So much for piracy," I said, and held her close to me.

"Thank God you were here, Jack. Without you we'd probably all be dead."

"Probably," I agreed. "Now go back to the cabin and try to sleep. I'll join you after Field Day."

"Field Day?"

"Navy for cleanup time."

As we walked toward the companionway she said, "Think Mother will be all right?"

"Why not? She wasn't shot, and now she's got a great chance to impress Mehmet by nursing him back to health."

"Dear, you can be so cynical."

"Uh-huh, so don't worry about Mom, okay? She's the original survivor."

I heard the diesel engines shudder into life, then the anchor winch began dragging anchor cable from the depths. I kissed Melody goodnight, and joined the First Officer on the bridge. He said, "Captain Staloniku told me to take my orders from you."

"What's your name?"

"Kitsos."

"Very well, Captain Kitsos, set course for Izmir, get out of Greek waters as soon as possible. Radio silence. Incidentally, where's the radioman?"

"He was one of them—you killed him." He gestured at the foredeck.

"Your Second Officer navigates?"

"He does."

"Good. After he gives you a course, I want him to question this pirate." I looked down at the dying man on the deck. "We know who the informant was, but we don't know who bribed him, set up the operation. I'm disposed to let this fellow live awhile if he answers promptly and truthfully. Otherwise—"

"I understand."

"Have two or three men come to the bridge. After bodies are disposed of I'll have you brief the crew. None of them saw me do any shooting—not even you if it comes to that—so the story is the thieves had a falling out, killed each other." For a moment I felt myself back in the Everglades sending corpses out to sea. That was a rehearsal for this. "Nevertheless," I went on, "the crew is not to discuss the incident ashore."

"I'll caution them."

The anchor clanked into the eye and the acting captain touched the controls. The yacht moved smoothly ahead and the Second Officer came onto the bridge. Captain Kitsos spoke to him in Greek, the officer nodded and began drawing a course on a chart overlay. After he had given the course to the Captain I said, "While you're questioning this unfortunate I'll take care of disposal."

Three crewmen came onto the bridge, touching their caps respectfully. "The idea," I said, "is to load all the corpses into the cargo net, weight it with, say, four amphorae, and drop the load in deep water." I paused but Kitsos said nothing. The Second Officer said, "Very practical, sir."

Kitsos gave orders to the crewmen who picked up the dead man and carried him down to the foredeck. I said, "Did I mention two in the owner's cabin?"

"Yes, sir, you did."

"At first light I want the decks hosed and holystoned."

"Yes, sir," the Second Officer responded, "I'll see to that." He knelt beside the dying man and began speaking to him. I pulled the spare mags from my waist and set them in the gun rack, then the AR-15, keeping the silenced Beretta. My S&W was probably still in Mehmet's suite. If he'd used it on the sixth gunman he wouldn't be flying to a Cretan hospital, a bullet in his leg. I considered his suffering a form of reprisal for his thievery.

"Also," I said, "I want those coins guarded, no souvenirs."

"Aye, sir," the Captain said, and after a few minutes told me the yacht was on course at twenty-two knots. "I'll hand over to the helmsman now."

"The Captain's bunk is bloody, so have the linen changed before we reach port. And the owner's suite needs attention."

With that I went down to the foredeck where the bodies were being collected. The boom swung the cargo net down into the hatch where it was loaded with amphorae. Then up to the deck where the bodies were rolled onto the net and the top closed with line. The boom lifted the net and swung outward. I returned to the cabin and told the Captain to drop the net when we were over two hundred fathoms. Then I asked the Second Officer if he'd gotten anything out of his questioning.

"Nothing worthwhile. This chap is from Minos, so were two of the others. Usually they robbed or hijacked sailing vessels. Their leader—now dead— had them on standby since yesterday. They were to capture this yacht and take owner and passengers prisoner, hold them for ransom. They planned to take the gold with them."

"Ask him if they didn't leave from a mother ship. That rubber boat isn't great for the open sea."

The Second Officer slapped the man's check, but his eyes seemed focused on the overhead. As I watched, I saw death cloud them, and pressed his carotid. "Gone," I said, "so I guess we'll never know."

The Second Officer shrugged. "Six men down," he said in a distant voice. "I never expected a massacre on this vessel."

"Who did? So you better draw up a new antihijack plan and drill the men. Another time I won't be aboard."

"I'll do that," he said respectfully. "What's to be done with this one?"

"Bring down the net and add him to it. I'll take care of the boat."

On the fantail I reached through the railing and untied the snub line. As it dropped into the water I shot four holes in the rubber pontoons and watched the boat settle beyond the phosphorescent wake. Of the pirates' expedition nothing remained.

Two stewards were cleaning Mehmet's suite. My .38 was on Mehmet's bed so I retrieved it and bade the stewards goodnight. Then I went into my cabin and found Melody asleep. In darkness I stripped off my pirate garb, cracked the port and dropped the garments over the side. Then I got in bed beside Melody and cradled her in my arms.

"Honey," I said quietly, "we can't get married at sea, so I think it's time we went home." Then I drifted off to sleep wondering what misfortunes could befall us when we reached Izmir.

BOOK THREE

NINETEEN

IT WAS after eleven when I woke. Sunshine streamed in through the port, the yacht was running smoothly over a placid sea. Melody was nowhere to be seen. I sat up and found my mouth tasting like an ash heap. Standing under the shower, I let spray cleanse my mouth, then dried off and poked around for clothing.

While I was dressing Melody came in with a pot of steaming coffee and a smile. " 'Morning. Feeling okay?''

"Too soon to tell." I drank from the china cup and asked, "Where are we?"

"Off some Turkish town with an unpronounceable name—we've been in Turkish waters since just after dawn. So the Second Officer tells me."

"What else did he tell you, love?" I managed a weak leer.

"The chopper pilot called from the hospital where Mehmet and the Captain are resting comfortably. Mother's there, too, and I'll talk with her later."

"Tell her we're going home, you and I."

"Are we? Terrific." She clapped hands. "We can get married in Miami."

"That's the idea." I finished my coffee and added more to my cup. "Be a dear child and fetch Añejo from the bar."

"Anything you desire. The whole crew regards you as a hero—me, too."

"The crew isn't supposed to know I did anything."

She shrugged. "Word gets around. Oh, the pilot wants to know if he should stay at Iráklion or return to the *Cygnet*."

"He ought to stay there until Mehmet can travel, then fly everyone to Izmir. Our host will do better at home."

"What about us—you and me?"

"Considering the contraband aboard, I want to get off as soon as we dock. The acting captain may know how to get all that loot to Mehmet's manse—I want no part of it.'' I glanced out the port and saw coastline that looked no more than a mile or two away. Melody left the cabin and I finished dressing. She brought back the Añejo bottle and I poured a substantial slug in my coffee—about half a cup. It vastly improved flavor. Melody said, ''I told the chief steward we'd have breakfast on the fantail so we can watch the sights. He said it would take a while to set up the buffet, so I told him to just fix us some eggs, bacon and croissants.'' She smoothed her dress and I thought she'd never looked lovelier. ''Miss Mom?'' I asked.

She frowned. ''I guess so, a little anyway.'' Then she smiled. ''Know what's funny? The grown-ups are gone, replaced by a younger generation—us. We're giving the orders now.''

''As it should be. Let's go eat.''

Seated in the open, we were enjoying breakfast when Acting Captain Kitsos appeared. He looked drawn so I invited him to join us. ''Coffee only,'' he said, and sat across the table. ''The navigator says we ought to reach Alsancak Harbor sometime mid-afternoon—that's Izmir. Hugging the coast and picking our way among these islands makes slow going, but you wanted to stay in Turkish waters.''

I nodded. ''I'll want the Rolls unloaded and a driver to take us to Mehmet's place. I don't know how the amphorae are to be handled, that's your problem.''

''I understand. The cargo will be off-loaded and transported with great care.'' He smiled. ''While port officials are looking elsewhere.''

''Any late bulletins on the patients?''

''Third Officer Konstantinos says they can be flown to Izmir in two days.''

''Welcome news. Until then Miss West and I will amuse ourselves around town. Did the gold survive the night?''

''Two men guarding it.''

''I want it crated, the silver, too.''

''Separately?''

I shook my head. ''Let Mehmet sort it out.''

Kitsos stood up. ''The navigator sends his respects, he's occupied charting us safely to Izmir.'' He gestured at the coast. ''That town is Tanihisar. Presently we'll round Cape Karine. It's a narrow passage with the Greek island of Samos off to port. Is there anything else, sir?''

''All traces of the incident removed?''

''Yes, and the weapons rack rebuilt. Oh, Mehmet's secretary, Giorgio, wants to speak with you.''

''I'd forgotten about him. Where was he during last night's action?''

''He locked himself in the office where he works. Came out this morning.''

"Prudent," I remarked. "I'll see him whenever it's convenient. He may have some ideas about the contraband."

"Yes. Doubtless Mehmet gave him confidential orders."

Kitsos went away then, and I laced a final cup of coffee with Añejo. It was going to take big trucks to transport the loot to Mehmet's place, and Giorgio probably knew how to manage the transfer.

Before I finished my cup a slim young man with curly black hair and a thin, olive face presented himself to us with a bow. "Giorgio Nicolaides at your service."

Melody got up. "I'm going to give myself a shampoo, get the salt out of my hair, then a manicure. See you later."

I told Giorgio to be seated and sized him up as a delicate young fellow. He said, "I want to thank you for saving all our lives."

"Whatever gave you that idea?"

He blushed. "The crew says you killed all six pirates."

"What an idea. Go on."

"I understand you're taking my employer's place while he is away."

"Someone has to."

"Of course. I'll continue my usual routine, then, checking markets, fax messages."

"The big job," I said, "is getting all those amphorae off the yacht and taken to Mehmet's place. Is that something you can arrange?"

He nodded. "I know which Customs officials to pay off, and the right trucking firm."

"Anticipate any problems?"

"No, sir."

"And there's a crate of coins."

"So I understand. I plan to ride with the truck that carries it."

"I don't want crew members ashore until all that's completed. They can have shore leave tomorrow. Tell Captain Kitsos."

"Yes, sir. And allow me to say I regret that your wedding could not take place as planned."

"Thank you. By the way, Miss West and I will be flying out day after tomorrow. To Miami. Can you make reservations?"

"Easily. I suggest flying THY—the Turkish airline—to Istanbul. Transfer to Olympia and change planes at Athens. Then direct to Miami. Will that be satisfactory?"

"It will."

We walked forward, parting at the companionway. I went up to the bridge and found the Second Officer instructing the helmsman. He acknowledged

my arrival and gestured at the restored gun rack. Wood paneling now replaced the shattered glass, and bloodstains had been cleansed from deck
linoleum. I said, "I don't suppose you've had any sleep."

"Not yet, sir. That comes after we reach port. Is there anything you need
or want done?"

"Mainly I'm concerned about getting the contraband ashore. I've dis-
cussed it with Captain Kitsos and Giorgio, who anticipates no problems."

"There have been none in the past." He consulted the chart and had the
helmsman make a course adjustment.

I said, "We were introduced when I arrived, but I'll confess I can't
remember your name."

"Costas. Stefanos Costas, I come from a small town in Northern Greece
near the Bulgarian border—the name is unpronounceable."

After we shook hands he said, "My parents were killed by Communists
and the Government sent me to the naval academy. I served five years in the
regular navy, then transferred to the merchant service. I was fortunate to be
hired by Mr. Kurdlu. I understand he is making a good recovery."

"So far." I glanced aft at the radio shack. Unoccupied. At some point the
radioman had made a fatally wrong decision.

He said, "If you like I'll notify you when we enter the Gulf of Izmir."
I nodded and left the bridge.

In my cabin a steward was taking out clothing to press and launder.
Melody was shampooing in her shower, and in that moment I found life very
good. After we married it was going to be even better.

Captain Kitsos joined us for lunch on the fantail, and pointed out the Izmir
lighthouse as the yacht turned into the Gulf. "Almost there," he said, "and
I'll be glad when this day is over. You'll be staying at Mehmet's palace, I
understand—you and Miss West."

"Palace?" Melody inquired.

"We call it that. Actually, the place was built years ago on the foundations
of an old fortress that was erected four or five hundred years ago during the
Crusades. By the order of the Knights Hospitalers of St. John." He gestured
to starboard. "That's Mount Pagos, associated with Alexander the Great. Today it's a good place to picnic, with olive groves and a fine view of the sea."

"Alexander the Great," Melody echoed. "Think of it."

"Izmir—which used to be called Smyrna—is supposed to be Homer's
birthplace, and it's a mix of cultures: Greek, Persian, Byzantine, Ottoman.
And like Bern the city symbol is a clock tower, the Saat Kulesi in the central

square. Only a hundred years old—modern as things go in this part of the world—but the design is pure Ottoman.''

"Fascinating," Melody responded. "I'm sure we'll see it before we leave.''

"The beaches are among Izmir's best attractions, you should visit them and enjoy the sun and water. Drive along the shoreline promenades by day or night. Restaurants, too.''

"You make it sound very inviting," Melody observed.

"Although I am Greek I must admit that the Turkish side of the Aegean is equal to the Greek coast. And many fewer tourists so there is less crowding.''

As the yacht proceeded into the Gulf we could see the city, the way its buildings rose from sea level into a backdrop of green hills. I excused myself, went to my cabin and got out the silenced Beretta. Reluctantly I dropped it out of the port; it was an excellent weapon and had served me well. But though you could explain a pistol, there was only one use for a silenced one—assassination by stealth. If our cabins were searched, I didn't want the Beretta found.

Topside, the Rolls's steel container was being opened, the limousine backed onto a cargo pallet for transfer to the dock. I spoke to the driver, then moved ahead to the cargo hatch. Below, two armed crewmen were seated beside a large wooden crate. Mehmet's metal treasure. Amphorae had been stacked next to a bulkhead to limit rolling. I estimated over a hundred in all, and thought they must represent one of the largest collections ever raised. It was going to take a lot of trucking to get them to Mehmet's palace.

The yacht was slowing, heading toward a long dock space. On the foredeck crewmen were readying cables to toss to waiting longshoremen below. The yacht began backing, then the bow cable dropped and was secured around a double bollard. The bow winch turned and sprung the yacht to the dock. Then the aft cable was secured. Even before the gangway went down, the Rolls was lifted and swung ashore. Stewards carried our bags down the gangway and the driver opened the trunk, held the door for Melody.

When we were seated the Rolls purred away from the yacht and I glanced back, remembering what had happened on board only fourteen hours ago. A memory I wanted to erase.

Until the a/c kicked in I opened the rear windows and watched breeze ruffle Melody's short hair. "You look about fourteen," I told her. "Are you ever going to grow up?''

She snuggled against me. "Does it excite you?''

"Everything about you excites me—the way it did when I first saw you.

Remember? You were diving in the family pool, and when you surfaced I could hardly breathe.''

"Liar—but I love it. Then you took me to a saloon, forced me to drink strong waters, and when I came to we were naked in bed and you'd had your will of me. What an insensitive brute you were—that cheap, hot-sheet motel on the Beach.''

"Wasn't cheap, they charged by the hour. Dirty movies extra. Anyway, my recollection is you suggested the saloon, and the motel.''

"You popped my cherry there so it's only right you marry me.''

"Don't be gross.''

"Well, you did.''

"But you said you'd had—experience.''

"I knew you wouldn't bed a virgin—especially an underage one.'' Her voice lifted and she crowed, "I was jailbait, San Quentin Quail.''

"That you were.''

"But I never held it over you.''

"Also true. *Basta* with reminiscences, sweetheart. Today is the first day of the rest of our lives.''

"Uh-huh—look how clean the city is, aren't you surprised?''

The driver was following a broad street that branched off and sloped toward the hills. I wondered how things were moving on the *Cygnet.*

The higher we rose, the more impressive the view of city, harbor and sea. We ascended a few minutes more, then the driver turned onto a paved access road and slowed to a halt before a wide grilled gate. He punched a remote control and the gate began rolling aside. When we were through it he pressed the control again and the gate slid shut. Melody said, "I love this Rolls, dear, can we afford one?''

"We can. But you're so frugal with your inheritance I'll have to pay the whole thing. And will—unless you think a Rolls is too ostentatious for the law school parking lot.''

"A Bentley, then—no, it's not top of the line.'' She paused. "How about a big ol' Mercedes?''

"It'll be my wedding gift to you. Incidentally, I'll ask Manny to be best man, and Lucy can give you away. Carmen and Rosario will be flower girls or whatever.''

"Wait a minute. Mother has to be there.''

"If she'll come.''

Melody shook her had. "Damn! I didn't think of that. If I know her she won't want to leave Mehmet's side.''

"Her problem, not ours. The Montijo family is dependable, let's plan on them." With a pang I suddenly remembered Pilar. She'd have to show as part of the family. Not knowing there was ever anything between us, Lucy would insist on it.

"Look!" Melody's cry interrupted my thoughts, and when I saw where she was pointing I gulped. On a promontory, Mehmet's residence looked every inch a palace. Walls of light sandstone matched the original foundations, distinguishable by wind erosion. Broad steps led up to a wide, carved-wood doorway set back under a Mediterranean-style entrance roof. On either side flowers and vines climbed the stone support columns. Swallowing, I said, "I think your mother can be happy here."

"Very happy. Hey, here comes the staff."

Uniformed servants filed down the steps and stood facing each other, porters and butlers on one side, maids on the other. As the driver opened Melody's door a tall man in dove gray cutaway descended the steps to meet us. "The majordomo," the driver whispered. "Kozan."

Reaching us, the majordomo bowed gravely. "Welcome to Yarin. We are here to serve you."

We both said, "Thank you," and nodded to the servants as we went up the entrance steps.

The central corridor was spacious and columned Graeco-Roman style. To the right was an open-sky atrium with floor tiles and a fountain representing the Three Graces. They were clustered together, faces upraised, mouths open. The soaring waterspout gave the impression they were barfing at the sky.

The corridor was lined with heroic busts on pedestals and life-size statuary representing figures from Greek mythology. Here Diana, there Odysseus, Ariadne further along. Homer, Herodotus, Sophocles, Euripides, the ancients stared at us with stone-blind eyes. Behind us the major domo said, "Miss, I believe you will be comfortable in your mother's suite. Sir, there is—"

"Wait a minute," Melody countered, "my husband will be with me."

"Oh, beg pardon, Madam. I did not—"

"No problem. Why don't you lead the way?"

He came from behind and ascended the sweeping balustrade that led to the upper floor. Turkish carpets covered the marble flooring the length of the hallway. At the end, Kozan turned and opened a door that gave out into the sitting room of the suite. Beyond, an immense bedroom. Like the sitting room its walls were tapestried, but so far I had glimpsed none of Mehmet's fabled art collection. That would be elsewhere, doubtless behind lock and key, and I wondered what security was in effect. If any.

Ceiling fans stirred the air and I noticed that our windows were screened and barred. Porters set our bags on racks and two maids came in. Kozan said, "They will unpack for you if you like."

"I like," I responded, but Melody shook her head. "I prefer doing mine."

"Very well." He spoke to the maids and one withdrew. The other, a young woman of thirty or so with a hairy mole on her left cheek, opened my bags and began distributing the contents among dresser drawers and the walk-in closet.

Kozan said, "As you see, the bath is beyond."

I nodded. "As you may know, a shipment of *objets d'art* came on the *Cygnet*."

"I am expecting it. You may take your meals at whatever time you choose, ordering what you prefer."

"Thank you," Melody said. "Right now a bottle of iced champagne would be welcome."

"I will see to it at once." He stepped back, bowed slightly, and closed the door.

Hands on hips, Melody stared around our suite. "It gets better and better, doesn't it? After cabin living this is going to be just fine."

"Agreed. I'm going to check out the shower."

"Not alone, you aren't." She kicked off shoes, pulled off her dress, slip and bra, and was naked before I had my pants off.

As we soaped each other in a shower with vertical and horizontal sprays, I said, "Afterward, what's our program?"

"After—? Oh, dumb me. Well, let's kind of laze around, order dinner for nine or so, and take a drive around town in the cool of the evening."

"Sounds great. What do we order for dinner?"

"Red meat for me—a big, juicy steak. After all that seafood I need sustenance. Say, some asparagus Hollandaise, and a salad."

"Double the order and I'll choose the wine."

Kissing, we let the needle sprays rinse our bodies, and tried to make love standing in the shower. But the wet footing was too slippery and I didn't want passion to end in slapstick, so I grabbed towels and pulled Melody into the bedroom. We were too wet for the bed, and settled down on the thickly carpeted floor. Melody said, "Why do I always have to have a pillow under my hips?"

"It's the way we're made."

"Cave people didn't have pillows," she complained. "How did they get it on?"

"Doggy-style. Now give me those pretty lips so I can smother them with kisses."

*   *   *

When we walked down to the waiting Rolls I heard noises from in back, and went around to investigate.

Two heavy trucks were backed up to the open door of what looked like a large garage—a separate building, anyway. A forklift was hauling amphorae from the trucks and taking them inside the building. Standing at the entrance was Giorgio, pad in hand, checking amphorae numbers. I called to him, and he glanced around, waved, and counted the next load. The coin crate was probably already stored. I went back to the Rolls and got in beside Melody. "The jars are being stashed," I told her, and wondered if their transfer from yacht to trucks had drawn attention. To the driver Melody said, "Just take us around, please. You know the city. Let's start in the center by the clock tower and come back by the promenades."

"Very well, ma'am." He steered down the drive and opened the gate. As we descended into the city two palace-bound trucks strained up the grade. No wonder the galley sank with all that weight.

You would have to care more for clock towers than I do to appreciate Izmir's symbol, the Saat Kulesi. We drove around it and then headed for the promenades. Karsiyaka Promenade reminded me of Nice with its palms and broad waterfront. There were alfresco tables and small specialty restaurants whose lights reflected from the calm water. Across the Gulf, the dark outline of Mount Pagos reminded me that we ought to go sightseeing there tomorrow.

By nine we were back at Yarin, a name the driver told us meant Tomorrow. "I like that," Melody had said, "because we ought to believe everything will be better tomorrow."

The formal dining table could seat a dozen couples with ease. We sat at one end, across from each other, and enjoyed the chef's best efforts. As ordered, our steaks were thick and juicy, the asparagus tender, sauce tart, salad crisp. Each of us had a waitress, and a wine steward stood ready to add more Burgundy to our crystal glasses. We took coffee and cognac on a balconied terrace overlooking the city and Alsancak Harbor. The night was still, no blatting powerboats, no multijet aircraft landing and taking off. In short, we lacked the sounds of Miami, and I didn't miss them. I said so and Melody nodded agreement. "This is such a tranquil spot that I hope Mother will be able to invite us back from time to time." She turned to me. "When do you suppose we can view Mehmet's art gallery?"

"When he returns."

"But we'll be gone."

"I know. Oh, I could have it opened for us but something tells me that's not a great idea. If there was a theft we could be thought responsible, and there's this: I have a feeling Mehmet Kurdlu is one of those international collectors who collect stolen goods. You know—a Rembrandt disappears from The Hague and isn't seen for twenty years. Then an industrialist dies in Singapore and the painting surfaces as part of the estate." I shrugged. "Thieves don't steal notable paintings for pleasure or satisfaction. They do it because there's a lucrative subterranean market they can tap into. The buyers don't exhibit their acquisitions in public or even admit possession, so the thieves run very small risk of blowback."

"My, you know a lot about artistic crime."

"I read the literature, hon. One other thing about stolen art: if thieves can't find a corrupt collector, they'll deal with the insurer, but for a lot less money." I paused, reaching for something, then connected. "Here's something I picked up in my former profession: there's often a connection between art theft and narcotics—big-ticket items paid for with illegal money."

"But I don't believe Mehmet buys stolen goods."

"Why not? You and I, we sat over an ancient cargo vessel while Mehmet plundered it. But for the pirate attack I think he'd have brought up even the nails. The pirates foiled what was to have been the *pièce de résistance*—raising the wreck's statuary Mehmet thought would be more valuable than all the other booty." I sighed. "He'll keep the choice amphorae for his clandestine gallery and sell or trade the rest—after subtracting the coins."

She looked at me. "I'm surprised you think so poorly of Mother's friend."

"Do I have to remind you your mother qualifies as a poor judge of character? Remember that Larry fellow she was seeing even before husband Paul got himself killed?"

"Larry—*ugh*—Parmenter." She made a face. "You're pretty much right. For Mother a man has to be handsome or wealthy, and she seldom finds the combination in one man. At least Mehmet is wealthy."

"No question." I sipped more cognac. "But nobody's told me how he got that way. You were on the yacht with him—did you learn anything?"

"Not really—Mother said he was an entrepreneur, an investor—I wasn't investigating him, after all."

"But for your mother's sake, maybe we should check him out in Standard & Poor's. I'll do it in Miami." I paused. "Absent your objection."

"Go ahead," she sniffed, "and I'm sure you'll find he's perfectly kosher."

I laughed. "Look at me—eating his food, drinking his wine, using his Rolls . . . making me an ingrate."

"Don't say that. You saved his life. That entitles you to find out what kind of life you saved." She clasped my wrist.

"For openers we know he's a thief. And if that isn't bad enough his thievery postponed our wedding."

"In Miami how long will it take?"

"Couple days for license and blood test. I don't know any friendly judge but I know a minister in North Miami who was a Woodstock hippy until he found the Hallelujah Trail. He plays guitar and would toss in a protest song for free."

"Jack, you're outrageous."

"But practical. In biker days his handle was Big Billy. Now he's Billy the Preacher—how's that sound?"

"Terrible. Be serious."

"I am." I hadn't told her Big Billy had been busted for possession with intent, or that he'd done a deuce at the correctional center where I'd interviewed Tito Gallardo. "Anyway, think it over."

"I have, and the bride vetoes it."

"Okay, I surrender." I glanced up and studied the indigo sky. "The stars tell me it's after eleven, meaning bedtime."

"Is that all they tell you?"

"One message per night is what you get without a telescope."

"I never learned that in college."

"Lots of things you didn't learn. But in years ahead, 'round our fireplace, I'll read you most of the things you need for a full and rounded life."

"I have that already. Will you read to the children, too?"

"If my voice holds out." I patted her rump. "Let's hit the sack."

Hand in hand, we strolled along the great hall by the atrium and stopped at what looked like a stone lectern. On it was a thick book bound in leather and brass. Its pages were open for guests' signatures. I dipped a quill pen in the small inkpot and inscribed us as Mr. and Mrs. of Coral Gables, Florida. Melody murmured approvingly and said, "I wonder if Mother signed in." She began turning back the heavy pages, finally spotting her mother's signature: Mrs. Delores Diehl. When she pointed to it I said, "Have to be a sharp-eyed bank clerk to read it," and turned the preceding page to scan it, without knowing why.

In the middle of the page were three signatures: Pasquale, Paolo and Gaspare Cuntrera, Segesta, Sicilia.

I stared in disbelief. These were the three *mafiosi* partners of General Padilla, the ones who had opened the New York heroin franchise to him. Last heard of, they were being tried in Italy, so they must have visited Yarin before their arrest. No date on that page or any page in the guest book.

I was surprised that the brothers could write their names, then noticed all signatures were in the same schoolboy script. One of the swinish brothers signed for the others.

Discovery of their joint visit channeled my thinking along new lines. Was Kurdlu bankrolling the Cuntrera operation? Was he a partner in their billion-dollar enterprise? Was Turkish poppy being processed in Sicily into happy dust sold in Harlem? If the answers were Yes, I'd uncovered a fascinating connection.

In all of it Tito Gallardo had been Padilla's loyal lieutenant, his gofer, and I wondered if he knew the details of the Cuntrera-Kurdlu association.

Melody jiggled my elbow, I flashed back to the present, and she said, "You *are* sleepy. What is so interesting, love?"

"Thought I recognized a name," I lied, and walked with her up the grand staircase. As we neared our suite I tried putting Cuntrera-Padilla out of my mind but when I was lying in bed waiting for Melody I found myself wondering if the pirates had really been after Phoenician gold, or whether they were a six-man Cuntrera hit team dispatched to kill Mehmet Kurdlu.

Vengeance and retribution were sacred among thieves. If Mehmet had crossed Padilla or the Cuntrera brothers they would send assassins until their target was dead.

Our windows were barred but I felt uneasy, and I told myself that the sooner we left Kurdlu's domain the safer we would be. Then Melody was beside me, warm thigh against mine. "Remember me, your bride? Wherever you are, come back to me."

I turned and drew her young, taut nipples against my chest, stroked the soft silk between her loins. "Nice," she murmured, "oh, so nice . . . Now make sweet love to me."

An invitation I couldn't refuse.

TWENTY

Over breakfast in our sitting room I said, "I know it means a great deal to you and your mother that she attend our wedding."

Buttering a croissant, Melody nodded. "So?"

"So I think you should insist she come to Miami."

"I thought you were delighted she wouldn't be with us. And you call *me* changeable . . ."

"Well, circumstances change things, and I realize now that in years ahead you'd blame me for your mother's absence—and I don't want that. So, call her and insist she meet us in Miami."

She gazed at me with narrowed eyes. "You're not telling me everything, Jack, come clean."

"What can I say? I have no relatives and you have only one—your mother, so it's essential she stand up with us."

Melody thought it over. "I was going to call her anyway," she said after a while, "ask about Mehmet and the Captain, so I could easily slip that in."

"Great."

"But remember one thing: Once I invite her I can't cancel the invitation. Won't."

"I wouldn't ask you to." I rang for the majordomo, and when he appeared I told him we wanted to call Kurdlu's hospital room. "Actually," Melody said, "I want to speak first with my mother."

"Of course, madam." While he was placing the call I refilled my coffee cup and carried it into the bathroom. I was shaving when Melody appeared. She said, "Mehmet and Mother will definitely be arriving here tomorrow evening. Shouldn't we stay and greet them?"

"Giorgio dropped off the tickets for our flight. Leaves tomorrow noon."

"Reservations can be changed."

"Sure, but it's a pain in the ass." I lowered the razor. "But I'll do it if your mother will fly with us."

Melody shook her head. "She feels she should stay and be helpful to Mehmet, smother him with attention—you know."

"For how long?"

"Didn't say—my guess is a week or so."

"Then she'll definitely come?" I resumed shaving.

"If we set a date—say ten days from now—she'll have no excuse for not coming."

"Good thinking. Okay, we've gone the extra distance and it's up to Mom."

Melody blew a kiss and walked back into the bedroom.

Showering lather from my face, I decided my strategy was working, if incompletely. Kurdlu's Cuntrera connection and the attempt on his life made his palace dangerous for us and for Melody's mother. To Melody I'd disguised my motive but felt the deception justifiable. As soon as I got back to Miami I was going to huddle with Manny and have him check out Mehmet Kurdlu and his apparent link to the Cuntrera family. Even if all three brothers were jailed, like Padilla they could place contracts. Marginal to my life as Mom was, I didn't want her killed with Kurdlu; Melody would never forgive me.

We took a picnic lunch in the Rolls, and the driver showed us the Cesme Peninsula that formed the south coast of the Gulf. On one side, unspoiled beaches; inland, fields of artichokes and other produce, orchards of fig and gum trees dotting the landscape. We stopped at a taverna for thimbles of syrupy coffee and fried pastry stuffed with cheese, then took the road back to Izmir.

In downtown Kemeralti Market a jeweler set Melody's Phoenician coin in a gold-chain necklace, and expressed admiration for the unusual souvenir. I clasped the chain around her neck reluctantly, for the sight of the coin gave me bad memories. Eventually the necklace was going to turn up missing.

She bought a handmade straw hat, and I selected a switchblade with a horn handle and a five-inch blade. "For slicing salami," I explained, and had the knifemaker whet the edge extra sharp.

From the marketplace we drove round the Bay to the foothills of Mount Pagos, ascended through groves of olive, pistachio and pine to a cleared overlook from which we could look down on Izmir and the Gulf. There were rustic tables and a stone cooking grill set under lofty pines. Melody spread a cloth on the table and opened the picnic basket. We shared lunch with the driver: wine, roast chicken, fresh bread, olives and tangerines, and afterward Melody and I lay back on a bed of pine needles and watched blue sky through the branches above.

At four the driver woke us, gathered up our picnic remnants, and took us back to the palace. Melody ordered dinner at eight, and we napped for an hour.

After dinner the driver took us to a casino on the Kordon Promenade, where I exchanged dollars for Turkish lira, and we played blackjack and roulette. Between losses we sipped champagne and devised new gaming strategies with no better results. By eleven, having contributed five hundred dollars to the local economy, I suggested it was time to leave, and half an hour later we were back in our suite at the palace.

As we stood on the balcony for our final night view of Izmir, Melody said, "I really don't think it would hurt if we stayed another day, Jack. Someone should be here to greet them."

"There's a houseful of servants to greet them, honey, plus guards in that treasure storehouse out back. Mehmet doesn't need us, he needs peace and quiet."

"Still, I'd like to see Mother, confirm she'll be with us in Miami."

"Call her again."

"A call from you might be more persuasive."

"She'd suspect ulterior motives. No, talk to the mother who bore you—whimper if you have to. It always works with me."

She stepped back and surveyed me. "You *are* in a mood, aren't you? Which makes me suspect you do have hidden reasons for wanting Mother in Miami."

I spread my hands innocently. "Just call her, honey. Can't hurt, and you could say goodbye."

"Suppose—I stay another day . . ."

"Then I'd have to say our marriage would fail due to lack of trust."

"You mean that, don't you?" Her lower lip began trembling. "It's such a small thing."

"Size has nothing to do with it." I put my arms on her shoulders. "Call her."

She turned away, went into the bedroom and picked up the telephone. I half-listened to her side of the conversation but I was thinking that one commando strike having failed, the optimum time to launch another was while Mehmet was immobilized by the leg wound. I was indifferent to his fate, but not to Mom's. I wanted her out of here and fast.

The call ended and Melody came out on the balcony. "She'll definitely come for the wedding. Leave here in a week, travel a day and be with us the day before.'' She looked up at me. ''Satisfied?''

''Yep. You did the right thing. Thank you for humoring me. Now let's get to bed.''

Through the barred window I could see a crescent moon free of clouds. Whatever happened to Mehmet Kurdlu would be the result of his own doings. And I thought how appropriate it was that *kismet* was a Turkish word.

We rose early, packed our bags and went down to breakfast. Before leaving I tipped all the servants—double to Kozan—then we got into the Rolls for the short ride to Adnan Menderes Airport, and gave the seaman-driver a hundred in Turkish liras. After a short wait we boarded a DC-9 for the Istanbul leg, and landed at Atatürk Airport in ample time to check in at the Olympic counter.

I always enjoyed First Class travel on a 747, and after takeoff we climbed the spiral staircase to the lounge. There we had cocktails and snacks, and after a while Melody said, ''Now that we're out of Turkey suppose you tell me why you really want Mother to leave.''

''You don't believe what I told you?''

''Uh-uh, uncharacteristic. Level with me.''

I drained my Añejo and looked at her. ''I'll never be able to deceive you, so, okay, here's the story.''

I told her of finding the Cuntreras' names in the palace guest book, and explained who they were and their relationship to General Padilla. I mentioned my suspicion that the pirate strike had been a planned hit on Kurdlu disguised as robbery-hijack, and reminded her that if I was right other attempts would be made—until Kurdlu was dead. ''Lame, he's at his most vulnerable, and if the palace is bombed or slammed by rockets I don't want your mother harmed. So I want her anywhere but with Mehmet.''

''Oh, Jack, you could have told me.''

''I didn't want you inadvertently letting the cat out of the bag. Our wedding is the best possible reason for getting your mother out of a situation she doesn't realize is dangerous. And there's another factor: Mehmet doesn't know I've learned of his Mafia connections. Remember, it's a deep secret, one that could destroy him if revealed. It's one thing to have hit men trying to kill him, another to have him putting out contracts to silence us.'' I took a deep breath. ''Forgive me?''

''Oh, honey''—she kissed my cheeks moistly—''of course I do. But I had reason to be suspicious, didn't I?''

I signaled the bartender for refills, and we worked on them until the Captain ordered all passengers back to their seats for landing.

There was no reason to go into Athens airport, so we stayed in our seats during stopover, and after a while new passengers came down the aisle, jet engines started and we lifted off above Piraeus and the Aegean.

Next stop Miami.

Often as I'd flown in to Miami after dark, the sight of the sparkling coastline and the jutting skyscrapers that formed the city's new skyline never failed to thrill and energize me.

As flaps and wheels shuddered down I woke Melody and said, "We're home."

"Already?"

"You slept most of the crossing."

Blinking, she roused herself, opened her purse and began dabbing at her cheeks. We were curving out over the 'Glades for final approach, and I thought of the poachers' camp where I'd found Manny. All that seemed years ago, and—but I didn't want to reprise the yacht firefight because I'd prevented a hit on a man who probably deserved to die. "Tomorrow," I said, "we'll go to the license bureau and declare our intentions. Then I guess there's a blood test."

She nodded. "Do you know a doctor? Do we have one?"

"Manny's. Dr. Horatio Ing."

She looked at her watch, still on Izmir time. "By now Mother must be at the palace. I'll call her as soon as we're home."

"Just don't say anything that might frighten her."

" 'Course not." Stretching, she said, "I need a shower and a gallon of Scope."

"I need a drink."

"After all you had since Athens?"

"Alcohol metabolizes fast."

"Please don't become an alcoholic, love."

"Alcoholics are born, not made."

"Who says?"

"Me." Through the window, tarmac lights were rushing by. We touched down with a bump and a screech of tires, and slowed. Through the loudspeaker a voice enjoined us to remain in our seats until the aircraft stopped at the gate. The announcement was repeated in several languages and then cabin lights dimmed.

We filed off, cleared Customs and emerged into the hot, humid night. Wary of gypsy drivers from past experience, I flagged a long cream-colored limo, asked if the a/c was working, and helped Melody in.

The ride was cool and comfortable and I counted the fifty dollars well spent. At the house, interior lights showed through the blinds, turned on by the photo-sensor. Melody opened the door and I lugged in our bags. She turned down the thermostat and cool air began blowing from vents as I carried our bags to the bedroom. After dropping her dress Melody began opening our luggage and I headed for the bar. Glass, ice cubes and Añejo. I inhaled the first slug, poured another and felt better than I had since the last one.

The message machine was blinking but I didn't feel like dealing with callers, though I hoped Pilar was not among them. But prudence dictated that I clear the tape before Melody got to it.

When she came out of the bathroom I said, "Shouldn't you report to law school in the morning? We'll hit the license bureau after lunch."

"Unless I have a scheduled class. By the way, where are my books?"

"In your closet."

"Oh. Was there a reason to hide them?"

"No," I lied, "just getting them out of the way."

"Are you telling me the truth or should I be looking for lipsticked Kleen-exes?"

"Look all you want." I'd made a careful search for telltale items before closing the house.

She sighed. "Okay, I'll believe you. Trust has to start somewhere."

I finished my drink before getting into bed. Lights out, we agreed we were too tired for lovemaking and settled for close bodily contact.

Before Melody woke I made morning coffee and I listened to the message tape at low volume. A roofer and a landscaper offered their skilled services, and a dealer in precious metals guaranteed fast return on silver ingots. A law school registrar wanted to know if Miss West was planning to attend this semester, and finally Manny's voice came through. "Thought you'd want to know," he said, "that Tito Gallardo was repatriated, sent back to Venezuela *via* the prisoner-exchange program. He's supposed to serve the rest of his sentence there, but he'll probably find a way not to. Anyway, welcome back, you and Melody, and congratulations on your marriage. Call me."

His was the last message, nothing from Pilar, so that concern evaporated. I woke Melody, told her to get over to law school, and while she was dressing

I cooked sausages and scrambled eggs, toasted muffins, and set the table. She ate quickly and said, "I'll call about lunch. Is the car functional?"

"Will be." We went out and I connected the Miata battery, kissed her and watched her drive off; the law student on her way.

I called Rosalia, the housekeeper, and asked her to come for the day, then phoned Manny's office, left my name with his secretary and considered Manny's news.

Gallardo's deportation was the good part; the downside was realizing Tito was not necessarily in a Venezuelan prison. He blamed me for the murder of his girlfriend, Marlena. A Blue Panther biker had slit her throat and was now equally dead; but if Gallardo sought misguided vengeance, how could I dissuade him? No way. He was back where he had access to unlimited funds, and a few thousand would lay a contract on me. Pocket change for him.

During the flight from Athens I'd thought of visiting Tito at Lewisburg and exploring the Padilla-Kurdlu connection, but I hadn't known the bird was flown. I thought I could take care of myself, but I had a loved one who would shortly be my wife, and his twisted mind might figure I should lose her as he had lost Marlena.

So when Manny called I got quickly to the point. "If Gallardo isn't on the Caracas watch list, how about adding him?"

"Yeah, but what's your concern?"

"Remember his girlfriend, Marlena?"

"Sure. She's dead."

"Well, Tito got it into his head I was responsible. So if he disappears from his usual haunts I'll want to know."

"That's reasonable. Say, what happened to the wedding?"

"Long and complicated, but we plan on about a week from now. Delores will be matron and you're best man, okay?"

"Absolutely."

"But harking back to realities, Delores has been kicking around the Mediterranean and Aegean seas with an interesting elderly Turkish millionaire who has a genuine palace in Izmir. Mehmet Kurdlu."

For a moment he said nothing. Then, "*The* Mehmet Kurdlu, I presume."

"Uh-huh. I don't like to mouth sensitive stuff by phone, but I may have uncovered an unattractive side to the gentleman. If you can stop by—Melody has the car at school—I'll tell you about it, and a bunch of other stuff."

"I've got a loaded desk, but when I can shake free I'll give you a call."

"Right. Just to stay ahead of the curve, how about running a printout on the fellow? I won't say more now, but he has some low-life friends."

"Check later." He hung up and I felt as though I'd gotten something moving.

Chimes sounded, and I let Rosalia in. She picked up mail I hadn't got around to, and laid it on the coffee table. "Do your usual thing, *mi amor*," I told her, "and I'll stay out of your way."

She looked around. "Is the *señorita* here?"

"At the university."

She frowned. "You should marry her."

"Soon," I replied and began opening bills while she got busy with breakfast dishes.

Writing checks always increased my heart rate so I downed a preventive dram and finished paying the most pressing bills. Melody called to say lunch was out, it looked like a long day and she'd be home when she could, probably not until evening. I expressed appropriate sorrow, and after hanging up told myself I might as well get used to my wife's long hours away. Well, we'd apply to the license bureau tomorrow, early or late.

Manny rang from his car phone, said he was en route, so I got into clothing and found a can of Coke for him. On duty he wouldn't have even a Corona.

We greeted each other with fraternal *abrazos*, then settled down on the sofa. Coke for him, a touch of Añejo for me. I told him about the *Cygnet* attack, and my suspicion that the pirates had been commissioned to hit Kurdlu. "Reinforced," I concluded, "by finding some interesting names inscribed in the palace guest book.

He sipped thoughtfully. "How interesting?"

"All three Cuntrera brothers."

"That *is* interesting." He sat forward and drummed fingers on the table. "As to Kurdlu you're right about one thing—he's got a lot of money. Real estate in Turkey, Malta, Cyprus and Rhodes. A hotel and two restaurants in Athens. A shipping company headquartered in Piraeus that works Aegean and Mediterranean ports . . . and an investment firm in Monaco. Clean as far as anyone knows."

"Except for the Sicilian connection."

"The *possible* Sicilian connection."

"Kurdlu wouldn't host strangers."

"No, he wouldn't. So how does it shape up to you?"

"I think his money is dirty. I think he's been financing poppy-growing for the Cuntreras, whose product Padilla pushed in Manhattan."

"Theory."

"Admittedly. So why not check Cuntrera associations and see if Kurdlu figures. Or his Monaco investment firm."

"That's reasonable. And you figure some pissed-off associates put a contract on him."

"Someone did. Let's try this: maybe the Cuntreras paid him for a big load of gum opium. They got jailed and Kurdlu never delivered. They hit him because he didn't return the money." I paused. "It's not a unique scenario."

He grunted. "And your mother-in-law-to-be has been palling around with him."

"Hell, you know Delores. The guy's got a yacht and a palace. For her those are big bona fides. I wanted her to come with us yesterday, but she agreed only to show up for the wedding. If she's still there when *pistoleros* try again, tough luck, Mom."

He drank from his glass. Somewhere unseen Rosalia was humming a Paraguayan forest tune. Manny asked, "How much does Melody know?"

"Everything I've told you. She knows her mother is in a possibly dangerous situation, and it worries her."

"Naturally. Well, you've given me a few things to work on. Incidentally, Cousin Pilar wants Carmen to finish her schooling in Spain."

"Sounds like a splendid idea."

"Also, I get the strong impression that Pilar misses you more than she would some casual acquaintance."

"She's a fine young woman," I observed, "and her family will do all the right things for Carmen."

"She'll go with Pilar over Christmas vacation."

"Good decision." I drained my glass and set it down. "Did you add Gallardo to the Caracas watch list?"

"I did, and asked for confirmation that he was jailed on arrival. If he's released I'm to be notified."

"Shugrue giving you any trouble?"

"He's been pretty subdued since I got back, but I expect him to stab me whenever he can."

"Jamey okay?"

"I see more of him when Rosario's home than at the office. Yes, he seems to be doing all right."

"Good. I know his intentions are honorable."

"I inferred as much, but so far I've heard nothing officially."

"Meaning what?"

He shrugged. "He hasn't declared himself to me, and Rosario is close-mouthed."

"Manny, they're not rushing toward marriage. They're sober, serious young people and they're giving proper thought to a possible future. Leave them alone, they can find their own way.''

''Wait'll you have daughters,'' he grumped.

''Hold on. Jamey did considerable to help me locate you—at the risk of his job, I should add. Now, if you want a stand-up guy for a son-in-law you could do worse.''

''I didn't know he helped.''

''We kept it quiet—for obvious reasons.''

''Well—thanks for telling me. Stand-up guy? Hmmm. Always came off kinda meek.''

''You terrify him. Listen, Manny, I know you didn't like Washington duty, but you and your family might be better off there than in Miami.''

''By 'better off' you mean safer?''

I nodded. ''That's the translation. Take a nice house in Spring Valley and let Rosario transfer to American U or George Washington.''

He smiled. ''Suddenly you're my career counselor.''

''I've been that all along.''

''Well, I'll give it some thought.'' He got up.

''No time for lunch?''

''Sorry—still got a lot of catch-up to do. Plus what you've laid on me. Just let me know the date, the place and the time. I'll be there.''

''I'm counting on you. No reception plans yet, but there'll be one, and your family is invited.''

He eyed me. ''Cousin Pilar, too?''

''If she likes. Call you for lunch.''

I locked the door after him, reflecting that he'd confirmed what I'd feared—being back in the same milieu with Pilar wasn't going to be easy. Not for me, probably not for her. But I was fully committed to Melody, a fact that had to stay foremost in my mind.

That thought segued into the realization that I'd never bought Melody a ring, engagement or wedding. We'd simply reached the point of deciding to marry and I hadn't been thoughtful enough to do the conventional thing. Well, there were plenty of jewelers in the Gables where I could find a nice platinum-mounted rock for my honey, with matching wedding band. In Bern I'd been too obsessed trying to collect from the Guats to think of rings. As Melody occasionally said, Dumb me. Well, now that I was finally aware, I was ready to make amends.

Too, at law school she was among males who were a lot younger and brighter than me, and the right ring on her finger was insurance against approach.

Around three Melody returned with a satchel of books and a dazed expression. "Honey," she said, "this is pretty formidable—I'm not sure I can stick it out."

"Sure you can. They say first year law is the hardest."

She dropped her books and plumped down on the sofa. "I'm famished—anything I can gnaw on?"

"Aside from your lifetime supply of yoghurt, not much. But check the freezer and I'll lay in real food later."

"Mother call?"

"Not yet." Chimes sounded and I went to the door. Through the peephole I saw the distorted figure of a man apparently well dressed. "Yes?" I called.

"Braman Motors. Delivering."

"Braman?" My thoughts flashed back to Jay Gerschwin's secretary, Mrs. Margolis, but he held up a small envelope inscribed with our names. Curious, I opened the door and the man stepped aside. In the drive stood a silver Rolls Corniche with a black fabric top—a twin of Kurdlu's except for the color. Behind me Melody blurted, "What's this? What's going on?"

He handed her the envelope. "Keys, ma'am, the Rolls is yours."

TWENTY-ONE

SHE STARED at the sleek Corniche, dazzling in the sunlight. "Mine?"

"I believe there is a card with the keys."

Slowly she opened the envelope. The white card bore a message in calligraphic script: *From Mehmet and Mother. Congratulations on your marriage, and long life.*

She turned to me. "Jack, I don't *believe* it!"

"Believe it. Solves the second-car problem, but—" I drew her inside and said to the Braman man "—this is a shock so give us a moment or two."

After closing the door I hugged Melody. "Honey, we can't keep it."

"We—can't? Why on earth not?"

"We'd be hypocrites, me anyway."

She frowned. "Maybe you better explain."

"Sure. Mehmet's corrupt and I want him destroyed. How could I accept a gift from him?"

"Well—it's from Mother, too," she objected.

"Realistically, from Mehmet Kurdlu. With dirty money."

She bit her lower lip. "You could think of it as payment for saving his life."

"Something I've been regretting. No, the car goes."

"Jack, I can't believe you're doing this. Don't I have anything to say?"

"Haven't you said it? You want the Rolls, I don't, so let's compromise." I opened the door and spoke to Braman's man. "It's a fantastic car, but right now we have no place to shelter it—and a Rolls invites vandals. So, until we're in a position to keep it safely we'd like it under your care."

"I see." He shifted uneasily. "I suppose we can accommodate you though it's quite unusual." He drew out a sheaf of papers and a pen. "Please sign acknowledgment of delivery."

I passed the pen to Melody. She hesitated, then slowly signed the form and handed back the keys. Reluctantly. The man gave us a business card. "Call me when you're ready to take delivery."

"We will," I said, "and thank you. We'll get all our Rolls from you."

"Glad to oblige," he responded, went down and unlocked the driver's side door. The engine started so silently we couldn't hear it from thirty feet away. Then it slid down the drive like molten silver and I closed the front door. Melody stamped her foot. "Bastard! Where do you get off refusing to take *my* car?"

"Jointly owned. It'll be safe pending ultimate disposition."

"Whatever that means. Jack how can you be so *cruel*?"

"It's best to establish ethical standards at the onset. We don't accept presents bought with dirty money. Not ever. I'll print a sign to that effect, hang it in our bedroom if the point needs further emphasis."

She turned away, walked toward the kitchen. "You can't prove Mehmet deals narcotics."

"Give me time, I haven't begun to try."

She jerked open the freezer door, drew out a frozen dinner and slammed it into the microwave. After setting the timer she turned to me. "You're very high-handed, you know, macho and chauvinist."

"And insensitive. Okay, we've had our first disagreement and it's over. Let it lie. Have lunch and study if that's on the time-line. We'll go out for dinner."

"Where? Burger King?"

"Joe's."

"I'll accept—as a peace offering. Shouldn't I call Mother now and thank them for the present?"

"You should."

"What time is it in Izmir?"

I glanced at my watch. "After ten PM. Encourage her to come earlier, say you miss her dreadfully, need emotional support."

"After what you just did I certainly do."

"Call her."

The Rolls was gone from the drive but my Miata was at the curb. I got into it and drove to the Gables, where I bought red meats, fresh fruits and vegetables, breads and frozen supplies. By the time I got back to the house, Melody was snoozing on our bed, and Rosalia was tiptoeing around to avoid waking *la señorita*. I wished Rosalia was equally considerate of me.

We were getting ready to leave for the famous stone crab restaurant when the phone rang. Melody answered, then handed the receiver to me. "Manny."

"Speak to me, *compadre*," I said cheerfully, then frowned at what he had to say. "Jack, the Caracas office reports Gallardo arrived by plane and was taken off in a police van. Only he never got to the prison."

"Rats!"

"Yeah. So he could be anywhere."

"Used the van as a taxi home."

"Looks that way. The office will report any sightings."

"Please make sure he's on our port-of-entry watch lists."

"I have."

"Thanks for letting me know. If he comes after me or mine, his body bag is waiting." I replaced the receiver and Melody asked, "Bad news?"

"Unwelcome." As we drove over to the Beach I told her how Gallardo figured in Manny's abduction, and why he might try to harm me.

She sighed. "It's almost as though you never left DEA. I do hope we'll have a tranquil life together."

"God knows, I do, too."

At Joe's I turned the Miata over to the valet and we went in and enjoyed a fabulous meal of the regional delicacy. Then home, where I watched TV while Melody cracked her books.

Next afternoon we went to city hall and applied for a marriage license. Afterward Dr. Horatio Ing came to the house and drew blood for the tests, said he would send the results by courier. Melody suggested sounding out the minister of a small Protestant church in Coconut Grove. "I went there a few times while I was at Ransom Everglades School and I liked the atmosphere."

"Whatever you choose, hon."

"Afterward we can hold the reception at the Grove Isle Club—I think Mother's still a member. How many will there be?"

"Well, you, me and Mom, plus Manny and his family—four or five."

"I thought it was just Manny, Lucy and the two girls."

"Well, a Montijo cousin is over from Spain, teaching at FIU. Oh, and there's Rosario's boyfriend, Jamey, who works in Manny's office."

"Ten, then. Is the cousin as nice as Manny?"

I nodded. "Even looks like a Montijo. That branch makes wine and brandy." I got off the subject fast. "Do you want to stop by the church tomorrow?"

"I could do that after classes. Or you. And I'll ask Mother about the reception. Honey, I really need to study now. We'll just have a small, quick dinner, okay?"

When she was at her desk I opened the floor safe and got out two packs of currency, ten thousand in all, and drove down to Miracle Mile. At Riviera Jewelers I told the saleslady what I wanted and she brought out two velvet trays of platinum-mounted diamonds. After narrowing choices I paid for a three-carat brilliant-cut stone, with matching wedding band. "If the size isn't right my fiancée will come in."

"That's customary," she assured me, and began gift-wrapping my purchase while the cashier vetted each of my hundred-dollar bills. A wise precaution considering the amount of Iranian-made queer circulating in Miami.

Back home I grilled lambchops, made salads and set the dinette, then called Melody. She noticed the small ribboned package on her plate, and said, "What's this?"

"Peace offering."

"Really?" She undid the wrapping, stared at the velvet box and exclaimed, "Oh, darling! If it's what I think it is—"

"Open it."

She did. I put the diamond on her finger and she dissolved in tears. Finally she dried her eyes and said, "It's beautiful, and it makes everything real. You didn't need to, you know." She turned her hand and lights made the facets sparkle like tiny flames.

"Compensation for the Rolls," I said. "No, that's not so. Actually it's because I love you and you should have had a ring long ago."

"And what a ring!" She gazed at it admiringly. "Must have cost a fortune."

"Let's say it's affordable. Now, what kind of car would you like—other than the Rolls?"

"The Miata's fine."

"I was thinking of something larger, for trips. Space for bags, diving gear, fishing tackle."

She nodded. "Good thinking. Anything but a pickup, dear."

"Promise. Now let's eat."

In the morning, after Melody left for law school, sparkler on her finger like a talisman to ward off evil, I phoned Braman's and asked for Mr. Ostergard, who had delivered and taken back the Rolls Corniche. Rather frostily, he asked, "Are you ready to accept your Rolls?"

"Not yet. Today I'm interested in a BMW."

"Lease?"

"Buy. If you've got a four-door, black, white or ivory, in stock I'd appreciate your bringing it here—with all the papers."

Much more warmly he asked, "Is there a color preference, sir?"

"Basic black is always acceptable. Ivory next, then white. Can do?"

"I'm sure I can meet your requirements."

"Waxed, polished, a/c icy, oiled, lubricated and full tank."

"I understand. Ah—how will payment be made?"

"In full on acceptance."

"Very good, sir. Before noon."

I resisted tossing him a fruity *toute à l'heure*, and complimented myself for restraint. Okay, that much accomplished. Unless Melody had Saturday classes we were free to travel tomorrow or do whatever the hell we wanted. I had in mind a day's fishing out of Tavernier or Islamorada, but Melody might prefer diving at Abaco and overnighting at the Inn. I'd enjoy that, too. Months had passed since I'd strapped on tanks and gone down. That image recalled Kurdlu's divers plundering the Phoenician galley, and I was glad I hadn't joined them on the seabed. Eyeballing the site would have made me more complicit than I already was; if interrogated I could honestly say I'd seen amphorae lifting from the sea, nothing more. Though I didn't expect Kurdlu would ever be charged with looting antiquities.

The telephone interrupted my thoughts, and it was Manny with a disturbing report. Tito Gallardo had been spotted leaving Caracas on a flight to Mexico City under the alias Juan Peralta. "Bad news," I remarked. "He's getting closer to Florida, and he won't have to cross at a legal entry point. Not when he can join a gang of wetbacks and wade across anywhere along our two thousand mile border."

"Unfortunately true. As of now he's on the Federal fugitive list."

"Big deal," I grunted. "I don't have overpowering faith in the Marshals catching him."

"Me neither, *hermano*."

"Thanks for the warning."

"I'll stay in touch."

After making fresh coffee, I poured a mug and added a splash of Añejo. One day Cuba would be free and Bacardi would again be distilled at Santiago, though the Puerto Rican variant was passably good. Meanwhile, the blend steadied my shaving hand, and while I was dressing the door chimes sounded and Jamey was there.

"Just a welcome home visit," he said as he came in. "Everything okay?"

"Seems to be. Melody's at school, and you're invited to the wedding."

"So Manny told me—thanks, look forward to it. What day?"

"Wednesday or Thursday, whenever Melody's mother arrives. Montijo ladies okay?"

He nodded. "All of them. Incidentally, it looks like Carmen will be finishing school in Spain, courtesy of Cousin Pilar and her family."

"I endorse the idea," I said, not mentioning I'd originated it.

"And I'm looking forward to meeting your fiancée—everyone knows her but me."

"Maybe not until the wedding, Jamey, she's not here much, and when she is she's studying."

"Yeah. Always heard first year law was a bastard." He looked around. "Enjoy the cruise?"

"Mostly."

"I thought you were planning on getting married on the yacht."

"We were but—well, the owner was hospitalized, so we came home."

"Well, anything I can do, give me a call."

"As before."

He drove off and I opened my floor safe, extracted forty-five thousand green and waited for Ostergard to arrive.

He pulled up shortly before noon, in a black four-door BMW polished to a mirror finish. I kicked the tires, listened to the almost-silent engine and felt the a/c's frigid blast, before telling him I'd take it.

"But, Mr. Novak, you never asked the price."

"I must have been too excited."

"Oh. Well, the sales manager said because you already have a Braman Rolls you get a five-percent discount on the BMW."

"A twofer, eh? Terrific. Got the papers? Let's go inside."

He showed me the bottom-line figure, which included an alarm system, cellular phone, tag and impact fee. I gave him cash, and after counting it he said weakly, "I don't think I've ever seen so much currency at one time."

"Then you weren't around when the Cocaine Cowboys flourished."

"No, I was working in Duluth."

"Not a bad place to be in those years." I got up. "The Rolls is secure?"

"Yes, sir. Under nylon dust covering. Ah—have you any idea how long before you'll want it?"

"Not really. Thanks for taking care of everything."

"A pleasure to do business with you. Any little problems, just let me know."

"Depend on it."

He gave me the keys and the alarm remote, showed me how to use it. "There's an option I didn't think you'd be interested in, so I didn't mention it."

"What's that?"

"Remote ignition and door opener."

"You mean, so I can start the engine from a safe—ah, from across the street?"

"Even farther. Are you interested in the option?"

"Definitely. Installation take long?"

"If I take back the BMW now, I can return it by, say, six o'clock. Will that be satisfactory?"

I gave him back the keys, watched him drive away.

At least in his eyes I didn't fit the profile of a customer who might want or need an anti-bomb device, but with Tito Gallardo on the loose I wanted whatever edge money could buy.

True to his word, Ostergard had the BMW back before six, and gave me a remote-starting demonstration that persuaded me the extra money was well spent. When she arrived, Melody said she was delighted with our new car. While we were discussing its features I pressed the remote starter and the unexpected sound startled her—until I showed her the control. "Now you can unlock doors and start the engine from a distance. So you won't be vulnerable getting out keys—I'm thinking of you in some parking lot after dark." And me anywhere, anytime.

"I'm certainly impressed, dear. Is the new car mine or yours?"

"Ours, precious. Fifty-fifty, we share everything right down the middle." As we began walking into the house, she said, "I stopped off at the Grove church and met the minister. He's young and sort of progressive, but he said he'd be glad to meld us—his word. Thursday evening okay?"

"If your mother's here."

"She promised. Reception at the Grove Isle, so tell Manny and Lucy, okay?"

"Great. Any classes tomorrow?"

"No, but I ought to spend time at the libe."

"Then let's get away Sunday, go down to the Keys."

"Wonderful."

Saturday evening we ran the BMW 740 eighty-five miles to Islamorada and checked into the Oceanside, an upscale resort on the ocean side of the Key. After unpacking in our suite, we had a drink on the balcony and looked out over the darkening Atlantic. Then we drove to the Green Turtle for conch fritters and broiled yellowtail, and turned in early.

Overnight, wind had picked up, and offshore whitecaps told us there'd be no fishing or diving today. No sun either, so we visited craft shops and bought a few handmade silver items for Melody: brooches, pendants and bracelets, all with marine themes. Devoured Florida lobsters at the Crack'd Conch along with conch chowder, alligator soup and key lime pie. Then we drove back to Miami, well before the northbound rush began.

On the way, Melody said, "Think we ought to have a weekend hideaway in the Keys?"

"If you like—I had one but Andrew blew it away, so I'm reluctant to invest in another. Besides, if the Keys have anything it's comfortable resorts, the advantage being the rooms are always ready and there's no maintenance, no overhead."

"I suppose you're right—still, so many people have condos and hideaways we ought to consider it—okay?"

"Okay."

The Miata was occupying the garage, so we pulled into the drive, and I suggested having a canvas canopy installed to shelter the new car from the elements. "Want plain color or stripes?" I asked as we walked toward the entrance.

"Stripes, I think, green and white."

"I'll order it tomorrow," I said, thinking it would enhance frontal appearance for Mom's approval.

As I was unlocking the door I heard a car coming slowly down the street as though the driver was looking for a street number. Something made me turn and watch the black four-door Lincoln as it came by. And though the windows were tinted I thought I saw something glinting—like a gun barrel—so I pushed Melody inside and ducked down. The Lincoln speeded up and tore down the block, tires screeching as it took the turn. No taillights, so I couldn't read the license tag, and I realized what had made me watch it was the absence of headlights; not a casual passage. I got up and Melody peered out, saying, "What was that all about?"

"Sorry. Lotta drive-by shootings, hon." I shrugged. "Probably only burglars casing the area." I carried our bags inside and locked the door, then armed the alarm system. The car's lack of lights, stealthy approach and fast getaway convinced me the driver knew exactly where he was, knew where I lived, and had spotted me.

While Melody settled in at her desk for study, I poured a long drink of Añejo, gulped half of it, and wondered how in God's name I could protect her.

TWENTY-TWO

A<small>FTER</small> M<small>ELODY</small> drove off to class in our new BMW, I got on the phone and called four Yellow Page advertisers of driveway car shelters. One's phone had been disconnected, and the other three said they were swamped by post-hurricane business, call back in three months. The last fellow I spoke with said business had never been better, and referred to his product as *porte-cochères*. I thought that was a pretty toney description of what was essentially a low canvas tent raised on gas pipes, but every business has its own jargon and deceptions.

I poured the last of our breakfast coffee, spilled a bit of aged rum into it and pondered how to deal with last night's drive-by occurrence. I doubted that Tito Gallardo was at the wheel, or even riding in the blacked-out Lincoln, but there was no shortage of thugs ready to kill for pay. Why hadn't they sprayed us with bullets last night? Because they were on reconnaissance, surveying target accessibility, and maybe hadn't gotten final word to take me out. But if Tito was behind them, trouble could come very soon.

I got out my .380 AMT backup pistol and checked its five-shot magazine, jacked a shell into the chamber and added a cartridge to the mag before homing it in the grip. Six dependable *amigos*. Then I strapped a black Cordura nylon holster around my right ankle and slid the backup into it, securing the pistol with a Velcro strap. My trouser cuff concealed it nicely.

When Rosalia arrived I told her I'd be gone for several hours and she should keep doors locked and alarm set. My instructions didn't upset her because she'd heard them before, so nodding understandingly she began tidying the living room while humming an unfamiliar tropical tune.

The Church of the Divine Reconciliation—Melody's church of preference—was located off Main Highway a few blocks from Melody's old prep school. Of dark weathered coral, the small church stood in a clearing surrounded by tall ficus and Australian pine. I parked the Miata around back and walked to the door of a separate one-story dwelling I took to be the parish house. Through open windows I could hear music—flute and piano—so I waited until the duet ended before knocking.

A pleasant-faced young man opened the door. For his youth he had very little topside hair; he wore rimless lenses, a blue denim shirt over a white turnaround collar, and held a long silver flute in one hand.

"Peace, brother," he greeted me, "how may I serve you?"

"You can marry me next Thursday," I told him. "Melody West's fiancé, Jack Novak."

"Yes, yes," he nodded. "You have the secular forms?"

I handed them to him. His lips pursed as he read the official boilerplate. Then he squinted at me. "It's customary to interview the groom as well as the bride before the church sanctions the ceremony, but the moment is inopportune." He smiled apologetically. "I'm rehearsing liturgical music, and my accompanist is only briefly available."

His head turned and I looked beyond him to a spinet where sat a comely lass of perhaps eighteen summers. Like the padre she wore rimless lenses and a patient expression. Hands rested demurely on the folds of her flowered organdy dress. She was a busty child and I wondered if her mother knew where she was, but said, "I understand, padre, another time, then."

"Yes, yes," he responded in relieved tones. "Oh, I'm Father Fedder— Miss West may have told you. Father Peter Fedder." We shook hands. His was warm, damp and limp. "Ah—I might mention that during the post-nuptial reception—Grove Isle, isn't it?—Charity and I would be pleased to provide a musical background."

"Splendid idea," I replied, "and I'll check the bride's desires." Gazing at the pianist, I said, "I ought to mention that alcohol will be served."

"Oh—oh—" He managed a smile. "I get your meaning. That is not a problem."

Charity struck a chord with I thought excessive force, and called, "Peter, we really must continue."

"At once, my dear." Another reassuring clerical smile and the door closed. I walked back to the Miata unprepared to certify that the parson had a good thing going with the pianist, but circumstances looked about right. A couple of generations back, it would have been preacher and organist getting it on in the choir loft, but perhaps I was doing flautist and pianist an injustice. My snap judgments were often terribly wrong.

From Coconut Grove I picked up US 1 and followed it south past the Metro Detention Center, where I'd first encountered Tito Gallardo. Then all the way to Florida City and El Rancherito, the dope-dealing biker hangout where I'd questioned and paid the late Marlena Gomez.

It was the same sleazy rustic-style building whose signs advertised Good Eats, Country Music, Nude Dancing and half-price Ladies Hour. All that plus Icy Cold Beer. *This Is The Place* proclaimed the sign over the entrance door, and that hadn't changed either.

On my previous visit there had been three bikes, two cars and a pickup in the parking lot. Today's numbers were reduced to two pickups with light bars and antler gun racks. I'd downsized the biker gang by several members, and a resentful rattler had terminated another, so I wasn't surprised at the shortage of motorcycles. Only one was visible, a heavily chromed, gussied-up antique Harley, modern helmets on the seats. I mounted board steps to the plank porch and entered the drinking premises, asking myself if I'd come on a fool's errand.

The dim interior bore the same musty smell of stale beer, sour barbecue sauce and rancid fry oil. An old man was sweeping paper plates and cups from the dance floor, where weekend revelry had been unrestrained. He looked dispirited and arthritic, like a DEA quality informant.

Seated on bar stools were three men and a woman. The latter was fitted into a black leather jacket, black Spandex shorts and black leather boots. A black SS cap crowned her cropped black hair. All the leather apparel was brightly studded—including the wide choker around her neck. From it trailed a chrome-link chain long enough to touch the floor. Her biker boyfriend was similarly attired, except for black trousers stuffed into boot tops. He laid down a short, thick cigar, and got ready to arm-wrestle one of the other men.

The female bartender eased toward them to watch the contest. She was a different bartender than Trudi, who had directed Marlena to my booth a month ago. Trudi had colored tassels on her nipples, and suede shorts that emphasized her sex. This one wore a bandeau-type half-bra that showed the aureoles of her oversized globes. Well, this was the day's early shift and things could get lots worse.

I slid onto a stool a couple of yards from the arm-wrestlers and the bartender collected stakes, easily twenty-five dollars. She glanced at me and tossed her head. "Get to you soon's this's done, okay?"

"Okay."

"Hey, wanna bet a few?"

"Wouldn't mind. Who's who?"

"This here's Wheeler"—she gestured at the male biker—"and this other piece-a-shit's Orlando.'' At that everyone laughed, including me. The biker femme's came out as a manic shriek. When things calmed down I asked, ''Odds?''

''Wheeler's two ta one.''

I laid fifty on the bar. ''Orlando.''

She snatched up the bill, laid down ten. ''You're covered an' you're crazy.''

''I'm backing Orlando.''

Her face screwed up as though her brain was permuting an insoluble problem. Finally her features relaxed. ''Why?''

''Been a loser,'' I told her. ''Let's see how it goes.''

Orlando gave me an appreciative nod. The bartender lifted a glass and let it drop on the counter sink. At the crash the contest began.

Wheeler took an early lead, angling the smaller man's forearm downward, then Orlando began gasping, veins bulged in his forehead, and inch by inch he forced Wheeler's arm up until both were vertical, a hollow A. Standoff. Wheeler's lips drew back, showing yellow teeth, he grunted like a carabao, and put his back into a second try. Orlando was ready for it, and in the split second it took Wheeler to tense up Orlando pushed hard and Wheeler's hand hit the bar. The biker swore and reached under his jacket but by then I was off my stool and standing between them. ''Fair fight,'' I said, ''and my loser won. So forget the money, I'll buy the drinks.''

Orlando wiped sweat from his forehead. ''Thanks for backing me, mister.''

''Yeah,'' the biker growled, ''that gave him the edge, bud.''

Bottles and shot glasses appeared on the bar. The biker femme, who hadn't said anything, gazed at me with interest. Her face was hard and angular with a thin pinched nose, but her eyes were soft and corrupt. She lifted a shot glass, tilted it toward me and downed it in a single toss. The biker didn't like that, so he snatched her collar chain and yanked it down. Her chin hit the bar and she yelped.

The biker laughed and jerked her chain again. ''Cocksucker!'' she screeched, and began to sob. Orlando and the unnamed third man poured shots and nodded thanks. The bartender spread her arms, palms on the bar, and asked ''What's yours?''

''Corona, if you got it.''

''Bud.''

''I'll take Bud.''

She handed over a dripping glass and uncapped the bottle. ''What'd you come for?''

"I like arm-wrestling."

"Shee-it," she said scornfully, "tell me a fuckin' other."

"The sign says nude dancing. Meaning I get to dance nude?"

She thought that was pretty funny. "If you wanta—but this ain't no gay bar."

"Maybe you're the nude dancer?"

"Could be—only this pays better." She looked at the biker couple who were reconciling in a tight embrace. Wheeler had one hand in her tight pants and was working on her crotch. "Hey," the bartender called, "ya wanta fuck, go outside." The femme looked at her with glassy eyes.

The bartender turned to me. "Saturday night a guy was eatin' out his girlfriend on the bar. Right here." She slapped the spot for emphasis. "Lucky no cops'n deputies around." She poured a Crown Royal for herself and kicked it back. "Hey, Wanda," she said loudly, and the femme blinked, sat up. "Yeah?"

"Stranger came in for nude dancin'. You wanta fill in for Shirley Ann?"

Wanda looked at Wheeler. "I dunno. Where's Shirley Ann?"

"Ridin' the calico pony. Well?"

Wheeler said, "What's in it for Wanda?"

"Thrills," I said, "and ten bucks."

"For twenty she goes."

I laid two tens on the bar and he grabbed them before she could, then pushed her off the stool. To the bartender Wanda said, "Let's have some music."

"Sure." She shoved a tape in the player and a heavy beat blasted from corner speakers. Trailing her chain, Wanda moved unsteadily to the platform. In a low voice the bartender said, "We had a real great stripper but she got knifed."

"No kiddin'. Boyfriend trouble?"

"Somethin' like that—who knows?"

With very little grace Wanda was shedding her costume. Cap, boots, jacket—and finally she peeled off the tight shorts. Her bush was thick and black. Collar still on, she twirled the link chain while making a series of pelvic thrusts. The men applauded.

Her small breasts were about the size of limes, with pointed nipples. She caressed them with her hands, grasped the pole and began sliding up and down it erotically. Her buns were taut and muscled from cycle-riding and one showed a Blue Panther tattoo. Overall, her naked hipless figure was slim and dykey.

She was gyrating awkwardly, and her bumps and grinds lagged increasingly behind the pounding beat. Finally she grasped the pole with both hands and slid to the floor, legs splayed. I led the applause until Wheeler strode to the platform, grabbed her leash and yanked her to her feet. He slapped both cheeks hard and yelled, "Dumb cunt, don't ever try that again!"

Whimpering, Wanda stooped over, picking up her costume, and the bartender cut the music. To me she said, "Wasn't worth no twenty, right?"

I nodded. "That stripper you mentioned—the good one who got knifed—name wasn't Marlena, was it?"

Her head jerked back. "How'd you know?"

"*Shit!* I did time with her boyfriend—he told me to see Marlena if I needed help."

"Who's the boyfriend?"

"Tito."

She nodded. "Seen him lately?"

"They put him on the Lewisburg bus before I got out."

She looked away, then back. "What kinda help you had in mind?"

"I'm not particular—anything that pays."

She leaned closer. "Anything?"

"So long's it pays."

Still on the platform a dejected Wanda was putting on her costume. Wheeler was back on his stool pouring another Crown Royal. The bartender said, "Let's get acquainted—I'm Bernice, they call me Bernie. What's your handle?"

"Pete." We shook hands.

"Well, Pete, I got nothin' for you right now, but check back in a day or so, okay?"

"Sure."

"After I check with Tito."

I stared at her. "What—?"

"He's out an' movin around. With a hard-on for the guy who cut Marlena."

"Serious?"

"Yeah—don't ask me how he got loose, but he did."

I shook my head in wonderment. "You saw him?"

"This time yesterday." She gestured at the biker. "Wheeler saw him, too. They talked a while, went out together."

"With Wanda?"

"Yeah. You like Wanda?"

"Why?"

"For ten you can take her back in the dressing room."

I grunted. "Not with Wheeler around."

She laughed and pushed back from the bar. "Smart. Very smart."

Orlando and his pal left the bar and went outside. Probably to sit on a park bench, watch the girls go by and count wedgies. I asked for another Bud and studied Wheeler with new interest. His unshaven face was squarish, with close-set eyes and heavy brows. A beer-belly bulged over his studded belt. He licked thick lips and poured another shot from the bottle. Bernie uncapped the Bud and filled my glass. "You could ask Wheeler," she suggested.

"Rather talk to Tito. When's he around?"

She shrugged. "Like I say, he come yesterday."

"I'll call you."

"Before eight, Pete. I get off at eight."

I pulled out my roll. "What's the tab?"

"You already paid," she said, but accepted a ten and tucked it away in deep cleavage. I swallowed half my beer and got off the stool just as Wanda arrived. "How'd I do?" she asked me.

"Great," I told her. "Professional."

Wheeler snorted. "You like Wanda? You shoulda seen Marlena—big hooters an' all the right moves. I c'n get hard just thinkin' about her."

Plaintively Wanda said, "I can't help I was born with little tits."

He grabbed her leash and pulled her face down between his legs. "Who you callin' cocksucker, bitch? Let's see who sucks cock around here."

While he was opening his fly I said, "Gotta go," and walked off through the swinging doors.

Outside air jolted my lungs and cleared my head. I got into my car and drove out the way I'd come.

Leaving Florida City, I reflected that the Rancherito visit had produced more than I'd expected. I'd won an arm-wrestling bet, seen raunchy nude dancing and confirmed that Tito Gallardo had returned to his former haunts.

With a burning desire to kill me.

TWENTY-THREE

WHEN I got back to the house I found a note from Rosalia saying her sister had taken sick, and so she'd left early. Well, my shirts could wait ironing another day or two. But Melody's slacks, I noticed, had been starch-ironed and folded neatly on her bureau. More evidence of domestic discrimination.

Twelve-thirty. I phoned Manny's office and learned he'd left for lunch, the purpose of my call. So I moped around and made myself a salami-and-cheese sandwich, downed a glass of milk and heard the door chimes. Manny?

Hardly. Professor Pilar Marisol de la Gracia y Montijo, looking fresh and even more lovely than when we parted. "Pilar!"

As she stepped inside she gave me an odd look. "You *are* expecting me?"

"I—ah, well . . ." I swallowed, feeling totally inadequate.

She put down her purse. "Jack, don't you *ever* clear your message machine?" I glanced at it and, son-of-a-bitch, the red light was blinking. Angrily, it seemed to me. "I feel like a fool," I admitted, "despite which I'm very glad you're here."

She looked around. "Melody? I came to meet Melody. Since she knows the rest of the family I wanted to meet her, too—before the wedding."

"Please sit down. Listen, she'll be desolated she wasn't here, but she's in class at law school."

She smiled wickedly. "Have you ever considered what it will be like married to someone who thinks logically?"

"Meaning I don't?"

"You tend to act before you think—impulsively, emotionally. Not that it's a completely negative trait—you're still alive, after all."

"And you're biting me to bits. Forget that, I can't tell you how glad I am to see you. Here. Before the wedding." What was I saying? All was confusion. "I think," I said, "I better have a drink. You?"

"Why not? I have no classes this afternoon—arranged for a substitute so I could meet your fiancée."

"Tres Reales?"

"Um—I think a bit strong for midday. Is there *manzanilla?*"

Light wine for her, brandy for me. I brought back our drinks. Our glasses touched, and she said, "Tell me about your Mediterranean cruise."

"Aegean, actually—Manny tell you anything?"

"Nothing. Why? Something I shouldn't know?"

"Well, we didn't get married at sea, as planned. Obviously. Our host, a Turk named Mehmet Kurdlu, had to be hospitalized, and well, Melody was missing classes, so we came back." I licked my lips. "Melody's mother will arrive in a day or so."

"Church ceremony, I believe?"

"Grove Reconciliation. Fadder Fedder—I mean, *Father* Fedder." I shook my head in disgust at my tongue-tied confusion. "Anyway, small reception at the Grove Isle Club—you know everyone who—"

"Except your bride—and her mother, of course."

"She's, well, Delores isn't easy to take. Has a place in Bay Harbor, but likes traveling abroad. And Melody and I like it that way. Pilar"—I took her hand—"there's no reason you and Melody can't be friends. You have a great deal in common—I mean that."

She smoothed skirt fabric across her thigh. "We have you in common, haven't we? As for the rest—that remains to be seen."

I summoned enough courage to blurt, "I missed you. Thought about you constantly. Couldn't get you out of my mind."

"Interesting," she observed. "I missed you, thought about you far too much, and couldn't get you out of my mind." She sipped from her glass. "Where does that leave us?"

"God knows, I don't know."

She shrugged. "When you left, I thought we'd forsworn each other. Forever."

"So did I." I touched a stray wisp of hair, replaced it behind her ear. God, she was ravishing! No woman had a right to be so well-formed, intelligent and beautiful. I was hyperventilating, heart pounding.

In tones of resignation she said, "But it's not working, is it? I mean, I feel about you now as I did before you went away. Even so I tell myself I'll feel differently after you're married. And you, Jack, how will you feel?"

"I don't know—but if the past is prologue I'll be, well, remembering you."

For a while we said nothing, absorbed in common thoughts. Finally she kissed my cheek. "Is it likely we'll be caught *in flagrante?*"

"Unlikely."

"You have the most to lose—risk it?"

"Hell couldn't prevent me." I kissed her full lips then; her body stiffened, then relaxed. I unbuttoned her silk blouse and nuzzled her breasts. She moaned and pressed my head. "Can't wait," I said hoarsely, and pulled off my trousers. Her back arched as she drew down her panties. Roughly, I pushed up her skirt and, unbelievably, we were making love.

In the aftermath I felt physically drained, psychologically shaken and entirely whole. Quietly I said, "You're right, I *am* impulsive."

"And I'm glad." She raised my hand to her lips, kissed each finger in turn. "Guilt?"

"Not now—you?"

"No, Jack, we're two people who care deeply about each other. Desire was natural, and we quenched it."

"Not entirely."

"I hope not." She stretched and sat up. From the confining sofa we'd moved to the floor near our discarded clothing. I got up and filled our glasses, brought them back. Taking hers, she said, "Your body has some interesting scars. Line of duty?"

"Mostly, the rest unofficial."

"Working for Manny?"

"Working for myself."

Her brow furrowed. "In what way?"

I settled down beside her. "It goes like this. Manny's office—the DEA—is interested in recovering or destroying narcotics. They don't care about the money involved. So I do the narcotics job and liberate the money."

"You keep it?"

"I try."

"Is that—ethical?"

"I never asked—but I know this, I can't spend thank-you notes." I hesitated. "Why? Do you care?"

"Curious mostly. Because I never knew anyone like you—even faintly resembling you. So I try to analyze what makes you—you. I hope you don't mind."

"Nothing you could ever do would disturb me."

"Nothing?"

"Never seeing you again."

She breathed deeply. "We must be realistic, *querido*. Your wife will

deserve all your attention and affection—that's how it has to be. I don't want
a clandestine affair, and I think you're too honorable to pursue one.''

I stroked her hair. ''That's your line in the sand.''

''It is. Please honor it.''

I swallowed. ''In the future.''

''That's what I meant.''

I drew her down on the carpet, held her tightly. We kissed, passion rose,
and presently we made love again.

Dressing in the bedroom, I heard Pilar singing in the shower. She came out
drying her body and then put on her clothing. ''Look how wrinkled my dress
is.''

''Casualty of a good cause.''

''I'm glad Melody won't see me like this.''

So am I, I thought, but said nothing. She took her purse to the bathroom,
powdered her face and put on lipstick. The Kleenex she put carefully in her
purse. ''Does Melody know anything about me?''

''She knows Manny's Spanish cousin is teaching here, not that cousin's
sex or name.''

''Well, you should tell her I came by to introduce myself—the message on
your answering maching will confirm.''

I nodded.

''It's after three, dear, I don't think we ought to push our luck.''

''I don't want you to go.''

''Obviously I can't stay.'' Together we left the bedroom and stopped in the
living room while she straightened sofa cushions. ''Don't forget the glasses,''
she warned, and smiled sadly. ''I could never be comfortable in a clandestine
love affair—the haunting fear of discovery, so many incriminating details to
attend to, conceal. The joy would drain away and I'd be just another adul-
teress.''

''I hate the word.''

She moved to the door. ''We've said our goodbyes, my love. To prolong
it—'' She swallowed. ''I'll see you at the wedding.''

''Yes.''

''And I want the two of you to share all the happiness in the world.''

''Thank you—for everything.'' I opened the door then, and watched her go
down the walk to her Jaguar. She unlocked the door, got in and waved to me.
When her car was partway down the street I noticed another car pulling away
from the opposite curb. Pilar turned left at the intersection and the other car,

a gray Mercury Marquis with muddy license plate, also made a left turn. Was Pilar being followed? I could think of no reason for it. There was no overt connection between us—she couldn't be endangered as Melody might be—so I dismissed the idea and for a while read mail, paid bills and tried not to think of Pilar.

Melody came in around four-thirty and I greeted her with the affection she deserved. After she'd unloaded her books I mentioned that Manny's cousin had come by to meet her before the wedding. She listened to the answering machine and turned to me. "*Girl* cousin? You didn't tell me."

"I didn't?"

"You did not."

" 'Cousin' is gender-neutral, sorry."

"Is she attractive?"

"Yes."

"Well, I want to see her."

"You will. I told her you'd be sorry you missed her."

After she rewound the answering tape I asked, "Did I do something wrong?"

"Hope not, lover. At this point in our lives I don't want female competition."

"Look, I saw her a few times while Manny was missing. She offered two million to ransom him, so—"

"She *did*?"

"Strong family feeling there. Now, let's have a drink and I'll do dinner."

"Make mine light—I have to study." Her head rotated and she said, "My neck is killing me from bending over books. The drink will help, along with a hot shower."

After dinner I rinsed dishes while Melody returned to her studies. Pilar's *manzanilla* glass was already in the dishwasher, and seeing it recalled our hours together—and how she'd driven away, possibly tailed by the gray car. I watched evening TV news, but the thought kept recurring until, finally, I phoned Pilar's apartment. No answer, but that wasn't necessarily cause for concern.

That came an hour later when Manny phoned to ask if I knew where his cousin was.

"No, but she came by at midday hoping to meet Melody. Haven't seen her since."

"Probably nothing," he said unconvincingly, "but it's not like her to miss a family dinner. Look, if she makes contact let me know, will you?"

"Of course—is Jamey there?"

"He and Rosario are getting ready to go to a movie."

"Have him check Pilar's place first. She could be sleeping, you know."

"Let's hope," he said, "but frankly, I'm worried."

"So am I. A lone female in a luxury car . . . around Miami anything could happen."

"Don't I know it. Well, if I hear anything I'll call." He rang off and I sat phone in hand, wondering if I should have mentioned the gray car. I was at least as worried as Manny, and with greater reason. Still, Pilar could have forgotten the family dinner and gone off to dine alone. Or returned to the university. Anything but what I feared most.

When Melody came out for a breather I told her about Manny's call. She said, "Aren't you two over-reacting? As a professor she's a responsible person, and—"

"Honey, this is Miami where cars are hijacked and tourists shot, it's not like Spain."

"If Manny's that concerned he ought to tell the police."

I poured a long drink and decided I ought to tell Manny about the gray car. I didn't want to add to his worries, but as family head he should know. I was reaching reluctantly for the phone when it rang. I grabbed it, expecting Manny's voice telling me everything was okay, Pilar was— Instead I heard a gruff male voice snarling, *"Novak, you killed my woman, I'm gonna kill yours."*

"Wait," I pleaded. *"Don't—"* but the line was dead and I sat alone in a silent room. Too stunned to react.

TWENTY-FOUR

WHEN MY mind began functioning—how long after the call I couldn't guess—I found solace that Gallardo had cut me off. Off-guard as I was, I would have blurted that he'd taken the wrong woman. If he believed me he'd have killed her forthwith. If not, he might let her live a little longer.

Melody came in asking "What were you shouting about?"

I told her and she abruptly sat down. "That black Lincoln last night . . . you warned me. Gallardo?"

"Yes."

"You have to tell Manny right away." Her features were tense, white spots above her cheekbones. "First Manny, now his cousin." She breathed deeply. "How could it be?"

"They've been watching the house, saw Pilar arrive, drive away. Never having seen you clearly, or her ever, they snatched Pilar."

"Thinking it was me." She shivered. "Jack, call Manny. Now."

After I got it all out Manny said heavily, "This is bad, Jack, very bad. Sure it's Gallardo?"

"I'm sure." With Melody listening, I told him of my return visit to El Rancherito and what I'd learned. For a while Manny said nothing. When he finally spoke he said, "Any ideas?"

"I'm still groping with reality."

He grunted. "You're our tracer of lost persons, *amigo*. You found me, you can find Pilar."

Alive or dead? I wondered, but said, "Okay, no publicity. Tell the Bureau and the Marshals that Gallardo's back, not mentioning Pilar's abduction. Get a printout on this biker, Wheeler. He's a Blue Panther, done time and could be on parole." I looked at Melody. "We've got a Catch-22. If and when Tito realizes Pilar isn't my fianceé he'll kill her and try for Melody."

"Does he know Melody's name?"

"Doesn't have to—she lives here, lives with me." I swallowed. "It may be too late for your cousin, but we can still protect Melody. She has to disappear."

Melody said, "I can go to the Bay Harbor house."

"It's empty. No servants, no protection. Manny, can you take her in for a while?"

"Of course, gladly. More than welcome."

"Because while I'm out roaming around I need the certainty that she's safe."

"She will be."

"And I may need help from Jamey, so fill him in."

"Will do. Anything else?"

"Two or three stun grenades."

"I'm going to the office for the printout, I'll collect them there."

"All right. I'll stay by the phone until I hear from you. Melody will leave now." I hung up and Melody rose. "I'll pack a bag, take my books." She touched my face. "I love you. And it frightens and confuses me that you're putting yourself in danger for a woman you say you hardly know, and I don't know at all."

"First, she's part of Manny's family. Second, she was kidnapped in your place. Remember that. And she's a prisoner—maybe dead—because she came here to meet you. Third, Gallardo's gone way over the line. It's one thing to threaten me, another to kidnap a woman he thinks is you. I didn't kill his Marlena, a biker did, but she's dead. Gallardo's crazed. There's no reasoning with him so he has to go down."

"Killed by you?"

"Someone has to. We can't live securely as long as he's alive. If he'd snatched you, threatened your life, I'd be going after him just as I am for taking Pilar." I gazed at her troubled eyes. "She's a complete innocent in all this, has no idea of the life I've led, the enemies I've made. I don't even want to think what may be happening to her. So be patient with me, tolerant. Because chance made Pilar the victim Tito intended to be you."

She swallowed. "I wasn't thinking—I'm sorry."

"I've given you the best answers I can. Now, Manny's family is waiting for you. I'll see you soon." Taking her in my arms, I gave her a long kiss. "I'll be thinking of you."

She was about to say something, decided not to, and went off to pack a bag. I stared at the phone as though it were a venomous reptile. Then I remembered my voice recorder, and set it up with a suction mike on the

receiver. Two rings would activate it, get the tape moving. Melody came in
with a suitcase and her bookbag. We kissed again and I let her out, watched
her go down to the BMW. She started the engine and unlocked the doors with
her remote transmitter. She drove away and no car followed. I locked the
front door and got busy.

With Velcro straps I taped my Izmir switchblade to my left inner thigh and the
AMT .380 in its nylon holster to my right ankle. From my concealed arms
cache I got out a MAC-10 and loaded the 9mm mag with Black Talon ammo,
whose possession by civilians was illegal. After adding a sling to the weapon
I decided to take along the cased night-vision scope. My Astra .38 pistol I stuck
in my belt, and put scope and machine pistol in a black athletic bag. Then I put
on a dark denim jacket to hide the Astra, and poured Añejo over a short glass
of cubes. By now, I thought, Melody was safe at Manny's, but I didn't want
to dwell on where Pilar might be. Not knowing when or how the night would
end, I placed the Añejo bottle in my carry-bag and waited for Manny to arrive.

Instead, it was Jamey with the Wheeler printout and a brown bag contain-
ing four concussion canisters—stun grenades. He said, "I went to Pilar's
apartment with Rosario, but the place was dark, nobody there." He glanced
at the recorder wired into the phone. "More calls?"

I shook my head and spread the printout on the coffee table.

"Wheeler" was the biker handle of Willard Whatley Skoler, age thirty-
four, eighteen arrests and four years incarceration between jails and prisons.
Member Blue Panther biker gang, involved in narcotics, robbery and car
theft. On parole for another three years. His parole officer was named but it
was too late to call the office. Skoler/Wheeler's address was given as a trailer
park near Florida City, no telephone.

"Not much there," Jamey remarked.

"Marginally useful. I think he's one of the men who snatched Pilar, could
be guarding her. Anyway, Gallardo contacted him at the bar hangout Sunday
and they left together."

"So if you find Skoler you can get to Gallardo."

"Maybe." I looked at the silent telephone. "I think Tito will call again,
taunt me. If Pilar's alive he may let me hear her voice to torture me." I wet
my lips. "Let's have coffee."

I got the percolator going and after a while we poured mugs and sat silently
until Jamey said, "I want to help, tell me what I can do."

"Been thinking about that. I want to switch cars with you, the Miata's too
visible by night."

He nodded and handed me his keys. I gave him the Miata's and stared at the telephone. Finally I picked it up, and dialed Information for El Rancherito's number. After five rings a woman answered and I asked for Bernice.

"Bernie? She quit at eight."

"Maybe she's still around."

"Yeah—who wants her?"

"Pete—just tell her Pete, okay?"

"Hang on, Pete."

The music was overpoweringly loud. Boot stomping and rodeo yells added to the din. Maybe a stripper was on stage. "Pete? Hey, howya doin' ?"

"Fair, Bernie, just fair. Lissen, anything come up for me?"

"Y'mean—work?"

"What I mean."

"Hey, I tole ya call in a couple days, din I?"

"Yeah but I got itchy, thought maybe you was strippin' tonight."

She shrieked drunkenly; too much tapping into the house sauce. "Me? My date wouldn' like that."

"But I would. Heard you got an A-Number-One figure. That right?"

"Who said?"

"Guy who claims to know."

"Yeah? Guess I know who, and he wasn' lyin'."

"So?"

"Not tonight, Pete. Hey, you got the hots for me or somethin' ?"

"Why'd I call you, babe?"

"Yeah, thoughta that. But tonight we don' connect—like, I got a date."

"My bad luck, uh—little Wanda there?"

Another cackling laugh. "You wanna take Wanda in the back room?"

"Not if you'll entertain me there."

"Hey, you're some character, don' care who you fuck. Yeah, I seen Wanda."

"Wheeler, too?"

"Nah, din show."

"Good. So if she's alone and lonely I'll stop by."

"Wait a sec, okay?" Pause. "She's at the bar. Yeah, I see her. Where you at, Pete?"

"Halfway down the Keys. Be there half an hour, but I don't go for no passed-out broads—tell her, willya?"

"Okay, Pete, see ya."

"Bernie, you're a pal."

After I hung up, Jamey gave me an odd look. "What was that all about?"

"Paving a path to Wheeler." I shrugged. "Not like I have a world of options."

"And Wanda is—?"

"His girlfriend."

"Got it." He smiled approvingly.

The phone rang, its shrill sound knifing through the room. Jamey and I looked at each other. After the second ring, when the tape was moving, I picked up the receiver. "Novak? This *rubia* says she ain't your woman. That right?"

"I'd have to see her to tell. Let me see her, Tito, then we'll do business."

"Business? What kinda business?"

"Anything you say. Put her on the phone."

"You tellin' me what to do? *Me?* I gonna kill her, then you. Slow."

"Killing a woman proves nothing," I said tightly. "Any *puto* can do that. You want me. I'll meet you any place, any time. Man to man."

In the silence while he thought it over some background sound came through. Finally he said, "You killed *my* woman, Marlena, who never did you no trouble."

"I didn't kill her, never touched her. Rusty did."

"Rusty?"

"Lozano's orders."

He paused before saying, "They're dead, *hombre*."

"So you should be happy. Let the *rubia* go, Tito. Meet me, and we'll talk—or fight."

"Fuck you, you lyin' *cabrón*. Ya wanna talk to the *rubia*? Listen."

A wail rose into a shriek of pain. *Pilar.* I stiffened and yelled, "Don't! Stop it!" The cries continued until Gallardo chuckled gloatingly. "Maybe I let you see her," and ended the call.

My hands trembled. Jamey was white-faced. "Jesus," he groaned, "oh, Jesus."

I rewound the tape, motioned him over. We listened intently, ran the tape again before I shut it off. "What do you make of the background sound?"

"Powerboat?"

I nodded, remembering my hours in Lozano's *Sabre.* "Or a big tractor rig barreling down the highway."

Jamey said, "Either he's near deep water or a heavy truck route."

"That covers most of Florida." I listened again, and said, "I wonder if he'd be crazy enough to use Lozano's place?"

"Why not? He doesn't connect you with it."

"All right," I said, "I'll check it out. If he's there I'll take him. If not—well, there's the Wanda card."

He got up. "I'll go with you."

I shook my head. "Stay here, monitor the phone. If he calls, answer and listen. Grunt like me. Okay?"

"If that's what you want."

"As long as he thinks I'm here he won't be watching his back." I opened my black bag, put in the stun grenades, and zipped it shut. I was ready to go.

"See you," I said, and went out.

Twenty minutes later I drove slowly past Lozano's house on North Bayshore. Moonlight showed the fire-destroyed dock; the house was dark. Around it, uncut grass stood foot-high and shrubbery was growing wild. There was a red band across the front door, and a white paper notice taped to it. The Feds had grabbed the property for forfeiture and neglected it. Neighbors were probably none too happy.

Still, it was possible Gallardo, his thugs and Pilar were inside, so I parked the Corolla three houses away, walked back and went slowly around the house, listening at each window. Nothing.

I went back to Jamey's wheels and drove over to I-95. Heading south, I prayed Wanda would be sober enough to talk.

She was the only lead I had.

And every lost minute drew Pilar closer to death.

BOOK
FOUR

TWENTY-FIVE

THERE ARE times when you think back and remember major mistakes you've made, and during the long drive south I enumerated and analyzed them. Pilar had called me impulsive and I had to concede she'd been right. Too often I'd acted without projecting consequences, so now with Pilar's life at stake I had to think things through, leave no margin for error.

Problem was I had no plan.

Mist drifted across the highway, clouds obscured the moon. My thoughts were of love and death and the curious conjunction they sometimes formed. I loved Melody; we'd been lovers so long that marriage was the inevitable outcome. And marry we would.

But I remembered Pilar, who said she loved me, and when we were together I felt I loved her, too. But a man was not supposed to love two women at the same time. Pilar's danger, I knew, intensified my feelings for her. When we were together she thrilled me. When I was with Melody I felt comfortable, which was not the same as being thrilled. I believed Melody and I could share a solid life but my passion for Pilar was unsought and irresistible. Like Sarita Rojas, my lost love, whom I would always remember and mourn.

Streetlights shone less frequently, the highway narrowed, and I knew I was nearing the place. An hour had passed since my call to Bernie the bartender and by now Wanda could well be too drunk to talk. Sobering her would take precious time, so I hoped she'd heeded Bernie's injunction to take it easy on the sauce.

I wondered if Gallardo had phoned again and what he'd said to Jamey. Maybe only more of Pilar's agonized screaming. I felt suddenly cold, and shivered.

Then I saw El Rancherito's roadside sign and slowed to turn in. The parking lot held maybe twenty cars plus pickups and two motorcycles, neither Wheeler's fancy Harley. I found an open space near the entrance, parked and killed the engine. Before going in I stashed my weapons bag in the trunk and locked it.

Show time.

A lively crowd was dancing to country music blasting from large corner speakers. Although the platform was empty I flashed to Wanda's less than exciting dance. I stood to one side of the entrance and looked the crowd over, finally spotting Bernie at a booth with a guy in soiled work clothes. Across from them sat Wanda, SS cap on her head, but no dog collar; master was missing tonight. Her hands toyed with a beer bottle, and I was glad she wasn't knocking back Crown Royal. Yet.

Bernie saw me coming, half-rose, and beckoned. Wanda turned and smiled. When I got there Bernie said, "Take a seat, Pete, took your time gettin' here."

"Accident at Largo, cops slowed everyone down." The excuse was standard; one stretch was called Death Mile, with reason.

"Say hello to Jason," Bernie commanded. "Jase, meet Pete." We shook hands though Jason's expression was far from welcoming. I slid in beside Wanda and said, "Sweet thing, I been thinkin' about you."

"Yeah? What kinda thoughts?" she challenged, her smile broadening.

"You want I should reveal them in public?"

Bernie roared with laughter. "Go on, Pete, tell it all."

I sighed. "Had to do with you'n me, Wanda." I hooked her arm with mine. "Now, y'all can use your imagination."

Jason said, "What line of work, Pete?"

"Like I told Bernie, anything that pays."

"Do cars?"

"Yeah."

"I got a connection when you got one."

"I'll remember that," I said, and flagged a waitress. "What'll it be, friends?"

Wanda said, "Crown Royal, Betty," and Bernie said, "Two of the same for us." I said, "Make it four."

"Will do." Betty pushed her way through the crowd, and I asked, "What y'all been doin' so far tonight?"

"Havin' fun," Bernie replied. Her pink face was damp, and mascara blurred her eyelids. Wanda said, "Nothin' much, Pete, but maybe things'll pick up now you're here."

"I'm for a good time," I declared, "and little Wanda's gonna see I get it. Right, honey-pie?"

"Damn right. I took a likin' to you when you was here before, so I don't see no problems between us." She snuggled against me. "You like a guy ready to fuck or frolic."

"At the same time," I agreed. "You, baby?"

"Hey, we're on the same wavelength, we gonna do fine together."

I squeezed her hand. "If the crowd was smaller I'd ask you to do that great nude dance for us, but—"

"You liked it, huh?" Her chin lifted proudly.

"Turned me on, babe, what can I say? But for the gorilla I'da carried you off to a lonely place."

"That so? Wish you had."

Drinks arrived, I paid with a twenty and told Betty to keep the change. Bernie leaned forward and spoke to Wanda. "I tole ya he was a free spender."

Shyly Wanda said, "Good lookin', too." She touched her glass to mine, and drained hers without blink or quiver. Sauce was an old friend to this baby, but I'd known that before. I patted her hand and said, "Honey, we gotta get outa here. Too much noise."

"An' too many people," Bernie said with a coarse laugh. "Treat her right, Pete, you'll be glad you did."

I laid another twenty on the table. "This oughta cover 'til we get back." I got up and eased Wanda off the seat. "Where we goin', lover?" she asked.

"Where you'n me can get to know each other a lot better than we do. Maybe you've got some ideas."

"Motel is a couple blocks away."

I shook my head. "No credit card, no ID. Let's try your place, sweetness."

"Well, it's kinda messy, but if you don't mind . . ."

We were on the porch and I steadied her down the steps. "Who needs a suite to play grabass?"

"Not me. So long as Wheeler don' come back, we're okay."

I unlocked the Corolla, let her in and went around the other side. I started the engine and asked, "He comin' back tonight?"

"Nah," she snorted. "Doin' a job for a friend."

Bingo.

She moved over beside me and stroked my thigh. "Easy," I said, "keep that up and we'll end up in the swamp."

She giggled and her hand lay still. "Turn right, an' it's maybe a half mile. I'll show you."

"An' that's not all you're gonna show me, right?" I smiled lecherously.

"Whatever you want," she said, and snuggled closer. "Guess you don' mind small titties."

"That pair o' lovin' mouthfuls' all I need."

"Jesus, Pete, you got a way a turnin' me on. Le's go faster."

We reached the Palm Tree Trailer Park—No Pets, No Kids—and turned into a lighted dirt road that led through two ranks of mobile homes, trailers and RVs mounted on masonry blocks. "Last one on the right," she directed, and I pulled around the dark side. We got out, I locked the doors, and followed her into the unlighted trailer. She turned on a dim table light, and latched the door. Bedclothes were rumpled and stained, dishes and cutlery piled in the sink. A roach scuttled across threadbare carpeting. "Want music?" she asked.

"Had all I could take at the bar. Anything to drink around here?"

She opened a cabinet and brought out a Crown Royal bottle that had been worked on. After rinsing two glasses she divided the remaining liquor between them, took a long pull and shook herself like a dog. I said, "Down the hatch," and sipped lightly. "I shoulda brought a bottle, right?"

"Manager sells bottles." She pulled off the leather jacket and a brown tank-top. Her small breasts seemed even smaller than before. Then she hooked her thumbs in the Spandex shorts and eased them off. In the dim orange light her skinny figure looked worse than I remembered it. This close I could see blue bruises and lacerations on arms, belly, thighs, and ass. A dark band circled her neck where the dog collar rasped her flesh. Another battered female. Wheeler should be flayed with a bullwhip.

She came to me, looped her arms around my neck and licked her lips. "Feelin' generous, Pete?"

"You'll see." Her crotch grinding against me made it hard to get out my roll. I peeled off five hundred-dollar bills and the grinding stopped as she gasped. "For me?"

"For openers." I sat on a folding chair. "Don't want to disappoint you, sugar, but I'm not in a sexy mood." I gave her the bills. She stared at them before sliding them in a boot. "Why'd you come? What's the dough for?"

"Information, honey." I counted out five more bills and fanned them. Squatting on her haunches, she stared up at me. "What information?" she asked querulously. "Like, about what?"

"The situation is this. Wheeler—I mean Willard Skoler—treats you like shit, drags you around like a dog, makes you give head in public, and keeps your money. The way things go between the two of you, one of you is soon going to end up dead, and it won't be Willard."

She licked her lips. "Who—who—are you?" she blurted. "Wheeler don't tell no one his name."

"With reason, because he's on parole for a long time. Another bust and he does life. The biker's handle is registered with law enforcement—which is how I know.''

Her eyes narrowed. ''You a cop?''

''Maybe,'' I said, ''but think of me as your savior. Why? Because I can get you out of this kennel before Willard murders you. That's point one. Point two is this: Willard kidnapped a woman on Tito Gallardo's orders. Maybe Willard doesn't know it but Tito plans to kill her. If that happens Willard will be guilty of felony murder which means a seat in Ol' Sparky. The strange thing is that Willard kidnapped the wrong woman, only Tito doesn't care. He'll kill her anyway. Wanda, you live here with Willard, you go with him, ride with him, you're known as his woman. When Willard goes down you go with him, and go a long way. Accessory gets twenty-five minimum, no parole.''

''I don't know nothin' about what he's doin','' she said hoarsely. ''Can't jail me for not knowin'.''

''Then you don't know the law. Ignorance is no excuse, so if you understand that I can help you.''

She got up, shielding her black bush with her hands. ''Help me? You lied to me, tricked me, got me here pretending we was gonna party.''

''And gave you five hundred for your time. Would an enemy do that?'' I waved the other five under her nose. ''I got you here because it's your home, where you're comfortable and not threatened. That's why we're not in a motel.'' I drew in a deep breath, my mouth and throat were dry. I swallowed more rye, coughed, and went on. ''I haven't threatened you, haven't touched you. But I could do bad things with a knife and leave you dead, drive away, and one day your murder would be on *Unsolved Mysteries.* But you don't want that because you're not as dumb as Willard says, not dumb at all. You've got five hundred now, and you ought to try for another five—plane fare anywhere you want to go.'' I touched her chin. ''A better life, Wanda. You hearing me?''

''What I gotta do?'' she whispered.

''Tell me where Willard is.''

''I—I dunno.''

I shook my head sorrowfully. ''Why don't I believe you? You were with Willard when Tito came in and made the deal. You went with them, heard it all.''

Her eyes welled and she began to sniffle. ''You—who tole you?''

''Not important.'' I had her on the downslide but couldn't push too fast. So I glanced around the trailer and said, ''Maybe I'll shake down this pigsty, find a little pot, some smack, a pistol. One call and you're in the slammer for prostitution and possession with intent. And if I can't get Willard for kidnap-murder he still does the rest of his time plus ten for parole violation, narcotics possession and firearms possession by a felon. For the next five years you can exchange letters—if he can write—and after you're out you can visit him Sunday afternoons.'' I paused. ''Or would you rather cooperate and leave here with a cool thousand in your boots?''

She looked down and toed the carpet, knuckled her wet eyes. ''Wheeler'd kill me,'' she sniffled.

''If you stay with him he'll kill you sooner or later. Look at your body, for God's sake, and realize all the punching and kicking is only a beginning.'' I shook my head. ''Ah, Jesus, Wanda, do something for yourself. I like you, feel sorry for you and want to help you.'' I paused to let the words sink in. ''But you got to help me save an innocent woman's life.''

She swallowed, looked at me tearfully. ''Would Wheeler have to know?''

''Not from me. Who's to tell him? Now, cut the bullshit and level. Where are they?''

She licked her lips again. ''I get the whole thousand?''

I laid the five bills on the chair. ''Talk.''

With a long sigh she sank down on the edge of the bed. ''Tito drove us from the bar—''

''What car? Lincoln? Mercury Marquis?''

Her eyes widened. ''Lincoln—how'd you know?''

''I know enough to tell if you're truthful. What color?''

''Black.''

''Where'd you go?''

She swallowed again. ''Near Homestead. There's a kind of a warehouse building beat up from the hurricane, nobody minding it.''

''Go on.''

''There's lights an' water, Tito's been stayin' there.'' She looked at me pleadingly. ''Tito tole Wheeler to steal a car an' go with one of his Spanish guys to Coral Gables, bring back a woman who lived with a man who crossed him.''

''Spanish guy have a name?''

''Soto—they called him Soto.''

''What's he look like?''

''Fat, thick arms, wears a mustache. When he took off his cap I saw he was pretty bald. Crooked nose like it was smashed.''

''And?''

''Tito said this gringo guy had sliced Marlena the stripper—Tito's girl-friend. That got Wheeler mad because he useta bounce the bitch when Tito was in jail.''

"So Wheeler and the Spanish guy, Soto, snatched the woman and took her to the warehouse."

"I dunno, maybe some other place."

I sucked in air, felt adrenalin rush hotly through my veins. "Get on some clothes, sweetie, we'll check out the warehouse."

Her cheeks paled. "Me?"

"You got to show me. Get decent, but leave off the SS cap."

She got up. "Why?"

"I've got Jewish friends. Now move your ass."

She picked up the second five hundred and tucked it in her other boot. Then she put on shorts, tank-top and leather jacket. I turned off the light and we went out to my borrowed car.

As I steered up US 1 Wanda huddled at the far end of the seat. Sex was no longer in the air, and she was scared. I said, "Relax, kid, you'll be fine. If the woman's there you can take off."

"Do I hafta go in—let Wheeler see me?"

I shook my head. "Stay in the car out of sight. When I come out with the woman I'll take you to the bus station in South Miami. Okay?"

"Okay. But—what if you don' come out?"

"You've got a thousand and walking boots. How far you plan to go?"

"Tupelo—got kinfolk there."

"And a change of lifestyle. No one needs to know about the Blue Panthers, Willard and the whoring. Stay clean, Wanda. And don't come back."

"I—I won't never. You give me a chance, Pete, been decent to me."

"I hope she's still alive," I said half to myself, and Wanda asked, "How you gonna get her?"

"Reason with them. Convince them they made a mistake."

"Yeah? I seen that piece in your belt."

"Sometimes I plink swamp rabbits, 'gators." And sometimes evil men.

After digesting the evasion, she said, "I figured it out: they took *your* woman, right?"

"A close friend, yes."

"Whyncha jus' tell the FBI?"

"Slow movers," I replied, and then she sat up, peered ahead.

"Gettin' close," she said, "but I was only here the once."

Another hundred yards and she pointed off the highway.

The field was littered with storm-blown trash, pieces of houses, tree branches, overturned cars. Beyond it stood a large building with metal sides. Roofing had been stripped down to tar paper, windows blown in. The warehouse looked dark and abandoned, but I hoped it wasn't.

I slowed to pull off the highway and braked on the slanted shoulder. Engine off, I could hear wind whispering around the car and the sound gave me an eerie feeling. "This may take a little while—you know how Latinos like to argue—so don't assume anything, okay?"

She shrugged. I put Jamey's keys in my pocket, opened the door and got out. "Lock the doors," I told her. "I don't want to come back and find you mugged."

The locks clicked shut and I went around to open the trunk.

I took the MAC-10 from my weapons bag, and two of the four stun grenades, leaving the night scope. The grenades went in my jacket pockets, and after closing the trunk lid I moved off in a crouch.

The footing was bad, puddled water was hidden by darkness and tall grass. Ten steps and my shoes were soaked. I gripped the machine pistol and wished I still had the silenced Beretta I'd tossed off the *Cygnet*.

My feet stirred up clouds of mosquitoes that settled hungrily on my face, throat and hands. I slapped away as many as I could and moved faster toward higher ground. Presently I was close enough to read flaked letters on the metal siding: Comfort Auto Repairs.

Still staying low, I moved to where I could make out the entrance. A pitted blacktop drive stopped at the wide, closed door into which a normal-size door was set. For a while I listened for human sounds, then crept closer to the door. Slowly and quietly I turned the knob, opened the door partway and slipped inside.

Moonlight filtering through high windows showed half a dozen vehicles in various stages of dismantlement, two welding rigs, and beyond them a gray Mercury with a muddied license plate. My heart began to pound, and then I saw the glint of motorcycle chrome.

At the far end of the building stood a windowless shed that must have served as office for what appeared to be a chop shop. Not that illegal operations did much bookkeeping, but mechanics and welders need a place to keep a coffee urn. As I stared at it I realized that what I'd thought was a vertical ray of moonlight was inside light showing along the door jamb.

The stolen Mercury was here, so was Wheeler's Harley. If Pilar was here, the shed was where she had to be.

I knew what I was going to do: kick open the shed door and toss in stun grenades, cut down any male I saw. So I slung the MAC-10 over one shoulder and got out both grenades, one in each hand. Then I moved forward.

I didn't get far because something hard bored into my spine and a rough voice growled, "Drop 'em."

The canisters thumped and rolled on the floor. I was a prisoner, too.

TWENTY-SIX

HE'D COME from behind a tall stack of tires and stepped out as I passed. Before I raised my arms he jerked off the MAC-10 and came around to face me, pistol in one hand, my weapon in the other. Digging it in my belly, he rasped, "Who are you? Watcha doin' here?"

"Security patrol," I said, and he snorted. On his head was a Marlins cap, he was short and fat, had a broken nose and a mustache. From Wanda's description, the Spanish guy, Soto. I said, "Who're you?"

"Whatta you care? We got no security patrol here."

"Then I made a mistake, sorry."

"Big mistake. See that office down there—that's where we're goin'." He noticed the Astra in my belt and yanked it out. Now he had three weapons to my one. Shrugging, I walked ahead of him, stepping over floor litter, angle irons and rusted tire rims, my soaked shoes making squishing sounds as we went.

I considered dropping and grabbing for my ankle backup pistol, but that would take four or five seconds, and Soto could shoot me in two. Bad idea. As we neared the shed I heard voices and shivered, thinking at least I'd tried to save Pilar.

Soto pulled open the door and prodded me in. Overhead light made me blink, but not before I recognized Wheeler and Tito Gallardo.

They'd been sitting at a small table, a bottle between them, and when they saw me they shot to their feet. *"Cabrón,"* Tito yelled, and Wheeler rasped, "Sneaky bastard." They both came toward me. Tito slapped my face and Wheeler drove his fist in my belly. Pain doubled me over, then Wheeler's knee slammed me upright but not before I'd vomited on Tito. He cursed, hit the side of my face with his fist and yelled crazily. Then he tore over to the corner lavatory and jerked open the door. I was hurting and dazed, but able to see the iron cot and the naked woman spread-eagled on it, tied by wrists and ankles. Her eyes were closed, she lay motionless, and I knew that she was dead.

Pilar. Rage suffused me. Then Wheeler sneered, "Your woman, huh?" and I kicked him hard in the crotch. He gasped as he dropped, and lay moaning. Then, from behind, Soto slammed something hard against my skull and I fell far and long into nothingness.

I wasn't dead because I could hear voices through the darkness. I was lying on a hard floor, wrists and ankles bound. I rolled over to sit up, and struck a cot leg. Remembered Pilar. "Oh, God," I breathed, "Jesus, I'm so sorry," licked swollen lips and laid my head against her thigh, sobbed brokenly.

"Jack," she whispered, "oh, my love, I wish you hadn't come."

"Had to. Thank God you're alive."

She began whimpering and it was the sound of a beaten child. I reached for my ankle, but the backup pistol was gone. All I had left was the switchblade, taped where I couldn't get to it. I managed to sit on the cot edge, then bent over and kissed her lips. "They're going to kill us," she murmured. "Why?"

"A mistake," I managed, and groped for a rough metal edge where I could saw my wrist ropes. Nothing.

My mind was beginning to clear from concussion fog. "I'm going to put my wrists on your mouth, try to free the knot." I hopped around to the head of the cot, and backed against it, lowering my arms until I felt her teeth take hold. Her head jerked back and forth as she struggled to slacken the cord, then she gasped, "No good. It gets tighter."

"Try another part," I urged, and felt her teeth bit in and tug again. Presently the pulling stopped and her head dropped. "Hopeless," she quavered, "so kiss me again."

Turning, I bent over and found her lips, stopped abruptly at a slight creaking sound from above. I looked up and saw boots coming through the narrow ventilator window, then the rest of Wanda's small body. Lithe as a monkey, she clung to the sill and lowered herself to the floor. "Pete," she whispered, "you here?"

"Over here. Oh, God, I'm glad to see you. Untie my wrists, fast."

In the dark we could barely see each other but her hands found the knot and undid it. I dropped my pants, tore off the switchblade and cut my ankle cords. Then I severed Pilar's bonds and raised her to a sitting position. She leaned against me unsteadily and her body quivered. Wanda said, "What'd they do to her?"

"What made you come?"

"Figured three was too many for you."

Gripping the knife, I tiptoed to the door and peered through the jamb space.

I could see two of them, Gallardo at the table counting out money while Wheeler watched. Soto appeared behind him, and Wanda touched my arm. "There's a switch box yonder on the wall. I'll cut the light and you go in. Okay?"

"Wait." I shifted position, squinted. My MAC-10 lay on the floor just this side of the table, about a yard from Gallardo's feet. I had to get to it before the men reacted. Then—"Okay. Hit the switch and hold it off for eight seconds." I gave her the switchblade. "When the light goes on this won't help me."

"Thanks, Pete." She kissed the side of my face. "You was good to me—I owed you." She moved over to the switch box, and I looked back at the cot, saw Pilar lying face down. "Ready," I said, heard the handle creak, and the light went out. I kicked the door open and dove for the table, snatched the auto and rolled away. Prone, I thumbed off the safety, and when light flared I shot at Soto's face. Wheeler had his revolver out, firing wildly at the door opening. Gallardo was running away until I shot him twice in the ass. Screaming, he fell forward, crawled on his belly like a sick gator. Wheeler pointed at me but I fired first. Three Talons ripped into his paunch and the revolver arced out of his hand. Gallardo was trying to get to his pistol but I stamped on his hand and jerked the pistol from its belt holster.

"I didn't kill Marlena, Rusty did," I told him, "and you made a fatal mistake." His hands were clawing at the bullet holes and he was howling so loudly I doubted he heard me. Blood flowed beyond his thighs and from the widening pool I surmised a femoral artery had been severed. Without immediate surgery he was going to bleed to death, and I wasn't a surgeon.

My first shot had caught Soto's forehead, blown off the top of his skull, and with it his baseball cap. It lay near what remained of his head, filled with bloody brains.

Wheeler was still alive. His bleeding was mostly internal, and he was a goner, too. Dull eyes fixed on me, lips moved, but I heard no words. Maybe Wanda would like to watch him die.

I went into the lavatory, saw Pilar sitting up, and looked around for Wanda. She was on the floor, back upright against the wall. Her leather jacket hung open, showing a dark wet circle on her tank-top at the level of her heart. Her sightless gaze was fixed on the doorway through which Wheeler's wild shot had come. There was nothing I could do for her. My throat tightened. *Think of me as your savior* I'd counseled her. Some savior; she'd never see Tupelo again.

From Pilar's throat came inchoate sounds. She was in shock and I had to get help for her. I ripped a worn army blanket off the cot and put it around her shoulders. Then I searched the main room until I found my Astra and ankle backup pistol—both were traceable to me. I put them where they belonged, slung the MAC-10 across one shoulder, and half-carried Pilar to the gray Mercury. The ignition lock had been punched out, leaving bare wires. I crossed them and they sparked, the engine started.

Tenderly I eased Pilar onto the passenger side and shut the door. Then I walked to the wide entrance door and opened it. After driving outside, I closed the door and got in beside Pilar. As I steered toward where I'd left Jamey's car Pilar spoke. In a high keening voice she wailed, "They raped me, over and over, they raped me."

"I know, I know, but you're alive. You'll be fine." Far easier for me to say than for her to accept.

Short of the highway I left the Merc in tall grass, and carried Pilar to Jamey's Corolla. Wanda had left the doors unlocked, so I didn't have to use the keys. When Pilar was inside, I got beside her and felt her clutch my arm with the strength of desperation. She was shivering so I turned on the heater and drove toward the only hospital I could remember. Every now and then Pilar would shudder and cry aloud, each cry a knife in my flesh. Her body seemed tense, almost rigid, and when I glanced at her pale face and fixed gaze, I sensed she was slipping into catatonia.

Finally a hospital sign and arrow. I pulled around the emergency entrance and honked until attendants appeared. "Rape case," I told them. "She's in shock." They wheeled down a gurney and laid her on it, covering her stiff body with blankets.

I followed as far as the ER, and went to the pay phone. I dialed my number and when Jamey answered I said, "Pilar's alive but in shock. I just got her to South Dade General. The bastards raped her, but don't tell the family. Just tell them where she is. And I'd like Melody to come."

"Right away. Jack, you okay?"

"Bumps and bruises."

He hesitated before asking, "And the—?"

"They won't be raping anymore. Now call the family."

I hung up, found a chair and sat down. Energy drained from me, and I could have slept sitting up but for the pain in my skull, belly and butt. A resident walked past me, stopped and turned back. "You in need of medical attention?"

"A few painkillers would help."

"Sorry," he said and walked on. After a while a nurse's aide approached me with a clipboard and asked me to fill out patient information. "Her family will be here shortly," I said, "I don't know her that well."

"Then who's going to pay for treatment?"

"Will five hundred help?"

"It will."

I peeled bills from my diminishing roll and laid them on the clipboard. The aide wrote out a receipt, and said, "What name?"

"Jane Doe."

She eyed me. "We prefer true names."

"So do we all—but rape victims aren't always eager to have theirs known." I stood up. "Snack bar open?"

"No, but there's a coffee vending machine down the hall."

"Yuk. How long will the patient be in ER?"

"It depends."

"Give a guess."

"I'd say another hour." She tapped her pen on the board. "Can you tell me how old she is?"

"No." I walked down the shadowed hall, found the vending machine and ejected a cold can of Sprite. It wasn't coffee, but it helped dilute the bitter taste of vomit, and I took it to the men's room.

There were mosquito bites on my face and forehead, the mirror showed red marks from Tito's welcoming punch, and my hands and clothes were grimy. Hot water and liquid soap improved my appearance and morale. I dried off and went back to the waiting room, found my chair and thought about Wanda. The little sparrow had died quickly, killed by her abuser, though by chance. *Consider me your savior, Wanda.* Wheeler, though, could still be bleeding his evil life away, and I wished him an agonizing end. If any Blue Panthers remained they could give him a big biker funeral. I never wanted to see their hangout again. Or the warehouse.

I hadn't tried to warn Pilar not to be specific about her kidnapping, rape or rescue, because her mind wasn't functioning well enough to understand what I was saying. Having killed her three rapists, I wasn't eager to answer questions about motivation, justification, and so on. Almost anything I said would incriminate me, so the best course was to say nothing.

Unintentionally, I fell asleep, and woke to someone shaking my shoulder.

"Jesus, *compadre,* you look like—well, I won't say it." Manny Montijo.

"Yeah, make me feel good." I struggled upright. "How is she?"

"Alive, of course, but mentally shocked. Ah—want to tell me what happened?"

"Not now," I said, as Melody leaned over and planted kisses on my forehead. Her cheeks were streaked with tears and I asked why.

"Because you're such a noble bastard." She began to cry. "Can't help it."

Then Lucy kissed me, Rosario and even Carmen. Jamey said, "Good to see you, Jack," and I tossed him his keys. "Where's Pilar?"

"In her room," Lucy told me. "Under sedation. We're all so grateful to you."

Carmen asked, "Where did you find her?"

"Down the road." I waved vaguely, and Manny said, "We're asking no questions. It's enough—more than enough—that Jack brought our cousin back."

I pried myself out of the chair and beckoned Manny aside. "If you haven't already, call off the Bureau and the Marshals."

"I have. Without explanation."

"Don't want them looking too hard for Gallardo."

"Oh."

Melody came over and linked her arm with mine. "Nothing more you can do here, precious, so let's go home where I can bind up your wounds and make you whole again."

"Do that," Manny seconded. "If Pilar needs anything we'll be here. Get some rest, both of you. Wedding in—what?—two days?"

I said goodnight to the ladies and Melody led me out to her car.

As we drove north toward the Gables I muttered, "I'm not even sure what day it is."

"Tuesday, dear." East, over the ocean, the horizon was turning gray. "I've been terrified for hours, do you feel up to telling me what happened, how you found her?"

"Not now," I said wearily.

"But sometime."

"Sometime." Possibly.

By the time we got home the eastern sky was pale. I trudged into the house and pulled off clothing while Melody filled the bathtub. Hot soap eased my pains, and a combination of pain capsules and Añejo helped even more. She undressed, got into pajamas, washed her face and brushed her teeth. Then she swabbed lotion on my mosquito bites and said, "Your shoes and clothes are a total loss."

"Out of fashion, anyway."

She steadied me out of the tub, dried me with a big fluffy towel and got me into bed. On her side, she lay against me, and I could feel the beating of her heart. "I love you," she murmured, "and I want you always to love me."

"I promise," I slurred, then sleep took over.

Around noon I woke and lay in bed for a while, gingerly testing joints and muscles before trying to sit up.

My belly, left cheekbone and skull delivered the most pain, so I tottered into the bathroom for more painkillers, and found a note from Melody taped to the mirror:

Had to go to class, sorry. I know you feel dreadful, so Dr. Ing will come at thirteen hundred hours to check you over. That's 1 PM. [She loved needling me for my Navy background.]

There's a Burger King breakfast in the micro, all timed, so just press the button when you're ready. Jamey's going to help out, be your gofer (his word), so I don't feel so bad about leaving you today. He'll be able to give you late word on Cousin Pilar.

Love you. M

I got into the shower, soaped well, and when I got out I dabbed alcohol on the worst insect bites, then padded to the kitchen for coffee.

Jamey was at the table. He'd covered it with newspapers and was cleaning my field-stripped MAC-10. My weapons bag was on a chair, the forgotten bottle of Añejo on the counter. "Morning," he said, "coffee's ready. Guess you saw Melody's note."

I nodded, poured a mug and added Añejo to the steaming joe. "See you're managing to keep busy."

"Imagine my surprise when I checked my trunk and found this illegal item plus your bag. I'll take the remaining grenades back to the office."

"How's Pilar doing?"

"Fair. Arm, thigh and ankle bruises—guess they tied her up."

"They did."

"Main problem is she's withdrawn, blocking all that happened to her. Under psychiatric care."

"At the hospital?"

He nodded. "The family wants her with them but the shrink says it's too soon. Keeps her pretty well sedated. And of course the Rape Center people are involved.'' He held up the auto's short barrel. ''Talon ammo doesn't leave much for ballistic analysis, but I figured the piece ought to be cleaned in case some LE type gives it the sniff test. Right now the barrel is shiny clean and smells of solvent and gun oil.''

''Thanks.'' I sat and watched him reassemble the firearm while I sipped coffee-rum. Soon I began to think I could face the day. After a while I said, ''I'd like to see Pilar.''

''No visitors, not yet. Lucy stays there all the time, and Rosario and Carmen alternate being with their mother.'' He smiled. ''Sorta leaves me at loose ends.''

''Not a bad way to be.''

''Guess not. Anyway, no one's been able to get a coherent story from Pilar.''

''She may black it out forever.''

''Would that be—healthy?''

''Ask a shrink, not me.''

''There.'' He finished wiping oil from the MAC-10 and laid it down. ''I emptied the magazine—six cartridges remaining.''

So I'd discharged nine altogether.

''I don't suppose Gallardo will be troubling anyone from now on,'' he mused.

''Guess not. Sort of isolates General Padilla up in the cold northwest. Meanwhile the Manhattan drug franchise is up for grabs.''

''The killing's started already. Mexicans and Dominicans battling it out.''

''Good news.''

He rose and said, ''If there's nothing more I can do for you I'll get back to the office, resume fighting the drug wars.'' He smiled bleakly. ''Glad you're out of it?''

''I've never been out of it,'' I told him, and thanked him for coming over.

As he left he said, ''Your Miata's in the garage, I enjoyed driving it, tank's full.''

He went down the walk and got into his Corolla; it had served me well last night and this morning.

I heated the fast-food breakfast: eggs, muffin, cheese, bacon and juice, ate what I wanted and tossed the rest away. Presently Dr. Ing arrived, and with him a technician for the portable X-ray unit. My skull was X-rayed from several angles, and the tech left with his equipment. Ing said, ''I'll have a radiologist's readout later today. How you feeling?''

''More or less like shit.''

I stripped and he poked and prodded me, *tsk-tsked* at my body bruises, and said dryly that he thought I'd survive. "But watch your urine for blood. Seen any yet?"

"None."

"And limit your alcohol intake, you're too young to have an enlarged liver." He drew blood for a complete workup including PSA for prostate evaluation, and gave me a tube of antibiotic with steroid for my bites. "Any malaria symptoms?"

"Not yet. Anyway, I've had malaria."

"Dengue?"

"If I had dengue I'd be in bed howling with pain."

"That's so. You can dress now, and my advice is to rest as much as you can."

"I'm low on painkillers."

Reluctantly, he gave me a small packet of Percodans, one every four hours, and closed his medical bag.

"How much do I owe you?"

"Mr. Montijo is covering it."

"That's not right, I'm not a member of his family."

"Well, he says you are. Nice people, aren't they?"

"Certainly are."

"You're getting married—when?"

"Thursday."

"By then you should look passable. Any problems, call me."

I promised I would, and after he left I phoned Manny.

"Some unfinished business to go over," I told him. "How about taking a coffee break here?"

"Sure." He paused. "I guess Jamey told you Pilar's not responding well."

"I don't think she ought to be pushed to remember. Won't help her, won't help anyone."

"There's that," he said thoughtfully, and by the time I was dressed Manny was at the door. He accepted coffee and we sat on the sofa where, only yesterday, Pilar and I had made love.

He opened the conversation saying, "How many were there, Jack?"

"Gallardo, a Hispanic rat named Soto, and the biker whose printout you supplied."

"Any possibility you'll be implicated?"

"I had to get Pilar to a hospital, no time for cleanup, so there's a possibility something could point to me. Can't rule it out. But what I wanted to take up with you is Mehmet Kurdlu, my yachting host. It offends me that he's free to finance big-time drug transactions."

"We have no evidence for an indictment."

"There's another way to neutralize him." I told Manny about the pillaged amphorae and their storehouse behind his castle. "Maybe your people could get the Greeks interested."

"You mean, have the Greeks interest the Turks."

"That would be hopeless—Mehmet would get tipped off and simply move his loot before a warrant could be served—if the Turks agreed to search his premises. No. His yacht could be seized in Greek waters and the crew interrogated."

"DEA isn't interested in stolen antiquities," he objected.

"Consider them means to an end. From jail he can't conduct his financing, ergo, reducing the flow of Near East drugs." I sipped from my mug. Manny thought for a while and asked, "Wouldn't want to get involved, would you?"

"No way. I'm getting married, remember? Anyway, the scale and ramifications are too big for me." I leaned forward. "But not for you."

He grunted. "Bottom line—you're outlining a big-time international operation. I don't know I want it."

"Well, all the elements are out there for an aggressive DEA officer to put together. Anyway, you should give it some thought."

"What's the yacht's name?"

"*Cygnet.*"

After a while he said, "I'll give it some thought."

I brought in the percolator and topped our mugs. Then I said, "Now I think about it, there's the Sicilian card."

"Sicilian? How so?"

"The Cuntrera brothers. They're facing long prison terms. DEA ought to have a good working liaison with Italian narcotics suppression. Maybe one of the brothers would be willing to cut a deal for less time if he implicates Kurdlu. Circulate a rumor that Kurdlu was a secret informant who gave evidence against them. Talk privately with one of the brothers and suggest he disclose what he knows about their money-man. That would satisfy the Sicilian requirement for vengeance, while doing himself some good." I paused long enough to add Añejo to my mug. "That would also be in Italian national interest by reducing drug flow. What do you think?"

"I like it better than dealing with Turks and Greeks because the Italians work well with us and they're determined to destroy the Mafia. Yeah, definite possibilities. Anything else?"

"Not of a professional nature. What's the prognosis for Pilar?"

He sighed. "Her father wants her back home, feels she'll respond faster in familiar surroundings. He doesn't know about the raping—that's for Pilar to reveal if she should ever decide to. All he's been told is that his daughter was kidnapped and maltreated. I think he's right about having her back in Spain. What's your opinion?''

"Eventually, not right away. The Rape Center can provide therapy that's probably not available in Spain—particularly rural Spain. Let her specialists determine when and if." I grimaced. "I'm carrying a large load of guilt for what happened."

"No one blames you—hell, you risked your life to save hers."

I grunted. "Least I could do under the circumstances. But having Carmen in Spain could be a painful reminder for Pilar."

"Maybe, but Carmen won't be around the family, she'll be at school in Madrid or Salamanca—I don't see it as a problem." He looked at his watch. "Anything I can get you?"

"Peace of mind." I got up and unlocked the door. "Any chance Pilar can come to the wedding?"

"You can ask her," he said and went out.

When Melody returned she kissed me between patches of antibiotic ointment and said, "Forgive me for abandoning you?"

"Of course. When classes call you gotta go."

"How are you feeling, love?" She unloaded her books and sank into a chair.

"Better by the hour."

"And your poor head?" She touched it lightly.

"Ing called to say no fracture. The bump'll go away." I could still hear the *whish* of Soto's weapon behind me. "I'll be fit to marry on Thursday."

"Before I left this morning Mother called. She's arriving late tonight or early tomorrow morning. I suggested she not stay with us—you know how she likes to spread out and take over."

"Only too well. Get her a suite at the Coconut Grove Hotel, she'll love it."

She nodded. "I've been thinking, dear. Mother wants to sell the house— why don't we buy it and establish a new lifestyle?"

"I like the one we have, but if that's what you want . . ."

"I'll work it out with her. We'll get an agent to sell this place and handle buying the other."

"After professional appraisal."

"Of course. And we wouldn't need all those servants."

"How many will we need?"

"A cook, and a maid to clean house and do laundry."

"Bay Harbor is a lot farther from law school."

"True, but I'd have the pool for diving practice, and we could swim together—nude."

"That's the convincer."

"Also, there's plenty of space for a nursery—when that time comes. My old room, for instance; I'd love to do it over in pink and blue."

I nodded. "Well, start by talking with Mom and I'll follow through."

She noticed the extra mug on the coffee table. "Jamey?"

"Manny came by."

"What's Pilar's condition?"

"Not encouraging. If you can spare the study time, I'd like us to visit her."

"I wish I could, honey, but it's not possible. Not with Mother arriving, and the wedding . . . Do you mind going alone?"

"I'll manage," I said, "and I applaud your dedication to the law."

So at dusk I drove to South Dade and found Rosario at Pilar's bedside. "She's been asking for you, Jack—almost the only words she's spoken."

"That's good, isn't it? That she's speaking at all?"

"It's encouraging. Since you're here I'll go out for coffee, make some phone calls. Can I bring back something for you?"

"Nothing, thanks." She went out and the door closed softly behind her.

A small table lamp provided the room's only illumination, giving Pilar's still features a waxy hue. I took her cool hand and her eyes opened. "*Querido,* I've been praying you'd come," she whispered.

"Of course, and here I am."

Something like a smile lifted the corners of her lips. "How are you, dear? How badly were you hurt?"

"Nothing to talk about. Mosquito bites were the worst of it." I pointed at my face. "More importantly, how are you, *mi amor?*"

"Not as bad as I've seemed. Doctors, even police, have been asking questions I didn't want to answer until I knew what you might have said."

"So far, nothing." I kissed her lips, her fingers ran through my hair, and she murmured, "I didn't see all you did at that dreadful place, just the results." Her lips trembled. "And that poor woman who helped us—losing her life like that . . . so unfair."

"She had a good heart, helped us because she knew I cared for you."

For a while she gazed at the ceiling, tears welling in her eyes. "I feel so dirty, so shamed and violated—will that ever pass?"

"It will. Faster when you're back with your family."

"I suppose that will help. But I don't think I'll ever get over my fear of Florida."

"That's understandable. This is a violent place."

She sighed. "I would make myself stay if you were—single. But—we've gone into that before."

I nodded.

"And understand each other." She lifted my hand to her lips and kissed the palm. "Before Rosario returns—what am I to say about what happened?"

"As much truth as possible. You went to a friend's in the Gables expecting to meet his fianceé; she wasn't there, so you drove away. At some point—you can say where—an old car forced you over and three men dragged you out and into theirs. They blindfolded you and when you struggled they knocked you out."

Her nails dug into my palm and her body shook. *"Oh, God,"* she breathed. I said, "I know this is hard for you, but we ought to keep going. If it's too much I'll stop."

"No, no, go on."

"When you came to you were in a strange place tied to a cot in a little room. They took turns raping you, threatening to kill you. It went on for a long time and you passed out."

She was shivering uncontrollably. "Pilar"—I touched her face—"stay with me. Gunshots brought you back to consciousness. You were in the dark, terrified, not knowing what was happening. Then the door opened and a woman came in with a knife. You thought she was going to kill you, but she cut you free. Then one of the men—looking like a biker—came in and shot her. You fainted. When you came to, everything was quiet, you were alone."

I poured ice water from a thermal carafe and made her drink.

"You covered yourself with the cot blanket and got out of the place— looked like a big garage—ran to the road, and finally an old pickup stopped for you. The driver was an elderly woman—maybe she was an Everglades Indian—and at a pay phone she called the only number you could remember—mine. She took you as far as the hospital where I met you. More than that you don't remember. Leaving the garage, you saw your abductors dead but you don't know who killed them or why. Don't speculate on drug wars or gang killings, let the police do that. You're a foreigner, aren't expected to know local crime.

"The next time you gained consciousness you were in this room, this bed, family members around you."

For a while she said nothing, but her body shook from time to time, and I realized she was reliving what really happened. I lifted her hand and kissed

it. *"Querida,"* I said softly, "I'd give anything in the world to have prevented it. None of it was your fault, you can't blame yourself, and above
everything you mustn't feel guilty or shamed. For a virtuous woman the
shock has to be horrifying and you're probably feeling forever defiled."

"I am, yes, I feel that way," she said with a harmonic of hysteria.

I kissed her cheek and forehead. "Think of it this way—you were at a
bullfight and someone you couldn't see spat on you. A nasty thing you
washed off and were clean again. Went on with your life."

"I—I'll try," she breathed, "and more than anything I'll remember that
you risked your life for me."

"A privilege," I said, then the door opened and Rosario came in.

"I've been talking," I told her, "and Pilar has been listening. She's feeling
better but not up to answering questions. Anyway, I've asked her to leave me
out of the story. She doesn't know where she was taken or who her abductors
were—didn't witness the gunfight. She was in and out of consciousness, and
when she realized she was the only survivor she fled the scene." I got up and
offered the chair to Rosario. "That's all anyone needs to know."

"I understand." She seated herself and took Pilar's hands, circled them
with a rosary. Pilar looked at me. "The wedding . . . ?"

"I hope you'll come."

She nodded and I left them together.

Driving back, I thought of all that had happened to Pilar and to me, and all
the things we'd left unspoken but were nevertheless understood. I'd asked her
to lie for me, and she would, knowing the consequence of truthfulness, and
perhaps out of gratitude as well. I was always going to remember Pilar
Marisol de la Gracia y Montijo and love her from afar. Depriving Melody of
nothing.

I thought of Mehmet Kurdlu and hoped that I'd started a chain of action
that would in time dethrone him. Delores would miss the yacht and the palace
and the art collection, but she was a resourceful woman who would soon find
another rich companion with whom to travel the world.

Late that night she called from the airport. Melody and I dressed and drove
there to meet her. We took her to the Grove hotel, saw her to her suite and
returned home to bed.

The next day Delores took charge.

TWENTY-SEVEN

WHILE MELODY and her mother were shopping in Bal Harbour for wedding attire I drove to the Gables and rented a tuxedo. For my wedding to Pam I'd worn Navy dress whites and had never needed a tux while working for DEA. I doubted I'd need one in the foreseeable future, so renting was the answer.

We met for lunch at the Grove Isle Club where Delores was accorded the awe and esteem due her exalted position as—what? A liberal spender was all I could infer. And while Melody and I lingered over *pousse-café* and tiny cakes, Delores huddled with the banquet manager and dictated the minutiae of our reception from hors d'oeuvres to silver candelabra, nuptial decorations, triple-tier cake and string quartet. Pastor Fedder and his winsome accompanist could soothe us during interludes. Delores was much in her element, the grande dame ordering as though for a hundred instead of the expected ten.

When she finally returned she said, "I do wish Mehmet were here. Jack, have you got the wedding ring?"

"I have, Mother," Melody chimed in, "and you haven't mentioned my engagement ring." She flashed it at Delores, who sniffed, "You haven't mentioned the Rolls."

"Pure oversight," I responded. "We're keeping it in a safe place until we can house it securely."

"I see. Well, you will come to the church in it."

"Unfortunately, there's a small part missing, so it's not driveable until the part—whatever it is—arrives from England."

"Good Lord!" she exclaimed, "and here I thought you two were enjoying it all this time."

"Apropos," Melody said, "there's a four-car garage in Bay Harbor, and an empty house. Jack and I would like to buy it—for a fair price."

Delores frowned. "Really? I've always liked the assurance of a *pied-à-terre* for Florida visits. Wherever would I stay?"

I said, "Mother, we plan on a perpetual room for you, isn't that right, dear?"

"Absolutely. Wouldn't have it any other way."

Delores shrugged. "Well, then, have it appraised and you can have it for whatever the figure is."

"And you'll hold the mortgage," Melody said firmly.

"Well, if that's necessary—of course."

I said, "If we're basically agreed, it would speed things along if you stayed on awhile. Save complications at the other end—consular visits to sign documents, and so on."

"Jack's right," Melody added supportively. "Then when you go back all the paperwork will be done."

She waved a hand dismissively. "Very well, though Mehmet needs me while he recovers. Poor lamb—I've really had to take over managing his household. Ever since the pirate attack he's felt dreadfully insecure—though I keep telling him there's really nothing to worry about."

How wrong you are, I thought, but said, "Where next?"

"Melody and I decided I ought to meet the padre—what's his name?"

"Fedder," I supplied. "Young and earnest. Committed to his vocation."

Her eyes narrowed. "Not a longhair, guitar-strumming hippie parson?"

"By no means," Melody assured her. "You'll see."

The church was only a few blocks away. I braked the BMW at the front entrance and turned off the engine. "I'll go find him," I said, and got out of the car.

After walking around to the parsonage I listened for the sound of music, heard nothing but human sounds and went to a side window, then peered in. What I saw made me glad I hadn't brought the ladies, because the incautious padre was seated in a rocking-chair, the winsome young accompanist—Charity, I remembered—sitting on his lap facing him. Her legs were positioned over the chair arms, and they were clutching each other in close embrace. Her skirt, I noticed, was flared modestly over his thighs and knees, and his clerical trousers were crumpled around his ankles. As they moved together the rocker squeaked rhythmically and they uttered small wordless sounds of joy and mutual delight.

Suddenly I regarded the couple in a new light. She was an Easy Rider, and he a bodacious risk-taker, a valorous rotary of the Anonga-Ronga, and a dedicated devotee of love in the afternoon.

As their movements grew more passionate I withdrew and returned to the ladies. "He's instructing a novice," I told them. "We'll call for an appointment."

"Can't we just wait?" Delores said irritably. "How long can it take?"

"I think he's only just begun—could take a couple of hours before they complete the . . . catechism." I started the engine and drove back home. On the way I reviewed the steamy scene and found myself hoping the good father had the kid on the pill. Otherwise he could find himself a father for real. But that was their affair, not mine.

Later, when I told Melody what I'd seen, she didn't think it at all funny as I did. As she denounced the daring dominie she used words like seduction, child molestation, statutory rape, taking advantage of ecclesiastical position, and so on. Finally I said, "Enough already. She wasn't trying to get away, she was having a hell of a good time, as was the padre. Lighten up, honey, there's enough sorrow in the world that two young people getting it on for mutual enjoyment shouldn't be reviled."

"Well, I hope her mother finds out."

"No you don't, not really. Suppose your mother had found out you seduced me when you were barely seventeen? We wouldn't be here today. Besides," I continued, "for all we know, they're engaged, so let's give them the benefit of the doubt, okay?"

"I guess."

"And be civil to them—both of them."

"If you insist," she sighed, "but when we're facing him at the altar I hope I'll be able to keep that other vision out of my mind." Then she giggled. "Jack, it *is* funny. You've made me as immoral as you are."

"With that in mind, get off that excess clothing and let's make the beast with two backs."

"Yes—and Mother can go meet him alone."

Next day the ladies came and went, alleging that there were final details to attend to. Manny called to confirm time and place and asked if I'd remembered the ring. "Absolutely," I replied. "Melody has it for safekeeping and I'll give it to you at the church."

"Nervous?"

"You could say that. Delores has all this kinetic energy to expend. So far she's visited the padre, returned to the club to revise the menu, and taken Melody back to Bal Harbour because her matron's dress needs a stitch in the sleeve. Or so she says. Ah—done anything with my Sicilian suggestion?"

"Prepared a proposal. Satisfied?"

"Amply. Now, how is Pilar?"

"*Compadre*, your visit worked wonders. They're letting her go to the wedding."

"Terrific. Finally Melody gets to meet her."

"And vice versa. I'm sure they'll like each other."

I thought for a moment and asked, "Got enough transportation?"

"Think so. I'm bringing Lucy and Carmen. Rosario is going with Jamey and they're bringing Pilar from the hospital."

"And I'm driving Melody and her mother. That takes care of everyone. See you there at, oh, five-thirty. Okay?"

"Okay."

Until almost the last minute Melody and Delores were adjusting their gowns, adding and subtracting jewelry, touching up makeup in what I decided was some sort of subconscious delaying tactic. Finally they said they were ready, we could go.

Very carefully I helped them into the BMW, ignoring Delores's comment about how much nicer and roomier the Rolls would be, and drove down into the Grove.

The Montijo party was already there. Manny introduced Melody and Pilar, who was looking much as she'd looked before, which was pretty ravishing. Everyone kissed each other and we entered the church.

Father Fedder greeted us at the entrance, and I saw Charity seated at the organ. She began "Oh Promise Me" and the padre formed us into a wedding procession. Cupped hand at my ear, Melody hissed, "Pilar *is* beautiful but you didn't have to kiss her so long."

"The Spanish are demonstrative," I muttered, "you know that. Besides, she needs comforting."

"Maybe so, and I understand she's grateful to you but—" Charity segued into the first chords of the "Wedding March" but before we could move down the aisle Manny whispered, "The ring, Jack. Give me the ring."

Hearing him, Melody clapped a hand to her mouth. "Oh, God, I forgot it. Jack, would you run out and get it? Glove compartment."

"No problem." I turned back and went down the steps toward the BMW parked around the side of the church. Hurrying toward it, I got the remote from my pocket and pointed it at the car. Pressed the button.

The blast shoved me backward. Shock wave slammed me to my knees as the car vanished in a huge ball of flame.

"Oh, God," I gasped, "Oh, God!" and picked myself up as Melody rushed to me. I pulled her back from the heat as the others stared, stunned, from the steps. Her arms circled me and she pressed close, crying uncontrollably. "I'm all right," I said, and kept repeating it until she glanced around at the flaming, disintegrated wreck. Her small fists pounded my shoulders, as hysterically she cried, "*Who did it? Who's trying to kill us?*"

"Padilla," I said hoarsely, and turned from the conflagration. Taking her arm, I began leading her back to the church, but she shook off my hand sobbing, "It won't ever end, will it? Never end?"

Shrieking sirens and the hoarse blatting of fire engines drowned out my reply.